WORLD
WITHOUT
END

TOR BOOKS BY MOLLY COCHRAN AND WARREN MURPHY

The Forever King
World Without End

WORLD WITHOUT END

MOLLY COCHRAN
AND WARREN MURPHY

A TOM DOHERTY ASSOCIATES BOOK

NEW YORK

TOR®

This work is humbly dedicated to the descendants of Atlantis who have preserved the great gift of their ancestors for the betterment of humankind. Their time has come.

We wish to thank Dr. Robert Stull; Patricia Hilliard, R.N.; psychic healer, Doloris Stevens; Captain Thomas Abbotts; and our indefatigable editor, Melissa Singer, for their kind and generous assistance with this book.

—M.C. and W.M.

WORLD WITHOUT END

A Tor Book
Published by Tom Doherty Associates, Inc.
175 Fifth Avenue
New York, N.Y. 10010

Tor Books on the World-Wide Web:
http://www.tor.com

Tor® is a registered trademark of Tom Doherty Associates, Inc.

Design by Patrice Federo

Library of Congress Cataloging-in-Publication Data

Cochran, Molly.
World without end / Molly Cochran & Warren Murphy.—1st ed.
        p.   cm.
"A Tom Doherty Associates book."
ISBN 0-312-85597-4
1. Lost continents—Fiction.   2. Atlantis—Fiction.   I. Murphy, Warren.   II. Title.
PS3553.O26W67   1996
813'.54—dc20   95-44006
                    CIP

First Edition: March 1996

Printed in the United States of America

0   9   8   7   6   5   4   3   2   1

THE MEMORY

The devil lived underwater in a place called the Peaks.

In the deep blackness of the Atlantic, ancient mountains crouched unseen, ready to spring up and tear a ship's hull to splinters. Below them stretched a bottomless valley that swallowed men whole.

Oceanographers said that the Peaks marked the northwestern tip of what is called the Bermuda Triangle, where for centuries seagoing vessels and their crews have disappeared without a trace. They explained that these phenomena were the result of navigational hazards due to the turbulent character of the Gulf Stream, the unpredictable Caribbean-Atlantic weather pattern, sudden thunderstorms, the shifting topography of the ocean floor, and human error.

But the leather-faced men who sailed those waters knew better.

The devil lived down there.

CHAPTER 1

THE SHIVERS.

Sam Smith felt them as soon as he saw the broken piece of pottery lying on the beach. Shivers, bone-wracking tremors that ran the whole length of his body and then settled somewhere inside his brain. They had nothing to do with cold, not *these* shivers. These were more like a second pair of eyes. Eyes he could never close.

They were what recognized the pottery shard. The shivers.

The piece wasn't much: a clay handle attached to a piece of curved earthenware, perhaps three inches square. It probably had once been a common pitcher in a common household—barely noticeable among the litter that the sea had cast onto the shore.

There had been some unusual seismic activity in the waters off the southeastern coast of Florida for the past two weeks, and the beach near Key Biscayne reflected it with nightmarish piles of weird debris, from rotting octopus carcasses to boulders weighing a ton or more. The beachcombers, who were out in force with their sifters and metal detectors, had not given the object a second glance.

But Sam could not walk past it. The shivers would not allow him.

He picked up the shard to examine it, and immediately felt the blood jump in his veins. His head felt as if it were exploding. Steadying his hands, he studied the small fragment. The faint trace of painting still visible beneath the cracked glaze was a simple design, a cross inscribed by a blue circle, repeated several times in a row.

It was old. Very, very old. The shivers saw that.

"Well, what do you know," Sam said aloud. The piece might be Greek, or even Mycenean—ships carrying all sorts of booty had sunk in these waters.

And then he heard music. Rather, he *felt* it, seeping out of the shard into his hands. It was as glorious as the sea itself, that music, a siren's song that called to him like a lover.

He had heard it all his life, in bits and snatches, always just out of the range of real hearing, just enough to let Sam know the song was for him and him alone.

Come to me, Sam

He closed his eyes.

My love, I have waited so long. . . .

When he opened them again, he was standing nearly knee-deep in the filthy water, facing a vast expanse of ocean.

"Oh, God," he whispered, backing up in panic.

He smacked into one of the beachcombers, apologized, then started to run down the shore.

Sam . . .

He thrust the shard into his pocket, and the voice faded. Ahead was a salvage boat with the name *Styx* painted on its prow. A flood of relief washed over him. Back on deck, he would be all right. He would be safe from his own craziness.

Maybe.

The shivers were still on him. He stopped to rest for a moment, his hands on his knees, his breath coming ragged. He turned his head toward the spot where he had walked into the surf in some sort of insane trance.

He had been facing southeast, where the Peaks were.

Where the devil lived.

Sam jogged toward the boat and willed his mind away from the sea.

Darian McCabe was pacing on deck—a sure sign that his negotiations with a prospective client had not gone well. The old man was in a foul mood.

"Cast off those lines and let's get the hell out of here," he growled.

It was a half hour before Darian calmed down enough to hold a conversation. Sam brought the piece of pottery out of his pocket and showed it to him. McCabe was standing behind the helm, his wary eyes scanning the horizon.

"What's that?"

"I found it on the beach," Sam said.

"Christian, whatever it is," Darian had said, uninterested. "All those crosses. Probably Spanish." He raised his arm to toss the shard overboard. "Junk."

Sam snatched it out of his hands. "Don't," he said. "I think it's old." His teeth began to chatter.

Darian snorted. "You think everything made before nineteen fifty is old."

"Older than Christian Spain." The shivers were bad now. Sam felt as if a cold wind were blowing through him. "I want to take it to the oceanographic museum to have it dated."

The old man shrugged. "Do what you want. Now go coil some rope."

An hour later, Sam heard the music again.

The same music, he thought. *It's always the same.* Shuddering, he went below into the galley of the fifty-foot salvage craft. At the small mess table, he sat down and pulled the piece of pottery out of his pocket to look at it. Through the old porcelain, his siren called to him.

Come closer, it seemed to say. Oh, yes. If he could just get close enough to hear it, hear it with his ears and not with whatever peculiar sense was perceiving it, he might . . .

Might what?

He knew what Darian would say if he knew. *Might just follow that music down to where the devil lives, isn't that right, Sam? Fling yourself headfirst into the ocean and sink like a stone. . . .*

"What the hell are you doing down here?" the old man shouted from the companionway.

"Nothing," Sam called, shoving the pottery shard inside his pocket.

"Then quit wasting time and boil up some water. I could use a cup of coffee."

"Sure, Darian."

He was glad to busy himself at the hotplate, even though his hands were shaking so badly he could barely pour the water. Every time Darian maneuvered the *Styx* through this area, the shivers came on him, but they'd never been as bad as they were today.

"Jesus Christ," the old man said, swiping at the spilled coffee as he picked up his mug. "You got a hangover?"

"No. Just a headache, that's all."

"Headache. Like you always get when we pass over the Peaks. You cold?"

"A little," Sam said. He joined the old man at the table.

"Hell, it's eighty-five degrees. You're shaking like a leaf."

"I'll be all right."

Darian slurped his coffee. "Coast Guard's out."

"Yeah? Where?"

" 'Bout a mile due east. Just seen them topside, coming in."

"What were they doing?"

McCabe shrugged. "Probably charting the bottom after those tremors we've had. Seaquakes can cause some big changes. Deep water fills up with silt, kills all the fish. Shallow waters suddenly turn too deep to dive."

Sam looked up. "I thought there weren't any shallows in the Peaks."

"There's some of everything in these waters," the old man said. "That's why it can't be dived."

All the sailors' kids had grown up on cautionary tales about sea monsters and ghosts. The old salts who hung around Eddie's Grill took pride in sailing the area which the general public had designated as the most dangerous stretch of ocean on the planet. They sailed it, but despite all the legends of gold and sunken booty, they never dived the Peaks. When asked why they were afraid of a patch of water, the old-timers would only wink and say they knew where the devil lived.

"I think it could be dived."

Darian's eyes narrowed. "Now, we're not going to talk about this again," he said.

Sam had been begging to dive the Peaks since the first time Darian had taken him over the area on board the *Styx*. At first Darian had laughed off Sam's pleas as the whim of a daredevil child, but over the years, they had become a real annoyance.

"You want to get yourself killed, find some other way."

"I'd stay in the shallows."

Darian waved him away.

"You said yourself there were shallows."

"Aye. That's where the shark come to feed."

Sam swallowed. "It's just that . . ." Unconsciously, he wrapped his fingers around the pottery shard in his pocket. "There's something down there."

Darian leaned back in his bench. "Such as?"

"Well . . ." He considered telling the old man the truth, then immediately discarded the idea. People who heard voices coming from the ocean ended up in rubber rooms. Suddenly an idea blossomed in Sam's brain. "Treasure," he said, smiling.

Darian laughed. "You sound like a tourist. Whatever's down in there's buried too deep to find without a bulldozer."

"Most of the time, yes," Sam went on excitedly. "But these tremors have shaken up the sea floor, just like you said. Things that have been buried for hundreds of years might be lying right on the surface now. And it isn't going to last long. In another week, it'll all be covered again."

Darian took another drink of his coffee, grimaced, and stood up with a stretch. "Damn. And I was hoping to buy a mountain in Peru."

"I'm serious, Darian."

"I know you are." There was a quiet threat in his voice. "We make a living finding salvage. We don't need no treasure. Forget about diving the Peaks."

But Sam would not forget. The shivers wouldn't let him.

As he had grown up, he had heard other people refer to the shivers in other ways : second sight. Telepathy. Clairvoyance. The Magic Eye. To Sam, they had been only one thing—a curse laid on him at birth.

He could not remember a time in his life when he had been free of them, where there had not come an unbidden moment when a sudden premonition had suffused his body and caused it to shudder uncontrollably. When he was seven years old, the shivers had alerted him that something terrible was about to happen to the orphanage in Pittsburgh where he'd lived since infancy. He had run screaming to the housemother, and the place had been evacuated in time—although not until a column of smoke billowed up the east stairwell. When it was all over, Sam had been blamed for setting the fire that he had only foreseen.

In the navy, where he was assigned to an underwater demolition team in the Persian Gulf, he had known that the mine one of his shipmates was arming was going to detonate. And it did, a split second after the knowledge came to Sam. There had been no time to save the other young sailor, whose remains had been so scattered that there had been nothing to send home to his family.

He had known, he had known, he had known. A thousand times in his life, the shivers had come upon Sam with terrifying urgency, and not once had they brought him the smallest measure of happiness.

But they *had* brought him to the sea. He had first felt the ocean's pull in the orphanage, where its salt kiss had awakened him in his bunk and brought him south, a runaway kid with no home and no name except for the institutional "Smith" which the authorities had assigned to him. The shivers had brought him over a thousand miles alone, with no real destination except for the constant singing of the sea growing louder with each step.

They had brought him to a pier in Jupiter Inlet, Florida, and to Darian McCabe. Darian hadn't wanted him, but Sam had known the old man—who had seemed old even then—would take him in.

Sam had begun as a hand on the *Styx*. Darian lived on the boat, then as now, and paid the boy with food and a bunk, and then clothes and a more than decent education at Maggie Waylan's school for the children of sailors. Even after Sam had reluctantly told about his past, Darian had not forced him back to the orphanage in Pittsburgh.

"Ain't going to find anybody works cheaper'n you," the old man had said when he gave Sam an old child-sized captain's hat. "And anyway, I expect you'll be moving on when you're of an age."

But Sam hadn't moved on. Darian was the only family he had ever known, and he had no place else to go. At twenty-nine, he still lived on the *Styx*, and in the past eight years since his return from the navy, Darian had made him a full partner in his salvage business. Sam's shivers had located six wrecks off the Florida coast.

Six they could get to, that is. There had been dozens of others, but all of them in waters too deep to chance. Darian was reckless enough to try an occasional salvage operation on an undocumented site, as long as it didn't cost too much, but he was not going to risk his life, or Sam's, in waters they weren't equipped to dive. Especially around the Peaks.

"You want to dive them waters, you get yourself a submarine first," Darian had once told Sam. "That and a prayerbook. I've known too many men who sailed into the Peaks and never came back. Real sailors, too, mind you, not them pansies with their silver cigarette boats."

Darian McCabe knew where the devil lived.

Sam took the pottery shard out of his pocket. The siren's voice poured through his body like warm wine.

She lived there, too, he knew. She called him from the Peaks.

You belong here, She sang. *You belong with me here*.

And though Sam tried with all his will not to listen, he heard Her.

By the time they reached their base at Jupiter Inlet, it was nearly dusk.

"Whole day shot to hell for nothing," Darian grumbled as he docked the *Styx* near Eddie's Grill, a fixture of the waterfront for the past fifty years.

Sam tied off, then joined him on the rickety wooden pier. "Buy you a beer?" he offered.

The old man grunted in reply and led the way to Eddie's.

Since it was summer, the tables were packed with tourists, but the bar was unchanged. The seamen who occupied the same stools every day of the year made room for Darian and Sam at the bar.

"You get that job?" a grizzled old-timer named Figg shouted to Darian from the far corner, a spot he had occupied for as long as Sam could remember.

"Mind your own business," Darian answered.

"Probably wanted a real sailor," Figg said and turned for approval to the group of excursion boat tourists seated at a nearby cluster of tables. His sailing days long behind him, Figg was glad to serve as local color for vacationers, as long as they bought the drinks.

"Hear the Coast Guard's out," he yelled.

"Aye."

"Looking for where the tremors started?"

"You want to know what the Coast Guard's doing, call the Coast Guard," Darian groused.

Figg was unfazed. "Happened once before, twenty-nine years ago," the old sailor said, slogging down the remains of what obviously had not been his first beer. "Seaquakes just like these here we've had the past couple of weeks. The whole bottom shifted. Hot springs started shooting into the waters. All the coldwater fish disappeared. Only thing it was good for was treasure hunters," he said with a wink. "Things what was buried under twenty feet of silt got pushed up like they was dropped overboard yesterday. Gold just a-laying there for the taking."

Sam looked tellingly at Darian.

"Here we go again," McCabe muttered.

Figg ordered another beer. He was drunk now, and loved having an audience of young people who hung on every word about what they considered to be the antediluvian past.

"Did anybody ever find treasure there?" one of the men in the group asked.

"Well . . ." Figg took his time rolling a cigarette and spitting out bits of tobacco as he lit it. "Fella from up north made a dive in the Peaks. Ever hear of them?"

"That's in the Bermuda Triangle, isn't it?" a pretty blonde woman asked.

"That it is," Figg said. "Ain't nobody ever dives the Peaks and comes back up again. Except this one fella, he did. And when he come up, he said he seen a cave glowing with light."

"Glowing?"

"That's what the man said. Guess he figured there'd be a pile of loot in there. Drove all night, and come back the next day with a helper and a truckload of special equipment—cameras, high-powered lights, underwater sleds, you name it." Figg took a swig of his latest beer.

"And?" the young man asked impatiently. "Did he bring anything up?"

Figg wheezed out a laugh. "Sharks ate him before he had the chance. His helper, too. Found an arm myself, up the shore a ways."

The old-timers at the bar exchanged smiles as the tourists recoiled in horror.

"Oh, that was a spooky time all around, that was, what with the cold water turning hot and the bottom of the sea flipping inside out like it did," Figg went on in the full glory of reminiscence. "Brought out all the kooks and hippies and what have you. There was even a bunch of them crowded onto one of the small islands out near the Peaks. God only knows what they was doing there."

The bartender glanced at Darian McCabe, whose face had suddenly grown ashen, and made a gesture for Figg to quiet down.

Figg paid no attention. "Anyhow, the whole damn place blew up. Boat ran aground or something, engine caught fire."

"Get you a drink, Figg?" the bartender shouted the length of the bar.

"Damn thing exploded right in their faces. Every one of them killed."

The bartender walked toward Figg. Darian's hand was covering his face. His fingers were trembling.

"Let's go," Sam whispered to him.

"Like flies in a trap, they was. . . ." The bartender had finally reached Figg, placed a hamlike hand on his shoulder, and spoke to him. Figg looked up, followed the bartender's gaze toward Darian's stool, then cleared his throat in embarrassment.

"I'm sorry, McCabe. Didn't know you was still . . ."

Darian got up and lumbered from the bar.

Sam knew better than to follow him.

He had learned about the accident from some of the old sailors. Twenty-nine years ago, a tourist in a rented powerboat ran over some shoals near a small private island. The boat spun into the air and crashed into a building where, as it happened, thirteen people were gathered around a dining table. The driver was killed on impact. Most of the thirteen died a few seconds later, when the boat's engine exploded.

Darian McCabe's wife and their twelve-year-old son were among the dead.

He never mentioned it. There was a faded photograph on the spartan bureau in the old man's bunkroom showing a much younger McCabe with a pretty woman and a small boy. The photo had been there all seventeen years Sam had lived and worked with him, but Darian had never once spoken a word about his lost family.

Sam was born in the same year Darian's son died. When he'd first come to Florida as a runaway, he'd been twelve years old—the same age the boy in the photograph had been when he was killed. What must it have been like, Sam had often wondered, for Darian to see another kid on his doorstep—a kid the same age as the son he'd lost? It was no wonder the old man had always been so protective of Sam, although McCabe would never admit to that.

He waited for an hour at Eddie's, then walked back to the *Styx*. Darian wasn't on board. He'd probably gone to another bar farther down the shore, Sam reasoned. Some place where the old-timers didn't hang out.

The moon was full. Its light made the choppy waves below look like golden shingles. In the distance, far out to sea, loomed the dim shapes of the small islands near the Peaks. Sam took the weatherworn piece of pottery out of his pocket and held it to his chest.

Its music—*Her* music—rose up in him again, and his breath caught with the beauty of it. *Come to me, Sam . . . Sam . . .*

"Who are you?" he whispered.

You will know me when we meet.

"Are you . . . are you the devil?"

No, Sam. I am your past and your future. And I will love you forever. But you must come. Soon, Sam. Now.

The music was driving him mad. "I'll come to you," he said.

Then he heard the heavy tread of Darian's footfalls on deck. He turned to see the old man swaying slightly as he walked toward the bridge. "What are you gaping at?" Darian growled.

"I'm not—"

"Well, quit standing around like a fool. Polish the metalwork or something."

Sam licked his dry lips. "Darian, I've got to make that dive," he said quietly.

"Dive?" Darian looked confused for a moment, and then his face set into a mask of stony rage. "You talking about the Peaks again?"

"Yes," Sam said.

"I told you, we're not treasure hunters."

"It's not about treasure. It's about my sanity." He looked at the shard in his hand. "Something's happening to me that I don't understand. I can't seem to get the Peaks out of my mind. It's as if something's . . . *waiting* for me there."

"That's bullshit." Darian spat over the rail. "Ain't nothing down there but sharks and bad water."

"Maybe. I hope you're right. But I've got to find that out for myself."

"Got to find that out for myself," Darian mimicked. "Since when do you make the decisions around here?"

"Darian, I've always tried to listen to you, and I know you're thinking of my safety—"

"I'm thinking you're an ungrateful fool I should have sent back to the orphanage."

Sam closed his eyes. "I'm just trying to tell you—"

"You don't need to tell me nothing! This is my boat, and I give the orders around here."

"Don't you understand?" Sam shouted. "I need to see that there's nothing there, so I can stop going crazy!" He pushed back his hair in a gesture of desperation. "Darian, please listen to me. If I don't make this dive, I don't know what's going to happen to me."

"I'll tell you what's going to happen. You'll get to work, and put this foolishness behind you." He picked up a rag and tossed it at Sam. "I want the metalwork done by morning," he said as he turned away.

Sam exhaled slowly. He had finally told the old man the truth, and it had meant nothing to him. "If you won't help me, I'll go alone," he said.

Darian wheeled around, his face twisted with anger. He grabbed Sam by his shirt and shoved him across the deck. Sam tripped over a coil of thick hawser line and fell sprawling on his back. "You won't dive the Peaks, do you hear me?" he screamed. His hands were closed into fists and his face was trembling with his rage. "Disobey me and you'll not be welcome on this boat."

He stared down at Sam for a moment, then stormed off the boat onto the dock and walked away.

Slowly Sam got to his knees.

The pottery shard was still in his hand.

Come, Sam. Come to me now.

He opened his palm, then closed it into a fist. He wanted to throw it away, pretend he'd never seen it.

But he knew he wouldn't do that. Not to Her.

For Her, he would disobey Darian, defy his own common sense, lose his job, his home, his friend, and perhaps his life.

He would follow Her song into the sea.

Sam stood up, clutching his stomach. The shivers were stabbing at his guts like knives. They would only stop, he knew, when he reached the Peaks.

CHAPTER 2

SAM SHIVERED.

He could not see them, but he knew he had reached the Peaks—or what was left of them after the seaquakes.

His teeth banged against his mouthpiece like jackhammers. They were nearly uncontrollable now, the shivers that made his hands shake and threatened to turn his muscles to stone. He looked at the depth gauge on his wrist, its dim light only barely visible in the dark water.

Fifty feet. Only fifty feet deep. Waters off the Caribbean weren't supposed to be this dark at fifty feet.

Dark as a tomb.

Okay, damnit, I'm here, he thought.

Somewhere above him was Tom Abbott's new Azimut, which Sam had borrowed and driven at top speed for an hour to reach the spot where he thought his heart would burst from his body. He had made the dive at night, without a dry suit or an air hose or anyone topside to help him in case he got into trouble. . . .

All for nothing. There was no ghost woman here, no siren calling his name.

No sunken ship filled with treasure. No sea monsters. Nothing waiting for him in the Peaks.

Just as Darian had said.

Still, the shivers were bad here.

Fighting to stay loose enough to move, Sam swiveled his light around. It was a tough plastic Brite-Lite that cast a hundred thousand watts—enough to throw a beam down several city blocks on land. Yet here, where the blackness of the sea was almost tangible, the light produced only a dim circle on the eerie rock formations a few dozen feet away.

Staying near some underground cliffs, he swam farther from the Azimut's anchor line. Around him, thousands of fish were making their nightly pilgrimage upward to feed. All around him were the creatures from the twilight zone of the deep—finger-long lamp tails, hatchet fish with iridescent bellies, shrimp of enormous size which blended in with the black water but, when caught in the beam of Sam's mercury light, shone a brilliant scarlet. Orangejawed whale fish pursued by tiny dagger-toothed monsters with binocular eyes rose past his face mask. A violet squid troubled by his presence shot out a puff of light blue ink to blind its enemies whose vision was accustomed to the profound darkness.

Beyond the fish, the dim circle from Sam's flashlight seemed to vanish from time to time as it fell on openings of pure blackness that sucked up the light.

Briefly he saw a faint luminescence inside the blackness. As three electric eels shot out into the light, he realized that the black holes were caves. The rock structure at the bottom of this part of the ocean was honeycombed with underwater caverns.

He realized, too, that he was alone. The sea life which had teemed around him moments before had suddenly vanished. *Shark?* he thought, swinging his light in a circle around him. No. There was no predator here. And yet . . .

Suddenly he felt flushed. If he had been on land, he knew, sweat would have been pouring off his body. He could not move. The shivers held him utterly, like a butterfly pinned to a wall, his legs dangling, the mercury vapor light held rigid in his hand as the water seemed to swell and grow around him.

Something's coming, he thought, panicking.

A moment later, it hit. An underwater wave, like a gigantic fist, hurled him far beyond the caves. The flashlight flew out of Sam's hand and bobbed on its lanyard, thumping against his thighs as he tumbled end over end like a toy. Somewhere, not far away, came a groan and a deep thump.

Hearing his own bubbles chuffing past his ears with each frenzied breath, he fumbled for the light and raised it until he saw a massive cloud of mud billowing toward him. It enveloped him quickly, blotting out the flashlight's circular beam. It was all darkness now. Sam could do nothing but hover blindly until the mud began to clear.

Seaquake. That's what it had been, Sam had no doubt. He'd been caught in the middle of one of the undersea tremors that had been plaguing the area for weeks.

He had no idea which direction he should take to reach the boat. Even the dial of his compass was invisible now.

Well, he thought philosophically, he'd just have to stay where he was until the water cleared.

He hadn't even thought about his air supply.

Now, crouching on the sea floor, Sam sighed in exasperation and immediately regretted it. He had been down too long to waste air. According to his best guess, he had another twenty minutes at the most, and that included time for his ascent. Another tricky matter. If he ran out of air on the way up, he would have to surface fast—a certain prescription for the bends. The bends could kill you. Or, if you were lucky, they might only cripple you for life.

Fortunately, the murk from the tremor was beginning to clear. In the light of his flashlight, Sam was able to make out the pocked surface of a wall of coral.

A reef, he thought, but as his hands moved along the rough expanse, he could feel its precise curve. He followed it for nearly forty feet. It was a gigantic cylinder of some sort, lying on its side on the ocean floor.

His heart beat faster. Nothing in nature held this particular shape.

Sam took the small knife he kept strapped to his leg and chipped away at the encrusted mass until the blade resonated with the ping of metal hitting metal.

He swam along to the end of the cylindrical structure. It was at least a hundred feet long. For a foot of coral to grow around it, the thing must have been in the water for hundreds of years, maybe thousands. What was it? An undersea cable? A pipe? *Made of metal?*

Then, through the clearing silt, he saw the dim outline of another structure, identical to the one to which he was clinging. But this tower was still standing, reaching up from the ocean floor toward the dark night sky.

Sam swam slowly toward it. The towers, or whatever they were, must have been buried under God knew how much mud before they were thrust to the surface during the seaquake. The mudstorm probably had been caused by the fallen cylinder when it keeled over and thumped onto the ocean floor.

The water here seemed oddly bright. He switched off his torch. No, it wasn't his imagination. The whole area between the towers was light, as light as it might be at twenty feet during daylight hours. As Sam neared the standing tower, he saw that it was resting on a plateau of rock no more than sixteen feet square. Around the plateau was nothing but water going down so far that, despite the strange brightness around the column, the light from Sam's flashlight could not penetrate to the bottom.

He had heard about these. The old timers sometimes talked about the valleys nestled near the Peaks—chasms of incalculable depth, from which even light could not return. He always had dismissed their existence along with most of the sailors' lore, but he was seeing one of the valleys with his own eyes.

Then he spotted something draped over the base of the column, something shiny that made him forget all about the topography of the ocean floor.

He blinked uncertainly, drawing nearer to it. The object looked as if it were on display in a store window: a chain of some thirty gold links, more than an inch long apiece, perfect and uncorroded. As Sam dived for it, the fine silt which already had begun to settle on it floated away.

And then he heard music.

He laughed aloud with happiness, sending up a burst of air bubbles around his head. It was Hers, the sea siren's, and she was making him a gift of it.

Take this, my wandering lover come home

He swam toward it, feeling the shudder in his belly turn to heat. His hand reached for it, trembling. He touched it. Inside his mask, tears came to his eyes.

Touch me, yes, take me

He picked it up. Dangling from the chain was a four-inch-long crystal, opaque with salty deposits. As Sam rubbed his thumb and forefinger along the faceted sides, it began to glow with a greenish light. His fist opened reflexively and the chain spilled out between his fingers. He dived for it, clutching the mercury light with one hand, grasping at the empty water with the other as the chain sank down, down, over the cliff of rock where the pillar stood, into the green warmth of the dark deep beyond.

Come to me, yes, yes, Sam, closer, yes

He dived after it.

Soon the pressure of the water was squeezing him, making his lungs labor with each breath. He caught sight of his questing hand in front of him. The fingers on it seemed to elongate into writhing blue eels.

He blinked hard, swallowed. His breathing was ragged. In front of him, a dozen images materialized at once: the kid with him on demo duty in the navy, looking like a burst balloon when the mine exploded and blew him to pieces; the headmistress of the orphanage in Pittsburgh, her features pointed like blades. There were others, Darian, others he didn't know. Through the twisted, caricatured faces he dove deeper, deeper, down to where the water seemed almost scalding and the light was as brilliant as emeralds.

Then he swooped down and caught the chain in his cupped hands, all the while making a sound in his throat like a man in the act of love.

Go *up. Got to go up now.*

Sam's air supply was low, and diminishing with frightening speed at this new depth. Panting, his breath sounding like the gasps of a dying man, he looped the gold chain around his belt.

On an outcropping of rock, a mass of blind shrimp wriggled like maggots on a corpse. Past them, where the superheated water met the cold, an intense green light shimmered like a desert mirage before the blackness beyond.

Yes . . . yes . . . yes . . .

The light emanated from a cave with a mouth more than four feet across.

But it had been so dark here, Sam thought. He looked upward, to where the column of coral-encrusted metal must be standing. There was nothing above him except blackness.

For a moment Sam hung motionless in the water, every muscle in his body rigid.

He heard music.

My lover

My lover

The song surged to life. It was no longer the half-remembered, teasing melody which had brought him to the Peaks. It was clear and wonderful, music that coursed through his blood like a drug, music that he could see as well as hear, music he could touch with his hands and that touched him back, on his lips, his eyes, hard in his loins and through his soul.

It was coming now from the mouth of the black cave.

Not far now, Sam, come to me, come to me

Still gasping, his movements a supreme effort against the crushing pressure of the deep, he swam, entranced, toward the cave. The music grew louder, the light brighter, inviting him, drawing him nearer until he passed through the cave mouth and instantly found himself in the middle of an underwater garden of fantastic beauty.

It was semicircular in shape, the calm warm water wafting lazily over what looked like flowers. Sam touched the strange vegetation, red-petaled blossoms on slim stalks, fernlike plants with lacy fronds that curled and opened with the movement of the waves. At his feet were pebbles of soft pastel colors. He felt as if he were inside an oyster shell, pearly and iridescent.

Against the far wall of the cave stood a block of stone nearly five feet high and six inches thick, furry with algae and encrusted with lichen.

As he swept his hand over its surface, the algae flew off in blindingly bright sparks. Sam followed them with his eyes as the tiny dots of light danced out of the cave. *They're what's generating the light*, he thought.

But when he turned back, the stone itself was glowing.

And on it, where the algae had been, was an image of a rocky shoreline.

He fell back. What was he seeing? How was he looking *at land*, standing as he was on the bottom of the ocean?

In the distance, around the bend of the shore he was observing, were dozens of large ships, enormous wooden-hulled vessels with square sails. At the very center of the horizon was a mountain flanked by two pyramids.

Pyramids? Get it together, now, Sam, he told himself.

In his excitement he had momentarily forgotten about the pressure in his chest, but he felt it now. He was in too deep. The sea was playing tricks with his mind.

Take a dozen of Figg's tall tales and let your air run out, and suddenly you've got an underwater TV screen to veg out on till you start sucking seawater.

There were people on the shore. They were dressed strangely in rough draped cloth. A man whose shoulders were hooded in a wolf skin, complete with the animal's head, came into Sam's vision and walked out of it again.

Get out, you dumb shit! Can't you see you're going to die down here?

He was answered by another voice, soft as velvet. Her voice.

Stay with me, Sam, stay with me.

Sam paused in the cave mouth.

Oh, Jesus, he thought. *What's happening to me?*

He looked at his air gauge. It read 150 feet. He had no air for such a dive.

In the scene playing before him, the people on the shore fell to the ground. One woman lifted a child and hugged it to her breast. The Earth began to shiver and tremble.

Sam trembled with it. He could hear the shrieks of women as a chasm opened in the earth. Some distance away, another line crazed across the landscape, and steam hissed skyward while the ground quaked and roiled.

Then the mountain at the far horizon erupted. The sky turned black, raining rock, capsizing the huge ships in the harbor. Lava streamed out of the shuddering volcano, glowing red as the ground opened a new jagged mouth to drink it.

Through the ash-blackened air, Sam could make out the figure of a man standing at the rim of the volcano, raising his arms skyward as the heat from the eruption melted his very flesh away.

Sam cried out, forgetting that he was underwater. A mass of precious air bubbles rose around his face. He staggered blindly back, out of the undersea garden, out through the cave mouth, even as the music he had heard was drowned out by the shrieks of dying men.

I*t isn't real*, he told himself. *Get out of here.*

Then the music came back, then and beautiful.

Sam.

He pushed her voice away, stumbling back into the darkness of the ocean.

The temperature of the sea suddenly dropped. It was freezing here, stabbing into Sam's muscles like daggers. He could not see. The light from his mercury lamp was a feeble mist in the overwhelming blackness. His shoulder smacked hard against a rock. He remained there, crouched, hoping to get his eyes to adjust to the absolute darkness.

Through his mouthpiece, he could feel his air resisting, coming slowly, the sure sign that he was near the end of his air supply. Gradually his eyes began to accommodate themselves to the inky darkness and he could concentrate on the dim column of light from his torch. He pointed it upward and began his ascent, slowly, taking care not to overtake his own bubbles, sucking gently on his mouthpiece.

He tried not to think of what would happen when his air ran out. By the time he reached the metal pillars, it was useless. Still he continued his ascent, breathing out slowly, knowing that holding his breath was the worst thing he could do, yet instinctively unwilling to let go of his last tie to life.

Come back, the voice called. It was sweet and full of promise. Her song. *You belong here, Sam, don't go don't go don't* . . .

Again he saw the image of the man's face above the volcano, his eyes ferocious in his melting flesh.

Sam

He slowed. His arm holding the torch lowered.

Why not? he thought. He was going to die anyway. Why not die in Her embrace, hearing Her song?

He looked below him into the blackness. There was the faint greenish glow from the cavemouth, extending upward in rays, like welcoming arms.

One breath. That was all it would take. One swift painful intake of water, one convulsive shudder . . .

Her music was louder now, throbbing with his heartbeat.

Sam

He dove.

C*oming I'm coming back I'm*

Something grabbed his leg.

Sam kicked, tried to spin around, clawed at the thing that held him.

No! You can't do this to me! Not now! He thrashed, fighting for all he was worth. He did not want to die here, like a drowned sailor, trapped in a web of seaweed for the fish to eat. He wanted to be with Her, in Her arms, surrounded by Her light.

Whatever it was that had him was encircling his neck. Black arms, slick and heavy, overpowered him. It pulled out his mouthpiece and thrust something into his face. Sam fought it, punching wildly at the thing. The black arms tightened. The last of Sam's air spilled out of him.

He wanted to sob. He had searched for Her all his life and when he finally found Her, he had been too afraid to stay. Now his chance was past. He would die like the coward he was, alone and in silence.

Hanging limp, he breathed in deeply, waiting for the shock of cold salt water in his lungs, but what poured into his throat was air.

Air?

He turned his head. The black arms loosened, allowing Sam to twist his body and face his attacker.

It was a man. He lifted a light to his own facemask so that Sam could see him.

It was Darian McCabe. It was his air Sam was breathing.

Darian pulled the mouthpiece from Sam and took a breath before handing it back. Then, holding Sam in his arms, like a baby, the old man kicked up slowly along the anchor rope toward the surface above.

Sam let his mind go blank. He was safe now, he knew. But somewhere behind his hearing, the music from the cave came back to him dimly, half-remembered, with each moment growing fainter and farther away.

CHAPTER 3

ON THE DECK OF THE *STYX*, DARIAN UNZIPPED THE TOP OF SAM'S WET SUIT and pulled off his face mask. There were deep red indentations on his skin at the mask's pressure points, and Sam's nose was bleeding.

But he was breathing.

Darian covered him with a scratchy wool blanket. Without removing his own wet suit, the old man started the boat's twin diesel engines and gunned the boat through the nighttime darkness to the Florida coast. He cast a disgusted look at the fancy speedboat that Sam had driven out in. "Screw it. Let it sink," he growled. He had no time to waste, not if he was going to save Sam's life.

Rapture of the Deep. He had seen it before. A diver gets too deep, stays too long, and the ocean drives him crazy. Darian had seen men cut their own air hoses with knives, laughing as they drowned.

The old man ran his hand through his wet hair. He should have known that Sam wouldn't listen to him. Whatever the reason, the Peaks had a powerful hold on the boy.

Is that why you knew to come here after him?

Darian squeezed his eyes shut for a moment. He had awakened in the middle of the night, so certain that Sam was gone that he had not even bothered checking his bunk. He had come here, out of all the vast Atlantic, to this very spot, at night, without so much as consulting a map or a compass.

But of course you knew the place. Jamie died right nearby, didn't he?

With a cry of anguish, Darian pushed the throttle full forward, set the automatic pilot, and went back to join Sam on deck.

To his astonishment, Sam was conscious. He was sitting up, holding a cloudy-looking, spear-shaped rock dangling from a golden chain.

"You're awake."

Sam nodded.

Darian didn't know whether to scream in rage or joy. By rights, he ought to be in a coma, or at least screaming with the bends. "I'm going to get you to the hospital to check you out," the old man finally said. "What the hell's that?"

Sam gave him the necklace. Beneath the thick deposits of crust on the crystal, it glowed faintly when Darian touched it. "Jesus Christ," the old man shouted, dropping it to the deck.

Sam lunged for it before it could wash overboard and offered it again. "It's gold," he rasped. "I want you to have it."

Darian grunted. He examined the necklace again, this time careful not to touch the stone. The clasp holding the pendant to the chain was in the shape of a squat cross inscribed by a circle. It was the same symbol that was painted on the shard of pottery Sam had found earlier.

"I'll be damned," Darian muttered.

"They came from the same place," Sam said quietly.

"You found the pot handle on the beach down near Biscayne."

"That's where I found it. But it came from the Peaks."

Darian looked at him sourly, but decided not to start an argument. "Probably more junk," he said. "Gold plated, most likely. Fell over the side of some pleasure boat yesterday."

Sam didn't answer.

"If it'll make you happy, though, I'll take it to the Oceanographic Museum so some faggot with letters behind his name can tell you that it's crap."

"It's yours. Do whatever you want with it."

Darian grunted, hooked the necklace around his diving belt, and went below to change into dry clothes. When he came back on deck, Sam was sleeping.

Mr. Smith."

Sam awoke, confused. The last thing he remembered was sitting on deck, looking up at the stars. He must have passed out. Only this wasn't the *Styx*. He appeared to be inside some sort of spaceship.

"You're in a hyperbaric chamber," a pretty dark-haired nurse said, smiling.

"Where . . . where's . . ." His voice sounded thick and muffled. It was hard to get his lips to work.

"West Palm Hospital," she said. "The sedation will wear off soon." She smiled again and took his forearm. "I need to get some blood." Expertly she slid in a needle.

Sam looked at his arm. There were three other puncture holes in it. "Why are you taking so much blood from me?" he asked.

The nurse shrugged. "Doctor's orders. He'll be in to see you soon," she said as she rearranged the pillow under his head. They were close; their eyes met.

Cute eyes, mister diver. Want to dive into me sometime?

"What?" Sam asked, surprised.

"I didn't say anything." The nurse's face reddened. She left the room quickly, air hissing out as she opened the chamber's heavy metal door.

The air was palpably heavy in the small, low-ceilinged room. He could almost feel it weighing down on his body. In chambers like this, he knew, divers who had been under too long were slowly returned to normal atmospheric pressure. This allowed nitrogen bubbles which had blown up inside their bodies to be slowly purged. If it worked and they did it in time, a diver might not wind up crippled.

He closed his eyes and remembered what had brought him here. The Peaks. The two towers. The strange scene inside the underwater cave.

Maybe they can fix my body, but my mind is beyond repair. I'm as crazy as a loon.

He always knew the craziness would take over one day. All his life it had been lurking in his head, right behind the shivers, waiting to come out. He had tried hard not to go crazy, tried to keep it at bay. But the ocean . . . the Peaks . . .

Two men and a woman, all wearing white lab coats, came into the chamber and headed immediately for the chart at the foot of Sam's bed, murmuring among themselves. The woman glanced up from the chart, her eyes meeting Sam's, and he felt his breath catch.

It was not just her beauty, although anyone would have called her attractive. She was blonde and gray-eyed, with the bigboned legginess of a runner rather than a dancer. But there was something about her that touched something inside Sam, some deep, vibrating chord that filled him with an odd mixture of joy and fear.

Her lips parted. They were sensually full lips that were at odds with her straight, pulled-back hair and absence of makeup or jewelry.

She feels it too, Sam thought, puzzled. The woman looked away.

"Hello, Sam. Good to see you with us," one of the men said, smiling. "I'm Dr. Cohen. This is Dr. Krantz, our head of serology, and Dr. Althorpe from our psychiatric staff."

So that's why she's looking at me, Sam thought glumly. *She's a headshrinker.*

"You're in a hyperbaric chamber as a precautionary measure against caisson disease," Dr. Cohen went on absently, flipping through the chart. "The bends. As a diver, of course, you know about that."

"I didn't have the bends."

"Apparently not, although it says here you were down deep, and long enough to use up your air supply."

Sam shrugged.

"You did have quite a lot of nitrogen in your blood when you came in, but that's almost gone now."

"Then I'm all right?" Sam asked.

"Oh, your health seems quite sound," the other doctor, Krantz, answered. He was older than the other two, with a nervous way of moving that reminded Sam of a marionette on a string. "It's your blood that's of interest here."

Sam raised his eyebrows. "What wrong with it?"

"Nothing's wrong. It's just that it appears to be rather unusual, a type I've only encountered once before."

"They told me in the navy it was type O-negative."

The doctor shook his head. "Blood typing is a whole new thing since the days of four major blood types and all that. With DNA and more sophisticated testing, now we find many different strains. For instance . . .

He chattered on, but Sam was not paying attention. His eyes were focused on the woman, who was watching him intently.

"Your blood type may be one in a million." Dr. Krantz smiled encouragingly, as if Sam ought to be experiencing a sense of triumph over the makeup of his blood.

"Yeah? So?"

Krantz cleared his throat. "I suppose what I'm getting at is that I—that is, the medical community in general—would appreciate it if we might study your case at some length." He smiled ingratiatingly.

"You mean you want me to stay in the hospital?"

"Just for an extra day or two. For your sake," he added hastily. "Because of the quantity of blood we'd be taking."

"Whoa," Sam said. "You're not taking more quantities of blood from me than you already have. If there's nothing wrong with me, I want to get out of here."

The corners of Krantz's mouth twitched downward but he managed a resolute smile. "Perhaps an outpatient program. Once a week, say, for six months or so. . . ."

Sam laughed out loud. "You're not getting it, Doc. No more blood. I mean it." He swung his legs over the bed. "Where are my clothes?"

Dr. Cohen touched his shoulder and gently pressed Sam back into the bed. "You'll be released as soon as possible," he said gently. "But you can't leave until the sedation wears off completely. Get some rest."

"No more blood," Sam said stubbornly.

"Well, we wish you'd think about it," Krantz said.

"You said you'd run across somebody else with the same blood as me. Why not test him?"

Krantz hesitated.

"He's dead," the woman said, eliciting a dirty look from both male doctors.

"He was a diver, too," Krantz explained. "I saw him when he came in with a shark wound. But he died months later in an auto accident. His death had nothing to do with his blood." He directed his last remark toward the woman.

"Well, if I die in an auto accident, I'll will you my blood."

Dr. Cohen laughed and gave Sam a pat on the shoulder. "We'll leave you with Dr. Althorpe," he said. "When she gives you the okay, you can go."

Dr. Krantz, the serologist, looked crestfallen.

Dr. Althorpe pulled a chair beside the bed and sat down. Sam felt uncomfortable with the woman now that they were alone together. He tried not to look at her.

"According to the man who brought you in, you may have had an episode of nitrogen narcosis," she said quietly. "Rapture of the Deep. You're familiar with it?"

"I've heard about it."

"The symptoms sometimes resemble dementia . . . being crazy." She smiled, and Sam felt a little of his discomfort melting away.

"That so?" he asked nonchalantly.

"Yes. I want you to know that so that you don't think you lost your mind down there."

I don't think, I know.

"It's a purely physical phenomenon. So if you did anything strange, well . . . there's nothing wrong with your mind. And there's no reason for it to happen again."

Strange? Strange has been happening to me all my life.

"You don't seem convinced."

"Sure. Whatever you say. Can I get out of here now?"

Dr. Althorpe sighed. "It's usually helpful to the patient to talk about it."

Sam folded his arms over his chest. "And you're not going to give me my walking papers until I do, right? Look, there's nothing to say. I stayed down too long and I came up too fast. That's all."

"Was your vision distorted at times?"

Sam didn't answer.

"Did you see things that weren't there?"

"I don't know."

"Images, memories? Did your thoughts become tangible?"

"What's that mean?" Sam asked.

She opened her hands. "This phenomenon affects people in different ways, much like drugs or alcohol. Sometimes the things people see in this condition take on unusual aspects. They appear physically different or imbued with emotions. Ordinary fish can suddenly become sinister and menacing. Or even comical. Or you can picture things that have been stored in your mind for years. Your mother's face. A long-lost pet."

Slowly, Sam nodded.

"What did *you* see, Sam?" She leaned forward intently.

Hesitantly he began. "People, mostly. Things from a long time ago. The people looked kind of like cartoons."

"Yes," she said. "That's a pretty common occurrence. Sometimes people suffering from this narcosis see entire scenes, almost like dream sequences in a movie."

Sam was silent. Dr. Althorpe said, "And you did too, didn't you?"

Sam began to recount what had happened to him underwater. He was tentative at first, watching the doctor for a sign that she considered him a crackpot. There was none. She put the clipboard down and listened without taking notes, encouraging him. As he spoke, he felt freer, although he knew he could never disclose anything about the shivers or the music he heard or the voice calling him back to the depths. But she had been right: Just talking about the strange visions made him feel better. Finally he told her about the cave, about the island he saw, the people on it, the erupting volcano.

"A. . . . volcano," she repeated in a whisper. It was the first time she had spoken since he had begun his recitation.

"It was in the center of the island. I think it was an island, anyway. It was big. The volcano was pretty far away, but when it blew, it destroyed everything." He wiped his face. "And there was a man. He was standing right beside the volcano. Don't ask me how I could see his face. I don't know, it was like a dream or something, but I could see him. He ... he melted."

Dr. Althorpe put her hands to her eyes and swayed in her seat. After a moment she looked up, startled. "I'm sorry," she said quickly. "It wasn't anything you said. I was just feeling a little faint." She smiled, though her face was still ashen. "I shouldn't have skipped breakfast."

"Oh. I thought you were freaking out at what I said."

She shook her head. "Not at all. But tell me. . . ." She bit her lip. "Where were you diving?"

"Southeast. Near the out-islands. You know, the one where all those people were killed way back when. The area's called the Peaks."

"I know it. I used to go out there." She cleared her throat. "Would you allow me to conduct some tests with you before you go?" She saw his reaction and added hastily, "Psychological tests. Nothing distasteful, I promise."

Sam lay back on the bed and sighed. "So I am crazy after all," he said.

"No, not at all. It's just . . . just that business with the volcano. I've encountered that particular image before, with other patients."

He sat up. "You're kidding. Inside the cave, too?"

"No, that part's your own. But the volcano . . ." The doctor clasped her hands together. Sam could see them trembling.

"Are you all right?" he asked.

"Yes, of course." She took a deep breath. "At any rate, I'd like to do those tests to see what you have in common with other people who've seen the same thing."

Sam nodded. "Just standard, huh?"

"Yes." She stood up and smoothed her skirt mechanically. "Just standard."

CHAPTER 4

NOTHING IS STANDARD ABOUT THIS, CORY ALTHORPE THOUGHT AS SHE rushed through the hospital corridors to her office. The Peaks. The volcano. The island. The blood.

Oh, God, Memory Island. And the blood.

In her office she rifled through her file drawers and came up with the folder on the dead diver whose blood was so similar to Sam Smith's. December '92. The man's name had been Mark Cole.

Attacked by a shark and admitted to the hospital in a deep coma, Cole had not been expected to survive a single night. Yet, to the amazement of the hospital staff, he had made a full recovery.

While he was recuperating, he had told Dr. Althorpe about the visions he saw while unconscious. They were not the usual tunnel-white light-dead relatives experience reported by most people who had come back to life after their normal functions had terminated. Mark Cole had seen a volcano.

So had others. They had all seen a volcano. They had all had the same type of blood. And they possessed one other common factor.

They were all dead.

In the back of the file cabinet was a small bound volume, its pages musty smelling and yellowed with age. Cory took it out and opened it to the first page.

EDWARD BONNER, it read in her grandfather's angular hand. 1966.

Cory had been seven years old then. Eight when he died a year later.

She turned the page: MAY 14, 1966. I HAVE 17 WILLING PARTICIPANTS, ALL WITH THE SAME X FACTOR IN THEIR BLOOD, AND ALL PSYCHIC AS THE VERY DEVIL.

Edward Bonner had been a prominent internist who had devoted the last fifteen years of his life to the study of psychic phenomena. He had been convinced that there was a physical common denominator among people who exhibited a high degree of extrasensory perception.

The year before his death, according to his journal, he finally had found something to support his belief. He had located seventeen subjects of outstanding psychic ability who also seemed to be unusually resistant to infection and who healed faster than normal people.

Although blood testing was not well developed in the mid-sixties, Bonner—with the help of a small federal grant, enough to hire a young serologist to serve as his assistant—managed to find one factor in the blood of the seventeen that was different from "normal" blood.

In April of 1967, Bonner brought the subjects together on a small island off the coast of Florida. The island was his personal property, inherited from his father. There the seventeen participants learned that what each could do alone was magnified a thousandfold when they worked together.

They were able to perform feats of what could only be called magic. During the last night at the conference, the group spontaneously called forth a vision they all saw: a volcano erupting, with a man standing in the middle of the fiery blast. Not one of the subjects understood the vision, but it had been somehow familiar to each of them.

They had experienced a group memory.

The seventeen had felt nearly as exultant as Edward Bonner. They called themselves the Rememberers, and named the place where they had come together Memory Island.

How true the name turned out to be, Cory thought, blinking back tears as the image of her grandfather came unbidden into her mind. Her memory of him was too painful. She had loved him more than either of her parents. He had been the one she shared her dreams and fears with; the one to cradle her head during the fierce summer storms that changed the face of the island every year, though the small frame house had stood, seemingly forever . . . until the day it exploded and burned in a spray of blood and bodies.

Even now, almost thirty years later, the blood was still there, turned black on the planks of rotting wood, but still there.

In the end, the blood had been Edward Bonner's testament. The press, with its infinite capacity for stupid callousness, had interpreted the tragedy as a bleak joke, with Bonner and his obsession for "hocus-pocus" as its butt. His brilliance was forgotten, his files destroyed, his program ridiculed. All that was left of Edward Bonner's work were the pages in his personal journal that the young Cory had found in the bedroom of his farmhouse in Vermont.

From the time of the triumphant mass vision of the volcano to the accident some months later, the Rememberers had used all their skills to determine the meaning of that single, ineradicable memory.

A camaraderie grew among them. A husband-wife pair of doctors, Lars and Marie Nowar, even told the group shyly that she was pregnant and that the baby had been conceived on Memory Island. Unfortunately, the group had only had enough time to distill one idea about the otherwise meaningless volcano vision: the sea. Somehow, they all knew, the sea was involved.

This prompted Bonner to focus his experiments on just one of the Rememberers, Jamie McCabe. Although the boy's father, a "colorful but stone-headed local," according to Bonner's personal notes, had denounced the project from the beginning as a foolish waste of time, Jamie was the obvious choice. Among the seventeen subjects, he was the only one who had grown up around the sea. And despite the fact that he was only twelve, his extrasensory perception was by far the most highly developed of the group.

One day, in a small powerboat that the boy could pilot like an expert, he led Dr. Bonner to a place in the ocean off the coast of Memory Island.

"It's here," he said.

"What is?"

"I don't know. The memory."

Dr. Bonner had asked several divers to explore the area, but all had refused. Apparently there was some superstition attached to it. They referred to the area as the Peaks.

Cory closed the book. There were no more entries. She knew the Rememberers had held only one more group session after the last entry was made, but what went on was not known because Bonner's notes were destroyed in the explosion.

His files, kept in his small office in West Palm Beach, had been packed away somewhere. Cory had tried to locate them after graduating from medical school, but no one in the family had had any idea where they were. Her grandfather's program had been a waste, after all, they had said with disdain. A complete embarrassment, of no interest to anyone.

Yet, twenty-five years later, the dead diver named Mark Cole had seen a volcano. And so, just last night, had Sam Smith.

She telephoned Dr. Krantz in the serology lab, trying to keep the distaste she felt for the man out of her voice.

"About Mr. Smith," she said.

"Who? Oh, the nitrogen narcosis. Did he change his mind about giving blood?"

"Not yet, but I'm working on it. I'm calling about his physical condition . . ."

"What about it?" Krantz snapped. "I'm very busy."

"The level of nitrogen in his blood seemed very high upon admission."

Krantz snorted. "That's why he was put in the H-chamber."

"And yet he's had no ill effects. Not even a trace of the bends. Is that usual?"

There was a pause. "Nitrogen affects people differently. But overall, no, it's not usual. You'd expect him to have some kind of symptom." He paused. "Get him to stay for more tests. Use your charm."

"Thank you," Cory said coldly and hung up.

Seventeen subjects, all unusually resistant to illness and injury, she thought, running her finger absently along the spine of her grandfather's journal. *All psychics.*

And what does that make me?

Cory had never suffered a cold in her life and never had a cavity. She had broken her leg once when she fell from a horse, but she had never been what one would call sick.

The first time she had seen her own blood was when her grandfather drew a small amount from her finger to show her the powers of the great electron microscope in his laboratory.

"Now, that didn't hurt a bit, did it?" he had asked, preparing the slide.

She shook her head proudly. At eight, she would have endured any pain just to be with him among his huge, secret tools.

"All right, now there it is at five thousand. Doesn't look like blood at all, does it?"

She stared through the microscope at the curved wall that was one of her corpuscles. "Wow."

Bonner chuckled and adjusted the controls as he lifted Cory onto his lap. The image on the slide was so enlarged now that she could see designs on the surface of a single blood cell.

"Those squiggles are what make your blood a little bit different from everyone else's," he said. "And a little bit the same, too. They're like little signs. What I'm working on is finding out if some of these signs can tell you what a person's brain thinks like."

"You can tell that just by looking?"

"Not yet, but maybe some day." He moved her aside to peer into the lens himself. "Now, what I'm looking for these days is one particular—" He stopped abruptly.

"What is it, Grandfather?"

Silently, he lifted her off his lap and placed her on the floor, then adjusted the microscope for more power. Cory shifted from one foot to the other. She would never disturb her grandfather in his work, but he seemed to have forgotten she was there.

Finally he lifted his head and stared at her. His gaze, puzzled, fascinated, was frightening to the girl.

"Is everything all right, Grandfather?" she ventured.

Bonner smiled. "Yes, honey. Everything's fine." He switched off the microscope, held out his big wrinkled hand, and led her into his office. There he took out a box filled with rectangular cards. He placed five in front of her. One had a circle on it, another a square. The third was a star, the fourth a triangle, and the last a set of parallel wavy lines.

"Let's play a guessing game," he said, taking another card from the box and putting it face down on the desk. "What's this card?"

"A star," she said without hesitation.

"And this one?"

"A square."

When she had gone through the box of cards four times, Cory asked, "Did I get any right?"

"Fifty."

"Just fifty?" She was disappointed.

"Fifty's good. About a million times better than most." Cory beamed, but her grandfather was not smiling. "Tell me, Cory . . . do you ever know things that other people don't?"

She squirmed in her seat. "Like what?"

Bonner shrugged. "Like . . . oh, I don't know . . . like something's going to happen before it does?"

She wrung her hands. "Well, I always know when Daddy isn't going to come home for the weekend. Mommy cries."

Bonner harumphed. He had never cared much for his philandering son-in-law.

"And I always know when it's going to rain," she said brightly. "The air smells different." Then she looked down at the floor.

"What's the matter, honey?"

"It isn't a good thing," she said.

"If it's the truth, it's good. That's what science is all about."

A fat tear trickled down her cheek. She wiped it away.

"What is it?" her grandfather asked gently.

"I can tell when people are going to die," she whispered.

Bonner blinked.

"I don't try to do it. It just happens."

"When does it happen?"

She sighed. "Like when Jody Alexander got sick at school. She said she just had the flu and got over it, but I knew. She didn't come back after summer vacation. Everybody was surprised when she died except me." Her breath exploded out of her in a sob. "Because I knew."

Bonner came across his desk and knelt beside her. "Cory, just because one time—"

"It wasn't one time. I saw a policeman outside a store and I knew it about him. Then that night I saw his face on TV. Somebody shot him. And there were other times too. Lots . . ."

She gasped. Around her grandfather's head was a dark corona, like a halo of black light.

"What is it?" Bonner asked.

Cory moaned and buried her face in his neck. "Please take me home, Grandfather," she said.

Less than six months later, Edward Bonner was dead.

It means nothing, Cory told herself. This had been the first time in years that she even remembered the incident in her grandfather's laboratory. And people remembered incorrectly. Nowadays, the courts were cluttered with cases filed by people who "remembered" things that never happened.

Bonner probably had not spent a long time examining the slide of her blood. Children were impatient. It was probably just a few seconds. And she knew from her own work that getting fifty correct answers out of a hundred Zener ESP cards was possible for anyone, given a single test. Had she repeated it, she might well have scored the normal twenty percent or less. And the fact that she had never had a cavity was undoubtedly due to good hygiene and proper food. People raised in comfortable circumstances rarely had bad teeth.

She replaced Bonner's journal in the file cabinet and locked it. Sam Smith, in the throes of caisson's disease, had seen a vision. It had nothing to do with her.

"Bring in Mr. Smith from Room seven fourteen," she snapped into the intercom.

CHAPTER 5

THE OLD MAN WALKED INTO THE CURATOR'S OFFICE, SAW A WASTEBASKET, and spat into it.

"Darian McCabe," he announced.

The secretary's gaze moved slowly from the wastebasket to the man's weather-lined face with its arrogant, arched nose and clear gray eyes as wise as the sea. Her first impression of him was that he was made out of bronze, like a statue incongruously clad in blue jeans and a none-too-clean T-shirt. He seemed bigger than life, utterly motionless, yet somehow filling the room with his presence.

"I believe Dr. Woodson is expecting you," she said, rising to show him into the inner office.

"I can get there by myself," McCabe said.

When he entered, Woodson looked up from his desk. To McCabe's surprise, he was a black man. He stood up and walked over to McCabe with a limp so pronounced that his whole body seemed as twisted and gnarled as an old tree.

"Harold Woodson," he said curtly, extending his hand. His voice and face were young—no older than fifty, Darian surmised—although the rest of him might easily pass for ninety. "You have something you want me to see?"

Darian liked the man at once. No phony smiles, no chit-chat. When he called the Oceanographic Museum for an appointment, he had expected some twerp with a Rolex watch on his wrist and a Greenpeace poster behind his desk.

"One of my men found this." McCabe produced the pendant from his pocket, careful to hold it by its chain.

Woodson took it the same way, then placed it on a square of black velvet near a small sofa and motioned for Darian to sit down.

He examined it with a magnifying glass. "Where'd your man find it?"

"Out a ways."

"International waters?"

"Aye. Belongs to the finder. Nobody else."

Woodson glanced at him sideways with half a smile, then turned back to the object. "The bale's unusual."

"Spanish cross, I figured," McCabe said, testing.

The black man shook his head. "No way. It's too stark. Modern, almost. Yet . . ." He fell silent.

"Think it's worth anything?"

"Well, I'm pretty sure it's a gold chain, so that should be worth a chunk. But any other value . . ." He shrugged while he scraped lightly at the cloudy stone with his fingernail. "You can't carbon-date gold. And the stone . . ." He put the magnifying glass down. "I can have it analyzed to see what the stone is, but I don't think there's any way we can determine the age of the piece. I don't know. Maybe the deposits on the stone might tell us something."

Darian snorted. "I told him it was nothing." He dug into his pocket again and came up with the pottery shard Sam had found on the beach. "He picked this up, too."

Woodson's eyebrows raised. "Come from the same place?"

Darian cleared his throat. "Might have."

Woodson seemed more interested in the shard. "The same design as the bale," he mused. "That's weird."

"Christian?"

"Not necessarily. Many cultures used the cross as a symbol for different things. Actually this is more like an X on its side or a plus sign. And it doesn't appear without the circle around it. It might even be Greek. Some early Mycenean work looked sort of like this."

Darian looked down his impressive nose at the man. "You don't find Greek antiquities in these waters," he said.

"No, not usually," Woodson agreed. "Of course, it might have washed off a sunken ship. Ships have gotten lost in some areas of the Atlantic. Out a ways."

A halfsmile crossed Darian's lips. "That came from a place called the Peaks. Heard of it?"

Woodson nodded. "Know it well. There's a lot of seismic activity going on out there right now. The coast guard's out keeping an eye on things."

"We seen 'em."

"Well, who knows? That's why this shard may be an impressive find. It might have been unearthed from a great depth during a quake." Woodson picked up the pendant again and placed it in the palm of his hand. "And this, too," he said. "Mother of God!"

He dropped the pendant. Its glow dissipated slowly as it fell back onto the black velvet.

Darian laughed. "Took me a spell to get over that myself," he said.

After a long moment, Woodson pulled his gaze away from the stone to look at McCabe. "What is that?" he whispered.

Darian shook his head. "Don't know."

"You said it came from the Peaks?"

Darian grunted agreement. "Now you're not going to give me any of that Bermuda Triangle hogwash, are you?"

"No, of course not." Woodson touched the stone again, lightly with the tip of his finger. Its green light flickered. "But what the devil could cause *that*?"

"Never seen anything like it myself."

"Do you mind if I have it analyzed?"

"Nope. Long as you give it back."

"Well, naturally. Is there more?"

"Just the two pieces. My man got the Rapture. Nearly drowned. I had to bring him up."

Woodson forced himself to look away from the pendant. "I'm sorry. I hope he's all right."

"They say at the hospital he's fine. Got him in one of those spaceship rooms."

"Hyperbaric chamber," Woodson said.

"Only he ain't got the bends."

"He's lucky."

Darian leaned back, sizing up the black man. "That's what you got, ain't it?" he observed.

"That's right," Woodson said tightly.

"Still dive?"

"Every chance I get."

Darian smiled. "The sea's a mean bitch. Once she gets you, she don't want to let you go."

"She almost didn't," Woodson said with a rueful smile.

Darian stood up to leave. "You're better'n I expected," he said, extending his hand. Woodson shook it and looked searchingly at McCabe's face.

"What's the matter? Tobacco juice on my chin?"

"No, no. I'm sorry. It's just that you look familiar to me. We might have dived together once."

"Doubt it," Darian said, shaking his head. "I'd remember a man of your color on a dive. It ain't usual."

Woodson smiled. "I keep forgetting. We aren't supposed to be able to swim."

"Maybe, maybe not. But I'd have remembered." Darian grasped the doorknob, but Woodson's hand closed over his own.

"It was on the island," the black man said softly, the remembrance a shock to himself, even as he spoke the words. "Memory Island."

A look of acute distress crossed Darian's face. Woodson was immediately sorry he'd spoken. "Forgive me. I know how painful that must be for you."

"Do you?" Darian snapped.

Woodson looked out the window. "I was one of them."

The old man stood, silent, for a moment. "The Rememberers," he said at last, his voice thick with bitterness. "That's what Jamie used to call you . . . you people. Like it was some kind of social club."

Woodson said nothing. The silence between them seemed almost palpable.

Darian finally broke it. "How'd you get away?" he asked flatly.

"I was in the john. When the explosion hit, it blew the wall out and me with it. I was out cold until it was all over."

McCabe was looking past Woodson's head, his steely eyes watching something deep within his own mind.

Suddenly Woodson wished to God that McCabe would go. He had not meant to speak of the island. It had taken years of effort to erase it from his memory. Yet it came back now as fresh and terrible as it had been twenty-nine years earlier. The bodies, the blood. The kid—Darian McCabe's son—blackened like a cinder, his body thrown over his mother's.

"Jamie was a fine boy," Woodson said in a rasp. "Exceptional."

Darian grunted. Yes, Jamie was exceptional, all right. All of the Rememberers had been psychic, but none like Jamie. That was what that lunatic Bonner had told the McCabes—that their boy might be a "pure strain," capable of unimaginable things. Darian had been against the experiment from the first, yet he had permitted the boy to participate because Jamie had wanted to so badly. He belonged with these people, he had said. At last he belonged somewhere.

And then he was dead. The strange mental gifts of Darian's brilliant son had ultimately killed him and his mother, who had only been on the island to look after her child.

They had killed Darian too, in every sense that mattered.

"The past is done," the old man said. He left the office without looking at Woodson.

Is it? Harry Woodson wondered.

The past was obviously not done for Darian McCabe. But he had no idea how bad it actually had been. McCabe didn't know that the accident that had killed his son had been no accident at all.

Except for Woodson, no one knew that not all of Bonner's seventeen Rememberers had been present on the island that night. Four had not come to the conference. But they had died all the same. Different people, different places, all in one weekend. A New England minister torn to shreds by a thresher on his farm in Maine. A hillbilly woman from West Virginia, stabbed by her crazy husband. Two doctors, a husband and his pregnant wife, killed when their car drove over into a swamp.

And then all the Rememberers were dead. All of them except for Harry Woodson.

His name hadn't been Woodson then. He was born Harrison Wood, Jr. Dr. Bonner's experiment had cost him his name, his family, his past, the future he had planned . . . and more. He looked down at his crippled hands which were never without pain. Much more.

On the day of the deaths, all of them seemed to have known that something bad was going to happen. Jamie had been silent and pale all day,

It was odd, Woodson was to think later. Thirteen psychics, all developed to peak ability, and yet not one of them had dared trust his or her instinct of doom. It was as if it were all still a game to them, with no relation to real life.

That certainly had been true in Woodson's own case, at least in the beginning. He had come to Memory Island strictly in vacation mode. He had never believed in psychics, and had assumed from the beginning that

all the Rememberers were reveling as much as he was in splashing around
on a Caribbean paradise while getting over on the U.S. government.

Those were the halcyon days of the sixties, when being black was the
ticket for everything he wanted. White people, particularly educated ones
associated with institutions, automatically assumed that Harry came from a
fatherless home, lived in poverty, and suffered from low self-esteem, and
bent over backward to make his life easier. Teachers understood when he
failed to turn in assignments. The administration closed its eyes when he
and two other students were caught hiding a camera inside the women's
locker room in the gym building. And long-haired blondes threw themselves
at him, doing their part for Equal Opportunity.

Naturally he kept very quiet about the fact that his father was an aerospace
engineer for NASA and his mother a concert pianist, and that Harry himself
was the product of elite private schools, summers in Europe, and a home
life of warmth and discipline.

In undergraduate school, his instructors routinely were amazed by his
good grades. Part of the dreadful existence he was supposed to have led,
he surmised, included being an academic zero; but on this he could not
pander to the expectations of white folks. His father, Harrison Wood, Sr.,
would have had no qualms about rewarding a failing grade with a year's
hard labor.

As it was, he had tried to defy his father only once, when Harry had first
fallen in love with diving. Young Harry announced at the dinner table
that he had decided to forego college and instead take up a career as an
underwater photographer.

His father had politely ordered him out of the house.

After three months of being a bonafide black man living at poverty level
with no prospects, he came home prepared to listen to his father's lecture
about choosing something "worthwhile"—which meant engineering—to
do with his life. He was reluctantly working on his masters in civil engineering when Bonner's program came to light.

Harrison Wood, Sr., definitely would not have considered participating
in a psychic experiment "worthwhile." So Harry didn't tell him about it,
just as he never told his father that he smoked pot, dropped acid occasionally, grew his hair into an Afro, wore tie-dyed dashikis, and had taken up
his own brand of African mysticism which basically involved stroking the
bared limbs of gullible coeds in order to drive evil spirits away.

He had found that he had a genuine talent for "reading" his subjects. It
was pleasant and convenient that girls were so crazy about having him drive
away their evil spirits, but occasionally a feeling would steal over him
and he found himself inside the young women's heads, hurting, striving,
suffering from things that, as a man, he had never encountered.

That had ruined everything for him. He saw the pain of a beautiful girl
from Colorado whose stepfather had beaten her mercilessly for nine years;
he felt the shame of a slender Japanese from Radcliffe who had consented
to sex with a professor in exchange for a better grade. He understood how
desperately some of them needed the real answers that he was not able to
give.

Harry stopped the African witch doctor scam then, but not before one of the girls had given him a newspaper clipping about Dr. Bonner's search for people with psychic ability. More than half drunk, Harry showed up for the test—about which he later could remember not one thing—and amazingly was invited to join Bonner's group.

"Have wet suit, will travel," he told his roommates, flashing his free plane ticket to Palm Beach. His friends shook their heads with admiration. Harry had just raised the art of deceit and scam to an entirely new dimension.

And yet, for all Harry's cynicism, he too had seen the volcano. And he realized that he had never before felt such a closeness to anyone as he did to this motley group of seventeen misfits brought together by the blood they had in common and the freakish gift this blood seemed to carry with it.

The Rememberers.

Harry looked down at his hands. They were holding the pendant. It still glowed faintly with its odd green light.

He called the lab. "I've got a couple of pieces here I'd like you to clean up and try to date," he said.

He set it down with a sigh.

The driver of the boat that crashed had been burned beyond recognition, as if he had been soaked in gasoline. The boat had gone straight to its mark, as if it had been set by remote control.

But why would anyone want to kill psychics on a remote island? Except for their unusual blood, the Rememberers were the most ordinary sort of people, not rich or famous or threatening to anyone in any way.

But if Harry had any doubts at the time that the dozen deaths had been murder, they were dispelled shortly afterward. Minutes after he came to, two men with guns drawn pulled into the dock at Memory Island to inspect the bodies.

They want to make sure we're all dead, he remembered thinking.

Blindly, unthinking, he ran. In a small cove on the island, Bonner had kept a small motorboat. Harry had taken it out the day before to go diving. He jumped aboard and, using a small emergency oar, paddled out into the ocean until he was sure the boat's motor would be out of earshot of the armed intruders.

But he was wrong. Moments after he started the engine, he saw the big speedboat back away from the island and come racing after him. He had no chance now. It was daylight and open sea. They couldn't miss him, and his little boat could not possibly outrun the big speed craft.

His only chance was underwater. His scuba equipment was still in the boat and he knew the tanks still contained some air. He dove into the water backfirst, dropped to the shallow bottom, and began swimming back toward Memory Island. The previous day he had discovered that the water near the island ranged from forty to two hundred feet in depth, with very little gradation. The bottom just seemed to drop out in places. Now Harry dove into one of those deep canyons, there to wait and hide until his pursuers had left.

He had not counted on them having their own divers and equipment aboard. Five minutes later they were on him. Before he even saw them, one of the men had looped a heavy nylon rope around Harry's shoulders like a lasso.

Harry struggled violently, but the two men were big and obviously experienced. They dragged him down to a deep spot, wedged him into a ledge of coral, and pulled out his mouthpiece. As he flailed in panic, the bubbles from his tanks billowing up around them like a reverse waterfall, the two men carefully twisted the rope around him, then followed it back up to the surface.

Harry tried to reach for the mouthpiece with his teeth, but that was useless. He wriggled frantically, trying to free his arms from the coral ledge, but the living reef clamped tightly around him like a giant tooth-filled mouth. With a feeling of utter despair, he saw the bubbles from his tank shrink. The huge billows slowed to a trickle and then stopped entirely. Their roiling noise stilled.

Harry was alone and the silence had come.

Thin streams of blood, colored green in the dim deep water, rose out from his legs and chest and back where the reef had torn his flesh. His lungs were burning.

And then, to his amazement, somehow he twisted free.

He felt himself falling out of the ledge, entangled by the mass of rope. He bit down hard on the inside of his cheek to stay conscious as he extricated himself, slowly, methodically, repeating to himself in a mental drone that buzzed inside his bursting head. *Do not panic! Do not panic!*

He got out of the rope. His hands shook like pieces of paper in the water as he ascended, fast, as fast as he could, blowing out his air, tasting the blood in his mouth, hoping he could reach the surface before he blacked out, feeling pain, cramps, getting worse but not caring. *Do not panic!* The pain, the pain the pain the pain. . . .

He rose out of the water screaming.

The other boat was gone. The two divers had tied the end of the long rope which they had used to harness Harry around the cleat of his own small boat.

I'm supposed to be dead and it's supposed to look like an accident. Like I got tangled in my own rope. But why?

He knew the answer. Because, for some reason he could not fathom, none of the Rememberers was supposed to live.

He still could not recall how he managed to get to his family's home, up the Florida coast, near Patrick Air Force Base. All he remembered was the constant pain.

His father immediately got him into the Air Force Base hospital which had a hyperbaric chamber, but by then the rogue nitrogen in his blood vessels had already done its damage. Though Harry always had healed quickly, this time too much injury had been done to his system. The doctors said it was amazing that Harry had lived at all. It was small consolation for the fact that he would be crippled for life.

A few nights later, he told his father everything. The two of them tracked down the four Rememberers who had not been on Memory Island and found that they had all died mysteriously on the day of the explosion.

Harrison Woods, Sr., wanted to contact the FBI, but Harry was scared. Someone had killed all the other Rememberers. If Harry let it be known that he was still alive, they would come after him again.

After some thought, Harry's father agreed. They settled on a radical course of action: Harry would have to change his name, forget Yale, and move out of the country. It was bizarre, but it seemed like the only way to keep him alive.

In Panama, he took up diving again and found that in the depths of the ocean, his back unbent and the everlasting pain in his joints abated. Only in the sea that had destroyed his body could he be whole again. He started from scratch as an undergraduate at the University of Panama and studied oceanography.

There Harold Woodson was born, full grown, out of the sea.

*D*estiny, he thought as he picked up the pendant again. Here he was, a different man from the one who had participated in the Rememberers experiment—a different name, a different body, a different line of work— and he had just met Jamie McCabe's father. *The circle goes round and round. Is it ever broken?*

A technician from the lab knocked before coming in, a valise like a tool box in his hand.

"That it?" the technician asked.

Woodson passed it over to him.

"Interesting." He held the crystal on his palm and turned it over. "Etruscan, maybe."

Woodson murmured assent. "It was found in Caribbean waters, though. Along with this." He gave the man the pottery shard.

"Ooh." His eyebrows raised. "Now that *is* interesting."

He opened the case, took out some cotton wadding which he wrapped around the shard, and placed it carefully inside. Then he picked up the pendant again.

"What's the stone? Quartz?" He scratched it with his thumbnail.

"You tell me," Woodson said.

The technician wrapped the pendant and put it into the case with a smile. "Will do, chief."

As he left, Harry followed him with his eyes, frowning. Something odd had happened. Very odd.

The pendant had not glowed when the other man touched it.

Not a glimmer.

CHAPTER 6

"WHAT IS IT?"

"A circle."

"This one?"

"Triangle."

"Now?"

"Square. And the next one's the wavy lines."

Dr. Althorpe looked at the next card in the diminishing pile and sighed. It was a star.

"How much longer is this going to take?" Sam asked, bored.

"Only a few more cards."

"Is this the last time around?"

"Yes."

She tried not to show her irritation, although one side of her jaw clenched in an involuntary rhythm as she presented the final cards.

Circle, circle, star, triangle, wavy lines.

All wrong.

A perfect score. Zero.

She gathered up the cards. Sam tipped his chair onto its two back legs and sat with his arms crossed, beaming.

"How'd I do, Doc?"

"I think you know," Cory said curtly.

"How would I know? Think I'm a mind reader?" His grin grew even broader.

"Very funny." She placed the cards neatly back into their box, yellowed with age. They had been her grandfather's Zener cards for ESP testing, the same set he had shown Cory when she was eight years old.

She had gone through the twenty-five cards four times, just as Bonner had in his experiments. He had always been scrupulous about his testing methods. An average person, without ESP, would score on average twenty percent correct, although occasionally "lucky" scorers could do much higher or lower. But over time, twenty percent would be normal.

For Bonner, those who scored higher than twenty percent for two tests in a row were singled out for further testing. Of his Rememberers, some had come out of the Zener tests with scores of fifty percent and higher, according to the scant writings Cory had found from Bonner. The young boy, Jamie McCabe, had scored a phenomenal eighty percent in his initial tests. No one knew how much he might have improved over time, since all those notes on the Rememberers had been lost.

But no one, ever, had gotten all twenty-five cards wrong four times in a row.

Her head bent, she looked up at Sam. Her gray eyes flashed with fury, then slowly softened.

"What are you afraid of?" she asked quietly.

Sam rolled his eyes. "Boogeymen. Vampires. Dust-bunny monsters under my bunk." He brought his chair crashing upright. "Jesus, what do I have to say to get you to check me out of this place?" His face brightened. "My mother. That's it. I'm afraid of my mother." He leaped out of his seat and pulled wildly at his hair. "Help me, Doc. I tell you, I can't be held responsible if . . . oh, my God, it's coming over me gain. Aaaagh . . ." He pretended to choke himself in a fit of madness.

"The cards, Sam," Cory said flatly. "You ought to know that the chances of your getting every one of a hundred cards wrong are on the order of one in ten billion. You'd be more likely to be hit by a meteor."

Sam shrugged eloquently.

"What I'm saying is that a score of zero on the Zener test is as big an indicator of psychic ability as a score of one hundred. You faked every answer, Sam, and you know it."

"Oh, for crying out loud," he said. "You people will do anything to keep me here."

She stared at him for a moment, then sighed. "No. No one can make you stay against your will." She took a form from her drawer and started to write on it.

"You're turning me over now to Dr. Krantz in the vampire wing, I suppose."

She shook her head. "I'm signing your release papers. Working with you is pointless."

Sam grinned.

"You can leave whenever you like," Cory said briskly, "but I suggest you stay until tomorrow morning. I'd like you to be monitored at least overnight after coming out of the chamber."

Oh, Sam, Sam, there's trouble comin'

"What?"

Cory looked up. "I said I'd like it if you were monitored. . . ."

Hurry, not much time they're after you, Sam

He recoiled back in his chair.

Gonna kill you, gonna die just like your mama and daddy, Sam

"Stop it!" He slammed his hands over his ears.

"That joke's getting a little old," Cory said, turning back to her papers. She signed the form and held it out to Sam, but he remained in his chair, his hands covering his face.

"Sam?" she said quietly. She moved around the desk to him and pulled his hands gently away. His skin was waxy and pale, his forehead covered by beads of sweat.

"Tell me what's happening."

He was breathing hard.

"Tell me."

He blinked the sweat out of his eyes. "I'm hearing a voice . . . you . . . someone . . ." He turned away, ashamed. "Forget it."

"I want to know what you heard."

"Nothing."

"Like hell. Tell me what the voice said."

"So you can lock me up and drain the rest of my blood out of me?"

She pushed the release form into his hand. "That's yours, all right? Now tell me."

He closed his eyes. "Why?"

"So you won't have to hear the voice alone."

He wiped his face with the palm of one hand. "I don't know. Some crap about how somebody's after me. I thought it was you talking."

"It wasn't." She took both his hands in her own.

"I guess you know now that I really am crazy," Sam said miserably.

"Sam, maybe . . ."

Hurry Sam gotta hurry here I am but I'll find you be careful they're coming, Sam

Cory gasped and let go of his hands as if they were hot coals.

Sam's eyes met hers.

"You heard it, too," he said.

CHAPTER 7

REBA DOBBS WOKE UP IN A SWEAT, HER EYES BULGING, HER BREATH COMING fast. She had heard a shout, but when she woke, she realized that she had only heard herself shouting.

She did not remember what she had been dreaming. It had been bad, though. Her gaze wandered over the familiar things in the room, the ragged blue curtains, the cracked plaster walls, the jelly glass filled with wilted pink blossoms, and came to rest on a framed photograph of a young man with wavy blond hair and a cigarette clamped between his teeth.

Must have been about Bo. The bad dreams were usually about Bo.

Sometimes she thought he was calling to her from the other side. Sometimes she wanted to go. Her time was coming. She knew that. Reba was old now, long past sixty, even though she never did learn the exact date she was born. But life had been long enough. Her knees hurt near all the time and she was damned tired of living alone in this old place.

Not that she minded the house. She had been born here, right in this same bedroom, and it didn't bother her a lick that the place was practically falling down around her head.

But Stony Holler had changed. There used to be five other families down in the hollow but they were all gone now. Everyone but Reba. She had never been away, except for that one brief time in Florida with the crazy professor.

God, had it all been thirty years ago? Thirty years already?

She got out of bed, picked up the photograph of the young blond man, and dusted it with the sleeve of the sweater she wore both day and night. Poor Bo. He had been so young when he died, barely more than a boy.

The blood. There'd been so much blood.

A sound startled her back to the present, back to Stony Holler, where she was an old woman living alone, and Bo and the crazy professor and all the people they knew in Florida were just shadows in another life.

She patted down the gray wisps of hair that had escaped her kerchief and went to the door.

"Hello, there, Reba," Mrs. Turnbull said in her operatic voice. "I've brought along my friend, Mrs. MacInteer. She'd like a reading too, if you don't mind."

Reba nodded. "Glad to oblige." Her voice was froggy. "Been napping. Not much else to do." She smiled apologetically, let the two women in, and took a grimy deck of cards from the cupboard.

"Reba here's the best fortuneteller in the world. Isn't that right, Reba?"

They sat on wooden chairs around the kitchen table. Reba shuffled through the cards, feeling them speak to her as the women chatted amiably with each other.

"You got to touch these," she said, handing the deck to Mrs. MacInteer.

The woman giggled as she shuffled the cards. They always giggled, lest somebody think that they really believed in the Sight. Reba's gift was just a trick to amuse ladies on an afternoon.

"Well, am I going to win the lottery?" Mrs. MacInteer asked, tittering as she handed the cards back to Reba.

The Sight. It was a burden, really. It had never helped her. Five pregnancies, not one taken to term. Her husband gone. Her sleep filled with nightmares from the past. She read cards for foolish women because there were no babies to deliver in Stony Holler anymore. Because that was all there was to do with the Sight.

"Seems it ought to be just about the most powerful gift the Lord could give you," her grandmother had said long ago. She had had the Sight, too and, like Reba, it had done her little good.

"We ought to be able to predict rain, maybe even pick a pony once in a while," she had cackled. "But it don't work that way, do it, girl?"

"Nothing for ourselves," Reba had answered, parroting her grandmother's oft-repeated words. "But why did it, Gram?" she asked. "How come I was picked?"

"Don't rightly know. None of my children was born with the Sight. But when you seen the ghost coming for Grandpa, I knowed you had it, though you wasn't naught but five years old."

Reba had indeed seen a ghost take her grandfather's hand in a dream on the night he died. Since then, she had learned to use the Sight from the old woman. Even after Gram's death, she continued to talk to Reba from time to time.

She had spoken loud and clear after Bo's murder.

Get up, the voice had demanded.

Reba had been stabbed twice in the chest, once in her belly, and her arms were streaming with blood. Bo lay near the window, too far away for her to reach, his eyes open, already glazed in death.

"Gram, take me with you," Reba had sobbed. "Don't leave me here. Oh, God, Gram, it hurts so bad, just take me. I want to come with you."

But the old woman had been insistent. *You got more to do, girl,* she had answered sternly. *Now you get up, you hear? You get up now.*

And Reba had gotten up, although how she did she would never know, and later she had picked up *that baby that baby that baby . . .*

* * *

Three of hearts, things coming to a close," she said to Mrs. MacInteer. "Something you was worried about, maybe. . . ."

The baby, it was the baby then and he's a man now.

"Like you wasn't getting on so good with your husband. . . ."

"Well, I'll be," Mrs. Turnbull interjected. "Lillian, wasn't I just telling you?"

Reba touched her forehead with trembling fingers. It felt as if her brain was cracking inside, splitting apart.

"Five of spades . . ."

Go get him, Reba, he needs you.

"The baby?" she whispered.

The two ladies looked at each other.

"What baby?" Mrs. Turnbull asked.

You ain't thought about the baby all these years, have you?

"Reba, are you all right?"

He's going to need you again.

"I can't." Reba dropped the cards.

"Reba . . . Reba, you're looking poorly. Maybe we ought to be going."

You can reach him, warn him, you know how.

"I'm tired, Gram. I'm tired and older'n you was when you passed on."

The two women stood up, frowning. Mrs. Turnbull patted Reba's hand, then gestured toward the door with her chin. She took two dollars from her purse and left them on the plastic tablecloth in front of Reba, who was still talking to the empty air in front of her.

"Don't make me do this again," Reba begged, her eyes fixed on the far wall. "The last time it took Bo."

It was Bo's time, child.

Bo, young and handsome as a movie star, lying with his throat cut in a river of blood.

"Don't even know if he ever got buried proper," Reba muttered.

With a look at each other, the ladies let themselves out.

It had been daring and bold.

Young people always left the hollow because there was no work. Mostly they went to Wheeling, a far cry from Stony Holler, but still West Virginia. But Bo had rejected that idea. Wheeling, he said, was dead dreams that never came true. One day he wiped his oil-stained hands on a faded red rag and said, "I been thinking about Florida. Reckon I can fix a car there as good as I can in Wheeling."

So childhood sweethearts, freshly married, Bo and Reba Dobbs headed south. The money ran out near West Palm Beach, so that was where they stayed. Within one day Bo had a job, and Reba had found them an apartment near the growing Cuban section of the city.

Reba loved it. Salsa music blared out of cruising automobiles day and night. The neighborhood women kept up a constant stream of chatter from their windows. The spicy aroma of exotic foods filled the air. Reba worked as a midwife and told fortunes for her Cuban neighbors. Bo's boss at the garage said he was the best mechanic he'd ever hired. The two of them walked to the beach almost every night and made love in the sand.

And then one day she learned about Edward Bonner's experiments.

"Reba, Reba."

Reba looked up as Anna Quesada, who lived in the apartment across the hall, ran into her kitchen holding a newspaper.

"Look at this."

Reba glanced at the page. "I don't read my own language very good, I sure can't read yours," she said.

"It say a professor, this Dr. Edward Bonner, he is looking for people with psychic ability."

"What's psychic ability?" Reba asked.

"It's what you got," Anna had said. "And he's interviewing people at the big hotel."

"What's that got to do with me?" Reba asked.

"You go. Maybe this crazy professor, he pay good," the ebullient Anna had said. "But you don't do nothing without money, you got that? Tell him you're a professional. If he want a reading, he got to pay like everybody else."

Anna had accompanied her to the hotel, but had to stay behind when the battery of tests began. And Anna had been disappointed when Reba told her she would not know the results of the test for a while and, worse, that she had not been paid for her trouble. But two months later, when Reba was notified that she had been selected as one of the subjects and was asked to attend Bonner's conference on a tropical island, Anna Quesada and nearly all the other women on the block were ecstatic.

Bo, too, had been happy for her. They had little money and Reba was still depressed after yet another miscarriage, so he encouraged her to go. He even bought her a Kodak camera.

On the small island that they reached by boat, Reba had met her own kind. It went beyond how people dressed or talked or who their friends were. There was one boy, she remembered, black as coal, with his hair standing straight up on end. He was the first black person she had ever spoken to. And Jamie, the youngster. He was special.

But the people she got closest to were a wealthy young pair of doctors from Canada, Lars and Marie Nowar. They had both had the Sight in strong measure and they knew, without being told, that Reba had lost her babies.

"The last one went six months," Reba had said. "We was going to name him Sam, after my grandpa."

The seventeen on the island with Dr. Bonner all had the Sight. Some, like Reba and the Nowars, were comfortable with it. Others behaved as if the session on the island were some sort of joke. But still the air was charged with their presence, and they could all feel it. They were like family. Reba took pictures of all of them.

"He don't like having the Sight," she said of the tall young black man as she snapped his photograph.

Marie Nowar had smiled. "Who does?"

* * *

After some time, Reba got up from the kitchen table and took a dusty photo album from its place beneath the stairs. She dried her eyes as she opened the stiff yellowed pages, past the photographs of her youth: her Gram eating cotton candy at the county fair, her cousins in a photo booth, making faces. A few pages later, she found the photo of the wild-looking African boy who talked like a college professor and hadn't wanted to admit he had the Sight. She smiled. He turned out to be right handy, though. Back on that island, he had rigged up five showers out of some tubing and twine so that everybody could get clean at high tide. Reba remembered thinking that he and Bo could set up one hell of a garage together.

He had written his name beneath his picture. Reba went over the letters painstakingly. Har . . . Harrison Wood, yes, that was it. Harrison Wood, Junior. She wondered if he had lived.

She shook her head. Of course he hadn't. None of them had lived, except Reba herself. Not Harrison Wood, not Jamie, not even Bo, who wasn't even a part of things.

Here were the Nowars. She took their picture out of its yellowed plastic sleeve and studied.

Months later, when they were nearing the end of the their trips to the island, Lars Nowar had told Reba, "We're going to name our baby Sam."

"Sam . . ."

"For you," the pregnant Marie Nowar had said, taking Reba's hand.

Two fat tears dripped onto the plastic sheet covering the picture. Reba wiped them away with her arm. All of them dead, a sea of blood and tears later, all dead.

Except for the baby. He had lived.

Go find him, Reba, honey. He needs you.

Reba slammed the photo album shut. "I don't know where he is," she shouted irritably.

Listen. Listen deep. You'll find him.

She sprawled on the bare floor, clutching her head, wishing with all her soul that her grandmother's voice and its attendant pain would go away. "Oh, God. God." She rested her head on her arms. "What I am supposed to do with him?" she whispered finally.

Lead him, Reba. Lead him to the place he's got to be. Lead him and the rest will come, too.

"What rest? They're all dead but him."

There are new ones now, Gram said.

Reba opened and closed her eyes slowly. Gram's voice faded. The floor was cold but Reba was too tired to stand up. She shuddered. A strand of gray hair fell over her nose, tickling, but she did not move it. She fell asleep where she lay and did not awaken until the next nightmare.

CHAPTER 8

SAM OPENED HIS EYES AND SAW DR. ALTHORPE'S FACE. TWO HECTIC DABS of color brightened her cheeks and her eyes were large and frightened. Her hands, on his again, were warm and dry and comforting. The searing pain in his head had disappeared.

"It's gone," he said.

"I know."

They sat silently, looking at each other, as if each of them were drawn into the other's gaze. Finally Cory broke away.

"We know so little about telepathy," she said hesitantly. "What you . . . we . . . were hearing might have been anything. A radio transmission perhaps. Some people even pick up sound waves through their dental work."

Sam looked away. "Yeah. That must be it."

"Did you recognize the voice?"

"No."

That was what made it so weird. It hadn't been Her voice he'd heard. That twangy, raspy drawl sounded nothing like the siren who had called to him from the Peaks.

So now there were two voices that spoke to Sam. *Great*, he thought. *That's just great.*

"How do you feel?" the doctor asked.

"Tired."

Dr. Althorpe rose. "Sam, I'd like to—"

"No other doctors," he snapped.

"But . . ."

He grabbed her wrist. "I've got my walking papers, remember? I'm not going to be put on exhibit like some dancing chicken."

She looked down to where he was touching her. Sam released her wrist. "I'm sorry," he said.

"Don't let go!" She held his hand between her own. "Do you hear it?"

He listened. There was the beat of her pulse, deep and even. And then, behind it, he heard music. The same hypnotic, sweet music that had come to him in the depths of the ocean, soft as silken cords encircling him, binding him.

"It's in you, too," he whispered in astonishment.

"Have you heard this before?"

"Yes, but I always thought . . . that is . . . I thought it was a person. Or something."

So the sea siren had not been for Sam alone. The psychiatrist heard Her, too.

"It might be anything," Cory said. She grinned. "I'm going to think of something, Sam, and I want you to tell me what it is."

"Oh, man. Not another test."

"Just try, all right? I'm picturing a shape. What is it?"

"A triangle," Sam said flatly.

"Yes!" She squeezed his hand. "How about now?"

"A star."

"Right again. Here's something new."

He hesitated. "The name Otto."

"My God." A frown appeared between her gray eyes.

"Who's Otto?"

"My cousin," she said.

"No, he's not."

She laughed. "You tell me, then."

His fixed his eyes on hers. "Dr. Krantz. Otto must be his first name."

"That's amazing."

"I told you. No more doctors."

"Cory was silent for a moment. "All right," she said. "Have you always been able to read minds?"

"No. Never," he said honestly. "Yesterday the volcano. A vision. I've always had some sort of visions. But I've never gone into anybody's mind before. Those cards you tested me with. You looked at them and I saw the pictures the same time you did."

"And you answered them all wrong," she said. "Deliberately."

"I was afraid. I'm afraid now, if you want to know the truth."

He stood up, but Cory did not let go of his hand. It was getting hard for him to breathe.

Cory inhaled sharply. "I feel as if I'm drunk," she said.

"Me too." Sam moved closer to her, so close that he could feel the heat from her body.

The music grew louder, enveloping them both. He touched her lips with his own, feeling her warmth fill him.

Suddenly she drew back, releasing his hand. "I'm sorry," she whispered, blushing wildly. "I don't know what—"

A buzz from the intercom made them both jump. "Yes, what is it?" she snapped into the machine, grateful for the intrusion.

"There's a man here who wants to see you, Doctor. He won't give his name but he's—excuse me—sir!"

The door burst open. Darian McCabe strode in like some ancient pharaoh. Dr. Althorpe's secretary peered from behind him, looking exasperated.

"What are you doing with him?" he demanded.

Cory flushed a deep red. "We were . . ." Her voice came out high and squeaky. She cleared her throat. "May I ask who you are?"

"Genghis Khan," Sam said.

"I got here as soon as I could."

"Guess you did," Sam said, still reeling inside. "Dr. Althorpe, this is my partner, Darian McCabe."

Darian didn't acknowledge her. "When the nurse said you went down for tests, I thought they'd be poking you full of holes." He looked around the office suspiciously.

"They did."

"Actually," Cory said pleasantly, "the results of Mr. Smith's bloodwork were unusual. I was testing to see if there was a correlation between his blood and . . . well . . . a certain psychic ability he appears to possess."

"That night?" Darian asked, the corners of his mouth turned down in a snarl.

Sam shrugged. "Whatever. I don't know."

McCabe picked up the Zener cards from her desk. "You using these?"

"They're only for—" she began.

"I know what they're for," Darian interrupted her.

"What exactly is it to you anyway, Darian?" Sam growled. "What are you doing here? You could have waited up in my room."

Darian ignored the questions. "You feeling all right?"

"I'm fine."

"When can you leave?"

"Any time I want."

Cory held her hands together. "We were rather hoping, Mr. Smith, that you might be able to stay for a few more days."

Sam's head snapped toward her. "For blood? Is that what this was all about?"

"No." She pleaded with her eyes. "For what we discovered today."

"What was that?" Darian demanded. "More phony baloney voodoo horse-feathers?" He turned to Sam. "Guy at the museum's got the piece you found," he said. "He wants to talk to us about it. You can come if you want." He strode toward the door.

"Sam, listen to me," Cory whispered.

Sam shook his head. "I've got to hand it to you, Doc. Even when I picked out Krantz's name, I didn't know what you were getting at. You're smooth. Real smooth." He followed after McCabe.

Cory caught up to them at the elevator.

"I apologize for what happened between us," she said, ashamed to look Sam in the eye, "but that didn't have anything to do with the telepathy experiment. Your ability ought to be explored—for your own sake. No blood need be taken from you. I'll see to that myself. If you don't want to work with me, I'll find you another psychiatrist—a specialist in ESP. . . ."

"Don't bother," he said and touched her arm. For a moment, they both heard the music again, faint but distinct. It took an effort of will for Sam to pull his hand away.

"Sam, please . . ."

"I don't want it, understand? I don't want doctors nosing around inside my head. Just tell Krantz his plan didn't work."

"He had nothing to do with this," she said.

"No? If I offered you a couple of gallons of my blood, though, I bet you'd take it." He stepped into the elevator as its doors opened.

"What about the voice?" she called after him.

Sam smiled. "Like you said. It could have been anything."

The elevator doors closed after the two men.

She walked slowly back to her office.

"Where's the narcosis patient?"

She raised her eyes to Dr. Krantz's scowling face.

"He left," she said.

"You were supposed to keep him here! We need to do more testing. His blood . . ."

"We had no right to keep him here against his will. His condition had abated. I released him."

Krantz glared at her. "You are an idiot," he spat. He walked angrily away from her. "Stupid woman," he muttered.

Cory turned back to look at the flat black closed doors of the elevator.

Who was he, she thought. Who was this stranger who could see into her very thoughts?

And yet he wasn't really a stranger, was he?

For a moment, there had been something real between them, some connection that went deeper even than telepathy.

She remembered the music. It had come from him, of course; that was part of Sam Smith's psychic makeup. And yet when she first heard it, the music had seemed to well up from some distant place deep within herself.

Closing her eyes, straining to hear the forgotten melody again, she touched her lips and felt the stranger's kiss on them still.

THE GATHERING

Aidon St. James finished first.

His son, Liam, was twelve laps behind and gasping. Liam's tubular, unmuscled arms flailed in the water, slapping the surface with each stroke like logs falling on the surface.

Aidon pulled himself out of the pool effortlessly and dried off with a towel of the finest Egyptian cotton, embroidered with the name of his yacht, the Pinnacle. *Twenty-five feet below the deck on which he stood, the wake of the 140-foot boat churned white, making waves that sent lesser craft fleeing toward shore like bugs scurrying out of the path of an elephant.*

Off to port, the pink mirrored glass of the St. James Tower glittered like a jewel on the Miami skyline.

It was his. It was all his, anything he wanted, anywhere he wanted it. Aidon St. James always got what he wanted.

"Dad . . ." The boy was treading water in the middle of the yacht's swimming pool.

"Get your face back in the water!"

Liam obeyed.

The boy was a slug, Aidon thought with disgust, an accident of birth, a genetic tragedy. Aidon himself had always been an athlete—hurdles, sculling team at Harvard, an Olympic skier. Even now, at forty-three, his body was strong and taut, the muscles chiseled, the abdomen as rippled as a tiger's shoulders. Women still melted in his presence, even on those rare occasions when they didn't know who he was.

Time magazine had called him a combination of Cary Grant, J. Paul Getty, and Attila the Hun. That combination of good looks, financial wizardry, and an instinct for the jugular was what made a winner, and Aidon St. James was definitely a winner. He had started with the three million his father left him and parlayed it into ten million by the time he was twenty-five. On his last birthday, his worth was counted in the billions.

"Dad, I can't. . . ."

Aidon stared blankly at Liam until the boy got moving again.

And this was his legacy, he thought, shaking his head sadly. This bloated, pimple-faced sixteen-year-old dolt with the fortitude of rice pudding. And an only child to boot.

"Pitiful," Aidon muttered.

The poolside phone rang. It came as a relief. With luck, it would be something urgent and he could send Liam back to school. The boy had been with him now for nearly two months, and Aidon was beginning to loathe the sight of him.

"Yes," he said softly into the mouthpiece.

He listened without expression to the voice on the other end. "How big is it?" he finally asked. He shifted the phone to his other ear. "Yes. I'm just off Miami. Get a photograph and fax it to me."

He hung up without saying good-bye. Not urgent, but interesting nevertheless. Interesting enough to take his mind off the lumpen mass that was his son and heir.

"Forty-five laps, Dad." Liam was climbing up the pool ladder, his fat little arms

quivering with the strain of the swim, his broad belly as smooth and shapeless as the underside of a fish.

"We agreed on fifty, son. Fifty laps."

"I'll try again tomorrow." The teenager shambled toward a stack of towels. His feet pointed outward when he walked. His wet footprints looked like a duck's. His shoulders hunched over. There was acne on them.

"You disgust me," Aidon said. He turned away. Then, before his mind had even completed the thought, he whirled in a complete circle and tossed the boy back into the water.

Liam landed with a shriek and a colossal splash.

"Fifty," his father said. He picked up the phone and rang the captain. "Head for Jupiter Inlet. We might be laying over there."

Liam was still sputtering and coughing in the pool. He shot his father a look of anger and hurt.

"Fifty. Or are we going to fight over it?"

Liam stared a moment longer, then thrust his face in the water and began swimming.

"I didn't think so," Aidon said.

Aidon St. James always got what he wanted.

CHAPTER 1

Harry Woodson held the pendant on the square of black velvet. "It's a diamond," he said.

Darian sucked in his breath. "Pretty big," he said.

Woodson smiled. "At nine hundred thirty-four carats and flawless, it's the biggest cut diamond in the world. Or so the lab says." He set it down on the low table before Sam and Darian. The stone and chain had been cleaned, and both sparkled with an almost unearthly brilliance.

"How much do you think it's worth?" Darian asked.

The black man shrugged. "I wouldn't know. Some stones—great stones, I guess you'd call them—can be worth as much as five hundred dollars a carat in the rough."

Darian whistled. "But this stone isn't rough. So it'd be worth more, right?"

"Got me. The mineralogists here were all going on about how it's been cut."

"How's that?"

"Strangely, I gather. It's supposed to have more facets or something. A couple of them seemed to think the stone's been ruined."

"Ruined?" McCabe said suspiciously. "Just look at the thing."

"Mr. McCabe, this is a museum of oceanography, not a jewelry exchange," Woodson said crankily. "I don't know how much money you can get for the stone, and frankly I don't care. My interest is determining where it came from and how old the piece is."

"How old is it?" Sam asked.

"I don't know. A diamond can't be carbon-dated. Neither can gold. What we tried to date was the vegetable matter encrusted on the stone, but there wasn't too much of that left."

"So? What'd you find?"

"As I said, there wasn't much to work with. The tests may have been in error."

"Damnit, Woodson, say what you got to say," Darian barked impatiently.

Woodson sighed. "The preliminary tests—which, I repeat, are inconclusive—seem to indicate that the material around the stone was . . . well, it seems incredible, but more than ten thousand years old."

"I knew it," Sam said softly.

"Ten thousand years," Darian growled. "You're talking about the Stone Age."

"I know. That's why I sent for an expert in ancient jewelry. He examined the stone this morning and wanted to check some books. He'll be back in a few minutes."

Sam tried to hide his excitement. "What if it's true?" he asked.

"Its age? Well, it might be a find of great importance."

"Important enough for the museum to underwrite a dive?"

Woodson looked up from the stone. "Perhaps," he said cautiously.

"I'd have to be in charge of the diving team."

Woodson tried to hide a smile.

"I know where it is," Sam said, "and I know there's more down there."

"Like what? Did you see something else?" Woodson asked.

"You're not going down there again," Darian interrupted.

Woodson looked up at the big man, surprised.

"You have to let me head the dive," Sam said, pointedly ignoring the old man.

"It's really rather early for—" Woodson began when his secretary entered the room. "Mr. Eames, sir," she announced.

She was followed by a lanky young man with a shock of brown hair and owlish eyeglasses. "Nathan Eames," the gemologist said, shaking hands all around. He was sweating profusely, despite the chilly air-conditioning in Woodson's office. "Sorry I was delayed. I was on the phone with my office." He looked down at the pendant. "It's really an incredible find. An incredible stone."

"Is it old?" Sam asked.

"The stone?" Eames said and shrugged. "Well, all diamonds are millions of years old."

"The jewelry. The piece itself," Sam insisted.

"I can't tell you that," Eames said. He wiped his sweaty brow with a wrinkled handkerchief. "The problem is the cut of the stone. Or rather, the fact that it has been cut at all. You see, before the seventeenth century, diamonds weren't cut. They were polished."

Darian chuckled. "Modern. I knew it. Some heiress dropped it off her yacht during a drunken party."

"Maybe," Eames said affably, "although I can't imagine any modern jeweler cutting a stone this way."

"What way?" Sam asked. "Now that it's cleaned up, it looks like a diamond."

Eames pointed a finger at the stone. "Two things make it unlike any major stone I've ever seen. One is the shape. Its widest point is well above the center. Then it tapers to an almost daggerlike point."

Darian puffed out his lips, bored.

"The second," Eames went on, "is the number of facets. Sixteen. Eight tapering toward the top, eight toward the bottom."

"So what?" Darian said.

"Most diamonds are cut with fifty-eight facets. Oh, maybe some small piece of junk might be cut with fewer, but no jeweler would do that to a gem of this size and this quality."

"Maybe he was just a lousy jeweler," Darian said.

"Then he wouldn't have been able to cut it at all. Not into this perfect shape." Eames shrugged again. "It's just a puzzle."

"What about the gold work?" Woodson asked. "It looked almost Mycenean to me."

Eames smiled ruefully. "A lot of things look almost Mycenean, including art deco that was done yesterday." He touched the cross-within-the-circle design on the bale of the necklace. "This gold could have been worked yesterday. Or a thousand years ago."

"Or ten thousand?" Sam said.

Eames laughed. "That's stretching it. They didn't even have the wheel ten thousand years ago. I don't think they had diamond cutters and jewelry makers."

Sam looked at Woodson. "Some of the material on the stone was dated that old," the young man said.

Eames answered, "It happens a lot. A piece gets in the sea. Some algae calcifies around it and then the algae happens to stick to a piece of coral or something that's much older, and it messes up the tests. I saw it once with a French cameo found near a wreck. The material was dated to be almost two thousand years ago. But the cameo had Louis the Fourteenth's picture on it. So much for dating."

He smiled triumphantly. Sam looked crestfallen; Darian was indifferent. Woodson was frowning, distracted.

"Then we're not looking at a piece from an ancient civilization," the curator said.

"I doubt it very much." Eames lifted the pendant. "But we are looking at a great stone of immense value. Any major jeweler would buy it in a heartbeat." He fondled the stone, almost lovingly.

"And do what?" Sam asked.

"Recut it, certainly. And probably break it into smaller stones. There's virtually no market for a stone this huge. Not unless some monarchy is designing crown jewels."

He put the pendant back onto the velvet pad. "I want to thank you for letting me see this. I've already taken the liberty of testing the commercial waters, as it were, to see who might be interested in buying such an amazing stone. Later, if you need advice on its sale, please let me know."

He shook hands all around again, then left.

The three men stood in silence. A ray of sunlight landed on the pendant and set flashes blazing out of the great stone.

Sam picked it up. A faint greenish cast infused its pure clarity, then deepened into a luminescent glow. He passed it to Darian. The glow dimmed slightly, but remained. McCabe passed it on to Woodson, who held it in two cupped hands. Its eerie light reflected off the curator's dark face.

"Eames touched it," Sam said, "and nothing happened."

"Don't ask me why," Woodson said. "The mineralogists found nothing. Scientifically, there is nothing unusual about this stone."

"Except that it glows for us," Sam finished.

Sam and Woodson's eyes met and held. Finally Darian snatched the stone from the curator's hands and tossed it back on its velvet bed where it again sparkled, clear as water.

"There's something else you should consider." Woodson limped to his desk and brought back a glassine envelope containing the pottery shard Darian had given him along with the pendant.

"This we were able to carbon-date without question," Woodson said.

"And?"

Woodson's face was taut. "It was made thirteen thousand years ago."

A puff of air escaped Sam's lips.

"The lab's rechecking the tests, but if they're accurate, these two pieces together might—just might—be enough to mount the exploration you were talking about. As to your heading it, Mr. Smith. . . ."

"He's not going," Darian said.

"Stay out of this, Darian!"

Woodson cleared his throat. "We'd need somebody to direct us to where the pieces were found."

"They weren't found in the same place," Darian growled sourly.

Sam shook his head. "That doesn't matter. They belong together. I know it. And there's more. There has to be—"

"You found the damn shard on a beach," Darian shouted over him.

"Is that true?" Woodson asked Sam, his face suddenly blank.

"Yeah. But it came from the same place as the pendant."

Woodson raised an eyebrow. "May I ask how you know that?"

"He don't know nothing," Darian said. "He just wants to go back to the Peaks."

Sam turned his hands palm up as he spoke to Woodson. "Look. I know there's something else down there because . . ." He ran his hands over his face. "Because I have a sense about things. Now I know you're going to think I'm a wacko, but I'm going to tell you anyway. When I found this piece of pottery, it sang to me."

"It what?"

"Oh, for chrissake," Darian muttered.

"I knew where it came from then because I'd heard the same music before, when I was diving the Peaks."

"Music," Woodson said flatly.

"Yes, *music*. And the deeper I went, the stronger the music got, until . . ."

"Until what?"

"Until he went crazy," Darian said, "and started seeing moving pictures. Enough is enough, Sam. When I pulled you up, the Rapture already had you so bad you'd ripped out your own mouthpiece. Let's go."

Sam turned his face away. The curator felt sorry for him. "I understand," Woodson said. "I've been down deep, too."

Sam stood up. "Yeah."

"What about the diamond?" Darian asked.

"I wish you'd leave it here for more tests. After that, you can have it transferred to a bank or a jeweler. Whatever you'd like."

Darian nodded and walked toward the door. Sam followed him dispiritedly, then turned and said, "It glows for us. For all three of us. Explain that away."

Out in the hallway, he heard Woodson call his name. Sam waited as the man limped over. Darian had already started down the long curved staircase toward the museum's entrance.

"When you were down there, what did you see?" the black man asked softly.

"Would it make any difference?"

Woodson's eyes crinkled. "I don't know. Try me."

"I saw a volcano," Sam said, then turned and followed Darian down the steps.

CHAPTER 2

"THANKS, DARIAN," SAM SAID BITTERLY AS HE SLAMMED THE DOOR OF THE ancient Ford pickup truck and started up the engine. "Thanks a whole lot."

The old man grunted and adjusted himself among the debris on the seat. "Didn't say nothing that wasn't true."

"Just that I was crazy."

"Like I said." Darian chortled.

Red-faced, Sam wiped the grime from the rearview mirror with his sleeve, pulled out of the parking spot, and slid into traffic headed for Route 1, back to Jupiter Inlet. Through the nearly opaque side mirror, he could make out the shape of a black four-by-four behind him.

"Woodson could have arranged a dive," Sam said.

"In the Peaks."

"Yes, damnit, in the Peaks. People have gone down there before."

"Most of 'em ain't come back up."

"Darian, this would have been a museum-sponsored exploration, with dive teams and underwater communications. Good lights, film, auxiliary air . . ."

"Don't make no difference," Darian said stolidly.

Sam looked up at the rearview mirror. The black four-by-four still trailed him. It was a Range Rover. As Sam veered his small truck up the ramp onto the highway, the driver stayed right on his tail, only a few yards away.

Sam rolled down the window and signaled the trailing driver to pass, but the Range Rover held its position.

"M.D. plates," Sam mumbled. "You must have to take a driving test to get into medical school. If you pass it, they throw you out."

Darian looked out the back window. "I seen 'em dive, too. Same way."

"And fly. You know all those small planes that are always crashing? Doctors. I guess they figure . . ."

He glanced to his side. The Range Rover was pulling up alongside him. Sam again waved him ahead. "Go on, Doc, pass," he mumbled. "I'd like you better in front of me."

The Range Rover did not pass. The driver turned his head toward Sam and stared.

"Hey, I know him," Sam said. "That's the blood doctor at the hospital. His name's Krantz, I think. He wanted me to stay so—"

Krantz raised his right arm. There was a gun in his hand.

"Get down!" Sam yelled.

The bullet pinged through both the driver and passenger side windows. When Sam slammed on the brakes, another shot ripped past the front of the truck. He spun the wheel and the truck skidded off onto the soft sandy shoulder. The Range Rover pulled off onto the berm, then began to back up.

"Jesus, this guy's just not going to quit," Sam said as he jerked the truck forward again. He thought he was clear when the doctor caught up and stayed with him, the front wheels of their vehicles almost touching. Krantz took aim once again, amid a din of horns as traffic eddied around the two vehicles.

Finally Sam jumped on his brakes in a panic stop, and the Range Rover skidded on by. Sam saw Krantz's face as the doctor turned in the seat and raised the gun again. Krantz pulled off the shot, missed the truck entirely, then craned backward in the seat. He had both hands on the gun now, ignoring the steering wheel. The last bullet hit the truck's windscreen almost dead center, between Sam and Darian, and then the Range Rover crashed through the metal guardrail and soared off the embankment down toward the ocean. It landed on two wheels, then tipped and rolled on the rock and shell-strewn shore before finally coming to a stop lying on its passenger side.

Sam pulled up the handbrake and got out of the truck. The shoulder of the road was already packed with parked cars, and several people were running toward the Range Rover. Sam and Darian climbed over the guard rail and were picking their way down the rocks of the embankment when they heard another shot. As Sam rushed forward, he saw a woman screaming near the wreckage. The other people clustered around Krantz's vehicle were drawn back, their faces registering shock.

"I called the police on my car phone," one of the men volunteered when Sam approached. "I think you'd better wait for them."

Inside the Range Rover lay the doctor, his arms tangled in the steering wheel. The top of his head was blown off. The gun was still in his mouth.

Darian loped up behind Sam. "What in the hell was he doing?" he whispered.

"You tell me," Sam said.

He barely heard the police officer during the questioning that followed.

"You know him?"

"He was a doctor at West Palm Hospital. I was being treated there."

"Any reason he might want to go after you?"

Sam shrugged, numb.

"Where were you coming from?"

"The Oceanographic Museum."

"And you didn't see him until you were on the Coastal?"

"No. Well, I saw his car following me. I didn't think anything. It all happened pretty fast."

The police officer came into focus. He was writing down Sam's answers. Darian stood nearby.

"We'll check this out," the policeman said. "Not your typical highway gunman, though. Had all his ID on him."

"Why would he want to kill me?"

The officer made a helpless gesture. "Could be he just snapped."

"Snapped . . ."

Sam! Samsamsamsamsamsam

Sam bent forward, his face wreathed in pain.

"You okay?" the officer asked as Darian stepped forward to take Sam's arm.

Sam breathed deeply a few times, then nodded. "Headache."

"Nerves, maybe. It happens."

"Yeah."

The officer gave him a sympathetic smile. "Hey, take it easy." He put a hand on Sam's shoulder. "You were lucky. The guy was a rotten shot."

CHAPTER 3

SAM!"

The scream came from everywhere, everywhere in the world, it seemed.

Reba awoke on the scarred linoleum floor of her kitchen. She sat up, blinking rapidly, her heartbeat gradually slowing to normal. She smoothed away a limp strand of hair that had fallen over her eyes. Gray hair. She was old. And Bo, the only man in her life, was gone, long dead.

So it had been a dream, then. A dream of a dream.

The dream.

She had first dreamed it twenty-nine years ago. The terror had never left her because the dream had been real. The voices of those who would die had called to her in her sleep, called to her for help, but she had been able to help only one.

The baby.

His mother had spoken his name at the moment of her death, willing him out of her womb, and Reba had heard her.

"Sam . . ."

Bo had worked late the night before and was sleeping in their West Palm Beach apartment when Reba ran into the room.

"Bo, wake up! You got to wake up!"

He had opened his eyes instantly, the way he always did, without a trace of fogginess or confusion. "What is it, angel girl?"

"Voices . . ." She was shaking all over with fear.

Bo propped himself on an elbow. "Your Gram?"

She shook her head. "No. Lots of voices, all at once, all calling for help. Oh, Bo, how they was carrying on!"

Bo cleared his throat. He had never doubted Reba's gift. Every family in Stony Holler had called upon Reba and her grandmother at one time or another. "I don't know what it could be, honey," he said gently. "Your friends got out to Memory Island okay. I seen the boat at the dock this morning, back safe and sound."

"Then it's not them," Reba said, relieved. She lay back on the bed. "I should have gone with them."

"Why didn't you?"

"Gram," she said.

The previous morning, Reba had been dressed in her best and waiting to go to the island with the other Rememberers when the message came.

Don't go, lamb, Gram's voice had said. *You'll be needed here.*

Without hesitation, Reba had obeyed. She wished everyone a nice trip, especially young Jamie McCabe, who had looked as if he hadn't slept well. She had hoped to see the Nowars, the young married couple from Canada. They had left word with Dr. Bonner that they would be driving down for the session, but Marie Nowar was nine months pregnant, and no one was surprised that they didn't show up.

Reba had waved good-bye to everyone, and that had been that—until the next night, when the voices had started to shriek inside her head.

"Feel a little better now?" Bo asked.

Reba nodded. The terrifying howl had died away.

"Go to sleep." He kissed her, sweet and sleepy.

"All right, Bo. Guess it wasn't nothing. Indigestion, maybe." She fell asleep in his arms.

And the dream continued.

Sam . . . It was a cry of anguish.

Reba's body jerked stiffly. "Mrs. Nowar?" she asked. She snapped to a sitting position. Bo awakened instantly.

"What is it, honey?" he asked.

"She's dying!" Reba shouted. "Guns, blood . . ." Reba thought she would go crazy with the pain of it. "And the baby . . ." Bo held her tightly, and in a moment Marie's voice was gone, too, replaced by a thin wail.

A different voice. There was fear in it, but not death. This was a scream of life. New life.

"There's a baby, Bo," Reba said, suddenly dry-eyed. "His name is Sam. He's calling to me now."

"Where . . ." Bo rubbed his hands over his face. "Where is he?"

She pointed out the window, overlooking the apartments outside. "That way."

Two hours later, Bo's pickup was on an umarked road off Route 82, its headlights illuminating strips of desolate swamp on either side. He squared his shoulders and blinked to fend off sleep.

"Don't look like nobody's out here," he said carefully.

Reba sat like a statue beside him, her hands clasped together, the knuckles white.

"Reba, are you sure . . ."

"I'm sure," she snapped.

In fact, she was not at all sure. For some time, she had heard the baby's cry loud and clear, blessedly overshadowing the memory of those other, unwelcome screams. But more than an hour ago it too had grown faint, the small mewlings of cold and hunger, until by now she was not certain whether she was hearing anything at all, or was simply remembering the sound along with all the other spectral voices.

Apprehensively, she reached into a box she had prepared for the baby and took out a bottle filled with breast milk from a young mother whose child she had just delivered. Reba placed the bottle inside her dress, against her bosom, to warm it. The baby would need food. If he was still alive.

"Oh, Gram," she muttered. "You told me not to go to the island 'cause I was needed, but that don't make me no magician." If her grandmother wanted her to help the baby, she thought angrily, the old woman's spirit ought to give her a little more help.

Bo looked over to her and smiled. This was her way of praying, he knew, talking to her grandmother as if the woman were still alive and standing right before her. If Reba were ever to live among strangers, she would be branded a lunatic.

"So I'd surely appreciate it, Gram, if you'd let me know one way or t'other, 'cause this road's mighty long and dark and if you're tiny and naked . . ."

Suddenly she was silent. She grasped Bo's arm and squeezed it hard, unable to speak. To her right stretched a silvery path of light over the swamp grass, a path of moonlight, except that there was no moon.

Bo brought the pickup to a halt, but even before it stopped she was out the door, splashing through the marsh, running into the darkness.

"Bring the box," she yelled behind her as she followed a path that was illuminated for her eyes alone.

"Reba, wait! I got the light. You'll get lost."

He stumbled out of the truck with the flashlight and the box of baby items and ran after her as quickly as he could, but it was not until he heard Reba's low moan that he was able to find her.

In the beam of the flashlight he saw her face, drawn with horror, and then saw the two bodies lying in the fetid shallow water of the swamp. Their hands had been bound. The man had been shot in the head at close range. The woman, whose chest was covered with blood, was naked. Bo recognized her face from one of Reba's island photographs. It was Marie Nowar.

She had lived longer than her husband; long enough for her assailants to rape her, evidently. And then, after that, long enough to give birth to her son. Between her legs, on a bed of matted reeds and the torn remnants of her dress, lay a newborn infant, his unbilical cord still attached to his dead mother.

"It *was* them," Reba said numbly. "Marie and all the other Rememberers I heard. All of them dead . . ."

Woodenly, Reba knelt in the mud and picked up the baby, pressing it against her. Bo set the box on the ground, then took off his jacket and covered the child with it.

"Is he alive?" he asked.

Reba crooked her head to nestle the baby's head against her neck. "I don't know," she said. Then there was the tiniest movement of the baby's mouth.

"Get the knife from that box," she said, slipping the bottle of breast milk between the baby's lips. The liquid spilled down his chin. Reba tapped the tiny cheek with her finger. "Come on, Sam," she whispered. "That was what your folks was going to name you, did you know that?" She held the infant closer. "And the last breath your mama took carried your name to me."

Her tears dropped onto the baby's face, and she wiped them away tenderly. "We ain't perfect, Bo and me, but we'll love you just as much as your own people could. So you got to live, you hear?" She was sobbing. "Please live, Sam."

Sam swallowed his first mouthful, then began to suck instinctively, greedily. Reba dried her eyes and smiled. "Cut the cord, Bo. Right about here. It won't need no clamp. And get me that wool blanket. We got ourselves a baby to raise."

When Bo looked at her with concern, she held the baby closer. "We're his family now."

Oh, God, how she had wanted it to be true. But the new family had not even lasted till morning.

They had left the bodies in the swamp and driven back to West Palm Beach with the baby. Bo was silent during the drive, but Reba spoke incessantly to her grandmother, asking for a sign that it would be all right to keep Sam, begging for a word of assurance.

There was none. Gram did not speak, not until the rest of that terrible night had unfolded.

She had finally gotten little Sam to sleep in their bed and had gone out into the small living room of the apartment to be with Bo. They sat on the couch, side by side, holding hands, until there was a faint knock on the door.

"Must be Mrs. Quesada," Bo said as he got up to answer it. Their Cuban neighbors were in the habit of visiting at all hours of the day and night.

A moment later, she heard a thud and ran toward the door. She saw Bo's body lying on the floor, his throat cut, his stomach ripped open, and two men with faces like statues moving toward her.

Wordlessly they came at her, their knives still red with Bo's blood. Before she could even scream, they cut her bad, bad enough to die, and left her lying there. The last thing she saw was her blood mingling with Bo's on the slick linoleum floor. The last sound she heard was the creak of the door closing behind her killers.

The last thing she thought was, *They didn't find the baby*.

She never knew how long she lay there. But she moved when she heard Gram's voice again.

Get up, the old woman had ordered, and Reba had obeyed. Somehow she had bandaged her wounds—the wounds that she knew should have killed her—and then she took Sam out of the apartment on Sweetwater Street with Bo's body still warm in it. She had traveled north, far north, away from the forces that she understood now were seeking out the Rememberers one by one and killing them.

And then she had done the hardest thing: She had left Sam on the doorstep of an orphanage in a strange, cold city because she feared those same dark forces would one day come for them again. She abandoned him, leaving a note that revealed only the baby's first name and date of birth, and hoped that he would be safe.

It was all so long ago. She was an old woman now.

Yet nearly every time she slept, Reba still heard the dying cries of the Rememberers in her dreams.

She shuffled across the kitchen, her legs stiff after sleeping on the cold floor. "Land sakes," she muttered. "Sometimes I act like I don't got no brains at all."

Reba had been back in Stony Holler, back living in this tar-paper shack, for twenty-nine years. It was about time she stopped reliving the same night over and over, a night which had taken place so far back in the past. She sighed. She would if she could.

If she only could.

Outside the sun was setting, showing the rust on the old pickup truck. Thirty-five years old and still running. Bo would have liked that, she thought.

And Gram was talking to her again.

"Did I do right, Gram?"

Yes, Reba.

"That was all so long ago."

Not so long. Things was waiting.

"Waiting for what?"

For Sam, child. For you.

"You don't make no sense," Reba said crossly. Her head hurt.

You got to get to him, honey. You got to show him the way.

"The way where, Gram?"

To where he got to go. Lead him, and the rest will follow.

Reba tried to speak, then shook her head. "This is just crazy," she mumbled. "Maybe I'm crazy. Maybe you ain't my Gram at all, just some crazy voice a crazy old fool of a woman thinks is talking to her."

She listened, her chin jutting out defiantly, but the voice did not respond.

"Don't know what you're talking about, anyway."

No answer.

Sighing, Reba went to the kitchen sink and idly washed out a cup. She caught a reflection of her face in the cracked mirror next to the cupboard.

"Old fool of a woman," she repeated. "Can't even read a map. How'm I supposed to lead anybody anyplace?"

You'll know.

Reba set the cup down. Her hands were shaking. "I'm scared," she whispered. "What they did to Bo . . . to Marie and Lars Nowar . . . to all of them . . ." She swallowed. "They're going to kill me, too."

Her reflection looked back at her. She had aged badly. There were no rounded cheeks to kiss, no broad lap for children to sit on. She looked like what she was, a woman who had spent almost thirty years in absolute solitude.

A long life.

Too long, maybe.

"What about Sam? If I find him, am I going to have to watch him die, too?"

Lead him, Reba. The rest will follow.

She bent her head. The Sight had been a cruel gift. It had taken everything from her and given nothing. And it was still taking. That was the purpose of her life, Reba realized: to accommodate the Sight.

"Ain't never going to leave me alone, are you, Gram?" she asked grimly.

She packed a few belongings into an old valise, then felt beneath her mattress for her money. A hundred eighteen dollars, accumulated over most of a lifetime.

Stuffing the bills inside her dress, Reba walked out to the pickup. She did not lock the door to her house. There was no point. She knew she would never return.

Outside, the last of the sun hung red over the hills above Stony Holler. Black clouds scurried overhead like flapping wings. A brief gust blew up, and Reba shivered.

Like wings, yes. Something dark and ancient was folding itself around her, spreading its black wings.

With a final glance at the tumbledown building where she had been born, where she had lived as a bride and then grown old alone, Reba started the engine of the pickup and headed in the direction of the first flock of birds she saw.

"I'm coming, Sam," she whispered. "It's time."

CHAPTER 4

NATHAN EAMES ORDERED A RUM AND TONIC FROM THE POOLSIDE ATTEN-
dant and settled into his deck chair for some serious ogling. The best thing
about expensive hotels, he had decided, were the class of women who
stayed in them. They were pampered, sleek creatures, the late-model wives
of rich men who traded in their mates every fifty thousand miles. They wore
jewelry (which his expert eye generally regarded as tasteless but expensive
junk), orthodontically perfect smiles, Dr. Diamond noses, and thong bikinis.

Eames himself sported a hat, a wide-brimmed touristy straw that covered
the thinning spot on the back of his head, blue Speedos, and a pair of
Wayfarer-style prescription sunglasses. Slightly aloof, he told himself. That
was the look he was trying to cultivate. When his drink came, he signed
for it without acknowledging the waiter's presence, then raised the glass
in salute to a beautiful blonde in a tiger-striped bikini. She smiled back at
him.

God, he loved being rich.

He had never expected to make so much of himself. His father had been
a jeweler with a store in the Bensonhurst section of Brooklyn. Nathan became
one, too, although a degree in art history had given him a finer appreciation
of his work than his father possessed. Nathan Eames believed gems set in
finely worked gold to be the most beautiful objects on the planet. They
were the stuff of dreams, of an even higher order than fancy cars, sprawling
homes, and beautiful girls.

All of which he now had. At thirty-one, he had a house in La Jolla, a
much larger one in Switzerland about which the IRS knew nothing, and a
seven-thousand-foot villa in the Bahamas (also unreportable). His garages
held two Jaguars, a restored 1935 Mercedes-Benz, a Lamborghini, and a
utilitarian Porsche. His secret bank accounts held more than a million dollars,
and a safe-deposit box in a Cayman Islands bank contained precious stones
piled an inch deep.

He could have retired, except for one thing: The Consortium would not
let him. That was one of the conditions of his good fortune. He had to keep
working.

There were three conditions. The second was that he was to to keep his involvement with the Consortium a secret.

Nathan Eames slugged down his drink in one draught. It burned going down.

He did not like to think about the third condition.

The blonde in the tiger-striped bikini was kissing an old man who dyed his hair red. Why did the old geezers always pick *red*?

Nathan shouted for the waiter to bring him another drink. He felt expansive and good today. Maybe now he would be permitted to retire. He had found the stone that had been his special mission. He was sure of it. It had certainly been described to him often enough: a clear, sword-shaped diamond as long as a man's fist, hand-cut with sixteen perfect strokes.

Nathan had nearly wet his pants when he first saw it at the Oceanographic Museum. However rudely it had been cut, it was a masterpiece of nature. Larger than the Niarchos, more perfect than the President Vargas, its beauty had leaped out at him from its black velvet bed. He had had to remind himself constantly not to act too excited about it.

Of course, the two bozos who "found" it—a pair of thieves if ever thieves had lived—couldn't have known less about diamonds. Or about anything else worth more than a dollar ninety-eight, from the looks of them. But it wouldn't be the first time that a priceless jewel had changed hands through dirty middlemen. Serious collectors did business with anyone who had a stone. In these rarefied heights, ordinary rules of ethics did not apply.

This particular diamond, for example, had been well hidden. Nathan believed that he knew of every stone of importance, ancient and modern, since man first fell in love with gems—and he had never heard of this stone. He had been tempted to point this out to the Consortium when they first told him what it was his mission to find. But he had known better than to question them.

Finding that stone had been the reason Nathan Eames was invited to join the Consortium in the first place. The man who had extended the invitation, whose face Nathan had never seen, was his only contact.

At first Nathan had thought it all a joke, a prank arranged by a drunken friend with time on his hands.

If you accept, your membership will be for life.

Sure, sure.

But they had delivered. That was the weird part. Before he had even done anything for them, the offers had started coming in. A consulting job in New York's diamond district where no one with a last name like Eames had ever worked, the publication of an article on Egyptian scarabs in *New York* magazine, an interview on the TV news after the theft of some Scythian goldwork, a permanent post heading the ancient jewelry department of the Neumeyer Antiquities Museum. All before the age of twenty-nine.

Then the phone call.

"Are you pleased with the advancements in your career, Mr. Eames?" The voice was bland, unemotional, devoid of personality.

"What? Who is this?"

"I'm calling for the Consortium. We spoke six months ago. I suggest you learn to recognize my voice."

This is some kind of nut, Nathan thought. "Oh, sure. Sure thing. Now if you'll excuse me . . ."

"I won't call you often, Mr. Eames. But when I do, you must listen."

"No, you must listen, pal. I don't know what you've been smoking, but if you call here again, I'm going to get the cops after you." He hung up, feeling righteous.

The next day he was fired from both the museum and the diamond district job. No reason was given.

During the next few months, Nathan discovered that there was a limited demand for experts on ancient jewelry. He went back to work for his father. Immediately his father's business began to evaporate. When the store closed, Nathan went to work clerking in a jewelry mill, specializing in engagement rings with "genuine 25-point" diamonds, stones that were cloudy and flawed with so many occlusions that, under a jeweler's loupe, they looked polka dotted.

Six months to the day of his last conversation with the blank-voiced man representing the Consortium, the telephone rang again.

"We can give it back to you," the voice said.

"Who . . ." But he knew who it was. He would not make the same mistake again. "Thank you," Nathan said. "Thank you for calling back. I didn't know how to reach you."

"You never will, Mr. Eames. And later, if you comply with the conditions of membership in the Consortium, no one will be able to trace you either, if you do not wish it."

"Okay. Whatever. I mean, I'll comply. Just help me get my museum job back, okay?"

"We'll do better than that. *If* you meet the conditions of membership."

"Fine. I'll recognize your voice on the phone. I won't get snotty. I won't ask questions about your . . . group."

"You will never mention the Consortium, or anything about it."

"Great. Not a word. Count on it."

"Not to anyone. Not wife, not priest, not child. No one. If you do, we will know about it."

Eames wanted to ask how they would know, but decided that the question bordered on snotty and he did not want to take a chance on losing even the rotten job he still held.

But he did not have to ask. "We will know because we have members everywhere. They possess great wealth and great power. If word leaks out about the Consortium, not one member will be affected because we are all anonymous. But you will be dealt with."

Nathan laughed nervously. "What would you do? Kill me?"

"In the end, yes."

There was a silence on the phone. "What about before the end?"

"Don't find out, Mr. Eames," the voice said. "Condition two. You will work where we direct you. Rest assured, you will be highly compensated, but you must work. It is your skills we are interested in."

"As an appraiser."

"As an expert in historical stones. There is a stone we want you to locate, a large diamond of specific dimensions. It has not been seen in many years. It may have been lost at sea. If it ever comes to light, we must know about it. Pay special attention to ocean discoveries. That is your responsibility."

Nathan raised an eyebrow. "Well, I'll give it a try."

"Your very best try, Mr. Eames. Finding that stone is your first and only priority."

"What if I don't find it?"

"We hope you do," the voice said after the barest pause. "Now, the third condition."

"I'm listening."

"Look outside your door. I will wait."

Putting the phone down, Nathan walked to the door of his apartment and opened it. There was an envelope on the floor.

"I found a letter or something," he said into the phone.

"Open it, please."

Inside was a name and address. "George Westerman? I don't know him," Nathan said.

"No. You are to go to his residence tonight."

Nathan checked his watch. Ten after ten. "It's pretty late," he said. "Not to mention the fact that I don't even know this guy. What should I say to him?"

"You don't have to speak to him. You'll find the keys to his apartment in your mailbox downstairs. We've made it easy for you this time."

"Okay. So I'll have a key. Still, don't you think it might cause old George the tiniest bit of apprehension to see a total stranger standing in his living room in the middle of the night? What am I supposed to be doing there?"

The man's voice was quiet. "You are to kill him, Mr. Eames."

Nathan stared blankly at the wall.

"You may choose whatever method you like, but I would recommend putting a pillow over his face. Mr. Westerman has been a semi-invalid for several years. He won't offer much resistance."

Nathan coughed weakly. "You're kidding, right?"

"No. Do you have any other questions?"

"Yeah. What kind of crackpot are you? I was beginning to take you seriously."

"Your father will be dead by morning," the voice said. "Good-bye."

"Hey! Hey, wait!" Nathan jiggled the receiver, but the caller had hung up.

He'd been an idiot, he decided, slamming down the phone. He had become so desperate that he had been willing to believe anyone who would give him a lick of hope. Nathan poured himself a straight scotch and decided that his luck was just bad. People like to think there is always a logical reason for bad things happening, but there often is not. There's just bad luck or bad karma or bad breaks.

Or, he thought with a chill, a band of murderous millionaires called the Consortium.

When the phone rang again, he spilled his drink.

"Nathan." It was his mother. She was hysterical.

"Oh, God. Dad?"

"What? No, we're all right, but the police just left. The most horrible thing. A bullet came right through the window. From down on the street. It was just a miracle we weren't hit. Oh, Nathan . . ."

"Mom, it's all right." His stomach was cramping. He could taste his own bile. "Did the police do anything?"

"They said there was nothing they could do."

"Is Dad okay?"

"Depressed, but he's always depressed. Nathan, you have to find him a job. It would help him a lot."

"I'll try. I'll talk to you tomorrow," Nathan said. He hung up and the phone rang again while his hand was still on the receiver.

"What, Mom?" he asked.

"Changed your mind, Mr. Eames?" the bland voice inquired.

"What kind of monster are you?" Nathan asked numbly.

"We," the voice corrected. "You agreed to join us a year ago, remember? I told you then that your membership would be for life."

"I thought it was a joke." Nathan sobbed.

"It wasn't. Neither was the incident at your parents' home."

"Don't touch them!"

"That's up to you."

"You didn't say anything about killing people."

"Don't think of them as people, Mr. Eames. It won't be personal. The target you've been given is a stranger to you."

"*Target?*" Nathan shouted, his voice breaking. "Are you *all* killers, or what?"

There was no response.

"Are you?" he asked at last, needing to know. "Are you all killers?"

"We," the voice corrected again. "We all pay dues. Yes." The voice was silent for a moment. Nathan picked up his drink. His tears dropped into the scotch.

"Now for the next ten minutes there will not be a patrol car within sixteen blocks of your parents' apartment," the calm voice went on. "I strongly urge you to leave for Mr. Westerman's in no more than nine minutes. Try very hard."

Then the line went dead.

Nathan sat clutching his abdomen, alternately sobbing and cursing. Finally, with a small cry of despair, he stumbled out the door. A set of keys was in his mailbox, just as the voice had told him. Nathan put them in his pocket and walked out onto the street, feeling the air sting his wet cheeks.

There was an air of unreality about the city as he rode the subway downtown. The colors around him were too bright, the odors too sharp. "Please let this not be real," he whispered over and over in a kind of chant.

But it was real. George Westerman lived in an old but pleasant-looking brick building in the West Village. One of the keys fit the outer lock perfectly.

Westerman's mailbox had a business card taped to it. It read:

GEORGE C. WESTERMAN
HEALER/READER
TAROT CARDS
ASTROLOGY
CHANNELING

Nathan hesitated at the bottom of the stairway for several minutes. How could he even consider killing a perfect stranger this way?

But how could he *not* consider it? His parents' lives were at stake. And maybe his own future.

It won't be personal. The target is a stranger to you.

The target. It made things easier to think of him . . . it . . . as "the target."

The target was an invalid.

And probably a New Age weirdo.

No big loss, right? he told himself.

Nathan walked upstairs to 3B and turned the key.

The target was asleep. Nathan sneaked into the darkened room on tiptoe, sweating so hard he was sure he was leaving puddles behind with every step. Every few seconds, he was seized with waves of panic. What was he doing here?

I'm paying my dues.

Yes, that was it. Just paying dues.

Suddenly a light went on. Nathan gasped.

"Who are you?" the figure on the bed asked groggily.

Nathan wished the man had not spoken. It was now harder to think of him as "the target."

Westerman leaned over toward his nightstand, which was covered with pharmaceutical vials. For a moment, Nathan contemplated running before the man could grab a gun and blow his head off.

What Westerman picked up, though, was a rubber face mask attached by a tube to a green tank with OXYGEN stenciled on it. He fiddled with something on the mask, then held it to his face and breathed while the tank hissed.

"You gave me a start," he said, smiling weakly as he set the mask down.

Westerman was a pathetic sight. His hair stood out like straw from a skull-like head. He wore striped pajamas far too big for his skeletal body. His face was blotchy and his hands were covered with lesions. "Has someone sent you?" he asked Nathan.

Nathan shook his head, then nodded. "Sent me. Yes."

"Do you want a reading?"

"What?"

"The cards. Do you want me to read the cards for you?"

"Don't you want to know how I got in?"

The man shrugged. "Most of my friends have keys. I really don't mind visitors, anyway, at whatever hour. Go ahead. Bring the cards. They're over there."

Woodenly, Nathan went to a dusty end table where a deck of oversized, dirty-looking cards was lying face down. He brought the cards to the man in the bed. The target.

"Do you know your sign?" Westerman asked as he shuffled and laid out the cards on the coverlet.

"No."

"When's your birthday?"

"I don't know."

Westerman said patiently, "That's all right. Well, here's something interesting. The Hanged Man. It's not a bad card. It signifies uncertainty, indecision. There are a lot of major cards here. This is an important time in your life. A turning point."

"It is," Nathan said. "I've come to kill you."

Westerman looked up, his forehead creased. "What was that?"

"I said I've come to kill you."

Westerman dropped the cards and stared at Nathan for a moment, then bowed his head. "I thought I might be on the list."

"What list?"

"You don't know? Are you doing this just for money?"

"Tell me about the list," Nathan said.

Westerman sighed. "All right. A lot of people who pretend to be psychics are frauds. But there are some . . . a few . . . who are real. Who have real power. And each of us like that knows who the others are. I'm one of them. And for the last few years, somebody's been killing us off." He folded his arms across his chest. "You, I suppose."

"Aren't you afraid?"

"Look, I have more diseases that most people my age have teeth. Six of them are terminal. But I confound the doctors by hanging around. They poke around, they take blood samples, and then they shake their heads and tell me I should be dead, but I just don't seem able to die. One doctor thinks it's my blood." Westerman shrugged. "Who knows? But I've been supposed to die for so long . . . no, I'm not afraid of it. Not even this way. I would like to know why I'm being murdered, though. Can you give me that?"

"No," Nathan said. He moved toward the target.

"Well, just thought I'd ask," Westerman said. "By the way, this reading"— he waved to the cards spread on the bed—"indicates you'll be dead yourself in two years."

"Two years later than you," Nathan whispered. He took the pillow from behind Westerman's head and pressed it over the sick man's face. Westerman screamed into the pillow. His arms and legs flailed obscenely. Nathan turned his head away, his eyes squeezed shut, as he bore down with all his strength until the fragile figure lay still.

He was scared after all, Nathan thought, feeling a strong urge to release his bowels.

Westerman's eyes were open. Though it revolted him, Nathan closed the lids to stop the corpse from staring at him.

The corpse, he thought. *The target.*

As he walked out the front door and onto the street, he took a deep breath. No one turned to point a finger at him. Children did not scream that they had seen a killer. Life, strangely enough, went on. In time, Nathan thought, this would become just another day.

And it did. Within three months, Nathan was working as a consultant on retainer for three of the biggest museums in the world. He had moved to California, into a glass house on the beach. His father's jewelry store was open again and thriving.

One day, during his morning jog along the shore, Nathan found a pigeon's blood ruby which he sold to a private collector for three hundred thousand dollars. It was worth more, but the collector did not demand an investigation into the stone's provenance. So Nathan did not have to explain that he had found the stone on his back steps, wrapped in a note that read WELCOME.

His membership in the Consortium was complete.

Nathan Eames looked at his empty glass. He didn't remember drinking it. He stood up and put on the terrycloth jacket and loafers he'd worn to the hotel pool. It had been a pointless attempt at leisure, anyway. Ever since joining the Consortium, he had not enjoyed idle time very much. It made his mind wander. It made him remember.

Nathan shuddered. The summer breeze suddenly felt very cold.

"Nathan!" a voice called. He turned around. It was the geezer with the red hair, this time minus the tiger-striped blonde. He was grinning broadly as he swaggered toward Nathan, hand extended in fellowship.

"How ya doing," he said with a broad New Jersey accent. "Ed Doyle. We met in Dallas last year."

"Oh . . . sure." Nathan shook his hand, certain he had never seen the man before in his life.

Doyle hoisted a deck chair with one hand and clapped Nathan on the back with the other. "See you around, Nate," he said, and walked back toward the pool.

Nathan was still puzzling over the man when he got off the elevator. He had indeed been in Dallas last year, but for only one day at an antiques convention.

He reached into his jacket pocket for his key and found a piece of paper. On it was written a name, CAROL ANN FRYE, in block letters. The same kind of letters once used to print George Westerman's name.

"Oh, God, not again," he whispered.

The phone in his room was ringing. Nathan unlocked the door quickly and grabbed for it.

"The target is working at a carnival near the Metro Zoo," the familiar bland voice said.

"It's a woman." Nathan's voice sounded thick, as if his saliva had all congealed.

"Yes. She works with someone who calls herself Madame Zola. The target is fifteen years old. She has dark blonde hair and blue eyes. . . ."

"You're talking about a kid," Nathan said.

"Just a target, Mr. Eames. Find her tonight and take her to the stretch of beach south of Eureka Drive. There are two homes in the area, but neither will be occupied. Police will be nowhere nearby. You'll find a tool in your end table drawer. Also, for your protection, you may use a car parked at the Koehler garage two blocks away. Those keys are also in your end table."

Nathan closed his eyes. "I found that diamond," he said slowly. "I called the number you gave me and left a message."

"We know. The Consortium is very pleased with your work."

"Thank you. But I thought that . . . since I've done what I was brought in to do . . . well, I thought that I might be excused from . . . I might not have to . . ."

The phone was silent for a moment. Then the voice said, "No one is excused from paying dues, Mr. Eames. Ever."

Nathan put the phone down.

In the end table drawer of his room were the car keys and a 9mm. Glock semi-automatic with a web silencer and no identifying numbers.

It doesn't have to be personal, Nathan told himself. *It's only a target*.

To satisfy his curiosity, he called the hotel operator and asked to be connected to Ed Doyle's room.

It came as no surprise that there was no such person registered.

Nathan waited until dark, then showered and dressed. He wondered if the fifteen-year-old girl he was about to kill would offer to read his cards first.

CHAPTER 5

DARIAN WAS SITTING AT A BACK TABLE IN EDDIE'S WHEN SAM CAME IN AFTER using the outside telephone booth.

"Cops say anything?"

Sam shook his head. "They just verified that it was Otto Krantz, that doctor I saw in the hospital. Nothing else."

"What'd you expect?"

"Like why he wanted to shoot us, maybe," Sam said as he sat down.

Darian grunted. "Could have been a coincidence."

Eddie brought over a bucket of steamers. "That's what the police think. We just happened to be there when the guy popped." Sam shook his head. "I don't buy it, though. Not after the fuss Krantz made over my blood." He added, "And the woman, too."

The woman. She had a name, he knew, but it had a "doctor" in front of it, which put her way out of Sam's league. Still, he had kissed her. Cory Althorpe had allowed that, even if it was just a cheesy scam to get him to give up his blood to Dr. Krantz.

And when he had kissed her, she had filled him with the music of the sea.

He ate in silence.

After a while, Darian said, "My son Jamie had rare blood, too. And the Sight."

Sam looked up from his food. "The Sight?"

"Second sight, whatever you call it," the old man said uncomfortably. "He was in some kind of experiment for it. The doctors were always poking him for blood."

Sam pushed his bowl away.

"The bastard in charge of the experiment, Bonner was his name, thought maybe his blood was what made Jamie so . . . different." Darian looked away. "Never found out, though. Jamie and all the rest of them got killed. Least I thought they had, till I talked to that Woodson."

"Woodson? From the museum?"

Darian nodded. "He was there. Said he was one of them. The Rememberers, they called themselves. Rememberers." He spoke the name with disdain. "They weren't the ones had to remember."

Sam took a deep breath. "Then all this time . . . I never thought you believed me about my shivers."

"What difference would it make if I believed you or not? They never brought you no good, did they?"

"No."

"Nor Jamie, neither. He'd be alive today if it wasn't for Bonner and that weaselly blood doctor he had working for him." Darian pulled a clam shell with an angry snap. "Turns out *he's* the one who's still alive, the son of a bitch."

"Bonner?"

"No, the assistant. His name was Gerald Heaney. I found out after I buried my wife and my boy that he hadn't been on the island that day. I went to see him—I never did believe it was an accident, the boat exploding that way right in the thick of them, and I wanted to see if Heaney knew somebody who wanted them dead. But when I got to his office, the coward was already gone. Left the country, his secretary said. He'd moved to Europe to get away from the memories." Darian repeated the words with bitter mockery. He brought a clam to his lips, then dropped it back in the bowl. "I could move to the moon, and the memories would still be there."

"Excuse me, gentlemen."

Frowning, Sam looked up at a smiling man with blow-dried hair wearing a striped knit shirt with a polo pony embroidered on it. Sam disliked him immediately.

"Darian McCabe?" the man asked.

"Could be," Darian said.

The man smiled. "Mind if I join you?"

"Lots of empty tables here," Darian said, crossing his arms over his chest.

"Come on," the intruder said affably. "I've come here just to see you. That's my boat outside." He gestured toward an immense yacht that all but filled the vista from Eddie's window.

"Real impressive," Darian said, then belched.

The man stood back, his smile gone. "Okay, have it your way." He reached into his back pocket and pulled out a rolled up sheet of slick paper. He creased it so it would lay flat, then tossed it onto the table. It was a fax replica of the pendant and gold chain. Darian and Sam looked at it, then at the man.

"Eventually you'll want to sell that," he said. "I'll buy it. I'll pay you more money than you've ever seen in your lives." He paused. "You still have the stone, don't you?"

"Don't know what you're talking about," Darian said. He pushed the fax back across the table to the man, who took it, returned it to his back pocket, and tossed a business card on the table.

"You can reach me through my secretary when you decide to deal," he said. He walked away. A few minutes later, the yacht steamed from the inlet.

"Aidon St. James," Darian read from the card.

Sam nodded. "I recognized his face from television. He's the guy who owns all the casinos."

Darian hunkered down over his clams. "Where do you think he heard about the rock?"

Sam shrugged. "From Woodson's jewelry expert, probably. Look, we were talking."

"I'm done talking."

"Well, I'm not. What you told me about your son makes me believe more than ever that something's not right."

"Leave it alone," Darian said quietly. "That's why I told you what I did. Just leave it alone before something happens to you."

"Something's already happened!" Sam shouted, then lowered his voice at a gesture from Darian. "That crazy doctor just tried to kill us."

"He's dead now."

"What if he wasn't working alone?"

"Now you're talking crazy," Darian said.

"Look, a lot of crazy things are happening. What about the diamond? It *glows*, Darian."

"So? I seen algae glow."

"Does it glow for some people and not for others?" Sam shot back. "It didn't do a thing when the jeweler touched it."

"Could have been the light," the old man said.

"There's the volcano, too. You said that Woodson was part of that group of psychics. When I told him I'd seen a volcano at the Peaks, I could tell it meant something to him."

Darian tensed. Sam could almost see the screen going down behind Darian's eyes. "It means something to you, too, doesn't it," he realized.

"No," the old man grunted, wiping his mouth. "I said leave it alone." He stood up and tossed four one-dollar bills onto the table. "I'm going to get some sleep. You coming?"

Sam pushed himself slowly away from the table. "Yeah, I'm coming," he said.

Darian waited for him. When Sam had reached the door, the old man picked up St. James's card and stuck it in the pocket of his jacket.

CHAPTER 6

CAROL ANN FRYE KNEW THE WOMAN WAS DYING THE MOMENT SHE WALKED into the tent.

Probably anyone could have seen it. The woman's skin was gray, her lips had a bluish cast to them, her eyes were sunken, her hands trembled. Her hair was colorless and sparse in back, white around her face. It was cancer.

But Carol Ann did not need her eyes to see the symptoms. She saw the disease itself, glowing around the woman like a shroud. Her aura was dark, broken. The cancer had swallowed her like an amoeba circling food and she was trapped inside, watching death squeeze her more tightly with each passing hour.

"Two dollars," Madame Zola yawned, tipping onto the back legs of her chair and stretching.

Madame Zola, whose real name was Nadine Gorman, had spent virtually her entire life in one carnival or another, running every carny game from the Money Wheel to Three-Card Monte. Almost all of them had brought in more money than the Madame Zola gig, but Nadine wasn't as young as she used to be and fortune telling was a lot easier on her back than standing up for twelve hours a day at the Money Wheel.

The sick woman took a long time unclasping her handbag. The disease was in her bones, and every movement hurt. Finally, she held out two worn dollar bills. Nadine promptly stashed them in a cigar box and set her chair aright, assuming the position of mediumship, waving her hands over a chipped, greasy crystal ball.

From the corner of her eye she saw Carol Ann standing just inside the tent flap. She gestured with her head for the girl to get out.

Carol Ann had come to her as a runaway from somewhere near Philadelphia. Nadine had found her outside a blood bank where the girl had just sold a pint of her blood for food money, and had let herself be talked into giving the girl a job. All in all, Carol Ann was a good kid. She didn't take drugs, didn't steal, wasn't a hooker as far as Nadine knew, and helped out with all the heavy work and errands in exchange for a place to sleep in

Nadine's trailer and three squares a day. But she was beginning to get on Nadine's nerves.

"Okay, what do you want to ask?" she said, smiling at the ailing mark, showing the lipstick on her teeth.

"I want to touch her," the woman said, pointing a trembling finger at Carol Ann. "I heard she could heal with just her hands."

Madame Zola shot Carol Ann a dirty look. More and more townies were coming around just to see her.

Oh, the act was good. Nadine had to admit that. Business had picked up considerably since the kid started with her Jesus Christ and Lazarus routine. But Nadine would be damned before she'd let a fifteen-year-old snot-nose girl squeeze her out of a job.

"That'll be extra," Nadine said, but Carol Ann was already walking toward the woman, her arms extended.

"I'm thirty-two years old," the woman said tremulously. "I've got young kids. My husband left. . . ."

Carol Ann embraced her, feeling the woman's wracking pain course through her own thin arms. Her eyelids fluttered. She felt a shiver down her back.

"Oh, God, I feel it moving," the woman whispered.

The disease was bad. It flowed through Carol Ann like molten lead. Her legs buckled, and for a few moments she had to cling to the sick woman to stay upright.

"Now, don't you have one of your fits here," Madame Zola snapped.

Carol Ann couldn't hear her. She heard only the cancer, raging like a wild wind, pouring out of the woman's body and into her own, where it could find no purchase.

The woman gasped and whimpered. Her nose ran. Carol Ann held her more closely, willing into herself the shroud of disease.

When it was gone, when Carol Ann had absorbed all the death inside the woman, she released her and stepped away. Then, raising her arms, she expelled the evil through her mouth, her nose, the top of her head, the tips of her fingers, until it had all vanished, dissipated into the air. Then she shuddered and fell to her knees.

Madame Zola muscled her onto a chair. "That'll be fifty dollars," she said irritably to the woman.

"I . . ." The woman rummaged frantically in her purse. "I don't think I have . . ."

"What do you got?" the medium grabbed the bills in the woman's hand and counted them quickly. Thirty-six dollars. The kid could pull in a thousand a day, easy, and she wasted herself on thirty-six lousy bucks. "All right, come back tomorrow and pay the rest." She pocketed the bills. "Well, what are you waiting for?"

The woman stood stammering for a moment, then knelt down alongside Carol Ann's chair.

"Are you all right?" she asked.

Carol Ann's eyes opened. The woman's cheeks were flushed. The dull cast to her eyes was gone. She looked young again.

"I'm fine," Carol Ann said, smiling.

"You're so pale."

"I just need to rest a while. You go home, now."

The woman touched her own face. "I feel so different."

"You're not sick anymore." Carol Ann saw the woman's aura, now blue and strong. "It's all gone," she said.

The woman bowed her head. "I was dying."

"Look, do you mind?" Madame Zola asked, her hands on her hips.

The woman stood up and, with a final glance at Carol Ann, left the tent.

Don't you think you're kind of overdoing this crap?" Nadine asked.

"What?"

"With the fainting and all. The eyeballs rolling back in your head."

"I don't know how else to do it," Carol Ann said. "She was so sick."

"Hey, this is me, okay? I'm a carnie. I understand scams. All I'm saying is—"

"It's not a scam," Carol Ann said quietly.

"Fine," Nadine said in disgust. "You want to be Sarah Bernhardt, go right to it. But at least wait until I collect the money, huh? And don't go getting any idea that you're my partner. You work for me, understand? Any lip, and you're back on the street."

Carol Ann nodded as a young man walked into the tent.

He was well dressed. Nadine immediately assessed him as good for at least fifty bucks. "Sit down," she purred. "Let me tell you about yourself."

Carol Ann rose and walked toward the exit.

"Is she leaving?"

"My assistant?" Madam Zola tried to wipe the crystal ball clean. "No, she can stay if you want her to. It's an extra ten dollars, though."

The man opened his wallet to take out the money. When he did, Nadine caught a glimpse of his driver's license.

His name was Nathan Eames.

I see a woman with dark hair who is close to you," Madame Zola said.

Nathan was looking at Carol Ann.

The medium waited for a response, then saw that the young man was not paying any attention to the crystal ball. She raised an eyebrow and turned to Carol Ann. "And what do you see?" she asked.

The girl looked uneasy. "Nothing. May I go?"

"No," the man said. "What do you see, really?"

Carol Ann looked at him and their eyes locked.

"Dark forces," she whispered. "Something evil. A shining stone."

Madame Zola beamed in triumph, then immediately altered her expression into a more somber cast. "This is deep, very deep," she intoned. "It'll cost another ten."

"I can't stay here," Carol Ann said.

"Don't go." Nathan held her sleeve.

"Ten dollars, please," Madame Zola repeated.

"I'd like you to have dinner with me. Both of you."

"Dinner?" Madame Zola scowled. "Are you nuts?"

"I'd just like . . . well, more private circumstances. I'll pay you a hundred dollars."

"Each?" Nadine gave the young man her most brilliant smile.

"Yes. Each."

"In advance."

"Of course," Nathan said. He took two hundred-dollar bills from his wallet and gave them to her.

Carol Ann shook her head. "No, I don't want to . . ."

"Shut up." Nadine checked the bills to make sure they were genuine, then stuffed them into her cleavage. "Great. I'm starving. Let's go now."

This time, the killing was easier.

Nathan drove the two women through an attractive residential area toward the beach.

"Is this a fancy place we're going to?" Nadine asked. "Is she dressed right?" She crooked her thumb toward Carol Ann in the backseat.

"You're both fine," Nathan said. He pulled onto the beach and parked. "But first I want to show you something. My favorite place."

Nadine sighed and rolled her eyes. "All right, but let's make it quick, okay? They got fireworks at the carnival tonight and there's going to be a crowd."

"I don't think it'll take long." Nathan felt for the gun in the back of his belt.

She knew. The girl knew. He would have to kill her first. It was too bad that the woman would have to die as well, but he couldn't very well leave a witness.

He had covered his tracks by having them meet him outside the carnival grounds, near the zoo entrance. The Porsche had smoked windows so no one who might have seen the women get into the car could get a good look at him. After it was done, he would return the car to the garage and forget about it.

As he got out of the car, he looked at the lights of two houses on the beach. Both were modern with gigantic expanses of glass. Nathan hoped with all his heart that the Consortium was right about their being unoccupied tonight.

But then, he thought, the Consortium is always right.

"Come on out, Carol Ann," he said gently. To his surprise, he smiled. He was getting good at this.

It's just another day. One event among millions in my life. Like brushing my teeth or going to the grocery store.

Or killing George Westerman.

He held out his hand for the girl. She shook her head.

"You knew my name," she said.

"Of course," he lied. "We were introduced."

She reached for the door handle on Nadine's side and was half out of the car when Nathan shot her. The bullet went into her chest, throwing her into the door. When she slumped onto the sand, she left a smear of blood on the Porsche's white leather upholstery.

Don't think about it, don't think too much, just another day, just another target . . .

Nadine shouted and scrambled out of the car. "What . . . ?" she began.

Nathan shot her in the face. Her arms jerked into the air and he fired again, dead in the center of her forehead.

. . . Just another target, just another day.

He trotted to the water's edge and hurled the gun into the waves, then came back to the Porsche, turned up the volume on the radio, and drove away, leaving the bodies behind him like picnic litter.

Another year's dues paid, he thought.

Just another

Just another

CHAPTER 7

AFTER HER NERVE-WRACKING ENCOUNTER WITH SAM SMITH AT THE HOSPI-
tal, Cory Althorpe went home, took two sleeping pills, and passed out until
morning.

When she arrived for work at seven, the entire hospital was abuzz with
the news about Dr. Krantz's insane spree which had ended in his suicide.

"A terrible tragedy," Dr. Cohen told her. "He must have been under a
monumental strain."

"I heard the man he was shooting at was named Sam Smith," she said.
"Could it have been the patient we saw yesterday in the H-chamber?"

"Smith?" Cohen shrugged. "It might have been, although that's a pretty
common name. Oh, Dr. Althorpe, I wonder if you would speak with a new
patient in intensive care. A teenage girl with a gunshot wound to the chest.
She was brought here last night after being attacked on the beach."

"Is she well enough to talk?"

"That's what's so odd. The paramedics said she was comatose, and the
ER confirmed. Massive loss of blood, cyanosis. Even after a transfusion, no
one expected her to live more than a few hours. But when I arrived this
morning, she was conscious and talking. Quite remarkable." He clicked a
pen absently. "Funny you should mention the nitrogen narcosis patient.
Sam Smith . . ."

"He demonstrated the same sort of wildly accelerated healing," Cory
said.

"Exactly. That was what so interested Dr. Krantz."

"The blood," Cory said softly, thinking of her grandfather and his work
with the Rememberers.

"Evidently. As a serologist, Krantz must have been trying to find some
connection between Mr. Smith's blood and the unusual regenerative ability
of his body."

"There was another one," Cory said. "Two years ago. A man named Mark
Cole."

"Yes. I recall Otto mentioning that. Another diver, wasn't he?"

She nodded. "He'd been mutilated by a shark, but in two weeks he was
completely healed."

"It's very strange," Cohen agreed. "I rather wish Otto had talked more about his work."

"What's the name of the girl with the chest wound?"

He consulted his clipboard. "Carol Ann Frye," he read. "She's fifteen. She was working in a traveling carnival. The woman she was with—sort of a mother figure, from what I gather—was killed. It might be good for her to talk to you. Just don't be alarmed if she says anything peculiar."

"Such as?"

Cohen smiled. "She told me that she was going to heal herself. I wouldn't take that too seriously, though. She's a teenager." He smiled. "I've got three of them. They all say crazy things."

"I understand," Cory said mechanically, even though she could feel her heart racing.

As soon as she touched Carol Ann's hand, she knew there was something different about the girl. The same something that was different about Sam Smith. And maybe herself.

"Feel up to talking?" Cory asked.

"I guess so." Carol Ann propped herself up on an elbow.

"You don't have to sit up," Cory said.

"It's all right. I'm healing. It just takes a lot out of me."

Cory nodded. "Dr. Cohen said you told him you could heal yourself."

The girl fidgeted with the covers. "I shouldn't have said that. He didn't believe me."

"Is it true?"

Carol Ann looked up. "Yes," she said slowly.

"How do you do it?"

The girl's brow creased. "I don't know exactly. It just happens. I can feel it. Only usually I do it with other people. I don't get sick myself."

"What happened last night?"

"I already told the police."

"I mean afterward."

"After he shot me?"

"Yes."

The girl's expression was fearful at first, but she took a deep breath and spoke quickly. "I came to on the beach. Sort of."

"Sort of?"

"Not really, I guess. My body was still lying on the sand. I saw it."

"You saw your own body?"

Carol Ann licked her cracked lips. "I . . . thought I did. And Nadine's, too."

Cory poured some cold water into a glass and brought it to the girl's mouth.

"I went to Nadine, but there wasn't anything inside. She was dead." The girl's eyes filled. "I think I was going to die too, but then I saw something and it made me go back. To my body, I mean. Does this sound stupid?"

"No. What did you see?" Cory asked.

"I don't remember. It was kind of like a dream. All I know is, I went back and then the ambulance came. One guy kept saying I wasn't going to make it, but I knew I was. Especially after they gave me blood. It was weak, but I could still use it."

Cory cocked her head. "The blood? You can feel what kind of blood you have?"

"I knew what they gave me was different. It had to go through my heart a couple of times. But then it was my own."

"So it was your blood that made you heal? Not your mind?"

Carol Ann reached for the water again, grimacing as she lifted the glass. "I don't know what it is. When other people are sick, I can draw the sickness out of them. It goes into me, then out again. Maybe it goes through my blood. I just don't know. But I felt it working last night."

Cory shifted in her chair. "Have you always been able to do this?"

"Heal? Yeah, I guess so. But it's been getting stronger lately. In the last few weeks. Something's happening, I can smell it in the air. I can feel it. It's time for something."

"For what?"

Carol Ann shook her head. "I don't know. Just . . . something. And it's coming fast. . . ." Suddenly her eyes opened wide. "I remember," she said softly.

"What do you remember?"

"What I saw that made me go back to my body." She looked up at Cory. "It was a volcano."

Cory blinked. "A volcano?"

"And a man standing near it. He was . . . he was saying something." She shut her eyes tight. Her thin body trembled.

"What is it, Carol Ann? What did he say?"

"He said we would meet again. That the stranger would bring us together."

"The stranger?"

"That was why I had to come back. Why I have to stay alive."

"Who's the stranger?"

Carol Ann shook her head. "I don't know."

They stared into each other's eyes for a long moment. Finally Cory broke her gaze away and looked down at her notes.

"Perhaps we should talk about the man who assaulted you," she said. "Did you give the police a description of him?"

"Yes, but it doesn't matter."

"Why not?"

"He'll be dead soon," Carol Ann said.

"How do you know that? Did you know him?"

"No. I just saw it. The death ring." She reached out with her hand and touched Cory's shoulder. "You would have seen it too, I think."

Cory felt herself breathing hard. "Perhaps," she said, trying to force the memories of her childhood away.

Carol Ann smiled. "I'm glad I'm with you," she said. "There'll be more of us."

"Us?"

"Yes, you're part of this, too. But you aren't the stranger." Carol Ann's eyes grew glazed and distant. After a moment Cory reached for her pulse, but just then the girl's eyelids fluttered. She looked bewildered. "That's funny," she said. "I was in some other place just now. There were boats."

"Boats?"

"And smoke, and columns of water shooting straight up, and mud, a rain of mud . . ." Her face contorted with fear. "And the volcano."

She lay back on the pillow. "I'm tired," she said.

"I understand. I'll let you sleep."

Carol Ann held Cory's hand tight. "Stay with me for a while," she said. "We've got to stay together. That's the only way we're going to make it."

She closed her eyes. As she slept, Cory felt the girl's blood pulsing through her fingers.

The serology lab was in even greater disarray than the rest of the hospital. Krantz's two assistants, both young doctors, and two technicians were scurrying around, pausing occasionally only to curse Dr. Krantz.

"He never told any of us anything," one of the technicians grumbled when Cory tried to talk to her about Krantz's research. "Everything was a big secret. And now nobody around here can do dick."

"But your files are on your computers, aren't they?" Cory asked.

"The patients' files are in there. It's just the research he never entered."

"Would you mind if I looked through them? I have a couple of his patients whose bloodwork I need to know about."

"Help yourself, Doctor. Holler if you need anything."

Cory sat at one of the open computers in a corner of the lab. The code for accessing blood records was printed on the machine with Magic Marker. She got into the computer and called up the file for Carol Ann Frye.

Krantz's lab was thorough. Cory would certainly give them that. Even though the girl had only been brought in the previous night, her file contained a total blood profile. Type AB-positive, Cory read. She scanned the data for glucose, urea nitrogen creatinine, uric acid, anion gap, bilirubin, cholesterol, and a score of other variables. To her practiced eye, all the readings seemed in the normal range.

She called up the file on Sam Smith. His blood type was O-negative. His readings, too, all seemed to be in the normal range. There was simply nothing in a normal blood profile to indicate that there was anything unusual about Sam Smith's blood.

Except . . . she had almost missed the material at the very end of the report, under the heading "ICDL." A string of numbers followed. Cory pushed her chair back for a moment, racking her memory to see if she remembered anything about something called ICDL in blood work.

Ionized calcium? She rechecked the records. No, there was a listing for ionized calcium: 2.1, well inside the normal range.

Whatever ICDL was, she had never heard of it before.

She leaned forward over the computer again and drew up the records for Mark Cole, the diver who had exhibited the same quick-healing tendencies. His blood was A-positive, and everything was normal—except the listing at the bottom. *ICDL* again, followed by more meaningless numbers.

Cory called over the lab technician. "What does ICDL mean?" she asked.

The young woman glanced up and down the computer's chart. "Never heard of it." She turned and called out to the others in the lab, "Anybody ever hear of a blood factor called ICDL?"

The three others shook their heads. The technician said, "Sorry, Dr. Althorpe."

"Do you always do the blood analysis here?" Cory asked. "Did Dr. Krantz ever use another lab?"

The technician smiled slyly. "Oh, yeah, he did. Someplace in Switzerland. He would never tell us about it, but his secretary was always complaining about the secret calls to Geneva. He wouldn't tell her anything, either, but the calls always showed up on the phone bills. What a putz."

"I need to reach that lab. Can you get me the number?"

"Sure." The technician leaned past Cory and pressed several keys on the computer. A phone number flashed onto the screen. "Right in the directory," the young woman said. "Real big secret, huh?"

Cory scribbled down the number.

"I just hope Krantz gets replaced by someone who's not a total jerk," the technician said. "Know any cute serologists?"

"Afraid not. Mind if I use this phone?"

"Go ahead. It's hooked right up to the computer in case you have to transmit data. But if anybody bitches later about the bill, I'll have to tell them it was you."

"No problem," Cory said. While she dialed the number, she scrolled back to Sam Smith's name.

This is all I have of him, she thought. Yesterday, the two of them had peered together into the universe. Today, he was just a name and a blood workup on a computer screen.

"Laboratoire Geneve," a woman answered on the other end of the line.

"Could you give me the name of the director, please?"

"Certainly," the woman said, switching to English. "Dr. Gerald Heaney."

"I'm calling for Dr. Otto Krantz in West Palm Beach," Cory said. "Can you connect me?"

"Hold on, please."

Cory waited, and then heard, "Yes." It was a man's voice, curt and rushed.

"Dr. Heaney, this is Dr. Cory Althorpe. I was an associate of Dr. Krantz's in West Palm Beach. He died yesterday and . . ."

"Otto's dead?"

"Yes. I'm sorry."

"Have you taken over his duties at the hospital?"

"No, Dr. Heaney. I'm a psychiatrist. But Otto and I both treated a couple of patients whose blood work was sent to you, I believe, for analysis."

"Yes?" Heaney asked hesitantly.

"Well, both patients—Sam Smith and Mark Cole—have a sequence of letters, ICDL, next to their names in the computer files. Since no one in our serology lab seems to be able to identify this factor, I was hoping you'd be able to tell me what ICDL stands for."

"Were you involved with Dr. Krantz's research?" Heaney asked abruptly.

"Not directly, but—"

"Then surely you don't expect me to discuss his research methods, even if I knew what they were, with you over the telephone," he snapped.

"Perhaps not, but I'd like to rule out the possibility that this has anything to do with the fact that both patients were psychic."

Heaney didn't answer.

"You see, both Mr. Smith and Mr. Cole showed a markedly accelerated ability to regenerate damaged tissue, and they both also displayed strong evidence of extrasensory perception. I would have taken their histories for coincidence, except that now a third patient has been admitted with the same characteristics. This patient mentioned specifically that her blood was the factor that enabled her to heal so quickly."

There was a slight pause. "You said you're a psychiatrist?"

"Yes," Cory answered.

"Then may I ask what this patient's blood—or her so-called psychic ability, for that matter—has to do with psychiatry?"

Cory felt a twinge of embarrassment. For all his rudeness, Heaney's question had been legitimate. A hospital staff psychiatrist had no real business with either field of study. "Actually, it's not my work so much as my family's," she said. "My grandfather was Edward Bonner, whose name you may know and . . ."

The line went dead.

"Dr. Heaney?" She jiggled the phone. "Doctor . . ."

Before her eyes, Sam Smith's blood-work records vanished from the computer screen.

She scrolled back to the Cs. Mark Cole's name was no longer listed.

Somehow, Heaney had just erased the medical existences of two people from across an ocean. *How did he do that?* she wondered.

And why?

CHAPTER 8

DR. GERALD HEANEY PUSHED AWAY FROM HIS DESK, SWALLOWING TO FIGHT down the nausea filling the back of his throat.

Bonner. He thought he would never have to hear that name again.

He stood up, rubbed his palm along his clean-shaven chin, and squeezed his eyes shut in anguish.

Twenty-nine years. For twenty-nine years, he had kept his silence, met his obligations, performed his work like a good trained seal. The Consortium had promised him a new life, and had kept its promise in every respect. Whatever he had been was gone. He was a different person now.

For twenty-nine years, Gerald Heaney had lived without a soul.

He dialed a phone number. A calm, expressionless voice answered on the first ring, as it always did.

"Why wasn't I told that Otto Krantz was dead?" Heaney demanded.

There was a slight hesitation. "Our apologies," the blank voice said. "Dr. Krantz's death had repercussions. It was an oversight that you were not alerted."

"A damned serious oversight," Heaney barked. "Someone who says she's Edward Bonner's granddaughter just called me. *Here*."

There was an audible intake of breath on the other end of the line. "How much does she know?"

"I haven't any idea. She's gotten into Krantz's files, though, and has made a connection between two of his patients, both with the ICDL blood type."

"What blood type?"

"Oh, Christ," Heaney muttered. If the Consortium insisted on providing him with a baby-sitter, he wished it were someone who understood at least a modicum of what his work was about. "Could I speak with someone else?" he asked coldly.

"I'm afraid not, Dr. Heaney," the even voice answered.

Heaney sighed. "Then tell whoever it is *you* talk to that this woman knows about Bonner's experiments with ESP, and that she's traced Krantz's work in West Palm Beach to me. Oh, yes. And that she's got a patient now who's saying that her *blood* is what makes her psychic."

He hung up with a satisfying crash of the phone.

Resisting an urge to panic, Heaney rifled through the papers in his "in" basket, pulling out the lab reports that had come in during the night: London, Colorado, Maine, Moscow. Here it was. Florida, blind sample. That meant it had not come from a hospital. In this case, the blood had come direct, on a cloth used to wipe the white leather upholstery of a Porsche. A fifteen-year-old girl had been shot.

Somebody in the Consortium had been paying dues.

The target's blood had all the earmarks of the blood that set one group of human beings so dramatically apart from the rest of the species. Powerful blood, Bonner had called it. The blood of a super race, except that it transcended all known racial, ethnic, and geographical divisions.

If they ever learned what they can do . . .

That was the argument that had resulted in Professor Bonner's death.

Ironically, Bonner and his assistant Heaney had been the first to understand the danger of exploring Intracellular DNA-Linked (ICDL) blood. They knew that anything arising from their discovery would create explosive social issues, beginning with the premise that all people were *not* created equal. ICDLs had more of everything—more stamina, higher resistance to disease, greater stress tolerance. And that didn't even take into account their mental differences.

It was not intelligence. ICDLs were no more or less intelligent than any other random group. It was the extrasensory powers that these people demonstrated that were so frighteningly different from other human beings. They could heal with a touch and channel to different levels of consciousness. Often they were clairvoyant. They retained "memories" of existences other than their present lives. They could spontaneously generate energy, including fire. They could call up "spirits," by which they meant the energy reservoirs of persons no longer living, and speak with them.

In short, they exhibited commonplace signs of lunacy.

And so long as they were considered lunatics, there was no problem. But Edward Bonner's findings, proving scientifically that not only did ESP exist, but that those who could practice it were physiologically different from the rest of the human race, would have created social chaos of an unimaginable magnitude.

Not to mention what would happen if the ICDLs themselves—Bonner's "Rememberers" and their kind—ever discovered their own power.

They had come close. Heaney recalled one incident in which all seventeen subjects reportedly "saw" the same vision.

It was an odd one. Bonner had hoped for something like the spectre of a prophet or a clear symbol of some sort—a star, perhaps, or the enlarged view of a hydrogen atom. But what his Rememberers came up with was a volcano. No other explanation. Just an erupting volcano and some vague presentiment that the sea was in some way involved.

Nevertheless, what Bonner had both feared and hoped for had occurred. The group had thought with one mind.

And if they could think with one mind, they could, theoretically, act with one body.

That was the true danger.

Heaney smiled bitterly. Had he gotten it right? That was the party line. He had worked for years to make himself believe it: True psychics were dangerous. That was why it was necessary to eliminate them.

Sometimes he did believe it.

Sometimes he could sleep at night.

He was startled by the ring of the telephone. No one except members of the Consortium called him on his direct line. Almost all the callers were doctors filing blood reports. Only one, the nameless blank-voiced man, was not.

"Yes," he said.

"The patient you mentioned in Florida isn't dead."

Heaney picked up the blind sample report. "No. That's what Bonner's granddaughter said. I have her blood work here."

"And she's definite?"

"She's got the blood you're looking for, if that's what you mean."

"Fine. Her name is Carol Ann Frye. She's in the intensive care unit in West Palm Beach. Age fifteen. Chest wound. She wasn't disposed of properly."

"I gathered that," Heaney said testily.

"The woman you spoke with was Dr. Corinne Althorpe, age thirty-seven," the blank voice continued. "She's on the psychiatric staff at the same hospital."

"Thank you for sharing that with me. May I ask why?"

"You're to go to Florida immediately," the anonymous voice said.

Heaney felt his shoulders slump.

That was all. Just a slump of the shoulders. Time had a way of making a person accustomed to even the most terrible things. An order to kill two people, one of them a child, who were perfect strangers to him and had never done him any harm, produced no objection other than a slump of the shoulders. The screaming but unvoiced protest he had felt in the past had thinned to a dull throb.

Even Heaney's perception of the blank-voiced man on the telephone had mellowed over the years. For the first few years, he had thought of that expressionless drone as the voice of God, disembodied and disinterested, to be disobeyed at one's peril. Now he pictured its owner in a different way. He was rather stupid, after all, that vacuous being with the air-conditioned voice. He was venal, small-minded, and devoid of conscience. God, for Gerald Heaney, had evolved into a flat-voiced thug.

Nevertheless, God—or Benny or Frank or Joey the Spike, whatever his name was—had complete authority to murder him at will; and therefore was still in a position to be disobeyed only at Heaney's peril.

"I'm needed here," Heaney ventured.

"We are arranging for you to replace Dr. Krantz at his hospital." It was as if Heaney had never spoken.

"Do you have any questions, Doctor?"

"No," he said quietly. "No questions."

He hung up. *Don't ask questions. It's better that way.*

* * *

He smoothed his hands over the lab report about the teenager in West Palm Beach. Carol Ann Frye. He wondered what she had done to warrant getting shot in the chest. Predicted the weather? Bent a spoon?

No, the spoon-benders were almost always fake. Back when he first came to work as Bonner's serologist, his salary paid by a small federal grant, he had been amazed at how the quacks had arrived in droves to volunteer for Bonner's experiments, clearly convinced that they could manipulate whatever tests they were given.

But they never could. Not through all Bonner's tests. And they never had the right blood.

So the fakes were sent away to continue defrauding whomever they chose, while Bonner gathered up the genuine ICDLs.

No, Carol Ann Frye wasn't a spoon-bender.

Maybe she was a healer. The healers always had been special targets. He remembered a married couple named Nowar, who had been in the group. They were both oncologists, both with very strong indications of ICDL, and an unheard-of record of curing terminal patients. They came to Bonner as volunteers, determined to find other physicians with ESP with the goal of pioneering a new form of healing.

The Consortium had made sure the Nowars were disposed of "properly." When they didn't show up for the final, fatal encounter on Memory Island, the Consortium had sent out people to find them. Heaney had read about their deaths while he was enroute to Switzerland, carrying the research records he had stolen from Bonner's office files. The Nowars had been found murdered in a swamp, surrounded by footprints in the blood-soaked mud.

He pushed his intercom. "I'll be leaving for several days. Please rearrange my schedule."

His voice, he noticed, sounded frail, the voice of a timid old man.

Why am I surprised? he asked himself. That was what he had become.

At the time of Bonner's experiments, Heaney had been an eager young scientist, a brilliant serologist with a brilliant future. Once the evidence about ICDL blood started coming in, he caught Bonner's fire.

"I think the extraordinary talents of these people are imprinted on their blood cells," the old doctor had said early on. "But what is yet to be discovered is where these talents originated."

"Isn't it obvious?" Heaney had asked. "It's cellular, an evolutionary trait gone awry. . . ."

"You think early man was psychic?"

"It's possible," Heaney said. "Birds can sense when earthquakes are coming. Animals grow thicker coats in anticipation of a cold winter. Primitive man might have needed ESP to survive, then lost the ability over the next few millenia, when it was no longer needed."

Bonner paced about the office they shared. "Assume ancient man did have psychic skills at one time. Just as a guess, I would think that any such skills would have been reasonably low level. Early man wouldn't have needed a psychic tool as powerful as, say, telepathy to avoid freezing during an ice age."

Heaney was beginning to understand him. "And yet a significant number of the Rememberers are telepathic—is that what you're saying?"

"That's just what I'm saying. They're telepathic, precognitive, clairaudient. . . . Their abilities far surpass whatever might at one time have been necessary for survival." He stopped pacing and smiled. "I think these people are different, Dr. Heaney, different down to the very cells of their bodies. I do not believe they are mutations, or even that they have followed a normal evolutionary pattern."

"Then . . . where do they come from?"

Bonner laughed. "I doubt if we'll find the answer to that within our lifetimes. What we can find, though, is the key to the Rememberers' particular genetic differences. That key is in their blood."

It was an exciting time. With the advent of the electron microscope, the secrets of life had been revealed through a code of markings on blood cells. All over the world, scientists had been jolted into the realization that *everything* about a human being was spelled out in a series of complex codes literally written on each cell and each bead on a strand of DNA. The trick was to decipher the code.

Most of the scientists tried to crack the codes of the physical body. Through these cellular markings, protein configurations were discovered, as were hemoglobin AIC, a cellular predisposition to diabetes, and a means to determine tissue compatibility, which made organ transplant possible.

These scientists were rewarded for their efforts with prestige, a place in history, and the veneration of their peers. Only Edward Bonner, whose work had predated most of theirs, was treated with ridicule and scorn. Of all the elements of human life encoded inside the cells in a drop of blood, only the mind was ignored.

The scientific community could accept the idea that a human being might be born with a penchant for obesity, but not for psychic awareness. Edward Bonner became a laughingstock, his name an epithet for ridicule.

That was the work of the Consortium.

And Gerald Heaney had helped them.

"Your work is overshadowed by Dr. Bonner's" the voice said during the first call. "It will always be overshadowed, as long as you allow it."

Heaney had protested, as any reputable scientist would. "We do not work for personal glory," he had said loftily.

The arid voice had only laughed. He—God, that is, the voice that would come to rule Gerald Heaney's life—had terminated the conversation at that point, because He had accomplished His mission. He had planted a seed of discontent.

Because his work *was* overshadowed by Bonner's, damnit. The blood work was the important element in the experiments, not the old man's silly mind-reading games, and Heaney was the blood expert.

And so, because God had seen into Gerald Heaney's heart and found it filled with weakness and pride, Heaney was more receptive to the second phone call. And the third. At the time of the fourth call, the speedboat which had been rigged to explode on Memory Island had already begun its fateful journey.

That call had come right to the point.

"Bonner will be dead in a matter of minutes," the voice said. "If you wish to join the Consortium, collect all your office files and take a taxi directly to the airport. Now."

"Dead? But—"

"There is no time for discussion, Dr. Heaney. Go now or stay."

The caller hung up. Half dazed, Heaney shuffled from room to room, wondering what to do.

He could go to the police.

And tell them what? That his senior partner was going to be murdered by a group known to Heaney only as a voice on the telephone?

He could sit tight and do nothing. Pretend the call had never come. Hope for the best.

And if his worst fears were correct, die like Bonner.

He could fight, of course. Die for his work, for his honor.

Honor.

What a sad little word it was.

What he did, in the end, was to take all Bonner's files, leave the building, hail a cab, and head for the airport. There a ticket in his name was dropped at his feet by a passerby whose face he didn't see. The ticket was to Boston.

At Logan Airport, he answered a telephone page and received a message to check into the Copley Plaza. The next day, a packet arrived for him containing a passport—he had never had one—another plane ticket to Geneva, Switzerland, and a sheet of paper bearing only the address:

12153 COMMONWEALTH AVENUE.

A moment later the phone rang.

"Did you have a good trip?" the voice said.

"Why am I going to Geneva?" Heaney asked. "What am I supposed to do there?"

"That's where you'll begin your life, Doctor," the voice answered with cool assurance. "You will head the largest serology laboratory in the world. You will continue with Bonner's work, but for the Consortium alone. No press, no conventions, no scientific journals. Just us."

He frowned, but said nothing.

"Now, I would suggest you go as soon as possible to the address you've received, Dr. Heaney. It's an apartment building where a woman named Grace Bonner lives. She is Dr. Bonner's sister."

"Yes, I know. I've met her."

"Then it won't be difficult. Go and tell her that her brother is dead."

"Well . . . I . . . all right. I suppose I can tell her. And then what?"

"And then kill her."

"What?"

"Proceed directly to the airport after that. Your plane leaves at two."

"What . . . I can't . . ." He felt as if all the breath had been knocked from his body. "You must be insane."

"All members of the Consortium pay dues," the voice said.

"But—"

"You won't be caught, Dr. Heaney. We take care of these things."

Heaney sat in stunned silence, breathing heavily into the receiver.

"Do it, Doctor," the voice said at last. "You know there's no alternative now."

The connection was broken. Heaney squeezed his eyes closed with the finality of the click at the other end.

He had done it, of course. He would not be alive now if he hadn't. And he had continued Bonner's work secretly, scouring the world's hospitals and clinics and blood banks, seeking to identify people with ICDL blood.

Then those people were killed, either by others or by Heaney himself.

He had killed many, many times.

At this moment, in fact, he was setting out for southern Florida to kill again. Heaney walked slowly past his secretary, who wished him a pleasant trip. He did not respond.

He sometimes wondered how things might have been if he hadn't spoken to the blank-voiced man. The Consortium would have killed him, of course.

But at least he might have died with some sense of . . . well, honor.

"Honor." He whispered the word and walked to his waiting Rolls-Royce.

CHAPTER 9

THE SUN WAS SETTING WHEN SAM AND DARIAN NEARED THEIR DOCK AT Jupiter Inlet. It had been rotten work, diving into muck to find a set of unused utility pipes for a housing developer. But they had been paid. Sometimes that was the most they could hope for.

"Who the hell is that?" Darian grumbled as a figure silhouetted against the flame-colored sunset walked out toward their mooring.

"A woman," Sam said.

"Probably one of them Jehovah's Nitwits." Darian wiped his hands on his grimy pants. "That's all I need."

"I'll get rid of her," Sam said, judging from the old man's mood that it was probably best to avoid an encounter between Darian McCabe and the general public.

The boat nosed into the dock. Sam tossed the rope onto the pier, ready to jump out and tie up, but the woman picked up the rope and wound it expertly around the cleat. It was Cory Althorpe.

Sam tossed her the stern line and she made that one fast also. From the deck, Sam stared at her.

"What are you doing here?" he said finally.

"I've got to talk to you."

Darian pushed past Sam and lumbered onto the pier to check the lines.

"They're on right," Cory said.

Darian gave her a black look, checked the ropes anyway, then hopped back onto the boat. "We ain't had supper yet," he said.

"I'm sorry to disturb you, Mr. McCabe, but this is very urgent. You'll want to hear what I have to say, too. Please let me come aboard."

With a sigh of disgust, Darian turned his back. Sam nodded approval for Cory to come aboard, then led her down into the galley. "I can make you some instant coffee," he said, trying not to notice the music that followed her like traces of light.

"Just let her say what she's got to say," Darian boomed as he followed them below.

Cory took a deep breath. "It's about your blood, Sam."

"If you came here to get more of his blood, lady . . ." Darian threatened.

"That's not why I'm here."

The old man settled onto one of the hard benches with an air of discontent.

"Sam, there was a code on the hospital computer indicating that your blood work was sent to some laboratory in Geneva, Switzerland. The same code was next to the name of another patient with the same kind of blood."

"The dead diver?" Sam asked.

"Yes. Mark Cole. I didn't get a chance to tell you that he might also have exhibited some psychic tendencies."

"Are you going to start that crap again?" Darian said hotly.

"It's a factor in what I've learned, Mr. McCabe."

"Then get on with it. You got too many words for a woman."

Cory closed her eyes in exasperation, then turned back to Sam. "Okay. The codes on your blood work. I wrote them down. Then I called the director of the lab in Geneva to see if there was a connection between your kind of blood and the fact that you're psychic."

"What'd he say?" Sam asked.

"He hung up on me."

Darian snorted. "Can't say's I blame him."

"And a moment later, both your name and Mark Cole's were erased from the computer file."

"Probably pushed the wrong button," Darian said.

"I did not push a wrong button," she said evenly. "It was deliberately erased."

"Why?" Sam asked.

"That's what I wanted to know. So I got on the phone with a hospital in Washington. I know somebody in the serology lab there. I got the names of every patient admitted in the past two years whose blood records showed the Geneva code. There were four." She swallowed.

"Yeah?"

"They're all dead, Sam."

Darian looked up sharply. "What?"

"Every one of them died soon after his release from the hospital. Just like Mark Cole."

"Krantz said he died in an auto accident."

Cory opened her pocketbook and took out a piece of paper on which she had scribbled some notes. "Yes, a hit and run. The driver was never caught. A man named Allen Decker also died in a hit and run. June Codispot fell out a window. Romero Cruz suffered a drug overdose. Hiroshi Nakajima succumbed to carbon monoxide poisoning." She folded the paper.

"Could be a coincidence," Darian said.

Cory exhaled sharply. "Yes, it could. Is that what you want to believe?"

Darian tightened his lips into a thin line.

"So I called another hospital in Tulsa. They had two patients on file whose blood had the Geneva code."

"Dead?" Sam asked.

"Yes."

This time Darian did not have an answer.

"Dr. Krantz tried to kill me," Sam said quietly. "Was it for my blood?"

She shook her head. "I can't make any sense out of it. He didn't kill the people in Washington or in Oklahoma."

"Who's to say those people were . . . whatchamacallit, psychics, anyway?"

"I am," Cory said. "After Dr. Heaney hung up on me, I called the families of each—"

"Heaney?"

"Gerald Heaney. He's the director of the lab in Switzerland. As soon as I mentioned a possible connection between this ICDL blood and ESP, he panicked. And yes, I checked. All those other dead people were psychic. So their families said."

Sam looked at Darian. "Didn't you mention something about a guy named Heaney?" Then he remembered. "That's right. You went to see him after . . ." He didn't want to finish the sentence.

"Do you know him?" Cory asked, bewildered.

"Heaney was one of the scientists in an experiment with psychics once," Sam said. "They tested blood, too."

"That's nothing that concerns her," Darian snapped. "Happened a long time ago."

"Memory Island," Cory said.

Darian stared at her.

"That's where it was, wasn't it?" Her face was ashen.

"How do you know about that?"

"Oh, my God," she said. "They all died, too."

"I asked you how you know about that," Darian demanded.

"She looked at Darian with tears in her eyes. "It was my grandfather's experiment," she said. "I'd forgotten his assistant's—"

"Bonner!" Darian's eyes blazed. "Your grandfather!"

Cory closed her eyes slowly, then opened them again. "McCabe," she said breathlessly. "Your son was Jamie McCabe."

"Get off my boat."

"It wasn't an accident back then, was it?" she went on. "They were all murdered."

"It was your fool grandfather got my boy killed!" Darian raged. "If it wasn't for him and his ungodly meddling with—"

"You're blaming the wrong person!" she shouted back. "Don't you see? He was killed, too. His reputation was destroyed. All his work vanished. And now the man who worked with him is running a lab that can identify people like Sam. And people like Sam have been killed. How do we know they aren't *still* being killed?"

"I want you off my boat."

"Darian," Sam began.

"Take her topside. Now."

Sam's mouth set. "Look, I don't know how . . ."

"That's right. You don't know nothing. I'll not have Bonner's spawn on my property. Now get rid of her before I throw you both off."

Sam rose from his bench, angrily, but Cory stepped between them. "I'll go," she said. "I've said what I came to say." She picked up her pocketbook and walked gingerly up the narrow steps to the deck.

Sam followed her.

"I can see myself off," she said on the deck.

Sam stepped close to her. "Look," he said. "I'm sorry the old man was so rude to you. I guess I was, too, yesterday at the hospital."

"I'd rather forget everything that happened yesterday," she said. "My behavior with you was unpardonable." She placed her hand on his chest to push him away, but at the touch of his body, she felt the intoxicating music surge through her.

Sam closed his eyes. His breath escaped in a quivering rush.

"Don't," she said softly. Then, her face showing her pain, she pushed him away and clambered onto the pier.

In another instant, it seemed, she was gone, the red taillights of her car speeding into the distance.

Sam put his hand over the spot on his chest where her hand had touched him. He could still hear the music.

Darian came up behind him. "Is she gone?"

"I'm going to bed," Sam said, walking past him without a glance.

"No supper?"

Sam didn't answer him.

Darian thrust his hands into his pockets and walked to the stern of the boat, where he looked out at the night sky.

If only Sam hadn't dived the Peaks. The devil was coming after Sam, just the way he had come after Jamie.

Darian heard a voice, deep inside his head. *I'll kill you, I'll kill you all.*

The words were always the same.

There had never been a picture attached to the words, only a man's voice, clear and low, filled with evil magic. Darian had heard it at different times, in dreams, sometimes when he was sitting at a bar after too many beers, or when he was out alone on the *Styx*; but he had heard it often enough to recognize it when it came.

I'll kill you. I'll kill you all. You and your children and theirs, through all time, through all eternity. . . .

The words had come to him on the day his wife and son died.

And now he knew: it was a promise.

I'll kill you. I'll kill you all.

Darian's breath came ragged.

He rummaged inside the pocket of his jacket and pulled out a wad of paper. Scraps, all with writing on them. Appointments, jobs long finished, reminders. And a business card. AIDON ST. JAMES, it read in flowing italic script.

The diamond.

The devil had come back to life with the diamond.

Darian hopped lightly onto the dock and crossed the road toward Eddie's. He put a quarter into the pay phone, dialed, and waited.

"St. James residence," an English male voice answered.

"Darian McCabe. Let me talk to him."

"I'm afraid Mr. St. James—"

"Get him."

After a moment, the phone was picked up. "Well, Mr. McCabe. What a pleasure."

"I'll sell you the stone," Darian said.

C H A P T E R   1 0

DARIAN AND SAM WALKED INTO THE MUSEUM JUST AFTER 8 A.M. WOODSON was seated at his desk, the diamond pendant in front of him. Darian marched forward, crossed his arms, and growled. "All right, you're the one wanted to see us so bad. What is it?"

"Can I get you some coffee?" Woodson asked mildly.

"No. Just get to it. I might be able to line us up a job today, though I doubt it, having to run in here to do your bidding."

"I'm sorry," Woodson said. "I offered to come to you."

McCabe had told Woodson about the proposed sale in a predawn phone call to the museum official's home that morning. "Just want you to know we'll be transferring the stone to Aidon St. James. So's you don't think he's stealing it," he had said. It was then that Woodson had convinced him to bring Sam in for one last meeting.

"What time is your meeting with Mr. St. James?"

"Seven o'clock tonight. He wants us to come for dinner on that fancy yacht of his."

"And you're going to talk terms about the diamond?"

"I am if he offers more than five million bucks for it," Darian said with a grin, which quickly faded. "Is that what you called us here for? To make sure you get your finder's fee?"

"No, it's nothing like that. But the stone itself . . . the diamond . . ." Woodson spread his hands. "I'm not sure you should be selling it so quickly. It might be of more scientific importance than we'd thought."

Darian gazed heavenward. "Oh? So you're a big jewelry expert now? The last time we were here, you didn't know donkey-doo about gems."

"I've been doing some reading."

"On this diamond?"

"No. There *is* nothing on this diamond. That's one of the things that's so peculiar," Woodson said. "All the great stones are catalogued somewhere. They have histories. When some man in India showed up with a so-called unknown stone, it was recognized immediately as a fragment of the great Cullinan diamond that Napoleon's soldiers had stolen a hundred years before."

Darian's face was grim. "Are we supposed to be interested in all this?"

Woodson tried to ignore him, to address himself to Sam. "Your stone has no history. We've looked at every source, and there's absolutely nothing on a thousand-carat, shield-shaped diamond with sixteen facets. The stone seems to have come out of nowhere."

"It came from the bottom of the sea, for God's sake," Darian snapped.

"But it's cut. It's not a raw stone. It was a treasure of a civilized society somewhere. And yet there's no record whatsoever."

"Which means what?" Sam asked.

"Well, this sounds bizarre, but it occurs to me that it might have come from a civilization so remote in time that it was never recorded. If it did, then the stone and its pendant could be an archaeological find of stupendous magnitude."

Darian scowled.

"I'm just suggesting that you not rush into a sale prematurely. I realize that you stand to make a lot of money on the sale of this diamond, but if it can be proven to be a genuine relic and can lead to further discoveries, the pendant's value would be beyond price." He paused, a look of desperation on his face. "I'd hate to see something like that cut into jewelry. It would be a great loss."

The old man sighed. "Remember what your diamond expert said? Cavemen didn't cut diamonds."

"Yes, but what if there was a civilization before cavemen?" Woodson asked. "Sam, you saw the image of a volcano. I've seen it, too. I was part of the experiment on Memory Island."

"Darian told me that, but—"

"We all saw it."

Sam cast an accusing look at Darian. "Jamie, too?"

"Every one of us." He limped over to a shelf and picked up an open book. "We saw *this*," Woodson said, holding out the opened pages.

It was a photograph of a smooth stone wall engraved with the likeness of an erupting volcano. "That photo was taken almost seventy years ago in an underwater cave in the Western Pyrenees. Archaeologists have guessed the date of this drawing at approximately eight thousand B.C.E."

"Ten thousand years ago?" Sam squinted at the picture, feeling his temples throbbing. It was not *like* the volcano of his vision; it was the same one. It was flanked on either side by some kind of tall structure. To the right, below the hillside, was a mass of frothing waves. The extreme right section of the carving was badly eroded. Sam touched the area gently with his fingertip.

"Boats," he said. "There were boats here."

"Probably," Woodson said. "Look underneath them."

Beneath the eroded area were more waves. Among them, at the very bottom of the carving, was a shield-shaped object that had been chiseled deep into the cave wall.

"The diamond," Sam said with amazement. "That's the stone."

Darian snatched the book from him. "You got to have a damn good imagination to see a diamond in that," he said .

"It's got eight facets on its face," Woodson argued. "You can see them in the drawing."

"Look more like scratches to me," Darian said.

"Then what do you think it is?" Woodson jabbed at the object in the photograph with his finger.

Darian shrugged. "Stingray. A rock, maybe. Hell, it could be anything." He slammed the book shut. "Ten thousand years old, my ass. In case you two geniuses didn't know, people who live on mountains don't use boats."

He turned the book over to see its spine. It was old, its leather cracked and dry with age. The gold lettering of the title was nearly gone, but it had been stamped into the leather: LOST LEGENDS OF THE ANCIENTS.

"Oh, wonderful," he said. You want me to pass up five million dollars because you read something in a book of frickin' *legends?*"

"Let him talk," Sam said. He nodded to Woodson.

"The Basques, who live in the part of Spain where that cave etching was found, tell a story of a great stone called the Eye of Zeus," Woodson began. "At least, that's how it was translated."

"Zeus?" Sam repeated. "That's Greek, isn't it?"

"It might be 'Zos.' The origins of the Basque language are so obscure that the word is untraceable. But it apparently referred to some sort of deity, so the archaelogists used 'Zeus.' A little romantic leeway, I guess."

"Eye of Zeus," Darian scoffed.

"Anyway, the legend says that Zeus—or Zos, or whatever—had a magical stone the color of water and the size of a man's heart with which he defeated the armies of his enemies and created a kingdom which would rule the Earth forever. But the king was betrayed by his own kinsman who vowed to destroy him and all his descendants. A great flood came, the king was killed, and the kingdom which was meant to rule forever sank beneath the sea."

"The sea in the mountains," Darian said.

"Clearly this is one of the flood legends," Woodson said. "In addition to the one in the Bible, there are stories in nearly every country in the world about a great flood in the ancient past. There are so many legends of this type that historians have come to believe there must be at least a grain of truth in them."

"What a pile of crap," Darian muttered.

Woodson looked to Sam for some acknowledgment, but the young man had picked up the book again and was reading it, his forehead creased in a frown.

"There's more to the legend," Sam said.

"I was getting to that."

Darian shoved his hands into his pockets and walked to the window. "This ought to be good," he said.

Sam cleared his throat and read aloud. " 'From that day to this, the enemies of King Zeus have searched the Earth for survivors from that deluge, slaying them where they were found, in the temples of knowledge and among the common folk who themselves had forgotten the eternal land from which they came. But because the magical eye was lost, returning to the water from which it was made, these enemies had no stone to guide them, and they have been unable to destroy all the king's descendants." He looked from one man to the other. " 'No stone to guide them,' " he repeated. "What do you think that means?"

Darian strode across the room and ripped the book from Sam's hands. He flipped through it contemptuously. "Indian legends," he scoffed. "Prester John. Noah's Ark. Zeus's magic eyeball. I bet there's something in here about Goldilocks and the Three Bears." He tossed it onto the coffee table.

Woodson looked at the floor. "After everybody in Bonner's experiment was killed . . . "

"Everyone but you," Darian said.

"No fault of theirs."

"How's that?"

Woodson told him about the events following the explosion—the deaths of the Rememberers who had not been on the island during the incident, his own attempted murder. "That's how I got the bends," he said.

"Did you call the police?"

"No," he said quietly. "I hid."

Darian stared at him for a long, silent moment.

Finally Sam spoke. "I think it's happening all over again," he said. "Somebody's trying to kill—" he almost could not bring himself to say the word, but he forced himself "—psychics," he whispered. "People like you and the other Rememberers. And Darian's son. And me. And the diamond's got something to do with it."

"Well, you can stop worrying about that," Darian said. "After tonight, that stone's going to be somebody else's problem."

"Maybe it isn't the problem," Sam ventured. "Maybe it's the solution." He turned his hands palm up. "What I'm saying is, maybe it was meant to come back to us."

"Us? Since when did you become the owner of this rock?" Darian spat.

"I only meant that if it's the same diamond of the legend, then it's . . . special."

"Because some foreigners called it the Eye of Zip?"

"God, I wish Jamie were here," Woodson said softly.

Darian looked up. "What's that?"

"Your son, Mr. McCabe. I know you don't much hold with it, but Jamie had a true gift. Of all of us, he was the only one who really knew how to use his power. And that's what it was, power. That kid was . . . well, once you got to know him, you couldn't think of him as a kid anymore. He was more like . . . "

"Like what?" Darian asked.

"Like . . . well, a prophet, sort of. Or a . . . a god."

The old man looked away.

A god.

No, Jamie wasn't a god, nothing like it. But he was never a child, either. He had always known things that took most people a lifetime to understand.

That was why I let him go join Bonner's program. Jamie had needed to do it, and no matter what I said, he wouldn't change his mind.

"Something's coming, Dad," he told me. "I don't know what it is yet, but it's important, and I think I can help."

"By doing what? Teaching Bonner and those swamis and potheads of his how to play hopscotch?"

"By seeing things other people can't see."

So I let him go and he died.

He was a kid, that's all," Darian said quietly.

"I think you know he was more than that," Woodson answered. "After one of the meetings on Memory Island—the one where we all saw the volcano—Bonner asked me to take Jamie out in a boat. Your son led us to the Peaks."

"You took him to the Peaks?" Darian asked angrily.

"Jamie had insisted on going. He was the one who first said that the volcano we'd all seen wasn't a vision so much as a *memory*. That's why we called Dr. Bonner's place Memory Island. But Jamie felt that the volcano was just the beginning of this group memory we shared. He said there was more to it than we knew, and that we'd need a certain stone to see the rest of it. A stone that would make us all see with one eye, was how he put it, so that we'd be able to find our way to where the memory began."

"And the stone was at the Peaks," Sam said.

"Yes."

Darian sat back. "A stone that makes you see with one eye," he repeated caustically. "Just like your Eye of Zorro. That's really something, how you can recollect his exact words."

"When Jamie spoke, everybody listened," Woodson said, bristling. "Everybody except you."

The old man's hand snaked out and grabbed him by his tie. "You don't know nothing about how I raised my son, you crippled-up—"

"Quit it, Darian," Sam said, pulling him off. "Are you all right?" he asked Woodson.

The black man straightened his tie. "Yeah. It was my fault, anyway. I was out of line. It's just that it's so damned frustrating to talk to you, McCabe."

The old man glared at him.

"Did you make the dive?" Sam asked. "For the stone."

"No. The weather started to turn and I didn't want to get caught out there in a storm, so we went back. And afterward . . ." *Afterward, Jamie had been killed.* He said simply, "I never had a chance to bring it up again."

"So now we just have to take your word for it that that's what happened," Darian sneered.

"Damnit, you don't have to take my word for anything! I've spent my whole life trying to forget that experiment, forget what happened to Jamie and the others." He looked down at his own gnarled body. "Trying to forget what happened to me. But the fact is, I can't forget. And when I read that legend in the book, it made me think that maybe I shouldn't forget. That's why I wish you'd hold off on St. James for a few days. I'd like to find out what else is down there."

Sam sucked in his breath. "You mean the museum will underwrite a dive?"

"No, I'm afraid there isn't enough evidence for that. You found the diamond because of a feeling you had. That's not enough for the museum board, but it's enough for me. I'd make the dive with you."

"Oh, then you won't have anything to worry about this time, Sam," Darian said. "Old Woodson here's going to look after you down in the Peaks."

"I don't suffer the bends underwater," Woodson said, ignoring the sarcasm. "And I have a submersible, a small two-man submarine. It's equipped for decompression."

Sam gave him a crooked smile. "How'd you get the museum to buy a submarine?"

"It doesn't belong to the museum. It's mine. I built it myself. I've been working on it for eight years."

"How many times you take it down?" Darian asked belligerently.

"I haven't. Not yet. But I trust my own work. I'm willing to go. If we find something, the board might grant a full exploration of the area."

Darian laughed. "You mean you're willing to risk Sam's neck on your homemade tub so you can find another diamond for yourself."

Woodson slumped into a chair and wiped his hands over his face. "All right," he said at last. "I give up. I was hoping you'd see things differently after I told you my ideas, but I admit they're pretty strange." He stood up and offered his hand. "It's your stone, Mr. McCabe," he said. "Good luck on your sale."

"'Bout time you got your nose out," Darian said, shaking the man's hand. "Now give me the diamond. I'm taking it with me."

Woodson's expression was shocked. "You can't do that."

"Watch me." Darian picked up the diamond and stuck it in his pocket.

"At least alert St. James that it's coming. He can send a guard for it, or something."

The old man walked out.

CHAPTER 11

He's nuts," Woodson said.

"I know." Sam picked up the book, which had lain on the table beside his chair. It opened to the page with the picture of the volcano.

"You can keep that," Woodson said. "I won't need it anymore."

"You might," Sam said. "Still want to make that dive?"

Woodson looked at him incredulously for a moment, then grinned. "Hell yes. I just have to make a few last adjustments to the sub. Can you hold McCabe back on the sale?"

Sam shook his head. "Like you said, it's his rock. But we won't need it to find whatever else is down there." His gaze was pulled back to the book. " 'No stone to guide them,' " he said, reading from the text. "That's a lot like what you were telling us Jamie said about the stone in the Peaks. Seeing with one eye . . ." He squeezed his eyes shut. "It's so hard to make sense of all this, but I know it's connected somewhere. *We're* connected. You, me, Jamie McCabe, even Darian. And others, too. It's almost as if we're . . . gathering for something. . . ."

His eyes met Woodson's. "Two days ago I met Dr. Bonner's granddaughter. She says I have the same kind of blood as the Rememberers."

Woodson raised his eyebrows.

"She thinks that people with that kind of blood are being murdered all over the country."

Woodson coughed, then choked. "McCabe told me about the guy with the gun, but—"

"It isn't just me whoever it is wants dead. It's everyone like me."

"Good God," Woodson said. "Just like before." He swallowed hard. "But why? I was never able to figure that out the last time."

"Maybe that's what we'll find out at the Peaks," Sam said.

Darian was not able to find them a job for the day, since the undersea seismic activity had worsened and the Coast Guard was broadcasting continuous advisories warning boats to stay in port until the waters had calmed.

Instead they stayed on board the *Styx*, cleaning the engine room while Darian railed against the weather.

"It's the Peaks," Sam said idly. "Something's happening. You can almost smell it in the air—"

"Shut up!" McCabe snapped. "I'm sick and tired of your foolishness. Now it's volcanoes. What's next week? Men from Mars? I'm selling the diamond, and that's that. Afterward, you can go your own way."

"What? I didn't say anything about the diamond."

"You don't expect me to stay on this old tub shoveling sludge out of canals for the rest of my life, do you?" the old man ranted on. "You got an education. It's about time you used it. Get a regular job. Inland. Or don't. Whatever you want. Hell, you won't never have to work again. Spend your days at the dogtrack, for all I care."

"I'm not taking any of that money, Darian."

"You damned well better. You won't have me to support you after next week."

"What happens then?"

"You're leaving, that's what." He polished the engine so energetically that he was panting with the effort.

"Now wait a minute, Darian—"

"I said you're leaving!"

Sam tossed his rag over his shoulder. "Why do you want me to go?" he asked quietly.

The old man was silent.

"Why?"

Darian took a couple of swipes at the engine with his rag, then stopped, his hand trembling. "Jamie knew he was going to die," he said in a whisper.

"What?"

"He woke up screaming one night. His ma and me, we tried waking him up, shook him and all, but he couldn't seem to come out of whatever kind of nightmare he was having. He just kept screaming. Finally he woke up and he looked at us with those old eyes he had, eyes like somebody who'd looked into the gates of hell. . . ." Darian closed his eyes for a moment, remembering. "He said, 'I've come at the wrong time. It's no good.' And I told him he was still dreaming, but he shook his head and told me, 'I won't be here much longer, Dad.' Just like that."

"What'd you say?"

Darian wiped his nose on the back of his hand. "Oh, I don't know. Told him to be quiet and go to sleep, most likely. But I knew he believed what he said. He was so still inside, like a rock. Maybe part of me believed him, too. But I didn't do anything. I watched the devil come out of the Peaks and take my boy, and there wasn't a damned thing I could do."

He held onto one of the pipes so tightly that his knuckles stood out white. "Did you know he died on the same day you were born?"

Sam shook his head.

"When you showed up, it was like seeing him alive again." He stood up slowly. "Like getting another chance."

He turned around, his face set in a scowl, but his eyes betrayed the terror he felt. "Now the sea's turned inside out again, just like it did then, and I know what it means. The devil's coming. But he's not going to take you. That diamond's going to get you away from this place." He slapped his rag against the engine housing. "You're leaving next week."

"Darian—"

"Don't make me beg you," the old man said.

THE VOYAGE

For many generations, as long as the divine nature lasted in them, they were obedient to the laws and well affectioned toward the gods, who were their kinsmen: For they possessed true and in every way great spirits, practicing gentleness and wisdom in the various chances of life, and in their intercourse with one another. They despised everything but virtue, not caring for their present state of life, and thinking lightly on the possession of gold and other property, which seemed only a burden to them. Neither were they intoxicated by luxury; nor did wealth deprive them of their self-control . . . But when this divine portion began to fade away in them and became diluted too often, and with too much of the mortal admixture, and the human nature got the upper hand, then they, being unable to bear their fortune, became unseemly, and to him who had an eye to see, they began to appear base, and had lost the fairest of their precious gifts. But to those who had no eye to see the true happiness, they still appeared glorious and blessed at the very time when they were filled with unrighteous avarice and power. Zeus, the god of gods, who rules with law, and is able to see into such things, perceiving that an honorable race was in a most wretched state, and wanting to inflict punishment on them, that they might be chastened and improved, collected all the gods into his most holy habitation, which, being placed in the center of the world, sees all things that partake of generation. And when he had called them together he spoke as follows . . .

The manuscript ends here.

Plato (c. 375 B.C.)

CHAPTER 1

AIDON ST. JAMES HAD SENT A SMALL DINGHY TO THE DOCK AT JUPITER INLET to bring McCabe and Sam out to his yacht for dinner. The yacht, the *Pinnacle*, was visible out in the east, lit up and twinkling like a cruise ship.

The dinghy itself, bobbing on the turbulent water, was manned by two sailors in formal blue uniforms. "We've come to take you to Mr. St. James, sir," one of them called to Darian as they pulled alongside the *Styx*.

"Oh, have you, now?" Darian asked with unaccustomed sweetness.

"Yes, sir."

"Well, you two just prance on out of here," Darian barked. "There's no way we're going out in this kind of water in *that*. We'll take our own craft. You two boys can go back to that floating whorehouse you work on."

The dinghy pulled away quickly. It was a half hour later before Darian and Sam pulled their salvage boat alongside the glittering yacht which barely moved in the rough sea. Two crewmen in brilliant white uniforms lowered a gangway ladder from the *Pinnacle*'s deck.

Aidon St. James, wearing a navy blue blazer over a silk T-shirt, was on deck to greet them. "Thanks for coming," he said warmly. "I hope you haven't changed your minds."

"He's got nothing to do with it," McCabe said. "And no, I haven't."

Dinner was served in an opulent salon of mahogany and brass, with a crystal chandelier hanging over the long table. Sam thought it looked like the last night aboard the *Titanic*. He half expected a string quartet to start playing.

A half dozen servants were on hand to serve the four people present—Darian, Sam, St. James, and his son, Liam, who stiffly shook hands with the guests when introduced and then sat staring into his soup plate.

There was a vague likeness between father and son around the set of the jaw; both were square and massive. But the rest of St. James's features were quick and mobile, expressing a vast range of emotions in the twinkling of an eye, while Liam's face was as sullen and placid as a herd cow's. His nose was a shapeless, claylike lump, looking as if it had been broken long ago and never set. His skin, too, had the shallow, bumpy cast of someone who ate the wrong food, and, judging from the boy's pudgy body, too much of it.

But it was Liam's eyes that held Sam's attention. They did not fit with the boy's clean hair and well-made clothes.

Sam had always thought it had something to do with being rich. Ever since he was a foundling, Sam had been fascinated by "outside" kids, children who didn't live at the orphanage. Kids who had parents.

Sam would look for them in the park, during the Little League games when St. Anne's would play suburban community teams. There they'd be, the outside kids, trying to look tough and ignoring their folks in the bleachers on the other side of the fence, as if the cheering and waving didn't mean squat to them.

But their eyes gave them away. They were naive kid eyes, trusting, expectant eyes filled with confidence and hope. They were the eyes of kids who were used to having people listen when they talked. One look at them, and Sam had known that their little lives had been jam-packed from morning till night with adults who laughed at their jokes and hung their drawings on the kitchen walls. Sweet-smelling mothers who kissed them too much. Jerky dads who tossed them into the air like bags of flour, while the kids laughed like idiots.

Their eyes had filled Sam with longing. The kids at St. Anne's didn't have eyes like that. St. Anne's kids looked at you sidelong, assessing you, trying to figure out why you were there, what you were going to do to them, how they could get something from you before you took everything from them. They had eyes that looked in the mirror and felt ashamed every morning.

Liam St. James had those kind of eyes. St. Anne's eyes.

Just go over the side. Get it over with.

Sam jolted upright.

"Mr. Smith?"

Sam coughed, trying to get his bearings. Who had spoken?

"I asked if the soup was all right. You don't seem to be eating." St. James was smiling at him.

"Oh, no, it's fine." Sam picked up his spoon and forced himself to swallow. "Delicious."

Darian pushed his bowl away. "Tastes like celery juice." A servant scurried to remove the bowl. "I didn't come here to eat, anyway."

"No, of course not," St. James said. "Whatever's your pleasure."

"My pleasure is five million dollars," Darian said. "It's worth more, and you know it. I want cash or a cashier's check. When it's deposited in my account at the West Palm bank, the diamond's yours."

"I haven't even seen the stone yet," St. James protested mildly.

"But your stooge, that gem guy Eames or whatever his name is, did. You know what it is and what it looks like," Darian said.

"Mr. Eames is just a colleague who keeps his eyes open for items that might interest me," St. James explained. "Do you have the stone with you?"

"You take me for a fool?"

"I'm sorry about that. I had wanted Liam to see it."

"Plenty of time for that after I get the money," Darian said.

St. James opened and closed his mouth, then threw his hands up in the air as if conceding a victory. "Your price is fine," he said with a gracious smile. "You'll have the money tomorrow."

"Good enough."

Darian started to shuffle in his chair as if getting ready to leave, but Sam interjected, "I suppose you'll have the stone cut into smaller pieces."

St. James shook his head. "I want it the way it is."

"What'll you do with it?"

"I'll own it. That's enough." St. James sat back in his chair and bridged his fingers before him.

"Does this stone have any history that you know of?" Sam asked.

Aidon smiled. "What do you mean?"

"Well, the man at the museum said that most big diamonds have some sort of story behind them . . . who owned it, where it came from, things like that."

"They call it 'provenance,'" St. James said.

Sam nodded. "But his researchers weren't able to find out anything at all about this stone."

"Maybe that's what makes it so unique."

"Then you've never heard of something called the Eye of Zeus?"

St. James looked at him with a sharp intake of breath. "Where did you hear that?"

"I read it in a book. There were some cave drawings in Spain . . . or France . . . someplace." Sam shrugged.

"I'm afraid there are all sorts of legends about 'lost' diamonds, most of which never existed. The Eye of Zeus is a particularly elaborate tale, undoubtedly created to boost stock in treasure hunting expeditions."

"All it told about in the book was a story about how some king used it to defeat his enemies."

"Ah, then you haven't been able to enjoy the full thrust of the fairy tale," St. James said. "In the first place, it wasn't just any king. It was Zeus himself, ostensibly in the days when Mount Olympus was a real place, before it became the stuff of Greek legend."

Darian crossed his arms and grunted, visibly annoyed that Sam had prolonged this visit by bringing up Woodson's ridiculous legend.

"I read about that stuff in school," Sam said. He glanced across the table at St. James's son. "You ever read about that, Liam?"

Before the startled boy could answer, St. James waved his arms expansively. "Of course he has. Zeus, king of the gods, who ruled the sky with the aid of a thunderbolt. His brothers, Poseidon and Hades, who had charge of the sea and the underworld. His colorful children. Let me see." He sighed. "There was Hephaestus, the blacksmith, and Athena, goddess of wisdom. Aphrodite, a great beauty and goddess of love. Ares, god of war. Apollo, god of music and medicine and all things strange and lovely. And his twin sister, Artemis, the huntress . . ."

He spread his hands. "I'm afraid I can't remember the others. The Greeks borrowed most of these deities from other cultures," he said. "But their fabrication was so elaborate that the whole bunch of them remained intact as a religion for several thousand years."

"But the Eye of Zeus . . ."

"Oh, that. I guess some enterprising fellow, history's answer to a best-selling novelist, apparently took the Greek mythology one step further and claimed that the gods really had existed, as real people, during some point in European prehistory."

"How long ago could that have been?" Sam asked. "If it was true?"

"Oh, who knows," St. James said. "Pundits of that sort of thing say it had to have taken place before the beginning of the Egyptian civilization, since the Egyptians would have written about any contemporaneous society. And that's the hole in the story, because before the Egyptians, there was very little in the way of civilization."

"Cavemen," Darian suggested.

"Exactly. So maybe what really happened was that in some Neanderthal settlement, the ruler of a particularly large tribe was named something like Zeus. And maybe he found a big crystal one day somewhere, and all the enemies he fought thought the crystal gave him power. And there you have it—the Eye of Zeus."

"I saw a picture of a cave drawing with a stone like this one," Sam said. "It was a cut stone."

"It was a stingray," Darian grumbled.

St. James laughed. "I'm acquainted with the drawing. Unfortunately, it's been fairly well established that the so-called gem pictured in it was a much later addition to the original art." He looked at Sam with a mixture of pity and contempt.

"Oh," Sam said lamely.

"Sorry to disappoint you. It is a lovely idea. I wish it were true, too." St. James looked at Darian again and said, "I'm very sorry you didn't bring it with you."

As Sam looked at the millionaire, suddenly the vision in front of his eyes began to shimmer like a mirage. The handsome millionaire's blue blazer appeared to transform into a costume of bilowing black robes. His head was covered by a gigantic mask of exotic bird feathers which extended over his shoulders like a cape. In his hands, replacing his soup spoon, was an elaborate bronze dagger.

Sam's jaw dropped open as he stared dumbly at his host.

The devil, that's what he is.

"What?" His head snapped toward Liam. "Did you say something?"

The boy sullenly shook his head.

Sam wiped his forehead with his napkin.

"Are you all right, Mr. Smith?" St. James asked.

"I'm fine," Sam managed to mutter, noting that the millionaire was again dressed in a blue blazer and innocently eating his soup.

Fine, except that he was going crazy again.

He was not only seeing hallucinations, but he was hearing voices again, too. Since his release from the hospital, he had managed to convince himself that the plaintive call of the woman he had heard during his session with Cory Althorpe had been an outgrowth of the unusual psychic connection between himself and the psychiatrist. Together, he had decided, the two of them had picked up the transmission from a radio somewhere. But what he had just heard was a completely different voice.

A boy's voice.

He looked again at Liam, who was rising quickly from his chair. "Excuse me," the boy said. His hands lingered for a moment on the arms of the chair as if to steady himself. His face was waxen and pale. A drop of sweat rolled onto his cheek. St. James gave the boy a glance of annoyance as Liam bolted from the room.

Sam got up and followed him. "I'll be right back," he said.

There was no sign of the boy when Sam stepped out on deck, but the air felt cool and welcome. He stopped at the rail, breathing in the salt breeze in deep gulps.

Do it do it do it coward

"No!" Sam shouted. Without reason or words, he suddenly understood everything. He ran to the yacht's stern, knowing, simply *knowing* what the boy was about to do.

He heard the splash just as he turned the corner around the massive cabin. Kicking off his shoes, Sam leaped over the rail into the water twenty feet below.

Liam fought him, but the boy was not strong. When he tried to breathe in water, Sam clapped his hand over the boy's nose and mouth and yanked him upward to the surface, where he got the crook of his arm around Liam's throat and forced him to breathe.

"Why'd you come?" he asked accusingly, hanging limp in Sam's arms.

"I heard you talking."

The boy's head snapped toward him sharply.

Just then the first mate blew a whistle. Within another minute, a dinghy lowered from the deck and two crewmen pulled Liam and Sam into the small boat.

Almost before their feet touched the *Pinnacle*'s deck, St. James ordered the first mate back to the dinghy. "Get the boy to West Palm Hospital right away."

"I'm all right," the boy protested. "I just fell overboard, that's all."

St. James ignored him. "I'll call ashore and have a car waiting for you," he told the mate.

"I don't think he needs to go to a hospital," Sam ventured.

"I think I may be better qualified than you to judge what my son needs," St. James snapped. "Call the emergency room from the car phone," he barked to the mate. "Tell them I want a thorough physical examination."

He banged his fist on the rail, then turned meekly to Sam. "Forgive me for losing my temper just now," he said. "You see, it isn't the first time Liam has tried this sort of dramatics."

"He said he fell."

"He didn't fall. He staged a mock suicide, knowing full well he would be rescued before any damage was done. Unfortunately, it's his way of protesting my decision not to buy him a sports car."

The first mate whispered something to him. St. James nodded and the mate climbed down the ladder to the waiting dinghy. Liam, wrapped in a blanket, was pushed toward him. The boy never looked at his father as he passed him.

"Don't have children," St. James admonished Sam with a smile.

"Aren't you going with him?"

"No need." St. James touched Sam's elbow. "Thank you for your help. Now please come inside. I'll get you some dry clothes, and we can get back to dinner."

Sam looked back at Liam, huddled in his blanket on the dinghy. "I'm not hungry," he said, vaulting over the railing onto the ladder.

The mate looked to St. James, who shrugged disdainfully. "Let him go along if he wants," he said.

Sam scrambled into the dinghy next to the boy. "Did you pull that stunt because your old man wouldn't get you a car?"

The boy looked at him with dead eyes. St. Anne's eyes. "That's what he told you, huh?" A mirthless puff of air escaped his lips.

"Why's he lying, Liam?"

"Who knows? Just one of his mind games. What's it to you, anyway?" He shivered.

. . . Coming something's coming something's . . .

"What's coming?" Sam asked gently.

"The knife! The sacrificial—"

He looked up at Sam, suddenly aware that the man was hearing his thoughts.

Sam rearranged the blanket around the boy's shoulders. "Relax, kid."

Liam edged away from him. "I don't need you," he said.

Sam sighed. "I wish you didn't," he said softly.

CHAPTER 2

WHEN CORY ALTHORPE STEPPED INTO THE OPEN DOOR OF CAROL ANN'S room, a young man in nursing scrubs stood alongside the sleeping girl, looking at the green-screened monitors arrayed on a shelf behind the bed.

At first she was startled, then suspicious. She stood silently, watching the man, but he just seemed intent on scanning the monitors. When he saw her in the doorway, the young man flashed her a big grin. He walked toward her so that his voice wouldn't disturb the sleeping patient.

"Hi, Dr. Althorpe. I'm Brian Hartman, from the emergency room. I just stopped up to see how the girl's doing."

"You know her?" Cory asked.

The burly young man shook his head. "Just saw her when she came in last night. I wouldn't have given a dime for her chances then. She was hanging on by a string." He shook his head as he glanced at the monitor. "And now all her signs are normal." He grinned. "You doctors must be practicing some kind of medicine the rest of us don't know anything about."

He was so hearty and open faced that Cory relaxed in his presence. "I wish we were," she said. "It's as big a mystery to us as anyone else."

"Well, God love her," Hartman said. "It's good for people who work in hospitals to see miracles once in a while. Reminds us that we're human."

He checked his watch. "I've got to get back downstairs. Anything you'd like me to do with the patient?"

"Thanks, Brian, but no. I'm just going to hang around for a while and keep an eye on her."

"Okey-doke. If you need anything, call. I'm on all night."

She stepped aside to let the young man leave the room. Knowing someone as kind—and big—as Hartman was nearby made her feel comfortable for the first time that day. She had been on edge since her meeting last night with that log, Darian McCabe, and had felt too hellish to sleep.

Today she had checked on Carol Ann between every round, hoping the girl would feel like talking, but she had been asleep each time.

Cory pulled a chair alongside Carol Ann's bed and sat down. She was off duty now and had nowhere better to spend the time. Besides, she could not dismiss the possibility that the girl was in danger. If she possessed anywhere near the psychic ability Cory thought she did, Carol Ann would be a prime target for whoever was killing people like her.

She shifted her chair so that she could watch the sleeping girl and the doorway at the same time. Somehow, she knew, it was all tied in to that Swiss blood lab and its director, Gerald Heaney.

Heaney had been her grandfather's assistant. Once she had recognized the name, she had been able to put a vaguely remembered face with it: Heaney, an intense young man who had seemed to worship Edward Bonner.

But why would Heaney be behind a series of murders?

Cory looked over at Carol Ann, who was sleeping so deeply that she appeared comatose. Suddenly frightened, she picked up the girl's chart and read it. The chart indicated that the patient had been given no sedatives since the previous night.

Cory replaced the chart and then carefully studied the monitors over the bed. Carol Ann's heartbeat was slow and strong. Her respiration was deep and normal. She was sound asleep. Nothing more.

She's safe here, Cory told herself. If she had voiced her fears to the police, they would have laughed in her face. Who would go to so much trouble to kill a homeless teenager just because she saw visions?

She had to stop imagining things. There was no reason to panic just because circumstances didn't make sense at the moment. Everything would undoubtedly look better after a good night's rest, which she would get as soon as she left the hospital in an hour or two.

Yes, that was what she needed, a long soak in the tub and an early bedtime. She would feel better in the morning.

Cory leaned back in the chair and closed her eyes. A moment later she was asleep.

It was just a routine knifing.

Three floors below the room where Cory dozed, Brian Hartman and a doctor in the hospital's emergency room worked together with practiced precision to sew up a gash in the forearm of a man who had been brought to the hospital by police officer who had stopped a fight in a bar.

It was the first stabbing of the night, about two hours earlier than usual, Hartman thought. It was going to be a zoo.

He had never been able to figure out a reason for the periods of heavy traffic in the emergency room. It was usually worse on Friday because Friday was payday. More people got drunk when they had money in their pockets and more drunks meant more knife fights. But there were some Fridays when everyone in the ER could fall asleep without seeing a "customer," as the staff called the hapless victims.

The weather was another variable: Hot weather made people short-tempered. Also local events—jai alai games, boxing matches, baseball, football, rock concerts—all sometimes contributed to a busy hospital night.

Hartman mused over these vicissitudes of his occupation while he bandaged the knife victim's stitched inner arm because it took his mind off the man's 86-proof breath.

"You a doctor?" the man asked.

"Nope. I'm a nurse."

"A male nurse." The man snorted up the mucus that was running from his nose.

"That's right."

"If you ain't a doctor, I don't want you touching me."

"The doctor stitched up your arm. I'm putting on the bandage."

"You hurt me, I'll sue."

"Okay," Hartman said cheerfully. "How about if I stick my foot up your ass?"

"What?"

"Want to shut up, pal?"

The customer shut up. Not many argued with Hartman. It was one of the reasons emergency room doctors were always happy to have him on their shift. A civilized emergency room was a happy place to work.

He had just finished when the ER doctor returned. "Sorry, I had a phone call," he said. He examined the bandage. "Fine. You can go," he told the patient.

"What do you mean I can go? Just like that?"

"Just like that," the doctor said.

"Hey, I got *knifed*, man."

"I know. And we sewed you up. Change the bandage every day. Wash the wound with liquid soap. See your doctor in a week to get the stitches removed."

"*I* thought *you* were my doctor."

"Wrong again, mister," Hartman said, picking up the doctor's impatience. "There's the door."

"Yeah, well, maybe I'm going to die," the patient said defiantly.

"Only if you hang around here," Hartman said.

The patient slid from the examining table and ambled toward the door. He looked back suspiciously as if the hospital staff had implanted a poison capsule under his skin.

"If I die . . ."

"I know. You'll sue." Hartman waved his fingers at the man. "Good-bye."

The doctor sighed. "Thanks," he said. "We've got to clear out the area a little. Someone's coming in."

"Big accident?"

"No. A teenager. But a special one. That was the administration office on the phone. Aidon St. James is sending his son in."

Hartman whistled. "Honcho. What happened to the kid?"

"Fell off the family yacht, it seems."

"Poor baby. Has the ambulance phoned in yet?"

"It won't." The doctor tried to suppress a smile. "He's coming by limo."

There was nothing wrong with Liam St. James, at least nothing that a good diet wouldn't cure. He had not taken on any water, and his heart and lungs and blood and bones all looked fine.

Just to be sure, Nurse Hartman noted with disgust, the ER doctor checked everything twice. Meanwhile, the three men who had brought the youth in—two of them in luxurious uniforms and the third in blue jeans—watched the proceedings from a corner of the examining room. The one in jeans looked familiar, Hartman thought.

Finally, the doctor stepped back from the boy on the examining table. "He's fine," he told the waiting men.

"He'll stay the night anyway," a voice said from the door. Hartman turned and saw Dr. Cohen, the hospital's medical director, who showed up at night only for hurricane, plane crash, or flood, standing there. *Liam St. James was one big-time adolescent,* Hartman thought.

The man in jeans stepped forward. "I think that should be up to the boy," Sam said.

Dr. Cohen shook his head. "His father wants him to spend the night. I've already arranged a room for him."

Sam nodded and walked over to Liam's side. "Sorry, kid," he said. "I tried to get you out of here."

"Whatever Daddy wants, Daddy gets," Liam said bitterly.

The man wore a black robe. Over his face was a gigantic mask of feathers than hung down over his shoulders. In his hands was a dark knife that gleamed dully.

He raised the knife above his head with both hands and then plunged it down, again and again with repulsive enthusiasm.

Behind him stood another. He was younger, smaller, hidden in the shadows, but he seemed to be waiting his turn. The man in the black robe offered the knife to him. And as he stepped forward . . .

Carol Ann awoke with a gasp.

"What is it?" Cory Althorpe sat upright at once.

The girl slumped back onto her pillow. "Just a bad dream."

"Want to tell me about it?"

She shrugged. "Somebody was sacrificing people with knives. Cutting their—" she swallowed with distaste "—their hearts out."

Cory came over to the bed and stroked the girl's hair. "I don't think that's a particularly unusual dream for someone with a chest wound," she said gently. "How is it, by the way?" She pulled aside the opening of Carol Ann's hospital gown to look at the bandage.

"Looks good. No seepage."

"It's healed," the girl said.

"I don't think so," Cory said with a smile. "It takes a little longer than . . ."

With a swift movement, Carol Ann removed the bandage.

Not a trace of the bullet wound remained. The gaping rip in her flesh, incurred only two days earlier, was fully healed over, covered with fresh, glowing pink baby skin.

With a growing sense of shock and wonder, Cory touched the spot where the wound had been.

"I told you, I heal fast."

Cory felt herself sweating. "This is more than fast," she whispered. "This is miraculous."

"It takes a lot out of me," the girl admitted shyly.

Cory sat back in the visitor's chair. "Carol Ann, last night you told me about a vision you had when you were injured. A volcano. A man talking. Do you remember?"

"Some of it."

"You said something about a stranger. That a stranger would bring people together . . ."

Carol Ann's head swiveled toward the door. "You're not safe with me," she said suddenly.

Cory's eyes locked with the girl's, and for a moment she felt the truth in Carol Ann's words. She actually rose from her chair, prepared to bolt with this hospital patient before reason calmed her down.

What am I thinking of? she thought, feeling ashamed at her moment of panic. Psychic or not, the girl had suffered deep physical and mental trauma. Not to mention the unearthly concentration it must have required to heal a gunshot wound, if that was what had happened.

"Of course I'm safe here. We both are," she said. "Why wouldn't we be?"

"Something's coming." Carol Ann shook her head. "I don't know what it is, but it's bad."

Cory stroked the girl's hair. "I'll order some medication for you so you can sleep," she said. "I'd like someone else to look at that wound anyway." She reached for the buzzer to summon the nurse's station.

"No!" Carol Ann clasped Cory's hand. "No, I don't want anyone else in here. And I can sleep. Really."

"Are you sure?"

Carol Ann nodded. "I was just feeling paranoid. Like the dream I had. It's probably from getting shot. Bad vibes."

"Mmm," Cory agreed. "All right. I'll let you sleep. But I'll stay here for a while, just in case."

The girl looked somberly at her. "You want to protect me, don't you?"

Cory smiled. "From what?"

"That's a psychiatrist's answer," Carol Ann said, and closed her eyes. *And that's what's keeping you on the outside*, she added to herself.

Like herself, Dr. Althorpe had a gift. Carol Ann had known that the moment she'd touched the woman's shoulder. There was a power coursing through Cory Althorpe that was almost as great as her own, but it was contained, negated, reasoned away. Educated people often distrusted the gift. That was why so few doctors were real healers.

It was why Cory Althorpe couldn't help her now.

CHAPTER 3

THE TOURISTS HAD GONE HOME AND NONE BUT A HALF DOZEN REGULARS were left in Eddie's bar and grill. Normally they would have included Darian in their raucous conversations, but his position at the far end of the bar and the expression on his face told everyone who knew him that he wanted to be left alone.

After Sam had left St. James's yacht with the pimple-faced boy, Darian had finished his business with the millionaire.

"Eight o'clock at the bank," St. James had suggested as the point of sale. "The bank president will be there. So will my people."

"Just make sure they bring the money," Darian said. He had clambered down the ladder to the waiting *Styx*, ran it back to their dock, then walked over to Eddie's to wait for Sam's return.

But now it was nearing closing time, and there was still no sign of Sam.

Well, why not? he reasoned after six hours' worth of straight rye. Sam was young; he might have picked up a woman. He could take care of himself. And after tomorrow, when Darian had put a couple of million green ones in his bank account, he would be able to take care of himself a lot better.

Away from here, he thought.

When Eddie announced last call for drinks, Darian waved his hand at his empty glass, stood up, and left.

"Don't want to cross him, not in the mood he's in," old Figg said to Eddie.

"Yeah, something's on his mind for sure."

Despite the long night of drinking, Darian was alert as he walked briskly back toward the *Styx*. Alert enough to notice that there was a man lounging in a doorway, across from the dock, and another following casually on Darian's trail.

St. James's men, he thought, though he took no umbrage at their presence. If he had been St. James and about to spend five million dollars on a diamond, he'd put some guards near the seller too, if only to make sure the guy didn't get drunk and set himself afire.

When he hopped down onto the boat's deck, he turned back to the street and announced loudly, "I'm going to bed now, friends. See you in the morning."

The two men, who indeed were employed by Aidon St. James, did not hear him. They were simultaneously turning toward a battered pickup truck a hundred yards or so down the street.

The truck appeared to be racing full throttle crosswise over the pavement toward the curb and the pier beyond it.

The driver of the ancient pickup, they saw, was a woman. A fat old woman wearing a moth-eaten sweater and a kerchief. She held her hands over her ears.

"Stop it, stop it, stop!" she screamed.

For seventy-two hours she had driven through a tunnel of voices. First it was Gram's, familiar and comforting, goading her onward. Then came the voices of the Rememberers, the Nowars, and Jamie and the colored college boy named Harrison, voices repeating conversations from the past, ossified into memory.

A volcano . . .

A volcano, yes, I saw it, too. . . .

Jamie's crying.

Why?

Don't know. It scares me, though. He knows things. . . .

She drove faster. She tried to eat once but could not keep the food down. She had slept twice, for less than an hour each time, inside the truck.

But the voices never stopped, not even while she slept.

Somewhere in South Carolina, they grew louder. By the time she reached the Georgia state line, they were screaming, shrieking the final sounds of their lives over and over again.

"Gram, can't you help me?" she had pleaded. Her vision was obscured by the torrent of tears running down her face, but she never slowed. She knew that the voices would not allow her to rest until she found the place she was looking for.

"But where is it?" she had cried out as she turned blindly onto yet another highway. "I don't know what the baby looks like now! I don't know where he lives! I been driving south for three days but for all I know he might be in Alaska!"

Her voice was hoarse and raspy; her mouth tasted of bile. "Gram, oh, Gram, please make them stop."

But the voices only grew louder, ringing in her ears until she thought she would drive the pickup over that pier and into the ocean.

Yes, I'll do that, she decided. *Just drive right into the water.* She shook the sweat off her face, then gunned the engine and closed her eyes.

At the edge of the pier, the truck's motor went dead.

"Stop it, stop it, stop!" Reba screamed. Her voice reverberated through the pickup's passenger compartment, then was still.

Hesitantly she let her hands fall. There was nothing but silence.

Bo would have said it was dirt in the gas line that made the truck stop dead the way it did.

Reba knew better.

She looked around, blinking owlishly. Two men carrying guns approached her. One had a flashlight. He directed its beam onto her face.

"Land sakes," she said, squinting against the light. "Who are you, the police?"

"What are you doing here, ma'am?" one of them asked, politely but firmly.

"Why, I don't rightly know," she answered honestly. "Tell the truth, I don't even know where I am at the present moment."

The men looked at each other. The flashlight went out. "This is Jupiter Inlet," one of them said as they turned away.

"Shitfaced," he muttered to his companion.

"I am not shitfaced," Reba objected, but she was too tired to press the matter. She rolled up the window and leaned her head against it, letting the silence wash over her like clean water.

"Jupiter Inlet," she whispered. "This is the place, Gram, ain't it?"

Yes, child. The eye of the storm.

"I don't see no storm."

You sleep now, Reba.

The old woman smiled. The voices were gone. The pier was bathed in moonlight.

Reba Dobbs had arrived.

Something was coming.

Harry Woodson's eyes snapped open and he lay in the dark, feeling his heart pounding in his chest.

He couldn't remember the dream, except for that one central tenet: Something was coming.

Gradually his breathing slowed and his heart rate dropped back to normal. Only then did he let himself be conscious of the rest of his body. Everything hurt just the way it usually did, except that there was no pain in his hands or fingers.

With a sigh, Woodson rolled onto his side and then carefully, laboriously, lowered his feet to the floor.

Twenty years ago, when he had been known as Harrison Wood, Junior, he had been over six feet tall. But the bends he had suffered in escaping from his undersea attackers had reduced his stature to a bare five feet, eight inches. His limbs, too, had never been the same. The pain in his joints was always with him, but sometimes at night he would wake up and find that his fingers did not hurt. On those occasions, he would get up, as he did now, and go outside to work on his small submersible craft.

It was nearly finished except for a few minor connections and some soldering and bolting on the control panel, and it was only during these brief respites from pain that he could manage to do that fine detail work. The job might have been completed long before if he had hired someone to do it for him, but Woodson trusted no one but himself. The sea, as

God and he knew, was dangerous enough without venturing into it with equipment that was anything but perfect. He did his own work.

Woodson's house was on the inland waterway, about three-quarters of a mile from the ocean. He had started building the small submarine in his yard, but when it drew too much attention from neighborhood youths, he had built a shed over the adjacent dock and dragged the sixteen-foot craft inside. There he could work on it day or night, safe from prying eyes.

As he stepped out into the yard, under the bright moonlit sky, he realized how tired he was. He would rather be back in bed. But his fingers did not hurt. Deft as a surgeon's, they fairly flew over the tiny components, pushing him forward.

Something was coming. Woodson had no idea what that something was, but its approach was certain and, proof or not, he no longer questioned it.

He worked through the night. He was going to need the submersible soon.

Very soon.

Buttoning his pajamas, Liam St. James walked out of the bathroom toward his bed. Sam was perched sideways on to the window sill of the hospital room, looking out at the city below.

"Have they gone?" the boy asked.

"Your father's men?" Sam shook his head. "Just downstairs for coffee."

"I didn't think they'd trust me alone."

"Can you blame them?"

"Look, I didn't jump. I fell, all right? I just fell overboard."

"Save your breath, kid."

"Save yours. I told you—"

"You told me you were going to jump. You called yourself a coward and then you jumped. So you must have been right."

Liam stared furiously at him for a moment, then turned away. "I never said it out loud," he said.

"I know."

"So? What's your explanation for that?" Liam tried to form his lips into his father's sneer, but his eyes were intent on Sam. Intent and almost pleading.

He really wants an answer, Sam thought. *And I don't have one to give him.*

He shrugged. "Maybe we're psychic."

"We?" Liam arched an eyebrow.

"Yeah, we. You saw the knife, too. What was that about, anyway?"

"I didn't see any knife!" Liam shouted. "And I'm not a psychic, understand? You say that again, and I'll—"

"Okay, okay," Sam said. "I won't say it. But that doesn't mean it isn't true."

"It *isn't* true!" Liam's hands balled into fists.

"Look, I didn't want to face it either," Sam said. "About myself. I didn't even want to believe it existed. But it does. And some of us have it stronger than others. That's all I know." When the boy did not respond, he went over to him and clapped him on the shoulder. "Think of it as being special."

"Oh, I'm special, all right," Liam said. "You don't know how special."

"What's that mean?"

Liam sniffed and ran his hand over his nose. "Nothing. It didn't mean anything."

Sam sat on the bed next to him. "I want to ask you something, Liam. Do you ever have strange dreams?"

"Dreams? I guess so. Like what?"

"Like an exploding volcano. You ever dream about that?"

"No," the boy said. Too quickly, Sam thought.

"How about the knife? Did you see someone in a black robe? And a—"

"Get off my back, okay?" Liam shouted. "I'm sick of this psychic bullshit. Just leave me alone."

He lay back heavily and covered his eyes with his hands as if to shut out the overhead light. Sam waited for the boy to look at him again, but Liam seemed content to lie there, shielding himself from any contact with Sam or the rest of the world.

Sam sighed. *If he knows anything, I'm never going to learn what it is,* he thought.

"Okay," he said at last. "I'm going."

As he walked past the end of the bed, he accidentally knocked the nurse's chart to the floor. He picked it up and replaced it.

"Your two keepers will be back in a . . . ."

A line on the chart seemed to leap out at him. The line read PHYSICIAN: Beside the colon was a name.

Gerald Heaney.

"Gerald Heaney is your doctor," Sam said slowly.

"So? He's been our family doctor for years," Liam answered, peering out from behind his hands.

Sam felt a wash of relief. "My mistake. I was thinking of a Heaney from Switzerland."

"Yeah, that's him. He runs a blood lab in Geneva. I go to school there." Liam propped up on his elbows.

"Has he ever talked about any . . . experiments?"

"What, like some mad scientist?" Liam grinned.

Sam forced himself to smile back. "He ever take blood from you?"

"No. You know, you don't have to go."

"Yes, I do," Sam said. "Take care of yourself, kid."

The events swirled in Sam's mind. Dr. Heaney ran a lab that identified psychics through their blood. Psychics who ended up murdered. Another doctor connected with him had tried to kill Sam. And now Heaney turned out to be Aidon St. James's family physician.

At least the boy is all right, he assured himself. Whatever demons might trouble young Liam, Dr. Heaney was not one of them.

He quickened his steps, feeling the oppressive atmosphere of the hospital, weighing on him like an oppressive cloak.

It's all connected. The deaths, the diamond, the Peaks. All of it.

Sam needed to breathe. He abandoned his search for the elevator and ran down the stairwell toward the street.

* * *

Close. It's too close.

Carol Ann lay shuddering beneath the sheet on her hospital bed, waiting for Dr. Althorpe to fall asleep.

The psychiatrist wanted to understand, but she couldn't. Her mind was still imprisoning her with what it called reason, which was no more than a steadfast refusal to accept truths that could not be proven in a laboratory. Even after seeing Carol Ann's healed wound, she would not believe. Even though she felt it herself, she would not admit that danger was coming, a danger that would engulf everyone who had the gift.

Silently, with painful slowness, Carol Ann removed the sheet and slipped from the bed. She glanced in the empty closet, remembering that her blood-soaked clothes had been too damaged to keep. She would have to find others.

At the doorway, she looked back at Cory.

The farther away from her I get, the safer she'll be.

For now. In the end, she knew, none of them would be safe.

She peeked into the hall. It was empty. She walked quickly down the gleaming tiles, trying to plan an escape.

Find clothes and walk out, that's all. No one would notice her; people rarely did. She was about to turn into another corridor when an eerie wailing music sounded from somewhere deep inside her mind.

It sent a feeling like an electric shock coursing down her spine.

It's here. Close, real closerealclose

Swallowing to keep her breath silent, she darted into the nearest room.

Liam St. James lay in bed, looking up at her.

"I need your clothes," she whispered desperately as she closed the door behind her.

He grinned. "Making a break for it?"

"Please."

She walked closer toward him. She was a wraith of a girl, he saw, small boned and delicate as a fawn, with huge dark eyes and a cascade of flaxen hair that fell down her back like water with the sun on it.

The sun. That was it. She brought *light* with her. Just seeing her made him feel as if he had just walked out of a shadow into a pool of bright, warm light.

"Help yourself," he said quietly. "Sorry, they might be damp."

"That's okay." Quickly she put on his trousers, which fit her like a tent, and his white dress shirt.

Liam sat up. "Can I come with you?" he asked suddenly.

"With me?" She hesitated. "You'd better not," she said finally. "It wouldn't be safe."

He had known he would be rejected. It had been stupid to ask. "What'd you do, lift some Demerol?" he asked scornfully.

"No." She came over to him and touched his hand. "Thank you."

Liam felt his breath catch. Her touch was like liquid sunshine, filling him, soothing all the wounds that no one had ever seen. He felt his eyes welling with tears.

"You'll be all right," she said. Gently she let go of his hand and backed away into the shadows, toward the door. "Be brave."

Then she was gone, and the light with her.

Be brave? He laughed out loud. *Boy, does she have the wrong guy.*

He flopped back onto the bed, weeping silently into his pillow.

Liam loved his father. He tried to remember that: *I love my father.*

It was his father who raised him alone after his mother killed herself. Though he was one of the most important men of the twentieth century, Aidon St. James had spent every summer with Liam since he was seven years old. And not just nominally, allowing the boy merely to sleep in the same dwelling as he did, but purposefully, focusing his full attention on Liam, leaving his business and his fortune in the hands of others for three months out of every year so that they could spend the time together.

Granted, their activities were not the usual things fathers and sons shared—there was no basketball or bowling or forays to the miniature golf course. There were no video games or friends. No outings. No nights at the movies. No music lessons, no TV, no conversations.

There were lessons.

Strange lessons.

First, there was the Language. It had no name, other than the Language. So far as Liam knew, no one spoke it except his father. He had never seen a book written in the Language, although he knew its alphabet and had written and read reams of exercises.

No mention was ever made of it, nor of any of the other lessons his father taught him. Liam had learned the folly of that early on. Once, when he was eight years old, he had spoken at the dinner table in the Language. It was a joke about the boarding school he attended. He had meant for it to be something the two of them could share privately despite the presence of the serving staff.

His father had not appreciated the joke. He responded to Liam with a cold stare, which effectively silenced the boy for the remainder of the meal. Then, to make sure the silence stuck, St. James came into Liam's room at night, stuffed a silk scarf into his mouth, and beat him.

"The Language is a secret," he said while his fists pummelled into Liam's back. "The lessons are secret."

Liam screamed noiselessly into the gag until he lost consciousness.

The next day his father came to see him in his bedroom. "I've told the staff that you're to remain here for a few days, as punishment for something or other. You'll be well enough to walk by then."

Liam only stared at him.

"I didn't touch your face," St. James said.

Liam blinked.

"Well, don't you think you should thank me?"

Liam swallowed.

His father's face was expressionless. After a moment, he reached into his pocket and pulled out the silk scarf.

"Thank you," the boy said.

"That's better. Shall we proceed with our lessons?"

Oh, Daddy.

There were plenty of lessons. There was "history," which was a collection of stories he had never found in any books in the school library, "geography," in which he studied from maps of the world utterly unlike any he had ever seen, and, the worst of them all, the Practice.

His first lesson in the Practice occurred when he was ten.

He had been required to kill a rabbit.

He had slit its throat, opened its chest, and pulled out its tiny heart. Then he had thrown up.

There was another beating for that. For his cowardice.

After the rabbit, there was a cat, a fox, a lamb, a dog, all with the correct ritual, all with a litany chanted in the Language. He tried to perform them numbly, forcing himself not to gag on the stench of fresh blood.

Daddy no, please I can't I can't

His father never touched his face during the beatings.

Liam consoled himself with food. It was medicine for him.

Put something in your mouth to make the pain go away.

But they never stopped. Not the beatings. Not the lessons. Not the Practice.

When Liam passed into his early teens, it began to occur to him that his father might be insane. After a particularly brutal session, during which Liam had decided that he no longer cared whether he lived or died, he had talked back.

"Go ahead and kill me!" he screamed. "It doesn't change the fact that nothing in these stupid lessons exists for anyone except us."

He had prepared for the blow, eyes squeezed shut, breath held, but it never came. Instead, his father laughed.

Laughed!

"I wondered when you would realize that," St. James said. "You're such a dull child, I was beginning to despair that you'd ever think about anything."

Liam could only gape at him, open-mouthed.

"The fact is, the information only *needs* to exist for us. For you, particularly, when you take my place."

"Your place as . . . as what?"

"I can't tell you that now. But it is a position that you will be uniquely suited for when the time comes. A position of great honor."

Honor.

So I mean something to him, after all.

"Will I . . . will I be able to stop . . . the Practice?" His mouth felt dry. "I don't like killing animals, Father."

St. James looked at him blankly for a moment, then sighed. "Do you love me, son?"

"Yes."

"And I love you."

From his pocket he took a silk scarf.

CHAPTER 4

WHERE IS THIS PATIENT?"

Cory awoke to see a man in a long doctor's gown standing by her side, staring at her angrily.

She looked quickly around the room. Carol Ann's bed was empty. "She's—I don't. . . ."

"Who are you?" he snapped.

Her own anger brought her fully awake. "I think I should be asking you that question," she shot back.

The man looked down at his lab coat and brushed at the place where his name tag should have been. "Dr. Heaney," he said brusquely. "This is my patient, and I'd like to know where she is."

"Gerald Heaney?"

He inhaled impatiently.

I didn't think he'd look so old, Cory thought. "What are you doing in Florida?"

"Madam, are we acquainted?" His voice conveyed a bone-numbing boredom with the conversation.

"In a way. I'm Cory Althorpe, with the psychiatric unit. We spoke on the phone. I'm Edward Bonner's granddaughter."

"Yes. We were associates once," he said flatly. "Why are you here?"

She wanted to ask him why he had erased the computer files she was reading during their conversation, but knew instinctively that this was not the time for a confrontation. "I was visiting the patient on my off shift," she said, "and I suppose I dozed off. But she wouldn't have gone far. Are you her physician, Dr. Heaney?"

"I've succeeded Dr. Krantz as head of serology," he said.

She nodded. "And you've seen Carol Ann's blood."

"Whose? Oh." He looked toward the empty bed.

"She has a name, Doctor, this patient of yours."

Heaney turned without another word and left the room.

* * *

She knows enough to get me killed.

Heaney walked through the hospital corridors, hearing his shoes clack smartly against the floor.

Damn the Consortium. They should have told him when Krantz died. This could have been contained. Now she knew. She and how many others? How many links were there in the chain that would wind around his neck and choke off his life?

He walked faster, in a fury.

Steady, steady.

Althorpe had to be eliminated. Soon. She, the diver with the ICDL blood whom she had released, and this new girl. Three links in the chain had to be cut before he could breathe again.

But first the girl. She would be the easiest.

Find the girl.

The same thought was on Cory's mind.

Her casual dismissal of Carol Ann's disappearance had been pure theater. The girl had been terrified. *You're not safe with me*, she had said.

Why hadn't Cory listened?

It did not matter if the threat Carol Ann feared was real or imagined. The fact was, she feared it enough to bolt from the hospital. Outside the hospital, whoever shot her once might get a chance to shoot her again.

She had bolted. Of that Cory was certain. There was no way the girl could have been kidnaped from under her nose without her awakening. She had left of her own will.

But where could she have gone? As Cory walked across the parking lot to her small Mercedes, she tried to think of where the girl might be. If she could only talk with Carol Ann, she thought, find out why she was so frightened . . .

She healed a gunshot wound . . .

So frightened . . . and why was Gerald Heaney at the hospital?

She slid behind the wheel and took a deep breath.

"No," she whispered aloud. "I will not be pulled into this hysteria."

Just because Carol Ann was psychic did not mean that she had correctly assessed the magnitude of the danger posed to everyone with ICDL blood. Carol Ann was in danger, possibly, but more because of her weakened condition than anything else.

What about the others? The others, who are all dead?

"God, let me find her," she said. "Before anyone else does."

She searched the city for three hours, stopping at every convenience store and bar within a twelve-block radius of the hospital, but none of the people she talked to had seen anyone answering Carol Ann's description. Finally, frantic with worry and fatigue, Cory had driven aimlessly around the city, hoping for a glimpse of blonde hair. It was nearly midnight when she saw a familiar figure walking along the deserted sidewalk.

"Sam," she called.

He stopped and peered inside. "Working late tonight?" he asked.

"In a way. One of my patients ran away from the hospital. She has the same kind of blood as you, and I'm afraid . . . " She rested her arms on the steering wheel and lay her head on them. When she said nothing more, Sam realized she was crying.

"How long has it been since you slept?" he asked.

"I'm all right," Cory stammered, trying to dry her eyes while her whole body continued to sob. "It's just . . . just . . . "

He opened the car door and slid inside. "Move over," he said. "I'm going to drive you home."

"That's not necessary. . . ." she began, then smiled. "Thanks, Sam. I'd appreciate the company." She gave him her address, then sat back in the passenger seat. "Guess who just showed up as head of serology," she said, rubbing her eyes.

"Gerald Heaney," Sam said grimly.

Cory's head swiveled toward him. "You knew that?"

"I found out by accident. He's the family doctor of another psychic kid."

"Oh, no."

He pulled into the driveway of Cory's rambling beach house. "Mind if I make a phone call?" Sam asked.

"Go ahead. I'll make us some coffee. I'm too tired to sleep, anyway."

As she busied herself, relieved to have something to do with her hands, Sam dialed the phone number of the *Styx*, not expecting much. There was a permanent telephone hookup on the dock to which the salvage boat was tied, but most nights Darian forgot to connect the phone.

To his surprise, Darian had remembered. He answered, thick-voiced and sleepy, on the first ring.

"What the hell do you want?"

"I want to know how you left it with St. James."

"You rousted me out of bed for that?"

"I don't trust him, Darian."

"Hell, I don't either, but he's willing to pay me five million dollars for a rock, so I guess I'm willing to put up with him till tomorrow."

"Is that when you make the exchange?"

"At the bank. Until then, at least, I'm safe. He's got two law-and-order types watching the boat. Nobody's going to mess with me tonight."

"What about tomorrow?"

"I got a thirty-eight under my bunk that's going to worry about tomorrow for me."

Sam smiled. "I guess you can take care of yourself, at that."

"Damn right. How's the kid?"

"Liam? He's fine. At least on the outside."

"Whatever that means, and I don't care to have it explained. Now leave me be." He hung up.

Cory and Sam carried their coffee out onto the beach where they sat on the sand halfway to the water's edge. Cory kept her eyes scanning the shore, hoping against all reason that Carol Ann would walk by.

"Memory Island's out there," Sam said quietly, inclining his head toward the dark water. "Due east, almost straight ahead."

Cory lowered her cup. "It's all tied up with that, isn't it?"

"Somehow, yes." He took a sip of his coffee. "It can't be a coincidence that Heaney would come to that particular hospital."

"You're right. I think he's looking for Carol Ann."

Sam faced her. "To kill her?"

She nodded. "I've told myself that he doesn't have anything to do with the man who shot Carol Ann—he certainly doesn't fit the description—but something goes off inside me when I bring his face, or even his name, to mind." They were quiet for a moment and then she asked, "Do you get those, Sam? Flashes of intuition, just *knowing* something, even if you don't have a real reason for knowing it?"

He smiled sadly. "Story of my life," he said.

"Something's waiting for us. All of us. And it's out there." She drank her coffee. "Straight ahead, due east."

Carol Ann Frye hopped a small wire fence along the sandy beach.

It felt better out here, away from the buildings in town and the night people. Every other face she saw seemed to carry a hint of menace, a look of "them."

Who "they" were, she did not know. There was the man who had shot her and Nadine Gorman without reason or explanation, but he was not who she feared.

The truth of it was, it was not even death that she feared. She had seen people die before, homeless old folks who had been beyond her help, sick people at a mission in Philadelphia where she had worked after she'd first run away from the crack house she had called home. Death was gentle, a quiet event that brought peace and a strange sort of hope for those who were ready for it.

She had seen angels, bright beings filled with light, enfold the used-up bodies of the sick and release their immortal spirits.

No, it was not death she feared.

It was something worse.

Carol Ann sat down behind a cluster of concrete pilings which anchored a long stone breakwater. She took off the baseball cap she had found in an alley and ran her fingers through her hair.

She needed rest. The effort to heal the wound in her chest had been monumental. She would never have tried such a feat normally, but she had known that time was short and that she would be needed soon. So she had forced her body to accelerate its processes. Her fingernails had grown long overnight.

Idly, she picked a stone out of the sand. It was ordinary, small and gray, but held the power of the universe in it. All natural objects, she knew, exuded energy, as much as people or animals, but their life force moved more slowly. Rocks possessed the slowest-moving energy of all, so it was possible for people—at least for Carol Ann—to absorb it completely.

She took a deep breath as she felt the stone's sure, perfect balance seep into her body. There had been nothing in the hospital room to help her replace the massive amounts of energy she had been expending on her healing; now she could fill up again. The sea mist washed over her like balm. The sand beneath her conveyed the throbbing life of the Earth. The stone gave her its heart.

It's coming

It's coming

Carol Ann wasn't so afraid anymore.

The bottle of champagne was empty.

Nathan Eames nuzzled the redhead's neck once more before getting out of bed. Sucking in his belly, he picked up the empty bottle by its neck and padded toward the kitchen.

"Don't fall asleep while I'm gone," he teased.

The redhead arched her back so that he could see her glorious breasts in the shaft of moonlight that streaked over them.

"Mmmm. I'll be right back," he said. "And I do mean *right* back."

He felt like singing as he glided barefoot over the marble flooring of the glass and chrome mansion. In the distance, the lights of the La Jolla docks sparkled like party lights. Nathan Eames, boy nerd, had become a man.

Killing the girl had not been as difficult as he had thought, certainly not as difficult as killing George Westerman. And the old bag had been a chip shot. They had been targets, nothing more.

Targets . . . and sacrifices.

Because wasn't that what life was all about, sacrificing something to get something else? All Nathan had done was to make a sacrifice to the Consortium, and in return, the Consortium had brought him the life he had always wanted. Westerman for the pigeon's blood ruby. Madame Zola and the wan-faced girl for . . .

For what? What was next? A palace in Morocco? A villa in Tangier, complete with a harem of exotic mistresses vying for the opportunity to satisfy his every desire?

Hey, why not, he thought. The sky was the limit in this game, and God knew he deserved nothing less than the sky.

Sacrifice, that was what it was. He had sacrificed plenty.

He slapped on the kitchen light, and suddenly the image of a harem in Tangier faded and died.

There was a man sitting at the breakfast nook. He was wearing a raincoat, and the gun in his hand was trained on Nathan's head.

"Don't run, Mr. Eames. I'm a good shot," he said.

Nathan put down the champagne bottle. All he could think of was that he was stark naked.

"Take anything you want," he began. "I'll give you the combination to the safe. Just . . ."

"This isn't a robbery."

The man was in his fifties, with the puffy face and red nose of a chronic alcoholic. His hands didn't shake, though; he seemed to know exactly what to do with the gun.

"You're with the Consortium," Nathan said quietly.

"That's right."

"But why . . . I did . . . what I was supposed . . ."

"The girl survived."

Nathan felt his stomach cramp.

"The news probably didn't reach you here. It's all over the papers in Florida. Your description, too. It's just a matter of time before the cops trace you."

"Oh, God," Nathan moaned. "Can you . . . I mean, I'll finish the job, guaranteed, I'll go back tomorrow, tonight, but can you . . . can they . . ."

"We'll get you away."

Nathan shuddered with relief. "Thank God. I mean, thank you. I really appreciate—"

A soft pop sounded from the direction of the bedroom. Nathan jumped. "What was that?"

"Your lady friend. No, don't do that," he said when Nathan turned involuntarily toward the doorway.

"You killed her?"

"I don't think she felt anything. Get a glass of water."

"What? Hey, what's going on?"

The man did not answer. Nathan got the water. The man took a small paper envelope from his pocket, fumbled it open with one hand, and poured its contents into the glass. It was a sand-colored powder. "Drink it," he said. "It'll make it easier for you."

"But what are you going to do? I'll come with you, all right? No problem. I'm not pissed about the girl in the bedroom, if that's what you're thinking, although it might be a good idea to get rid of the body. . . ."

"Drink it and shut up."

Nathan picked up the glass and stared at it. "You're going to kill me, aren't you," he said in a small voice. He sighed. "I was at the top of the world."

It hadn't been a very long run, he thought.

He should have known. He had found the stone. His usefulness was over.

Nathan shook his head and grinned. He raised the glass in salute. "To the Consortium," he said.

The night was getting cold. Cory moved closer to Sam on the beach.

"Want to go in?" she asked. "You . . . you can spend the night if you want."

He looked at her. He wanted to, wanted to hold her and make love to her and love himself in her body. He wanted to forget that the singer in the sea had ever called to him.

But the time for forgetting was long past. They were caught up in something now that was going to turn everything inside out, the way a seaquake shook up the ocean floor, burying the present and exchanging it with the past.

Memory Island, Harry Woodson, Jamie McCabe, the diamond. All parts of the past come back for another turn.

"I can't," he said. "I've got to . . . to wait."

For Her.

Because She was behind it all, wasn't She? She, a phantom in his mind who had filled him with Her presence all his life, She who had made it impossible for Sam ever to love a living woman, She stood somehow in the vortex of the storm swirling around him. And She would never let him go.

"Okay," Cory said, visibly embarrassed. She stood and dusted the sand off her clothes. "I'd better get some sleep."

She went inside, bathed, dressed for bed, and went to sleep. Later, she awoke. The night table clock read 4 A.M. She went to the window and looked out onto the beach.

Sam was still there, his arms folded around his knees, gazing out toward the ocean. Due east.

CHAPTER 5

IT WAS FULL SUN WHEN REBA AWOKE.

"Got to find Sam," she said aloud, and turned the key in the truck's ignition. The engine started without a sputter.

It was only then that she remembered that she had gotten to where she was going.

There were no more voices. They had stopped last night, along with the truck.

Dirt in the gas line.

Reba smiled. She turned off the engine and got out.

A man who walked like he had a doozie of a hangover was puttering around on a boat down a ways. He was the only one on the pier except for the two young men who had confronted her with the flashlight the night before.

One of them was talking into a tiny telephone and looking at his watch. When he hung up, he latched the phone onto his belt. Reba clucked, marveling at the gizmos people used nowadays.

"Mister?" she called to the old man, waving from the dock by his boat. "Yoo hoo, there!"

The old man lumbered toward her, scowling. "What do you want?" he shouted.

"I'm looking for Sam," she answered.

"Sam who?"

Reba's face fell. It had never occurred to her to doubt that she had come to the right place.

"Don't you know him? Young feller, twenty-nine years old. He'd have brown hair, I reckon, and brown eyes, like his folks."

The old man looked at her suspiciously. "You selling something?"

"No."

"Then why do you want him?"

"Well, I can't rightly say. I just know I got to find him, that's all. He live here?"

"Who sent you?"

She was stumped on that one. If she told him that she had come at the insistence of her dead grandmother, he would like as not take her for a fool. "I'm not going to do nothing bad to him, if that's what you're worried about," she said, laughing. "I ain't as young as I used to be."

Just then the two young men strode up on either side of her and grabbed her elbows. "We'd like you to move on, ma'am," the one with the phone said as they hustled her back toward the truck.

"Wait," she protested. "I'm just trying to find the boy."

"Go look somewhere else." Together they raised Reba completely off her feet, and one of her shoes dropped off. Her heart was pounding frantically. "My shoe! Let me down!"

"You heard her!" Darian roared. As the men were settling her back on her feet, Reba turned around to see the old man standing on the pier, her shoe in his hand. He tossed it on the ground in front of her.

"Mr. McCabe, we've been sent by Mr. St. James to protect you," the man with the phone began, "and we can't take any chances. . . ."

"Don't you dare treat me like some pantywaisted buttered bun! I didn't invite you and I don't need you to protect me from the likes of her. Now git!"

"We're under orders to escort you to the bank . . . sir . . ."

Fists on his hips, Darian stood glowering at them until they backed away.

"We ought to be leaving soon, Mr. McCabe," one of them said.

"I know when the appointment is!"

They backed away farther. Then he turned his glare on Reba.

She only smiled. "I like a man knows his own mind," she said.

Darian's mouth opened once, twice, then snapped shut. It was pointless to shout at someone who took no offense.

"McCabe," the old woman said softly, a crease forming between her eyes.

"Yes, and I don't want nothing you got to sell, neither."

"McCabe. Don't I know you?"

"You do not."

Her face lit up. "Jamie," she said breathlessly. "You're Jamie McCabe's daddy. I thought you looked familiar, but I couldn't place you."

Darian stiffened. "How did you know Jamie?" he asked flatly.

"Oh, I'm sorry," she said, reaching out to him, but he shied away. "I was in a group with him once. We called ourselves the Rememberers. Your boy was . . ."

Darian walked away.

". . . real fine," she finished.

She knew how he felt. The thought of Bo filled her with hurt, too, and time didn't make it any better. Maybe if he had been sick or fighting in a war or even killed in an accident, she might have been able to accept his death. But knowing that someone you loved was murdered was too much to ask of anybody. When that happened, part of you just broke off and died, and nothing was ever the same.

She stood on the pier and said a prayer for Mr. McCabe.

When he emerged from the boat again, he was wearing a clean shirt and a rather ill-fitting brown blazer. His hair was combed. He looked unnatural, Reba thought, like a little boy dressed for Sunday school.

She tried to approach him again, hoping to make amends for bringing up the son he was trying to keep buried, but he did not even give her a glance as he walked purposefully toward the two men and got into their car with them.

"Mr. McCabe!" she called to him as the car backed out into the street. "I just need to know about Sam. You never did tell me if he lived here. I just want to know what boat he's staying at. . . ."

The car peeled away, leaving her coughing in its wake.

Reba crossed her arms and leaned against the truck. "All right, you old buzzard," she muttered. "I'll just wait right here."

And then she realized that she knew exactly where to find Sam. Sooner or later, he would come to McCabe's boat.

Because the fact that his son had died on the same night that Sam was born was no coincidence.

Gram had directed her true. She would wait. And when she saw Sam, she would know him.

Darian had met Aidon St. James twice and liked him less each time. But St. James's assistant, who had come to the bank to handle the sale of the diamond, set a new standard for loathsomeness.

His name was Mr. Penrose. Darian could not think of a more appropriate first name for the man than "Mister." He was in his late forties, with carefully pressed hair, yuppie eyeglasses that were too small for his face, and the manner of a maître d' in a cheap restaurant. Even his voice impressed McCabe as oily and dishonest.

He was waiting for McCabe and his two escorts at 8 A.M. inside the bank president's office. Although the building was not officially open at that hour, security had been alerted and the guard had unlocked the door and ushered them into the bank president's office.

The bank president's name was Jackson. Penrose made a point of standing near him, the two of them facing Darian as if he were applying for a job.

"You got your boss's money with you?" Darian asked, looking innocent.

Penrose tightened his lips before he spoke. "Mr. Jackson will explain the transaction to you," he said. "He'll try to keep it simple."

The bank president cleared his throat before Darian could respond. "What we have, Mr. McCabe . . . Darian . . . may I call you Darian?"

"No."

"I see. As I was saying, what we have is a five-million-dollar transfer of funds from Mr. St. James to this bank. We'll deposit it in whatever sort of account you wish. We have many different types of savings programs. . . ."

"What about cash?"

Jackson blinked. "Well, the fund transfer is as good as cash," he said, smiling nervously. "You can draw on it at any time."

"All five million?"

Jackson looked pained. "Yes. Although it might take me a few hours to get all that cash in here. Is that what you have in mind, Mr. McCabe?"

Penrose rolled his eyes.

"No," Darian said. "I only asked because I believe this guy and his owner are thieves."

Penrose's mouth opened in outrage.

"And perverts," Darian finished, unperturbed.

"So, Mr. McCabe," Jackson said quickly, "am I to understand you will open an account?"

"Don't have to. I already got a checking account."

Jackson gave a little grunt, as if someone had punched him in the stomach. "You want to deposit five million dollars into a *checking* account?"

"No, just five hundred thousand. I want the rest to go to my employee, Sam Smith. He's got a checking account here, too."

Jackson stared at him balefully.

"You got a problem with that?" Darian asked.

Penrose smirked and waved aside whatever objections Jackson might have voiced. "Let him do it," he said.

Jackson looked pained. "Very well. We'll deposit four and a half million dollars into Mr. Smith's . . . checking account."

"I want receipts."

"Certainly. I'll get them now." The banker stood up stiffly and left his office.

Penrose leaned back in his chair. "Do you have the stone?" he asked.

"Right in my pocket," Darian said, patting his jacket. "And that's where it's going to stay till I get the money."

Penrose looked away in distaste. In a moment the bank president returned with the deposit slips. As he handed them over, Darian brought out the diamond pendant hanging from its gold chain and placed it on the desk.

Tentatively, Jackson lifted the stone. Penrose took it from him, gazing at it with awe.

Darian noticed that it did not glow for either of them.

When Dr. Gerald Heaney was ordered to go immediately to Liam's room, he was a little unnerved at finding Aidon St. James there.

The boy was sitting on the edge of the bed, getting dressed in clothes that he plucked, one article at a time, from a shopping bag next to him.

Heaney tried to smile. "Feeling well enough to leave?" he asked.

The boy ignored him. "He's fine," St. James said. "Where's the girl?"

The color drained from Heaney's face. "I don't know," he said. "Dr. Althorpe let her go, as I told you."

"She'll be found."

"Yes, I'm sure she will."

"And when she's brought back here, I would appreciate it if you did not botch things again."

Heaney's jaw clenched. "She's just a young girl," he said.

St. James shot him a vicious look. Just then, there was a small buzz in the room. St. James took a cellular phone from his pocket.

"Yes," he answered. After a pause he added, "You have the stone?" He listened for another few seconds, then said, "All right. Now we can dispose of the loose ends."

He clicked the telephone shut and noticed his son, now fully dressed,

looking at him with curiosity. Heaney, meanwhile, was trying to look anywhere else.

"The loose ends, Doctor?" St. James said sharply before leaving with the
boy. "You know what they are."

Heaney could smell his own perspiration. It stank of fear.

Need a lift?" Cory asked.

She was wearing a white dress that billowed in the morning breeze. She
looked beautiful, like an angel in flight.

"Sure," Sam said, getting up from the damp sand of the beach where he
had sat vigil all night. "If it's no trouble."

"None at all." She extended a hand to help him to his feet.

"Look, about last night—"

"What about it?" she said.

"I didn't want you to think . . . well, that I wasn't interested. It wasn't
like that."

She laughed. "I got over those games in high school. Come on, I'm going
to be late for work."

Tyrone Davis sat drinking an Orangina at the outdoor cafe in West Palm
Beach, eyeing the young blonde chick at the fruit stand across the street.
She was wearing baggy pants and a baseball cap, but the hair beneath it
hung down her back and shone in the sunlight.

Skinny thing, he thought. She would cry a lot while she was giving it
up. When the public phone rang, he nodded and one of his underlings
answered it.

The underling was a fifteen-year-old who had just beaten his first murder
rap. Tyrone himself had beaten several, although he'd had to be careful
since he had now turned eighteen. Then again, his fee had gone up, so he
did not have to work very often. He was enjoying being an adult.

The underling hung up the phone. "They just left the house," he said.
"White Mercedes convertible."

Another underling, noted among his peers for his intelligence because
he could read a bus schedule, looked at the gold Rolex on his wrist.

"They'll be coming by in like nine minutes," he said. "Are we ready?"

Tyrone rose out of the chair until he stood his full six feet tall. He was
thin but well muscled, built like a switchblade. "We are ready."

Tyrone got into his twenty-year-old Dodge Lancer with its elevated wheel
base. The other two entered a battered maroon GTO directly behind it.
Together they waited.

When the Mercedes passed by, both cars moved out smoothly into traffic.

Carol Ann counted the change she had discovered in the pocket of the
trousers she was wearing. Eighty-one cents, enough for two apples. While
she was paying for them, she asked the owner of the market, a plump Cuban
lady with a nice smile, if any work was available.

"I can sweep up for you and unload the produce," she offered. "And I don't need much money."

Suddenly her head swivelled toward the open doorway facing the street. Two beat-up old cars were pulling out of parking spots.

That was all.

"I can't have nobody on the books," the woman said. "The social security, it kill you, you know what I mean?"

With an effort, Carol Ann pulled her attention back to the woman. "That doesn't matter," she said. "I just need . . . work."

She inhaled sharply. Her hands were cold. She felt nauseated.

It's coming, it's coming.

With a cry, she dropped both apples on the floor and ran out.

Reba Dobbs clutched her heart.

Hurry, baby, hurry, Gram said.

"Where?" What . . .?"

Go.

She whirled toward the truck, slipping on some loose stones, and her knees buckled beneath her. She hit the pavement hard, but there was no time to check her bruises. She pulled herself up by the truck's door handle, feeling her sweat slick on the rusted chrome.

Once inside, she started the engine and peeled out into the street, laying a strip of rubber twenty yards long.

The Mercedes had barely entered the business district when Cory noticed the green car racing behind her, trailing a cloud of exhaust.

"Looks like he's in a hurry," she said, turning off into an alley. Sam looked behind them.

"It's okay. We can get to the docks just as easily this way."

The wheels of the green Lancer squealed as it followed, knocking a rear fender against a corner of the building at the alley entrance, but it never slowed.

"What the hell . . ." Sam said.

The Lancer raced up and sounded its horn. Cory edged her car as close to the wall as possible. "I don't believe it," she muttered. "He's going to pass me. Here."

The Lancer pulled alongside them, then nosed in front of the Mercedes and swivelled right.

Cory gasped as she slammed on the brakes. The driver door of the Lancer swept open.

"Back up," Sam said.

She shot the car into reverse, but before she reached the end of the alley, another car pulled in. Its doors also opened. Three teenagers walked toward them.

"I don't like this, Sam," Cory said.

He got out. "It's not my favorite way to start the day, either."

The three surrounded him.

"Leave the woman alone," he said.

Tyrone flicked a blade in his hands and slashed. A split second later, one of his companions kicked Sam between his legs.

The knife came down again.

Carol Ann screamed.

She was running, elbowing aside whoever was in her way, when the scream gurgled up in her throat and rent the air.

"Jesus Christ," a young businessman said. He had been walking to work when the girl shoved him against a mailbox in her headlong dash down the street.

A woman with two shopping bags filled with doughnuts for the retirement home where she volunteered stopped to offer consolation. "PCP," she said. "I seen 'em before. They get crazy."

"You're not kidding," the young man said, brushing off his suit. "She could hurt somebody."

"Oh, they can. They have the strength of ten people while they're in that condition. That's what I've heard."

"Somebody ought to call the police."

"Yep. They sure ought to."

The young man went on his way. The woman picked up her shopping bags and proceeded down the street.

We'll drive you back, Mr. McCabe."

Darian squinted into the sun. "No thanks, boys. I'll walk."

Though their responsibility toward him had ended as soon as Darian had entered the bank, his escorts had waited patiently with the guard in the lobby while he conducted his business upstairs.

"You boys get some rest. You probably need it."

He was sauntering across the thoroughfare when an aged pickup screeched to a halt less than a foot in front of him.

"Damn you!" he shouted, raising his fist. "Can't a law-abiding citizen even cross the street anymore?"

Then he recognized the driver. "You!" He pointed a finger at the old woman at the wheel.

Reba rolled down her window. "Get in," she said.

"The hell I will."

"Get in. It's Sam. Something's bad."

"What are you talking about?"

A horn blared behind her. "Get *in*," she repeated.

Darian entered the truck and she sped away.

"What about Sam?"

"He's in trouble. He's . . . oh, where am I gonna go?" she lamented at an intersection.

The hesitation was momentary. Almost before the words were out of her mouth, she veered to the right at top speed. "Something . . . I don't know . . . he's . . ."

Then they both saw the yellow-haired girl screaming at the entrance to an alley.

"Here," Reba said with certainty.

She parked right beside where the girl was standing and reached beneath the seat.

"My husband's toolbox," she explained. "Grab yourself a hammer."

Cory was pinned against her car. As soon as the first blow against Sam was struck, one of the youths had gone to the Mercedes and dragged her out, sprawling his body across hers.

"You're next," he whispered through a grin as the knife struck Sam again and again. Every time Sam tried to stand up, the blade would come down across his face, his chest, his arms. He was red with blood, and each time it took him longer to rise from the pavement.

"Sam," Cory sobbed, trying to struggle free. The mugger was between her legs. Her wrists were pinned against the cloth roof of the car. The only part of her body she could maneuver was her head.

She took a deep breath and banged her forehead against the boy's. The force of the impact made her dizzy, but he only scowled.

"Bitch," he said. He spat in her face.

Sam was on all fours in the alley, unable to raise his head. The younger of the attackers kicked him. Blood came out of his mouth.

Then the other one, the one with the knife, stepped back. He put the switchblade away.

Thank God, she thought. *Just go away now. Please go away.*

"Come on, pretty boy, get up," Tyrone teased, beckoning to Sam.

Sam got up, one leaden foot following the other, until he stood upright, swaying. One nostril had been cut open. Two of his knuckles had been crushed beneath a heel.

"That's good." From the waistband of his jeans, Tyrone took a length of one-inch iron pipe and slapped it against his palm.

"No!" Cory screamed.

The sound seemed to fill the entire alley. The muggers themselves looked around. Even after Cory fell silent, the scream went on. And on.

Then Cory saw her: standing behind the maroon GTO, her hands clutching at her hair, her mouth emitting an unearthly shriek as if it were she, not Sam, who was being beaten to death. It was Carol Ann Frye.

Tyrone cursed. This was supposed to go down quiet, one two three. Some rummy passing by, maybe some folks moving real fast like they never seen nothing. Now this fool druggie girl takes it into her head to work off her jones right here.

"Stuff the bitch," he said. His companion loped off.

Tyrone smiled at Sam. "You and me, man."

"That's right," Sam answered, and lunged for the pipe.

He should not have caught it. He should definitely not have caught it because Tyrone Davis was fast. Fast as a blade.

But he did catch it and he yanked it out of Tyrone's hands and tossed it on the pavement behind him.

"Like you said, buddy, you and me," Sam said.

Fast as a blade, Tyrone danced out of his way.

Almost.

Sam caught him, barely, caught him by the sleeve of his shirt. And once he caught him, he yanked Tyrone toward him like a rag doll, then threw him against the brick wall. "My turn," Sam said, trying to blink away his fatigue. With the last of his energy, he slammed a bloody fist against Tyrone's nose.

"Jo Jo," Tyrone called in a wavering voice as he fumbled for his switchblade, which had fallen out of his pocket in the scuffle.

"Go visit him in the hospital." An old man and a fat old lady were walking toward them. They seemed to be carrying tools. The blonde screamer was with them.

"Shit," Tyrone said.

Sam was having trouble focusing. "Darian?" he asked, not quite believing his eyes.

In that moment the youth pinning Cory spun to the ground and picked up the blade. Cory tried to run, but the kid was too quick. He grabbed hold of her hair before she had gone three feet and yanked her back to him, the knife an inch from her throat.

"Back off," the boy said. "Or I cut her."

He was the youngest of the trio. His eyes were wide with fear. "You too," he said to Sam.

Sam backed away.

"Let's go," the kid told Tyrone.

Tyrone took a few steps toward the car, then assessed the situation.

None of these suckers was going to do a damn thing as long as they thought the kid was going to stick the lady.

He crossed his arms, wagged his head, and walked back for the iron pipe.

"Let's *go!*" the kid said.

"I'll get there when I get there," Tyrone said. He touched his nose. It was broken. He slapped the pipe against his leg. "Just taking my property," he said.

And then he moved. Fast. Holding the pipe like a bat, he clubbed Sam on the temple.

The impact sounded like an explosion. Sam went down.

"Go!" Tyrone shouted. The kid dropped Cory and dashed out of the alley on foot. Tyrone jumped in the green Lancer, backed up quickly enough to hit anyone who might be foolhardy enough to chase them, then sped out the far side onto the street.

Cory was the first to reach Sam. She checked his pupils, loosened his clothing, tried to find his pulse, listened to his chest. "Call an ambulance!" she ordered.

A knot of onlookers had formed at the entrance to the alley. Some of them left to find help, now that they themselves were no longer in danger.

"How bad is it?" Darian asked.

Cory's look of anguish told him everything.

Darian knelt down beside her. Blood was running out of Sam's ears. "Is he dead?"

Cory squeezed her eyes shut. "I don't know," she whispered.

"Can you do anything?"

"Not here. He needs a surgeon. All we can do is wait for the ambulance."

"No."

A small slender hand reached between them to touch Sam's chest. Carol Ann's face was somber. "There isn't time," she said.

She placed her other hand on Sam's head, over the crushed bones of his temple, and began to breathe deeply. Instinctively, the others moved away to give her more room.

Can't do it. Too much. Too far gone.

Carol Ann's fingers turned blue almost immediately. The light around Sam was cracking like glass, dissipating and washing inward. She heard a whooshing sound, like the flapping of birds' wings, or wind in a tunnel.

But there were no angels here, no good spirits filled with light and welcome.

"Don't let him go, child."

Carol Ann looked up, startled. There was an old woman standing over her.

Biting her lip, Carol Ann pressed harder on Sam's chest. She could feel no heartbeat.

"I don't think I can do it," she said.

Gently Reba placed her right hand over Carol Ann's. "We'll help you."

With her left hand, she took Darian McCabe's.

Darian reached out until he found Cory Althorpe's hand and held it.

Cory was the last. She looked at Sam, at the slashes across his face, at the terrible wound on his head.

"Please live, Sam," she whispered as she touched Carol Ann's head.

The circle was complete.

Carol Ann closed her eyes. She began to tremble; the power shooting through her was electric. A music rose out of it, big as the sea, carrying Sam's pain through all of them, swelling, threatening to extinguish them, then subsiding, shrinking, fading until it left their bodies and disintegrated into the air.

Sam groaned. He opened his eyes.

The circle broke. Carol Ann fainted.

When she came to, the old woman was smiling at her.

Carol Ann leaped forward into her arms and hugged her. "You're like *me*," she said, filled with a joy she had never before experienced. She looked at each of them in turn, the stony-faced old man, the handsome young one who was sitting with his elbows on his knees, Dr. Althorpe. Dr. Althorpe who had helped to heal, not with her knowledge, but with herself. Carol Ann felt as if she had been looking for them all her life.

"You're all just like me."

CHAPTER 6

"WITH A STRANGER IT BEGAN; WITH A STRANGER SHALL IT BEGIN AGAIN.'"

Aidon St. James looked up from the cracked parchment he held in his hands. It was a copy of a copy of a copy, although the parchment itself was more than two thousand years old. It had been copied by a distant, if direct, ancestor of St. James's. It was written in the Language.

Before him sat twenty-five men, plus St. James's personal secretary, Penrose. They had come from the far corners of the world: an Arab sheik, whose riches had been owned by his family for millennia; a Chinese entrepreneur whose ancestors had been warlords over vast domains; a German industrialist who still lived in the castle his people had owned since the Middle Ages. All were wealthy beyond the imaginations of ordinary people. All wielded a power that dwarfed that of their governments. All were killers, descended from long, ancient lines of killers.

They were the Consortium.

"Thus begins the testament," St. James said. He wore a long black robe splashed with gold around the shoulders and waist. The others were dressed in white. Ceremonial garments were always worn at these gatherings of the highest level of the organization whose members numbered in the tens of thousands. The robes eliminated any distinctions between the men.

They were a brotherhood whose allegiance to one another superseded all other loyalties. Family ties were nothing compared with their fidelity to the Consortium: St. James himself had proven that when he had eliminated his own wife because of her suspicions about his activities.

He stood at the front of the small auditorium, below decks on his yacht. The men before him were silent, listening.

"These words are a warning," he said. "Because the Stranger has not yet come to take our birthright of power away from us. We have successfully kept him away through all the ages of civilization. We have destroyed the temples of Heliopolis, where the knowledge of his kind was kept. We have discredited the teachings of the Egyptian seers. We have erased the writing of the Nazarene prophet. We have, through our own personal efforts, rid the Earth of most of those beings who might spawn another Stranger.

"For the past twenty-nine years, those efforts have borne abundant fruit.

Our enemies can now be identified by their blood. Few of them remain, and those who are alive have been rendered powerless. They are called 'psychics,' and have been dismissed by every population in the world as fools and charlatans, and their words carry no credibility.

"Yet still, they might one day rise to take over the Earth again, as they did in the distant past. The freakish force they possess is strong. Even without teaching or indoctrination into their alien ways, they are able to call upon their powers to use for their own ends.

"The prime directive of the Consortium has always been that these creatures must not be allowed to exist. Above all, they must not be allowed to exist *together*.

"And now, at last, after thirteen thousand years, we will be able finally to fulfill that directive."

St. James paused to make certain that each man was giving him his full attention. Then he moved slowly toward a seven-foot-long table covered with a cloth of black silk and opened a chest of solid gold which sat atop it. From the chest, he took the diamond pendant and held it up for all to see.

A collective intake of breath was the only sound in the chamber. The eyes of the white-robed men were focused absolutely on the magnificent stone, a stone that shone like a living star, as St. James lowered its golden chain over his own head.

"The Stranger will not come again," he said.

In a stateroom down the passageway from the auditorium, a Venezuelan shipping magnate and an American film producer helped Liam dress in a white robe.

Normally the teenager would have been embarrassed by this attention, but today he was beyond embarrassment. Something worse, much worse, was happening.

This was the day he had dreaded all his life.

"It will be your beginning, Liam," his father had told him as he had left the stateroom to prepare himself for the assembly. "All your lessons—and I admit that some of them have been harsh—have been to prepare you for this."

The lessons. The beatings. The Practice.

"Father, I don't think—"

"You will not contradict me," St. James had said evenly. "You are my son, and someday you will take my place with these men. It is the sole purpose for which you were conceived."

And he had left Liam to wait.

For what? Were all these men as crazy as his father? Did they all force their children to mutilate animals? Did they beat their kids when they cried because they did not like killing? If they did, he did not want to be part of their sick little club.

He did not even know its name. Through all the drill, all the inane lessons about the nonexistent history of a nonexistent country with its nonexistent language, his father had never once told him what it was all for.

Now he apparently was supposed to assume a mantle of some kind, receive the blessing of a bunch of rich wackos just for being the only son of Aidon St. James.

One of the men dressing him clipped a gold brooch on his shoulder. It depicted a bird Liam had never seen before.

He was frightened, scared to death. What would he be expected to do? What had the Practice been for?

Be brave, the girl in the hospital had said.

The girl who brought sunlight with her.

Liam had never told his father about her. He had explained away his missing clothes with a shrug.

"Guess somebody took them," he said. "What do you pay those bodyguards for, anyway?"

He had received a slap in the face for the remark, but he had not been questioned further.

Then his father and Dr. Heaney had spoken about a girl who had fled from the hospital. His father had told the doctor not to botch the job again.

What job was that? What did it have to do with the runaway girl? And why had Sam Smith looked so shocked when he saw Heaney listed as Liam's physician?

He closed his eyes. He did not want to think about any of it. He did not want to remember his father reminding someone over the phone that it was time to "dispose of all the loose ends."

He did not want to think about the yellow-haired girl who had told him to be brave.

Carol Ann refused to set foot inside West Palm Hospital, so Darian and Reba waited with her in a coffee shop across the street while Cory accompanied Sam to the radiology department.

"I tell you, I'm all right," Sam groused. "If my head were caved in, don't you think I'd feel it?"

"The point is, twenty minutes ago your head *was* caved in. I saw it happen. You're getting X rays."

Cory stole a look at Sam. It was amazing. The clothing he wore seemed to have sustained more damage than his body. The faint flaking scabs that crisscrossed his face in fine lines had been, less than a half hour before, deep knife slashes. Most astounding, though, was the spot on his temple where the pipe had smashed his skull.

Nothing remained of the wound. Nothing at all.

A miracle, she thought. Made by ordinary people and whatever power they had been connected to.

At Cory's request, the nurse on duty called the head of radiology from his office. He was a young fresh-faced doctor who seemed to be barely out of his teens.

"Morning, Fred," she said. "This is my friend, Sam Smith. Could you take a picture for us?"

"Sure. Anything special you're looking for?"

"He got hit in the right temple. I'm just trying to rule out fracture."

In one of the X-ray rooms, the radiologist had Sam lie on an examining table, then placed a lead body apron over him. He positioned the large chrome-plated camera over Sam's head. "Don't move," he said as they retreated behind the lead-shielded wall to the control panel.

After the brief buzz of the machine, the doctor removed Sam's heavy apron. "You just stay put a few minutes," Cory said. "We're going to develop this film."

Sam nodded as the two of them left. He sat up, took a brochure on radiation from atop a file cabinet, and idly began to read it.

Darian, Reba, and Carol Ann sat drinking their coffee without exchanging a word. The experience they had gone through had left them all shaken and drained.

Carol Ann was staring at her cup, her eyes unfocused, trying to regain her strength. In one hand, hidden from view, she still clutched the small gray stone he had found on the beach.

Reba looked around at the pretty luncheonette with its pastel colors, thinking how far she had come from Stony Holler.

Darian was exerting all his will to hold back the tears which had threatened to explode from him since Sam's first groan of life in the alley.

You're all like me, the girl had said, and he had seen the happiness on her face.

Jamie must have felt that way about the Rememberers.

God knew, the boy had not had that kind of kinship at school. His classmates had ostracized him from the very beginning. They had jeered him when he told them that the lights around their faces changed color as they spoke. They had beaten him senseless when he said they would lose the season's first baseball game to Miss Olsen's second grade class, and they did. His teachers, too, had constantly hinted to the McCabes that their son might be "troubled."

Crazy, they meant. Everybody thought Jamie was crazy.

That was why Darian had tried to bully the Sight out of him. If the boy never got any pats on the back for his wild talk, Darian reasoned, he might forget about it.

After all, what the hell was the use in seeing the inside of a tree, as Jamie insisted he could, or in hearing the voices that called to him. . . .

From the Peaks . . .

Darian cleared his throat.

Oh, son, if I could have told you that I understood, that they were all wrong and you were right . . .

Only the Rememberers had treasured Jamie for what he was.

"Were you on the island?" he asked quietly.

Reba knew what he meant immediately. "Not that day. I was with Sam."

"Sam?" Darian asked, shocked.

"He was born that night. I took him from the body of his ma in a swamp."

Her freckled, knotted old hand patted his softly. "Your boy come back to you, Mr. McCabe."

*   *   *

Well, I can't be a hundred percent sure, but look for yourself."

The young radiologist pointed his finger at the still-wet X-ray film hanging on a viewing screen inside his office. Cory leaned forward as he traced his finger over the image.

"No sign of current fracture. This line across the temple is from an earlier injury, clearly. If your patient is suffering from some sort of mental disorder, this might be the cause."

"Earlier?"

"Much earlier, maybe twenty years. But it must have been a beaut. This was a twenty-centimeter fracture with starburst shattering. It's surprising he survived it."

Dr. Gerald Heaney nearly sprinted toward the radiology department. He had received a call from a nurse on staff telling him that Dr. Althorpe had brought a patient into the hospital.

"Is the patient a teenage girl?"

"No, Dr. Heaney," the nurse reported, dutifully consulting her notes. "It was a man." She would be paid for this information, and made certain it was correct. "His name is Sam Smith. Possible skull fracture."

He had hung up at once and filled a syringe from a vial he kept in his medical bag. Then he ran for the elevators.

Sam Smith! Krantz's ICDL and the psychiatrist both! It would be tricky, he would have to work fast, but he could eliminate them both. Tie off two of the "loose ends" at once. It might make up for losing the girl.

No, it won't, he thought as he peered into each of the radiology rooms in turn. The Consortium didn't allow mistakes. Not even one.

The third room was the only one occupied. A young man sat on the examining table reading a leaflet.

Heaney tried to still his hands as he entered the room. "Don't let me disturb you," he said with a smile. "I just have to get something from that cabinet behind you."

With one hand he fumbled noisily with the latch on the cabinet, while with the other he reached into the pocket of his lab coat for the syringe.

What was inside it was a fairly simple decoction of digitalis and some epinephrine derivatives combined with a toxin developed at the laboratory in Geneva. It would bring on instantaneous cardiac arrest, followed within seconds by death.

Heaney had administered the injection many times, though never so publicly. Still, it would be possible to explain the sudden deaths of Althorpe and this Smith. During the investigation—which would be sure to follow—he would reveal to the hospital administration, in great secrecy, that ICDLs never lived long, and almost always died suddenly. Those facts were catalogued in twenty-nine years of research data in his lab. Sam Smith was already listed as an ICDL. It would be a simple matter to add Cory Althorpe's name to the list.

And Heaney would be believed. Because the data was real. And because someone in West Palm Hospital's administrative offices, perhaps the administrator himself, was connected with the Consortium.

But Smith was alone.

"Excuse me, you don't happen to be with Dr. Althorpe, do you?" Heaney asked.

"She's with . . . um, Fred," Sam answered. "The radiologist."

"Ah."

The radiologist, too. So there would have to be another death, Heaney thought with a sinking feeling. Another and then another and another after that. . . .

How has it come to this? he wondered sadly.

This was not why Gerald Heaney became a doctor. He had not expected to spend his life killing like a trained attack dog.

The syringe in his hand was shaking as if it possessed a life of its own.

Sam looked over, then launched himself off the table. "What the hell are you doing?"

Heaney flattened himself against the cabinets. The syringe hung between his fingers like a cigarette. He was panting, his mouth gaping.

"Hey, what's the matter with you?" Sam demanded.

Just then, the door swung open and Cory walked in. The radiologist was behind her.

She stopped in her tracks. "Dr. Heaney," she said.

"Heaney?" Sam put more distance between himself and the man with the needle. "What's he doing here?"

"They're going to kill you all," Heaney said. "They won't need me to do it."

Cory moved toward him. "Doctor . . ."

"Stay back." He raised the syringe.

"Who do you work for, Heaney?" Sam demanded. "St. James?"

The doctor smiled wanly. "Does everyone know, then?" His voice was faint. "He's got men all over the city looking for you. And he'll get what he wants." He blinked once, slowly, and licked his lips. "Aidon St. James always gets what he wants."

He unbuttoned his lab coat and one button of his shirt, then pressed the hypodermic between two ribs, directly into his heart.

"Holy shit," the radiologist muttered, running for the nurse's station.

Heaney slumped to the floor. Cory went to him. He was already gasping for breath. The hand that had held the syringe was twitching violently.

"Code blue." The announcement blared out of every loudspeaker in the hospital. *"Code blue. Radiology."*

Sam knelt down beside Heaney's convulsing body. Cory shoved him out of the way and began CPR on the doctor. Within moments, a team from the emergency room, two intensive care nurses, an EKG technician, a respiratory therapist, a nurse anesthetist, and an I.V. team streamed through the door with a crash cart. In their wake were several young residents, all hoping to be asked to participate in the procedure.

Brian Hartman, the hulking ER nurse, lifted Heaney onto the examination table, then set up the defibrillator atop the crash cart and affixed two gel pads onto Heaney's chest.

"Fine V-fib," he announced, watching the monitor with his practiced eye. "Very fine, I'd say. Like a flat line. This guy's deader than Keely's nuts."

"Defibrillate three-sixty," commanded the ER doctor. "Clear!"

Everyone jumped away as Hartman applied the defibrillator paddles. Heaney's body jerked up off the table.

During the proceedings, Sam was shunted farther and farther away until he was edged out into the corridor, where he collided with Darian McCabe.

"Jesus!" the old man roared. "I thought that commotion in there was for you. That blamed girl started to wailing, said you were in trouble again."

"It was Dr. Heaney," Sam said softly. "Bonner's old assistant, the blood man." He ran his hands through his hair. "He killed himself."

Cory came out a few seconds later, looking disheveled and shaken.

"There's nothing more we can do," she said. Seeing Darian, she asked, "Where's Carol Ann? Is she all right?"

"She was when I left her five minutes ago," Darian groused.

"Come on, let's get out of here," Sam said. "We've got to find a place to hide her."

Following a polite knock at the stateroom door, Penrose stepped inside. He examined Liam's costume fussily, adjusting and tucking like a mother hen while the two Consortium members stood back.

Liam despised the man. Penrose was like some kind of evil spirit, always hovering around his father. The fact that St. James hardly regarded his assistant as a human being did not make it any easier for Liam to bear his presence.

It had been Penrose who had chosen the Swiss boarding school Liam attended, Penrose who visited him on holidays, sighing and looking at his watch while he listened to the boy's excuses for his poor grades. It was Penrose who sent Liam's birthday and Christmas presents to him, regular as clockwork: subscriptions to *Boy's Life* in April, and a box of chocolates at Christmas, signed "your father" in Penrose's florid hand.

Even the summers, the sacred summers when his father left New York and traveled the world aboard the *Pinnacle* with Liam, did not exclude Penrose. He seemed to be wherever they docked, his notebook and pencil at the ready, his portable phone strapped to his waist like a sword.

Mostly, though, he hated Penrose for all the times the man had seen Liam bloodied and bruised after his father's beatings and had pretended not to notice.

"This is an important day, Liam," he said now in the air-conditioned voice he usually reserved for the Consortium's workers. "Your behavior must be impeccable."

"Oh, sure thing, Penrose, no problem. Of course, nobody has bothered to tell me what I'm supposed to be doing, but I'll make sure to do it impeccably. You bet."

"You're not supposed to know," the man snapped. "It's a test. A test of your courage and your manhood."

Like yours, Liam thought. "Give me a break."

"Would you like me to call your father?"

Liam instantly shriveled. "No," he said sullenly.

"Then you'll keep your smart-aleck remarks to yourself, thank you very much."

Liam rolled his eyes. He could not wait to get back to school. "Just tell me what this is about, okay, Penrose? Is that some kind of business club out there that I'm supposed to join? Do I have to learn a secret handshake or something?"

Penrose's hands, which had been adjusting Liam's belt, suddenly stilled. He kept his head down for a long time. "I'm not a member," he said quietly. Then he brought his head up, sniffed, and held open the door. "Good luck to you, Liam," he said.

The two men who had helped Liam dress now preceded him down the center aisle of the auditorium. As they moved in their stately procession, the men in the audience rose.

Ahead, at the far end, stood Aidon St. James. Though he was dressed outlandishly, in a black robe with long wide sleeves which hung down from his extended arms like banners, his eyes held a coldness and strength that made Liam shiver.

Then the procession halted. The men who had headed it fell away, melting into the audience. St. James lowered his arms and stepped aside.

Liam gasped.

Lying before him, bound by ropes tied to crude iron stakes that had been hammered into a long black-draped table, was a man.

He was naked. His head was lolling. His eyes were glassy, as if he had been drugged, but inside their depths was a stark terror.

Liam knew him. He was a gemologist named Eames who had come aboard the *Pinnacle* no more than a week earlier. He had been terribly excited then, so excited that he had begun to babble about a stone of some kind as soon as he had boarded the yacht, talking even in front of Liam and the crew. St. James had ordered him to shut up until they were alone.

The stone must have been a jewel, Liam had supposed. People with the amount of wealth his father possessed were always buying jewels as investments.

He looked over to his father. A massive dagger-shaped diamond hung from St. James's neck. *That* jewel.

Liam's face was pinched in bewilderment and fear. *What are you doing?* he wanted to shout. Why was this man here, like this? Why didn't anyone object?

His father turned slowly toward him, meeting his eyes. From his sleeve he took a small curved knife with a bronze blade and placed it into Liam's hands, which he covered with his own.

"Our sacrifice for the stone," he said.

Eames's eyes rolled wildly. His mouth worked. "Nuh . . . nuh . . ."

They were the only sounds he could manage.

Liam watched him, aghast, as the man strained his muscles against the ropes. St. James raised the dagger high.

"Remember the Practice," he whispered into his son's ear.

The Practice. The rabbit with its body split open, its heart still beating in Liam's hand.

Oh God, no, no I hate you, Father, don't, no, no.

"No!" he screamed as his hands were brought down into the man's chest.

CHAPTER 7

THE FIVE OF THEM, SAM, DARIAN, CORY, REBA, AND CAROL ANN, EACH CAR-
ried two supermarket bags filled with provisions and supplies as they walked
down the pier toward the *Styx*.

"Hope we got room for all this stuff," Darian muttered. "Not to mention
all of *you*."

Reba beamed. "Ain't it fine how we all come together like we did?" she
chirped. "It's like it was meant to be, all of us with the Sight and all."

"Speak for yourself," Darian said. Reba only laughed.

"But where are we going to go?" Carol Ann asked.

She rubbed her thin arms. In the coffee shop, while Sam and Cory had
been in the hospital getting Sam's skull x-rayed, a feeling of doom had
passed over her like a wave. Even when Darian had come back with them,
the feeling did not pass.

It was still with her, oppressive and nauseating: danger.

Cory moved closer to her. "We'll find someplace where you'll be safe,"
she said.

"That's not going to be easy," Sam said quietly, so that only Darian could
hear. "Heaney said that St. James has men all over town looking for the
rest of us, too."

"I can get you to any port along the coast," Darian said. "After that, you
better split up. Send the girl to a city, maybe. Someplace with enough people
so's she can get lost." He turned to Sam. "As for you . . ."

"Forget it, Darian. I'm staying with you."

"And getting yourself killed? Oh, that's using your head, Sam. Good
thinking."

"We got to stay together," Reba said.

"Stay out of this."

"I will not. I come near a thousand miles to be with you all, and one
thing I know is that we got each other and damned near nothing else to
fight what's coming. And it's coming, believe me. The air's thick with it.
That's why Carol Ann's looking so poorly."

"Yap, yap, yap," Darian said as he stepped onto the boat.

He led the group down the companionway into the galley. "Just try not to mess anything up," he called behind him. "Everything on this tub's got a reason to be where it is and—"

"Hold it, Mr. McCabe."

It was one of the young men who had escorted him to the bank. He was holding a gun with a web silencer on it. His associate stepped out of the shadows, directing the others to set down their bags and join Darian against the wall.

"First St. James has you protecting me, and now he sends you to shoot me. Is that it?"

"I'm sorry, sir," the young man said.

"Well, I can't say I'd expect anything more from the likes of that weasel. But these folks don't have anything to do with the diamond. Let them go."

"We can't."

"Are you Carol Ann Frye?" the other man asked. Carol Ann nodded, her teeth chattering.

"That's all of them," he said. "Plus the old lady." He looked to his companion and swallowed.

"What's the matter? Not used to murdering innocent people?" Darian taunted. "Stay with St. James. You'll get to be experts in no time."

"Shut up!" The man with the gun trained on McCabe backed up. "Make sure the door's closed up the stairs," he told the other.

The second man climbed up three steps of the companionway, then stopped with a sudden grunt and reeled backward. As the group watched, he flew back, sprawling onto the floor.

A yard-long spear quivered in the middle of his chest.

"What—"

A whistling hiss cut through the air, and a second shaft struck deep into the other gunman's heart.

Harry Woodson descended the companionway, a speargun in his hands. "Are there any more?" he asked.

The group shook their heads dumbly.

"Good." He set down the gun. "There were only two spears."

Darian snorted once, then guffawed. "What the hell are you doing here . . . with *that*?"

"I brought over my submersible," Harry said. "I was inside it working when I heard these two come on board your boat. I listened to them for a while before you got here. They were sent to kill you." He looked over the group. "All of you, I think."

"You got that right," Darian said.

"I would have called the police, but couldn't risk going to shore. So I grabbed the only weapon I had in the sub."

"Hell of a good shot," Darian admitted.

Woodson hefted the speargun. "I've had twenty-nine years to practice," he said.

"Twenty . . ." Reba stepped forward. "That's where I know you from. You're the college boy who fixed up our showers."

"Showers?" Woodson frowned. "I don't think . . . oh, man, it's Reba!" He grabbed the old woman in a bear hug, forgetting the gruesome sight of the dead men.

"Remember the showers you made for us on the island?" Suddenly she pulled away from him and sucked in her breath. "Harrison, honey. You lived."

He looked down at his wasted body. "Sort of," he said. "They came after me."

"Me, too," she said in a whisper.

They stared at one another in silence for a long time.

Finally Darian spoke. "Somebody give me a hand with these bodies," he said.

Fifteen minutes later they were seaborne. Woodson's submersible followed behind the *Styx*, attached by a tow rope. Woodson stood on the aft deck, watching.

"Does that thing work?" Sam asked.

"It goes down."

"That's a start. Does it come back up?"

"Don't bother me with details. I'm a policy-maker."

Sam squinted into the sun. "We're going east," he said, bewildered.

"Yeah?"

Sam ran to the bridge. "I thought you were going to take us north, up the coast," Sam said.

"St. James'll have men on the lookout, most likely," Darian said. " 'Specially once his shooters float back to shore. Wouldn't take a speedboat long to catch up with us."

"So where are you heading?"

Darian gave a small shrug.

"East. Due east . . ." And then he knew, although he could hardly believe it. "You're going to Memory Island, aren't you?" Sam asked in astonishment.

"Think I don't know what you plan to do with that hunk of junk of Woodson's? Least this way, I'll be close by."

Sam looked out to sea. The Peaks . . . deep inside his mind, he could already hear its song calling to him.

"What about the women? Your idea about us splitting up makes sense for them. They'd be safer alone, in different cities."

"That old bat's not about to budge," Darian said. He wiped his nose with the back of his hand. "Besides, she's right. The devil lives out there." He spat out the window. "We'd best face him together."

Our two men are missing, and Darian McCabe's boat is gone from the docks."

Penrose bit a hangnail. "When they last called in, they said that McCabe and several others were headed toward the boat. Sam Smith was with them. Also the psychiatrist from the hospital, a teenage girl who fits Carol Ann Frye's description, an someone else, an old woman they said had been hanging around the docks recently. I really don't know how McCabe could have known . . ."

"They went to the island," St. James said laconically from behind the desk in his office aboard the yacht.

"The—you don't mean Bonner's island."

St. James nodded. "Indeed I do."

Penrose was unconvinced. "Well, Dr. Althorpe does own it, but surely they know they'll be like sitting ducks out there. It would be smarter for them to head north, or south around Florida toward Louisiana, where they could move inland and separate. In fact, what's more likely is that they've set the boat adrift and are already going their separate ways."

"They won't separate."

Penrose exhaled in exasperation. "I don't think they'd be so stupid as to—"

"Intelligence is not a factor," St. James said. "They'll stay together. And others will join them."

"What?"

"They won't be able to help themselves."

Penrose looked away. He was not a member of the Consortium, he told himself. He was only its telephone voice. His job was to do what Aidon St. James told him, nothing more, nothing less. "Yes, sir," he said, somewhat dispiritedly. "Shall we send someone after them? To the island?"

"Just one boat with a diver. I'll take care of the rest."

"Yes, sir."

Alone, St. James opened a small gold casket on his desk and lifted the diamond from it. The stone's beauty was unearthly, perfect. It was already doing its work, the work it had been inspired to do since the dawn of time.

It was calling to its people.

It would call them together, sending their strange blood surging with life.

And then they would die. Together.

With Darian at the helm, they powered at high speed across the calm open sea. The five passengers were sitting on benches built around the gunwales on deck when Sam doubled over with a groan.

"What is it?" Cory called out, running over to help him.

"The shivers," Reba said.

Sam looked up. "You . . . know?"

"Your pa got them, too. He said it was why he couldn't be a surgeon. He never could tell when they was to come on."

Sam stared at her blankly, listening to the music inside him swell and then fade as they passed over the Peaks. "Did you say my *pa?*" he asked at last.

"Yes, Sam. Your folks was both doctors. I knowed them from a group I was in a long time ago."

"The Rememberers," Sam said. "With Harry Woodson. And Darian's son."

"And your parents."

"But how . . . how did you . . . I never even knew my own last name."

"It's Nowar, Sam. Your pa's name was Lars. Your ma was called Marie."

"Nowar?"

"They was killed for having the Sight, same as most of us. Harrison—Harry Woodson—and me, we're the only ones made it out alive." She blinked rapidly. "Your ma called out your name with her last breath."

Sam thought. "If I had family, why was I raised in an orphanage?"

"I didn't think you'd be safe with them . . . or me. The killers was everywhere those days, like now. You was in another room when they come for me the first time, but I figured sooner or later they was bound to find you. So I had to put you in a place where nobody knew your name."

"Nowar," Sam said, trying it out.

"So you're connected with Memory Island, too," Cory said. She stood up, cupping her palm over her eyes. "Look ahead. There it is."

Memory Island.

Sam took a deep breath. He had never seen it so closely before. Darian had not permitted the *Styx* even to enter the waters surrounding it.

On the few maps which showed it, the island was just a speck at the westernmost end of the Bimini chain. Technically, it was the closest foreign landfall to the continental United States, although that fact was of little interest to anyone except cartographers.

It jutted out of the sea like a shining rock less than a mile away. The whole of Memory Island was, in fact, more a rock than an island. Barely three square city blocks in size, the stony beaches along its perimeter were sloped gradually after centuries of bad storms and high seas. What scant vegetation existed was a far cry from the cultivated lushness of much of the Caribbean. There were a few clumps of trees with thin, snaky trunks, some scrub bushes, and, among the jagged rocks, hardy weeds growing tall.

Still, it exuded for Sam an attraction so strong he could barely control an impulse to shout in triumph.

Come to me, Sam, called the voice from the sea, its music strong and throbbing.

Inside his heart he answered it: *Yes, soon. Soon.*

Harry Woodson could feel his heart beating as he looked past the small cove to the charred remains of the building which had housed the Rememberers. All those present had all died there.

All except me.

He could still hear the explosion as the speedboat hurtled into Bonner's house with the impact of a bomb. He could still see the men with guns who came ashore minutes later to shoot the survivors, though they had found none.

That sound, that image, had haunted him for nearly thirty years. He had changed his name and switched his occupation; even his physical appearance had altered so radically that he would be unrecognizable to his closest friends from his life before that terrible day. And yet the fear had never left him.

For someday, he knew, they would come back. *They*, who had murdered a twelve-year-old boy who might have worked miracles with his genius. They who had raped a pregnant woman and then shot her to death.

And they had come back. They were here now, somewhere close by, and it was just a matter of time before they found Harry Woodson again.

Only this time I'm not going to hide, he thought. *This time, you're going to have to fight me.*

The fear had hardened him. It was the fear that had enabled Woodson to kill the two gunmen in Darian's galley without a shred of remorse. Even when their bodies were dumped in deep water, he had entertained no thought beyond extracting the speargun darts from their flesh without damaging the steel tips.

Yes, he thought, looking at the sun-splashed island, this time he would fight.

R eba covered her eyes with her hands.

It was too much, too much to bear. *Why did I have to come here, Gram?* she asked. Here, to this place where she could all but see the ghosts of the dead.

'Cause they're here, child, Gram answered. *You come to be with them.*

"Then I'm going to die, too," she whispered into the wind.

Maybe. Since when you been afraid of that? Gram chuckled, the way she did when she knew Reba was talking nonsense. *Honey, you know why you come.*

"Sam," she breathed. "I was supposed to lead him . . . someplace. . . ."

She dropped her hands. Memory Island stood shining in front of her. "Here?"

Suddenly the sun felt warm on her face. She looked around at the others, absorbed in their own thoughts. Gram had told her about them, too. *Others would come*, she had said, and here they were, the new Rememberers, coming to take the next step forward.

Coming home.

C arol Ann had never been to Memory Island. All she knew about it was what Reba had told her, that it had been a place of death and horrible destruction.

And yet, feeling the salt spray in her face as the rocky shore grew nearer, she felt suffused with a sense of peace and comfort.

I belong here, she thought. *We all do.*

A seagull swooped down close and landed on the rail in front of her.

It's coming, it seemed to say.

But "it" was no longer terrifying.

"Angel's wings," Carol Ann said softly, slowly turning her hand palm up. With one finger, she gently stroked the gull's white breast.

The place was filled with angels.

They would help the six who came to face the evil day.

The gull blinked at her with its little reptilian eyes, then released something from its mouth into her hand.

It was a seed.

Carol Ann looked at it with wonder as the bird flew away.

The last time Cory visited Memory Island, the blood had still been there.

That had been five years ago. It had taken Cory most of her life to steel herself to face the scene where her grandfather and the special people whose minds he explored with such fascination had died.

From the water, Bonner's house looked as if it had been flattened by a hurricane. Heaps of rubble were piled around long jagged planks of gray wood. Cory had visited the place with plans to remove all trace of the wreckage. She would hire a boat to take away the glass and appliances and wiring and plumbing. The wood would be burned, the stonework dropped back into the sea. Then, on the leveled ground, she would build another house, a place where she could come to be alone. She would build a windwall around it and bring in soil to plant a vegetable garden surrounded by orange trees.

This would be her home when she grew old. It would become the land of her dreams.

All that had changed when she saw the blood. It had darkened from red to black on the rotted wood that lay in splinters, but there was no mistaking what it was. There had been pools of it, washed away by the police after the bodies had been neatly laid on the ground, but the dark stains had never come off the floor. Even after two decades of weather, with weeds growing through the deep cracks in the cement slab underfloor, she could still see the death there.

Cory left that day and never came back.

Until now.

That blood will still be there.

She wanted to run to the bridge, tell Darian to turn the boat around. There was nothing for them here, in this place of ruin and tragedy. Whatever promise had once taken root here was dead.

There's nothing left.

Tears filled her eyes. Through her wavering vision, she saw the place as it once might have been, two gleaming pyramids rising out of the green land like beacons to the stars, and behind them the lush meadows and woodlands and the great cities. Beyond them was a dazzling archipelago of islands surrounded by ships with a hundred oars each, all dwarfed by the great mountain, the volcano towering over the world. . . .

What?

She clutched the rail with all her strength to keep herself from falling.

Woodlands? Cities? *Pyramids?*

She felt dizzy, utterly disoriented. Her ears rang sickeningly, blocking out the sound of the wind and the ship's engine and the cry of the circling gulls.

"The volcano," she said, unable to hear her own words.

* * *

Darian stared grimly ahead to the small mooring harbor. He had docked there twenty-nine years ago when he came to claim the bodies of his wife and son.

There had not been much left of them. He had recognized Jamie only because that particular mound of blackened meat was smaller than the others. Rose had fared a little better. She was wearing a pin Darian had given her for Christmas one year, a yellow enameled daisy with a small diamond chip in its center. The pin had been melted into her skin.

He felt his hands shaking as he cut the engine and began steering the boat into the harbor. Ahead, the charred ruins of the building where the power boat had exploded stood like a monument to the killers who had burned his family alive.

None of them had ever been caught.

I'll kill you, I'll kill you all.

His hands flew off the helm.

This was where he had first heard those words, the words which had sounded in his head for nearly thirty years afterward.

There had been a thick fog that day, which had made it difficult for Darian to negotiate between the police and Coast Guard cutters that had jammed the narrow inlet.

That's right, the fog, he thought. The fog had come out of nowhere.

Darian had hesitated stepping off the boat. By that time of morning, he knew, the flies would be swarming around the bodies. He had not wanted to see the flies.

Maybe the fog will cover them, he had thought.

Then he had heard a terrific clamor rising around him, bells and horns and screams, all from the sea around him. The fog had turned to smoke, smoke that burned his lungs, and ash that fell black on his face as he tried to maneuver the huge ship out into open water. His compass was no more than stones in a bowl of water and was useless in the roiling waves.

People were crowded in around him, screaming, panicked; on land, the very earth groaned as it opened up, swallowing those who ran toward the safety of the water. Water shot out of the ground in spouts nearly a hundred feet high. Great marble buildings collapsed like toys. In the distance, a massive monument exploded into framents.

And through it, through the ear-shattering noise and the carnage that was worse than any vision of Hell, came a voice through the fog, clear and low, filled with evil magic.

"I'll kill you, I'll kill you all. You and your children and theirs, through all time, through all eternity."

All eternity.

It had been nothing, of course. No smoke, no bodies in the sea. Just an illusion. When Darian had looked outside the bridge, the Coast Guard boats had still been moored in the foggy harbor. The only sounds were the faint voices of the law officers who had come to clean up after the massacre on the island.

And then, after identifying the remains of Rose and Jamie, he had forgotten all about the vision.

Craziness, he thought now as he set his hands deliberately back on the helm, unaware that the back of his shirt had turned dark with sweat. *Pure craziness.*

It had been excusable, he told himself. His wife and son had just been killed in what he had believed at the time was a freak accident. No one could be expected to think right at a time like that.

But that did not explain why gradually, almost imperceptibly, the bridge was now filling with fog again, and a bell sounded in the distance, growing louder, and from somewhere in the sea came the voices of people screaming. . . .

"Darian."

The old man clapped his hands to his ears. "No, damn you! I won't hear it! I won't hear it anymore!"

Sam stood before him, frowning.

Darian took one hand from his ear and slowly swatted the air. There was no fog now.

"I'll bring her in," Sam said, spinning the helm to turn the boat around. "Might as well dock ass-in. We've got the room."

Darian nodded, the movement of his head jerky and uncertain.

"We might want to leave in a hurry," Sam said with a smile.

Darian leaned against the far wall and wiped his forehead with his sleeve. "Damn hot in here," he said.

"Yeah, it's a scorcher," Sam answered, although he was not particularly warm. He maneuvered the boat into the slip, meanwhile calling out orders to Woodson, who pulled up the towline of the submersible.

Finally both craft were moored side by side.

"You all right?" Sam asked.

"Why wouldn't I be?" Darian barked.

"Okay. I'll go tie her up."

Darian heard the thumping of feet on deck, then felt the boat sway as the passengers disembarked.

When they were all well away, Darian emerged from the bridge. The wind was calm here, the sea blue and clear.

He stepped off the boat onto the dock. The rotting planks creaked beneath his shoes. On the shore he scooped up a handful of pebbles. Some of them were white. *Marble*, he thought. Marble in the Caribbean.

He let them sift through his fingers. With a sigh, he stuck his hands into his pockets and walked up toward the ruin of a house.

"Never thought I'd see this place again," he mumbled.

CHAPTER 8

DARIAN FOUND THE OTHERS STANDING IN THE RUBBLE OF WHAT HAD ONCE been the main room of the house. The end wall nearest the harbor had been torn out, and most of the roof had been destroyed by flames. Only a few charred beams were still in place.

The old man was seeing it for the first time. When he had come to reclaim his family, the fog had blessedly spared him the sight. But the place was plainly visible now. The speedboat had raced through the inlet, jumped the little strip of sand separating the house from the sea, and slammed into the wall. It had been carrying some sort of accelerant and had exploded on impact.

The heap of charred wood to Darian's left had been the dining tables. His son and his wife had been sitting there when they died.

Reba dabbed at her eyes with a handkerchief.

Woodson left the site without a word.

"We'll sleep on the boat tonight," Darian said thickly.

There was no disagreement.

After a moment, Sam clapped his hands. "All right. We might was well clear away this stuff, so we can stay on the island if we have to. We don't have much daylight left. And we've got to eat."

"There used to be an old wood-burning stove in the kitchen," Reba said. "If it still works, we can eat out here." She touched her fingers to her lips. "If that don't bother anybody."

"All's we got in the galley's a hotplate anyway," Darian said, picking up an armful of planks. "We'll take these down to the shore."

Sam and Cory did likewise. "On the way back, we'll get some of the provisions." Cory made a face. "Too bad it's all canned."

"I can catch some fish for us," Carol Ann volunteered.

"Give it a try," Sam said. "There are a couple of poles in the hold."

"Oh, I won't need those," the girl said, scampering off.

Sam watched her go. "Where's she from?"

"Philadelphia."

"That figures." Sam started down the hill. "Let's remember to bring a couple cans of corned beef hash."

On his fourth trip to the beach, Sam saw Woodson hauling a rowboat onto shore.

"Where'd you find that?" he asked.

"On the other side of the island. I remembered Bonner kept a few of them there, covered with tarps. This was the only one that stands a chance of staying afloat more than ten minutes."

With a final heave, Woodson grounded the boat. "I thought we might tow the sub to the other side of the island and submerge it." He made a small movement with his shoulder. "Just in case."

"In case someone comes after us?"

"Well, it's a possibility, isn't it? Here we are, right out in the open. I figure if for some reason we can't get to the boat, the six of us might be able to squeeze into the sub. At least for a few minutes," he added dubiously.

Sam smiled. "It's as good a plan as any. We'll tow the sub tonight."

By the time the sun had begun to set, Sam's muscles were twitching. He had not eaten or slept in two days, and was feeling punchy. With a grunt, he hoisted a canvas duffel bag filled with broken glass and debris over his shoulder. They would bury it all tomorrow.

At the site, Reba was sweeping the area clean. Below, Cory was staggering under the weight of a box filled with rubble as she followed Darian and Woodson, who carried a loaded tarp between them. They were all as grimy and sooty as chimney sweeps. Sam was making his way toward a section of beach as yet unfilled with detritus, when he caught sight of Carol Ann standing in a shallow lagoon, singing.

That's just great, he thought, feeling irritation well into anger. The rest of them were working their butts off while the flower child from Philadelphia was practicing arpeggios.

Then he saw, lying on the sand of the lagoon, a pile of fish.

There were at least a dozen of them, still wriggling with life as Carol Ann bent over, singing her wordless little tune, and snatched a shining grouper out of the water with her bare hands.

"I'll be damned," sam said, laughing. "A psychic fishing trip."

Hearing him, she looked up and waved, then gathered up the fish onto the wide apron of her shirt. When she reached the top of the hill, her cheeks were flushed.

"Think this is enough?" she asked, displaying her catch.

They ate sitting on the bare ground around the wood stove, which now stood incongruously in the middle of an empty plain, while around them the setting sun put on a grand show.

"I think that was the best meal I've ever eaten," Cory said, crumpling her paper plate into a ball and tossing it into the stove.

"Let's hope it's not the last," Darian growled.

"Now, you stop that," Reba chided. "We're going to be all right. You all know as well as me that we're meant to be here."

"I know no such thing," Darian said. "Truth be told, I think we're a bunch of damn fools sitting around waiting for somebody to use us for target practice."

"Why'd you bring us here, then?" Reba countered shrilly, setting her chin.

"Okay, guys," Sam interrupted. "There's no point in arguing about why we're here. The fact is, we *are* here, and we're going to stay here, at least until we come up with a better idea. So maybe we should quit bickering and go back to the boat."

They all lumbered to their feet, their exhaustion accentuated from sitting so long on the chilling ground. Sam helped Harry Woodson, whose crippled body refused to obey him.

"I think I'm going to need a few hours sleep before we tow the sub," Woodson said apologetically. "My joints aren't feeling so great."

"You'll get no argument from me, buddy." Sam worked his shoulder under Woodson's armpit and the two of them walked slowly toward the *Styx*.

"You were right to stop those two at dinner," Woodson said. "Still, I've been thinking the same kind of thing myself. We *are* waiting for something here. I don't know about the others, but I've been waiting for days, ever since—"

"The diamond," Sam finished for him.

"Yes. From the moment I first laid eyes on that rock, I've been . . . well, consumed is the word, I suppose, consumed with a need to finish that submersible. As soon as I put in the last bolt, I brought it to you."

"Just in time to save our lives."

"Exactly. It's as if pieces of a puzzle are falling into place at the precise moment when they're supposed to."

Woodson tried to move his nearly useless legs as Sam half carried, half dragged him toward the dock. "There's something else," the black man said. "I resigned from the museum."

"How'd you know we'd be leaving?"

"I didn't. I just knew it was time for whatever I'd been waiting for, and that whatever happened, I wasn't coming back."

"What do you mean?"

"I mean that for twenty-nine years I've lived in hiding, and I'm not going to hide anymore. If that means I get killed, I don't really care," Woodson said. "But I'm never going to take up that scared-rabbit life again. You're looking at a new man, Sam."

Sam shifted his weight beneath Woodson. "Weighs as much as the old one, though," he grunted.

Woodson laughed. "Let go. I think I can walk now." Wincing, he took a few tentative steps on the dock. "The sad thing is, it looks like we're the ones who've been chosen to fight whatever's coming. Some army, huh? A cripple, an old lady, a ninety-pound girl . . ."

Sam helped Woodson propel his ungainly body over the rail onto the deck of the boat. "I keep asking myself, why us?" the black man panted. "Why these particular six people?"

Sam looked at his hands. "I can't answer that, Harry. But I think it's right somehow."

"Yes. I feel that, too. Despite everything, this is the right place and we're the right ones to be here." His eyes shone. "Goddamn, I'm ready."

Sam slapped him gently on his bent back. "Get some sleep."

"We should go before dawn. St. James might already have sent someone out for a look."

"You got it. I'll wake you in a couple of hours."

Sam awoke at 2:45 with the music swelling around him.

For a moment, he lay curled in his blanket, listening, feeling Her, the siren in the sea, as She wound Herself around every molecule of his being.

Sam, you're close now, you're so close

What are you going to do to me? he silently asked.

Love you. I have always loved you. Always.

He felt his eyes cloud with tears.

Jesus, man, come off it, he told himself. He had a job to do. That was all. Tow the sub . . .

To the Peaks.

. . . to the other side of the island.

And then come back.

He got up and turned off the alarm he had set for 4 A.M.

After he had gathered up scuba gear for two, he woke Woodson. "Put your wet suit on under your clothes," he whispered, so as not to wake the others.

Woodson raised his eyebrows. He had not planned for them to enter the sub at all, but he did not argue. Sam usually had good reasons, even if he did not always articulate them well. Woodson put on the wet suit, then layered a heavy wool sweater and a pair of jeans over it.

Carrying the rest of their gear, they climbed quietly up onto the deck. A small light glowed in the bridge. Darian was awake.

"You going?" he asked.

"We'd better move the sub before daybreak."

"Be careful."

"Nothing to it."

"If you come back and I'm not here, stay put. I'll be back to get you."

"Sure thing, Darian."

The old man watched them step out onto the dock and head for the rowboat with the sub's towline. They fastened the line, pushed the rowboat into the water, then paddled into the darkness. Within a few minutes they were out of sight.

Darian stared out into the blackness of the night. *Will I ever see him again?* he asked himself. He had not gotten Sam away in time. He had hoped to protect the boy who had been sent to him as a second chance, but instead had brought him to the same place where his own son had died.

It did not matter now how that had happened. It made no difference that Darian knew, as did Reba and the others, that Memory Island was where they were all meant to be.

All he could think of now was that he had just given up his second son to the devil.

*   *   *

Woodson was a powerful rower, his oars cutting cleanly and quietly in the water.

"You tired yet?" Sam asked. "I can take over."

"I'm fine. You sure you know where we're going? I can't see behind me."

"I know. I've got a compass in my head."

"Yeah, well, I hope it's working. Because it seems like we've come out pretty far."

"We're almost there."

"If I'd known you wanted to stash it so far away, we could have ridden in the sub and towed the boat," Woodson complained.

"We need to save the sub's batteries."

"For what?"

"Want me to row?"

"I'll tell you when I'm tired, okay?" Woodson said irritably. He rowed in silence for another few minutes, then said, "I can't even see the island from here."

With his head, Sam gestured toward it.

"*Behind* us?" Woodson shouted. He laid down the oars. "You have got to be jerking me off."

Sam shook his head.

"We were supposed to take the sub to the other side of the damn island!"

Sam said nothing for a moment, then looked at him pleadingly. "I've got to dive the Peaks, Harry," he said quietly.

"*Now?*"

"Yes."

"Why?"

"I . . . I don't know. Something . . . someone is calling to me, Harry. It's music. The most beautiful music I've ever heard. And there's a woman's voice . . ."

"Oh, for chrissake," Woodson said.

"I won't be down long. Besides, that's what the sub's really for, isn't it? So that we can check out the place where I found the diamond?"

"The operative word here, Sam, is 'we.' Meaning I'm ostensibly a member of this diving team, too." Woodson's eyes bulged with outrage. "Now excuse me for being a stick in the mud, but I'm not really that thrilled about attempting a major exploration at the crack of dawn without so much as a map of the area."

"I told you. I can find it without a map."

"Not to mention all the seismic activity that's been occurring in the Peaks." Woodson looked around nervously. "Jesus H, even the Coast Guard's quit sending their boats out there. How far away is it, anyway?"

Sam sighed. "An hour. Maybe a little more."

"Good. We're turning back." He grabbed the oars.

"Harry, please." Sam touched Woodson's arm. "I've got to see the Peaks again." He strengthened his grip. "I've got to."

Woodson rolled his eyes. "So then why didn't you tell me back on the island? Or at least some time before we were five miles out to sea?"

"I didn't know then. At first, I just wasn't paying attention when you started going in the wrong direction. But then something inside me said, no, this isn't the wrong way, this is the *right* way, and you've got to keep going. . . ."

"To the goddamn Peaks."

"To the Peaks," Sam said softly.

"Where you got the Rapture."

"We have the sub now, Harry." He smiled. "Actually, we ought to give her a trial run, anyway."

Woodson's jaw tightened.

"Ten minutes, okay? I just want to go down for ten minutes. It'll be full light by the time we get there. Afterward, we'll bring her back to the far side of the island."

Woodson sighed. He drummed his fingers. He looked heavenward with disgust.

"Shit." He thrust the oars at Sam. "You row."

It was nearly five o'clock when Carol Ann sat bolt upright on the cot where she had been sleeping and ran barefoot up to the bridge.

Darian was fiddling with his radio, receiving nothing but static.

"They're coming," Carol Ann said breathlessly. "Lots of boats. Big ones, with guns and soldiers who kill for money. They're going to come onto the island. I saw them. . . ."

"Damned frequencies are jammed," Darian said, tossing down his headset. He looked at her, bleary-eyed. "What's this you're saying?"

"I had a dream, Mr. McCabe. Someone's coming for us."

Just then Reba entered the cabin. She was wearing one of Darian's old jackets over her dress. Cory was behind her.

"Mr. McCabe . . ."

"Don't you start, neither of you," Darian warned.

"Where's Sam and Harry?" Reba asked.

"They took that U-boat around to the other end of the island." He looked at his watch. "We'll give them ten more minutes. If they're not back by then, we'll leave without them."

"No," Reba said belligerently.

Darian met her eyes with equal ferocity. "Last time I checked, I was still captain here. I said we're leaving."

"We can't, Mr. McCabe." Reba's voice had softened. "It's got nothing to do with the boys. We were meant to be here. We got to stay."

"Reba, they're going to have guns," Carol Ann said. "I saw them. . . ."

"I did, too." Reba's chin quivered. "But we got to fight them here together."

"Bullcrap," Darian said. "If what you saw is true, we're getting the hell out of here." He started the boat's engine. "We'll pick up the boys on the far side of the island."

He pushed the throttle forward. Nothing happened. He threw the engine into reverse. He turned the wheel. The boat did not move.

"Damnation!" he muttered, smacking the helm.

"What is it?" Cory asked.

"Seaweed, most likely," Darian said. He turned off the ignition, then got up out of his chair with a sigh. "Something's got the propeller stuck. I'll have to go down and clean it up." He stomped down into the hold to put on his diving gear.

Twenty minutes later he was back on deck. "The propeller's been taken off," he said, unzipping his wet suit. "It's gone."

"You mean someone sabotaged it?" Cory asked.

"Looks that way. Must have happened while we were up on the island yesterday." He took off his flippers and threw them on the deck.

"It had to be that St. James," Carol Ann said. "Look, it's me he wants. The rest of you shouldn't have to go through this. When he comes . . ."

Darian waved her down. "It's not just you. Never was. Besides, it's too late to do anything about it now." Discarding his wet suit, he threw on his clothes. "Get some of these tools together," he ordered. "We'll have to build some kind of barricade on the island. No point in giving that turkey a clear shot at us."

He picked up two rifles. "Speaking of shooting, this is what we got in the way of weapons. Any of you ladies know how to use one of these?"

"I used to be pretty good with a squirrel gun," Reba said.

Darian tossed her one of the rifles. "Guess we better get moving," he said.

CHAPTER 9

ONCE THE EASTERN SKY BEGAN TO LIGHTEN, DAY BROKE FAST. BY THE TIME Sam set down his oars, the red ball of the rising sun was already tinting the ocean around them into a field of fire.

Woodson, who had been sitting silently for the past hour and a half with his arms crossed over his chest like an angry potentate, grudgingly took the oars.

"It's okay," Sam said, panting with exertion. "We're here."

Woodson looked around him. "How can you tell?"

Sam shrugged. "I just know."

Woodson shielded his eyes. "That a boat out there?"

"Yeah. Looks like a pleasure craft."

"Treasure hunters, no doubt," Woodson said. "Since the Coast Guard started coming here with the undersea eruptions, the papers have been dredging up the old stuff about the loot people found back in the sixties. I understand they've had their hands full rescuing idiots who've come diving out here unprepared." He looked pointedly at Sam.

Sam grinned and stood up in the rowboat. "Hello!" he called. There was no answer.

"If it's a diver, he's probably already down," he said. "I just didn't want to scare him."

"We probably won't even see him." Woodson pulled the towline until the submersible was alongside the rowboat. "He's too far away and we'll be on the bottom. Okay, let me brief you on how this thing works."

He pointed to a large riveted hatch on the top of the sub. "We get in and out through this escape hatch. Once we're inside, we secure the hatch and then kick on the pump switch. It's big and red, you can't miss it. It'll pump all the water out of the compartment. Then we can open the side door into the main section of the submersible. That's where we'll be for most of our ride."

"What about air?"

"I've rigged up an air recycling system, pumped up with some added oxygen. We should have enough to breathe down there for maybe five or six hours. After that, we'd have to breathe from our tanks and use the rest of our power to surface. The problem with submersibles, of course, is just like electric cars. The damned batteries don't last long enough. And half the weight of this machine is batteries. We'll be okay for ten minutes, though." He looked at Sam. "You did say you wouldn't be down for more than ten minutes."

Sam nodded reluctantly.

"We could do more if we had to," Woodson conceded.

Sam beamed. "If the sub works," he said.

"Guess we're going to find out." Woodson untied the towline, and he and Sam squeezed into the tight compartment. When the hatch was closed behind them, Sam felt a shudder of panic. After the brightening of morning, the little chamber was black as death and held precious little air.

Then Woodson flicked a switch and a small light, not much brighter than a night light, began to glow.

"That makes it homier, doesn't it?"

"Just like Grandma's."

Because the sub was still floating on the surface, no water was in the chamber so it was not necessary to use the pump. Instead, Woodson opened another hatch between the escape chamber and the main passenger compartment, reached inside, and tossed another switch to turn on the interior lights.

There were small fixed seats for two on either side of a long curved window which ran from the bow of the sub and down under it for almost half the craft's length.

Sam followed Woodson inside. After the hatch was closed and locked, they were sealed in the submersible's passenger section. Along the walls, Sam saw six scuba tanks and three sets of regulators and diving gear.

Sam settled into the seat alongside Woodson, who worked a series of switches on the control panel as the metal walls reverberated noisily.

"What the hell's that?"

"Relax. We're taking on water so we can dive," Woodson said. A moment later, the sub began to settle downward.

Through the curved glass, they watched the ocean around them grow darker with their increased depth. Then Woodson turned on a pair of outside spotlights, almost like a car's headlamps, and the scene lit up around them like a huge aquarium.

"How deep did you say this place was?" Woodson asked.

"About fifty feet, most of it. But I found a deep pocket. My gauge read a hundred fifty feet, but it might have been busted."

"Maybe not," Woodson said. "You're not the first to report pockets of that depth. That's why they call it the Devil's Triangle."

The devil lives here.

Sam shuddered.

Woodson turned on another switch. They felt, rather than heard, a small electric motor that propelled them forward as well as down.

"We watertight so far?" Woodson asked.

"No leaks that I can see."

Woodson turned out the interior cabin lights so that he and Sam could see without reflection into the ocean. They reached bottom in another ninety seconds, the depth meter registering forty-eight feet here.

"Any special direction you want to go?"

Sam was beginning to shiver. "No. You can just cruise."

"What are you looking for?" Woodson asked as he moved the craft gently forward.

"I'm hoping to recognize something from my last dive. There were two big long things, like columns . . . there!" he shouted excitedly.

"What's that?" Woodson asked, looking at the sea-encrusted cylinder on the seabed.

"The damnedest thing, Harry. Underneath all that coral and barnacle, it's metal. Man-made."

"Out here? Why didn't you tell me about this at the museum?"

"Go slow, now. When you reach the end of this one, we might find the other one. It's still standing. Or it was last week. . . ."

"I see it," Woodson said tensely. "I'll be damned."

"Whatever they are, they were buried until the bottom got pushed up during the seaquakes. This is where I found the pendant. And somewhere around here is the cave where I saw the volcano."

"Might be interesting to see what's in there now, without the Rapture working on you," Woodson said.

Sam turned to him. "Want to go swimming?"

Woodson laughed. "Best suggestion I've heard all day."

Together, Sam and Woodson swam toward the vertical metal column.

Things looked so different during the day, Sam thought. Although the sun was not high enough for its light to penetrate fully, the shapes of things were distinguishable, even away from the submersible's powerful lamps. There was none of the sinister mystery which had seemed to permeate the sea floor during his last dive.

Woodson, he could see, was jubilant. When they reached the column, he paddled around it like a fish, knocking it, holding his ear to it, then standing at its base, trying to take a measure of its immense diameter by comparing it with his outstretched arms.

The sight was startling. Under the pressure of the ocean, the nitrogen bubbles that were permanently in Woodson's joints shrank. Here his twisted body now stood straight and tall.

The sea owns him, Sam thought. *She crippled him, but he keeps coming back. Because when he's with her, she makes him whole again.*

He thought of his own siren who lived in the sea. He could hear her music now; it had been welling in his blood since before he awakened.

Is that what you're going to do with me—make it so that nothing's any good without you, so that I stay down longer and longer until one day I just don't come up at all?

He did not have time to listen for an answer. Inches from his head, something sped past and slammed into the column near Woodson. As it drifted toward the bottom, Sam recognized it as a spear just like the ones Woodson had used to kill the gunmen on board the *Styx*.

He spun around. Two divers were heading out of a ledge of coral toward them. Sam and Woodson both began swimming toward the submersible, but the other two had a better angle. Before Sam could reach the hatch, another spear flew at him from less than twenty feet away.

Collapsing his body sideways, he managed to avoid the hit. *St. James's men*, he thought. How long had they been here? How many speedboats like the one he had seen topside were dotted around the area of the Peaks, with divers below paid to kill him?

As the diver tried to reload the speargun from a pack at his side, Woodson swam toward him, pulling out the utility knife he kept strapped to his leg.

Seeing Woodson's powerful speed, the diver jabbed the spear in his hands at him, but Woodson's arms were too strong. He grabbed the spear with his free hand and yanked the driver toward him. With one stroke, Woodson cut the man's air hose.

A gush of white bubbles rose immediately around both men. The diver panicked, kicking up silt and mud in his rush to get away, but Woodson held him fast. Sam took out his own knife and turned in a full circle, looking for the other diver, but he was nowhere in sight.

He motioned for Woodson to come back. If they could reach the sub, they would be able to outrun a single diver, speargun or no.

But Woodson was not paying attention to anything except the diver he held tightly in his grip. While Sam swam over to them, Woodson reached over with his knife once more and cut the man's throat. Then, before the inky fluid and the churning mud completely obscured his vision, he brought the knife down again.

He's losing it, Sam thought. For Woodson, these were the same men who had attacked him underwater nearly thirty years ago. He wasn't going to stop until every drop of blood had left the man's body.

And maybe not even then.

Sam propelled himself, blind, into the thick murk, grabbed what he hoped was Woodson's knife arm, and pulled it back toward the safety of the submersible.

He pushed Woodson into the open hatch and was coming in behind him when another spear hammered alongside his head.

The impact knocked Sam forward and slammed the hatch shut. Dazed, he sank slowly to the ocean floor. He could see the blood from the wound above his ear floating past his eyes, but he felt somehow disconnected to it, as if his body no longer belonged to him. The steady hiss and churn of air from his tanks was hypnotic.

Sam . . .

Slowly he turned his head to look through the muddy water. Ahead, he could discern the shape of the dead diver on the feathery ocean floor. Already the sea was claiming the man, covering his body with silt. Beyond it lay a cave.

A cave glowing with a soft green light.

Yes, he thought. I knew I would find it again.

Now, Sam. Come to me now.

The music touched him like a kiss, then enveloped him. Nothing could harm him, no one could invade the glorious space around him. She was there, so close now, so very close.

Effortlessly he rolled away from the sub and began to swim.

Inside the escape chamber, Woodson had to lock the hatch and then wait for agonizingly long seconds while the pump ejected the water from the small compartment.

You're not getting away this time, you bastard, he thought, slamming his fist against the wall. *Not this time.* Then he opened the other hatch to the passenger cabin, snatched his own speargun, and reversed the entire process.

By the time Woodson got back outside, he could see no one. The sea around the sub was a thick, dark muddy soup.

He swam cautiously away from the lights, hoping the second diver would show himself in them. As he moved, a long shape brushed against him, touching the back of his hand with its sandpaper skin.

Shark.

Fear rushed through him as the fifteen-foot-long creature glided past without interest.

It was a tiger shark. Even in the muddy water, its striped markings were visible as it weaved sinuously toward the dead diver and the cloud of blood around him. It must have sensed the blood almost as soon as it was spilled, Woodson realized, regretting his rash action. At the time, he had only wanted to kill the man. He had not considered the possibility of drawing sharks.

Now the blood would bring yet more predators. And Sam was somewhere in the water.

With its wedge-shaped head, the shark nudged the body once, twice, waiting for it to move. Sharks would eat a corpse, Woodson knew, but they preferred their prey lively. They were equipped with electroreceptors which enabled them to pick up even the tiniest nerve twitch or muscle movement in the darkest water. A bleeding, frightened man was a perfect dinner.

Oh, Jesus, Sam, get over here.

Out of the corner of his eye, Woodson saw a small movement off to his left, beyond the stern of the sub. Instinctively he rolled into a ball as a spear whizzed nearby and struck the sub with an audible *chunk*.

The shark looked over at the sound, its round doll-eyes gleaming yellow.

But Woodson was no longer watching the shark. Steadying himself, he aimed his own speargun at the swimming figure, and fired.

The spear struck the man in the thigh. Dropping his own gun, he rolled over in the water, pulling at the shaft as ribbons of blood circled around him.

Woodson knelt on the bottom, preparing to fire a second time, when the shark left the dead diver and shot forward.

With a single snap, it bit off the wounded diver's leg. A stream of bubbles shot upward as the man's mouthpiece fell out and he screamed silently into the water.

The shark propelled him, still screaming, toward the light of the sub's headlamps. Woodson recoiled in horror at the sight of the diver's flailing body folded over the shark's snout as they swam together in a grim dance, with banners of blood and white bubbles trailing behind them.

Sam! he wanted to scream. *Where the hell are you?*

In the full light of the headlamps, the shark flung the diver aside. Woodson watched as it hesitated momentarily, then lunged, its triangular teeth exposed, to tear out the man's belly.

And then the others came.

The second shark was larger, close to twenty feet. Two others, young by their clear markings, followed behind. The big tiger nosed the first away, claiming the food as its own, but the original hunter was already crazed with blood. It spun around and tore a massive chunk out of the big shark's flank. The younger sharks joined in, now also intoxicated with the wild smell of death, indifferent to their own safety, intent only on feeding, as into the light swam four other sharks.

Oh, Jesus, Sam . . .

There was nowhere to go except inside the sub. As it was, the sharks might well attack it, too—in a feeding frenzy, they would bite anything, including metal and plastic—but Woodson knew he had no chance outside it, and it would be no more than a matter of seconds before one of them noticed him.

Don't come around now, buddy, he thought as he swam slowly upward toward the hatch. *Wherever you are, wait this out. I'll find you, I promise.*

Trying to keep his movement steady and slow, he released the hatch and crawled inside.

From behind the curved glass of the window, he watched as the sharks tore into one another, flopping and swirling in their crazed, mindless destruction.

Woodson felt a sinking feeling in the pit of his stomach. Sam was still out there. And then he forced himself to admit another possibility: *He's already dead.*

If he was, Woodson knew, it would be his fault.

Sam had brought him to the sub after he had killed the diver and had probably closed the hatch over Woodson because the second man was coming close.

And Woodson, instead of coming back out for Sam immediately, had wasted time getting a weapon.

He grasped his elbows. Without the pressure of the water on them, his joints were already beginning to ache.

My fault.

It had been stupid, selfish. He had left Sam alone and defenseless against a trained killer with a speargun, just because he could not bear the thought of letting the man get away.

"My fault," he whispered.

Then he saw it, some distance beyond the sharks: a cave mouth, glowing with the same phosphorescent light he had seen in the big diamond. And swimming toward it, illuminated by the faint green radiance, was a man.

"Sam!" Woodson shouted inside the sub.

Sam was swimming with such slowness that he seemed to be drifting, but it was not a dead man's float; Woodson could see the steady movement of flippers and a rhythmic exhalation of air.

Manipulating his stiff fingers as fast as he could, Woodson switched on the electric motor and eased the sub forward.

The sharks noticed. One of them darted toward him and thumped its snout on the sub's metal skin. The sub jerked slightly but remained undamaged. The other sharks spared it no more than an incurious glance, returning to feed on the carcasses of the two divers and the big tiger shark.

Woodson hoped the sub-attacker would lose interest and go back with the others, but it remained with the craft, swimming circles around the sub's nose, occasionally fixing Woodson with its big, dead-looking eyes.

"Get away," he muttered, slowing the sub even more. The last thing he wanted was to lead the shark to Sam. He veered the submersible away. "Come on, baby, follow me. . . ."

But the shark had sensed the moving flippers on the man near the cave. Its interest in the sub vanished utterly as its long upper tail lobe thrust powerfully in a burst of speed.

"Oh, God, no!" Woodson shouted, rising out of his seat. "Sam!"

Sam looked back, almost as if he had heard him. His expression was bewildered, like that of a man who had just been awakened from a dream. With a glance, he took in the sub, Woodson inside it, and then the shark coming at him like an arrow. His body arced in pure terror. Hands splayed, he cast about wildly.

Woodson strapped his tank back on, reloaded his speargun, and headed for the compartment with the hatch. A few moments later, he was outside and swimming toward the cave mouth.

The circling shark was some fifty feet from Sam and moving fast, while Sam seemed to be frozen in one spot. He turned his face toward the cave, then to the shark, then back to the cave.

Woodson shot one spear, but he was too far away. It bounced off the shark's tough skin like a rubber toy.

Get out of there, Sam, he pleaded silently, slicing through the water as fast as he could. *At least give me a chance to catch up with you.*

The shark swam closer.

Sam took a final look at the cave, then swam inside.

The shark was right behind him.

Jesus! Woodson thought. The cave would be like a barrel for the shark. It would nose Sam against a wall and finish him then and there. By the time Woodson could get there, Sam would be a drifting pile of raw meat.

Why'd you go in? he screamed inside his head. *Why in God's name did you have to go inside?* The seconds it took Woodson to arrive at the mouth of the cave seemed like hours. When he did, his speargun was ready. He had one shot; he knew it had better take. And then, if he killed the shark, he would bring what was left of Sam's body back to Memory Island.

Another death.

As he approached, the cave dimmed, as if whatever current had illuminated it had suddenly shut off. Woodson turned on his own safety light, raising and lowering it over the entrance. He had expected a storm of swirling silt, but there was nothing. The place was as calm as an underwater lagoon.

Slowly he swam inside, pressing the light against his speargun. The light fell on the shallow walls, crusted with lichen. On the sea floor, grasses waved with the soft current.

It was empty.

THE FOREVER LAND

He swam toward the light.

Yes.

Her voice, clear as bright water, guided him upward through the music.

Light . . . lighter . . .

He broke through the surface of the calm sea. And gasped.

He was there, in the place he had seen inside the cave. In the distance, two pyramids rose out of the green land, flanking a mountain whose flat top seemed dimmed by low clouds.

A volcano.

"My God," Sam whispered.

Then he saw a shark's dorsal fin break the water and make a large lazy circle around him.

The shark from the Peaks. It had followed him here.

Sam turned with it, watching its movements. He was reaching for the knife that was strapped to his leg when he heard a shout.

A large wooden sailing ship moved by so closely that Sam might have collided with it. Men stood on deck, watching him, watching the shark. Then one man strode forward, past the others, to stand at the rail.

Darian?

No, of course not. Sam thought in a welter of confusion. The man did not look anything like Darian, except for his granite-hard eyes.

Where was he?

In the moment it took Sam to unsheath his knife, the man held up what looked like a spear and threw it, the muscles in his right arm bulging, directly over Sam's head.

And then Sam saw that the weapon had not been a spear. Its three prongs quivered deep inside the shark's body as the creature thrashed in its death throes: a trident.

Dropping the knife, Sam swam quickly from the spreading circle of the tiger shark's blood toward the shore, but before he managed a dozen strokes, he felt a rope net dropping over him.

A moment later, he was hauled from the water like a giant fish, pulled to the deck of the big wooden ship, and dropped there.

The granite eyes gazed down at him.

"Where am I?" Sam demanded.

The sailor regarded him impassively. Then he turned to bark orders at his crew in a language Sam could not understand.

Except for one word. Sam had recognized a single, shocking word.

For what the man had said was in a language long forgotten: "Move on smartly, boys. On to Atlantis."

Atlantis.

Sam had arrived at his genesis.

CHAPTER 1

It began with a stranger.
With a stranger shall it begin again.

THE WORDS ETCHED ON THE GIGANTIC STONE PYRAMID SHONE CLEAR IN the bright sunlight.

Athena felt the heat beneath the thick silver headband she wore, but gave no indication of her discomfort. She was a princess of the royal line of Atlantis, attending the funeral of a hero. She would not sweat.

She stood on a balcony built into the front of the massive pyramid. Before her, past three perfect concentric circles of canals, the turquoise sea lapped gently onto the sand.

To her left, across the channel known as the River Styx, the Land of the Dead awaited its newest resident.

The dead possessed a pyramid of their own, identical to the other except for its truncated top where a slave now knelt, his head covered, his hands bound, awaiting impassively the sacrificial knife of the high priest.

The high priest Hades—who was, to Athena's perpetual dismay, her uncle—was mounting the thousand steps to the pyramid's apex. His face was covered by a huge and grotesque mask of red and gold, bounded by feathers. The slave would look upon that mask before he died. It would be the last thing he would ever see.

Athena turned away.

Beside her, Rhea, mother of the king, wept openly as the gilded funeral barge came into view. It was no secret that even before her husband, Cronus, had been deposed as king and exiled, Rhea had loved Prometheus. Even now, though Prometheus had been a commoner, she felt no shame in weeping at his passing.

The barge bearing Prometheus's body was flanked by drummers on either side of the canal, beating the slow, deep rhythm of a heartbeat. As the boat passed below her, Athena searched the crowd of mourners for the tall figure of Poseidon with his unkempt mane of curly gray hair, but there was no sign of him.

He'll be furious to have missed it, she thought. Her uncle Poseidon, of

189

all people, should have been present. He was the one who had brought Prometheus's body home, despite accusations that, as a traitor, the old soldier had no right to burial. Poseidon had fought that edict tooth and nail, finally getting his way only by giving his own tomb to house Prometheus's remains.

He could do whatever he wished with his chamber in the death pyramid, Poseidon had argued. And what he wished was to give it to the man who had been his second in command, along with all the pomp that would have been accorded Poseidon's own passing. The fact that Prometheus had been a common soldier born in a hut meant nothing to Poseidon. His friend would be given a prince's funeral.

"Make clear the path!" The aged boatman, Charon, shouted the words which had begun every royal funeral procession for the past thousand years. "For one of the Royal House passes on his way to eternity!"

Athena knew that both Prometheus and Poseidon would have had a good laugh over that. But to the common populace, it was a rare and wonderful thing that one of their own had ascended, even if in death, to the heights of the king-gods.

And so the commoners, who usually attended royal funerals only as entertainments, stood in silence, their heads bowed, as the funeral barge floated past.

Even the slaves, who silently rejoiced at the deaths of their captor-princes, halted their work and crept out of doors, venturing as close to the barge as they dared in order to catch a glimpse of the man who had died giving fire to the world.

For that, in the slaves' minds, was what Prometheus had done. It was of no importance that he had only lighted one torch to keep an injured slave woman and her children from freezing, or that even the most primitive tribes on the two continents flanking the islands of Atlantis already knew the use of fire. For them, the story had already reached mythic proportions. And the outcome had been the same as if he had indeed bestowed a divine gift upon the savages of the lands from which these slaves had come: Prometheus had been executed by his own countrymen for showing compassion to beings the Atlanteans did not consider human.

From the far fields of the plain, a lone slave began to sing. It was a song from the eastern mainland, perhaps from the very land where Prometheus had died. The even rhythm of the funeral drums accentuated the simple melody and strange words which carried to the mourners on the wind.

> The wind blows
> And we are scattered like seeds
> To clutch the Earth,
> To bloom for a moment,
> To die like dust in the wind.
> And the wind blows . . .

Someone near her in the royal mourning party picked up the song. It was her brother Apollo, his voice sweet and pure as a bell, his eyes half-closed as the breeze caressed his blond curls. He meant no disrespect for the soul of Prometheus by his singing. Athena was sure he was not even aware of what he was doing. He so rarely was.

Next to him, his twin sister, Artemis, looked fiercely ahead at the funeral barge, her hand held in a fist over her heart. If Artemis had not been a woman, she would have been the greatest of warriors. Her salute to Prometheus was a mark of respect for a man who had proven himself in battle over a span of more years than most people lived.

Near Apollo stood the black man called Hephaestus, the great builder and engineer. Like so many others, he owed his life to Prometheus.

As an infant, Hephaestus had "fallen" from the high priest's hands during his naming ceremony. Later, Hades would claim that the accident had been an act of the gods demonstrating that the brown-skinned son of the king and his African concubine was not welcome in the land of the living. But while the child had lain bleeding on the floor, Prometheus, alone among all the multitude who watched, had defied the priests' gods by picking up the baby and taking him to his mother.

Hephaestus's bones had been broken too badly to heal perfectly. He had grown up crippled and in pain. Yet the mind of this bent, slow-moving man had designed the strongest dams, the swiftest ships, the most sophisticated metalwork in the world.

But his greatest accomplishments, the one by which Hephaestus would be remembered to the end of time, were the pyramids.

They were marvels, these two structures whose floors hung as cantilevers from a central metal column anchored deep in the rock of Mount Olympus. Unearthly in their austere beauty, they had been built to last forever.

Two of them, Athena thought as the high priest reached the top of the thousand steps. Below him, the shining stone surface of the pyramid was streaked with brown blood. *One a king's palace, the other a sacrificial altar.*

Her eyes filled with tears of anger. To use Hephaestus's masterpiece as a killing ground was an obscenity.

T hings had not always been so. There was a time, long before Athena's birth, when no blood was spilled in the name of the gods.

But then, in those days there had only been one god, and She was a woman.

Athena had learned the legends from her mother, whose family had followed the old ways. Not many did anymore. Most of the citizens of Olympus did not even know the origin of the words on the great palace pyramid.

It began with a stranger. . . .

They had been the dying words of that same Stranger. The priestesses of the temple of Gaea had preserved the ancient paper on which they had been written for more than a thousand years. They had revered him as the true husband of Gaea, spirit of the Earth.

But the priestesses were all dead now. Their temple had been razed to the ground more than forty years ago. Gaea Herself had fallen out of favor, replaced by the stern religion of the god-kings. Now that her mother was dead, almost no one except Athena ever thought about the Stranger.

The Stranger. How fitting that he should have had no name.

He had no history, either. In the legends, he simply had come out of the void to shape the great civilization of Atlantis with the knowledge brought from his unknown land and by the Power held in his mind.

He could see into the future, the legends said. He could heal with a touch. He could discern a person's thoughts. This was the Power.

From his seed had come all the great kings of Atlantis: Atlas, Oceanus, Uranus, Cronus, many others.

To them he gave his knowledge, the tools to change Atlantis from a primitive island of half-humans into the glory of the world. The early kings developed wheat, domesticated animals, learned to forge metal out of ore, brought farming to a new level of productivity. They built ships which opened up the world to them, produced books which passed on the truths of science and mathematics to future generations, created music, fostered painting and architecture, invented devices which allowed them to examine the stars themselves.

But he had not bequeathed the Power to them. That he had given only to the goddess worshippers and their offspring, and they had guarded their secrets well. It was only in the temple of Gaea that the great crystals, resonating with the sounds and colors that could heal the sick or ease the troubled mind, could be found. It was only through the priestesses that the souls of the dead could be recalled. Only the women who served the goddess knew how to divine what was to come, and the place of mankind within All That Was.

Perhaps they should not have kept their secrets, Athena thought.

In time, the kings grew to discount the Power held by these women. They formed another religion in which their own ancestors, the deceased kings of Atlantis, were worshipped as the creators of the universe. After all, they had created everything of importance, they said. The king-gods brought wealth and peace and dominion over all other lands on Earth. They ensured lives of comfort and refinement for Atlanteans by providing foreign slaves to perform tedious work. Their concern was with the present world and its inhabitants, not some vague, all-encompassing cosmos which depended on the myth of a nameless man and his make-believe magic to exist.

People liked the new religion. Eventually, the priestesses were regarded as foolish women and their goddess the outdated remnant of a primitive time. And when Gaea the Earth spirit first grumbled that she was displeased, a slave was sacrificed to the king-gods, who silenced her.

CHAPTER 2

As THE DEATH BOAT BEARING PROMETHEUS'S BODY TOUCHED THE SHORE OF the Land of the Dead, all heads turned toward the thundering of hoofbeats.

Poseidon galloped a white stallion right up to the edge of the crowd at the base of the royal pyramid, then dismounted in a cloud of dust. He was dirty, still dressed in the short tunic of a seaman. Athena smiled. Her uncle had no doubt jumped directly from his ship onto the waiting horse.

Across the narrow channel, the priests lifted Prometheus's body from the boat. The drumbeats stopped, and in a voice that echoed over the crowd, Hades began to intone the prayer for the dead.

Poseidon's jaw clenched as he entered the balcony to join the family.

Hades had issued the order to kill Prometheus. Poseidon did not relish the idea of his friend's murderer praying piously over his body, but he took some satisfaction in knowing that Hades probably loathed having to do the praying.

But he did not regret for an instant having given up his own burial tomb. If there was such a thing as eternity, he wanted his brother Hades to spend it in the chamber next to Prometheus. At least then the old soldier would have a chance to get even.

A harsh chuckle rose in Poseidon's throat. *I wish I could see that*, he thought.

Beside him, Athena nudged him gently.

"Sorry," he whispered. "I was just thinking about Prometheus and Hades meeting in the afterlife."

She smiled and shook her head. "Uncle, you're incorrigible," she whispered back.

"Did you miss me while I was gone?"

"Terribly."

"Good. I brought back a gift for you. A man."

Athena slitted her eyes. Poseidon had been teasing her about her unmarried state for years. "I pulled him out of the sea myself. A most unusual type. He had the skin of a seal." He grinned, then saw his mother Rhea looking at him with eyes like steel daggers. Poseidon cleared his throat and arranged his face into a look of proper solemnity while Hades finished his droning prayer.

On the top of the death pyramid, two priests held the slave over the sacrificial block. He screamed, trying to resist, but the priests kept him down. Then Hades stepped forward, his knife held high. He plunged the blade into the slave's chest and brought out a still-beating heart.

Even Athena's presence could not mitigate the disgust Poseidon felt. In a lifetime at sea, he had watched countless men die, both on water and on land, but even in the most savage hinterlands he had never seen death administered with the inventive cruelty of Hades and his priests.

The crowd below let out a roar of approval. They loved the sacrifices. Since Hades had become high priest, the practice had grown to new heights. Even a commoner's wedding required at least one sacrifice. A royal marriage demanded a dozen or more. The birthday of one of the king-gods used scores. And for the great festivals, the pyramid in the Land of the Dead ran red for days on end.

Poseidon spat over the side of the balcony.

When the dead slave's body ceased twitching, Prince Ares, dressed in bronze battle gear and wearing a high crested helmet, stepped out onto the altar and accepted the heart from Hades's hands.

Strutting young butcher, Poseidon thought miserably.

Hades had issued the order to kill Prometheus, but it had been Ares who carried it out. He had tied the solider's wrists and ankles to stakes set into the ground beside a boulder, then slit Prometheus's belly so that the blood would draw predators. By the time Poseidon arrived, vultures had already plucked out Prometheus's eyes. His entrails had been eaten by wolves.

Poseidon found himself shaking with rage all over again as he watched the priests carry the coffin into the pyramid. *Ah, Prometheus, how could you die and leave me with this piranha as my second in command?*

It was inevitable now. As the king's eldest able-bodied son, Ares would take over Prometheus's position as land forces comander. There would be no shortage of slaves for Hades's sacrifices anymore. Worse, unless the king named another successor before his death, Ares would one day inherit the throne.

The gods help us all, he thought.

Athena saw the look of distress on her uncle's face and offered him her hand, cool and steady.

Poseidon regarded her calm features with admiration. *Now if this one were only a man,* he mused. There would be no question about naming an heir then. Athena was intelligent, level-headed, and serious. Though the king met daily with his council, it was not to them he turned when he wrestled with a particularly difficult problem, but to Athena. She spoke little, listened much, and understood everything.

And she could fight, too, Poseidon remembered with a smile. When Athena had first arrived in Olympus from the Atlantean out-island where she had been raised, she presented herself to her father the king wearing a breastplate and carrying a spear and shield. The court ladies had been shocked, but from that moment the king—and Poseidon, too—had loved her.

Yes, this is a ruler born.

A above them, a banner bearing the blue encircled cross of Atlantis unfurled to signal that the king was to appear, ending the funeral rites. The king ruled over the living; the time for the dead was over. Athena stepped back with the others to make way for her father and his wife, Hera, as the crowd below cheered.

Hera was vacantly beautiful. Next to her, the king looked like an old man.

He's dying, Athena thought.

When she first came to Olympus to meet the king, she had expected the exuberant, dynamic man her mother had talked about so often during their long years of exile. From the moment of his ascension, Metis had told her daughter, she had known that he was to be the greatest king Atlantis had ever produced.

Because none of the king-gods had ever possessed the Power.

None, until this one.

Until Zeus. The Thunderer.

On the day he took the crown, those of the old religion had fallen on their knees with gratitude to the Earth spirit Gaea. Here at last was the amalgam of heaven and earth: a king in whose body pulsed the pure blood of the Stranger.

Others carried the Power in their blood, Athena knew, even though the kings never had. She herself did, as had her mother Metis. Through the years after she had been forced to leave Atlantis, Metis trained her daughter in the use of the Power just as she had trained her to weave and read and throw a spear.

"You will find others like you in Olympus," Metis had told her. *"They have come to be with your father, drawn by the Eye of Zeus."*

She was referring to the massive diamond the king wore as a symbol of his office. Said to have been carved by the Stranger's own hands, every king of Atlantis had worn it. But only for Zeus had it come to life.

The stone had glowed upon his chest, Metis remembered, from the moment it first touched him. And with its indescribable fire it had drawn from others, as himself, a Power beyond anything human. Her mother's prediction had proven to be true. After Metis's death, Athena had returned to Atlantis to find the family she had never known, and with them, a wellspring of the Power.

Here she had met her half brother Apollo, with whom she could communicate without a word being spoken, even over long distances. And Rhea, the queen who had given birth to her son alone, in a forest, because she had seen death waiting for the infant in the royal palace. Athena had come to love Hephaestus, whose genius was so deep that it went beyond mere intellect, and Poseidon, who could sail any sea without a map or a compass.

But her greatest feelings of tenderness were for her father, the king. Because by then the Power he had been born with had already deserted him.

With a stranger shall it begin again. . . .

He was to have fulfilled the cryptic prophecy kept so long by the priestesses of Gaea. The people looked to him as the great king who would join the old religion with the new, and make Atlantis whole again. He was to have been the Stranger come back to life.

For a time, perhaps, he might have believed it himself.

He had been magnificent, a lion of a man with flowing auburn hair and the fire of the universe in his eyes. Under his leadership, Atlantis underwent a renaissance of art and technology. Beautiful new buildings graced the elegant streets of the capital city of Olympus. With his brother Poseidon, Zeus sailed uncharted seas to explore new lands, which he assimilated into the empire with the enthusiasm of a father welcoming a new child. Through new, far-seeing trade policies, he changed the face of the world. Mainland outposts once used only to harvest slaves were transformed into settlements where Atlantean tools and grain were traded for local ore, animals, and labor.

For the first time in more than five centuries, foreign workers came voluntarily to Atlantis. During their stay, which was limited to a year, they were well fed and housed, given medical care and educated. Then they returned to their homelands, respected and knowledgeable about the island archipelago where the gods lived.

Athena bowed her head. Those days were long past. She was grateful that Metis had never learned the truth, that one by one, Zeus's progressive trade policies had been reversed. That within half a year of Metis's banishment, slavery had resumed. That the world no longer regarded Atlantis as a land of gods, but of demons.

Zeus had not been the Stranger come back to life. To look at him now, he was hardly even a king. His broad back was bent, as if it carried an invisible weight upon it. His hair had turned white. The eyes Metis had remembered, filled with the fire of the Power inside him, were weak and rheumy. Even the amulet he wore, the fabled Eye of Zeus, had lost its dazzling brilliance. It hung around his thin neck like a worthless piece of rock.

Zeus the Thunderer, Athena thought sadly. *A dying god in a dying land.*

As the king and his wife waved to the crowd, the Earth began to shake.

In the city square surrounding the palace, the crowd of people who had come to watch the funeral threw themselves on the ground. Poseidon ran down the steps for his horse, which shied and whinnied, its eyes rolling wildly. Across the canal, on the pyramid in the Land of the Dead, the sacrificed slave's body tumbled off its pedestal and fell with a thud to the stone pavement.

On the balcony, Queen Hera shrieked and ran inside. Athena's eyes flickered over to her.

How could Zeus have discarded my mother for her? she thought with contempt.

Earthquakes were no longer uncommon in Atlantis. The tremors that weakened the buildings and broke the dams around Olympus had been going on for decades, but they had grown much worse in recent months. The sturdy mud-brick homes of the farmers now tumbled down with dismaying regularity. A special contingent of soldiers had been formed expressly for the purpose of putting out the fires that followed each quake. The pyramids themselves, though Hephaestus had built them too well to be damaged, were now often surrounded by a soggy mire.

The words echoed through Athena's mind: *a dying land.*

Beside her, King Zeus staggered on his feet as the tremor shook the very foundations of the huge pyramid, but he kept his arms upraised and his head high, as if a mere earthquake meant nothing to him. Within a few seconds, all was silent again. Slowly the people in the square got to their feet and saw the figure of the king, immovable and permanent as the sun in the sky, silently willing their fear away.

They went wild in a frenzy of adoration for him, shouting and throwing their hats in the air as they knelt in fealty to the white-haired ruler who, surely, would deliver them from harm.

"How I love you," Athena whispered.

She saw that his eyes were filled with tears.

CHAPTER 3

THE COMMONERS MOVED ASIDE AS ATHENA AND POSEIDON, LEADING HIS horse, made their way from the large plaza toward the royal park.

"Give an old man a few minutes," he said, smiling.

"I have all the time in the world," Athena said.

Her uncle sighed. "Unfortunately, I do not. After the council meeting—which I insist you attend, if for no other reason than to keep me from strangling Hades with my bare hands—the king will want to hear about my last voyage. I probably won't see you again for days."

Athena gave him a wry smile. The old sailor had women waiting for him in every city in Atlantis, and he was doubtless eager to visit them all. "I think you'll manage," she said, stroking the stallion's nose.

"Don't be pert." On the crest of the hill in front of them appeared a line of men in shackles, flanked at intervals by soldiers. "Damn," Poseidon muttered. "I was hoping you wouldn't have to see this."

Athena sighed. "The slaves would still exist, whether I saw them or not."

They waited in silence as the captives crossed in front of them on their way to the canal. From there they would be taken to the prison inside the death pyramid.

They were broken men, snatched from their homelands, brought starving and nearly naked to die horrible deaths for the glory of Atlantean gods whose names they did not know. Some of the prisoners were shaking with fever; others showed wounds which were already festering.

"They need medical attention," Athena said. "I can help them. Apollo and I—"

Poseidon shook his head. "Don't even bother hoping. Hades won't let anyone into the Land of the Dead. And it's just as well you don't know what goes on there."

The bystanders coming from the funeral jeered the foreign slaves. Children threw stones at them. As the slaves moved along, the Atlanteans turned up their noses or grimaced with the stink of the savages.

Poseidon pointed to the end of the line, at a slave with close-cropped hair. "That's the one I was telling you about, by the way. We removed the seal skin from him, along with a number of strange objects. I think he may be a spy."

"You'll never know."

"Why not? He may talk."

"There wouldn't be any point in it. He knows we'll kill him anyway. That's what we do to all foreigners in Atlantis."

"That's enough, Athena," the sailor said irritably.

Just then a stocky farmer, arrayed in his finest tunic, cleared his throat and spat in the face of the short-haired slave. The captive tried to make a retaliatory move, but the soldiers guarding him yanked the chains binding his wrists. He cried out in pain.

"Stop," Athena called. "Halt the line, Uncle."

The guard looked beseechingly at Poseidon, who shrugged. "Halt the line," he shouted. At the sound of his voice, the entire procession ground to a standstill.

Athena walked over to the farmer, her angry gaze boring through him.

"It is no more than a quirk of fate that you are not in this man's place," she said coldly.

The top of the farmer's bald head flushed crimson as he fell to his knees. He had been perfectly within his rights to spit on the slave, of course. But he had not thought that the Princess Athena would see him.

"Forgive me, my lady," he begged.

Athena turned from him and looked at the slave. The guards were still struggling to hold him back from the fat farmer, whom he regarded with blazing hatred.

Athena tore the hem of her dress and reached over to wipe the spittle from his cheek. As she approached, the slave turned his head toward her. He met her eyes straight on.

It felt like a hammer blow, that look. Athena stepped back suddenly, her breath caught in her chest. For in the slave's eyes was something like . . . *recognition*. Her mouth opened. The pounding of her heart was so loud she could hear it.

"Athena?" It was Poseidon, frowning, looking from her to the foreign slave. "What—"

Abruptly she handed the scrap of cloth to a guard. "Clean him off," she ordered. Then, careful not to look at the slave again, she walked quickly away.

"Take this one to the palace and have him prepared to meet the king's council," Poseidon ordered the guard. After the line shuffled forward once again, he walked his horse through the gates into the park. Athena was far ahead of him.

"If you go any faster, I'll have to ride to catch up with you," he called.

Finally she stopped and sat on a bench to wait for him. When he reached her, Athena's eyes were wide and frantic.

"Gods above, what's happened to you? Are you not well?"

"I'm—" She swallowed. "I'm fine, Uncle. Now that it's stopped."

"Now that what's stopped?"

"The . . ." She caught herself. "Nothing. Some random thoughts. Nothing." She smiled and squeezed Poseidon's hand.

She had not realized until she spoke that what had filled her mind since she had first seen the slave was music.

Music, as wild and strong as the sea.

CHAPTER 4

THE SOLDIER PRODDED HIM WITH THE POINT OF A SPEAR. SAM JERKED FOR-
ward, toward the gleaming white pyramid on the far side of the plaza.

A pyramid, he thought.

This was a dream. There was no question about that. What he needed
to know was how to wake up.

Because it was clearly no ordinary dream. As fantastic as the events in
it had been, he could account for every minute. Well, almost every minute.
He had passed out on the deck of the weird-looking ship, he remembered
that. When he had come to, he was somewhere in the hold, lying on straw
filthy with excrement and vomit, surrounded by men chained as he was.

Suddenly, without warning, a sob welled up inside his chest.

It's finally happened.

His worst fear had come true. His freakish mind had finally betrayed him.
He was insane.

He had always known he was crazy. Even the kids at the orphanage had
known it. Sam the bedbug, they called him.

He could not blame them. He had told them he heard voices. Sometimes
they even heard him answering them.

But he had learned to hide that. He tried not to act crazy. In time, the
boys at St. Anne's stopped staying up at night to hear him because he didn't
answer the voices anymore.

As he grew, he learned to hide the craziness better. Darian never suspected. When Sam had experienced his first, shocking wet dream, the old
man had never suspected that the boy had not been alone. He had been
with *Her*, the nameless faceless voice who filled his heart and body with
music.

Even Cory Althorpe, who should have known better, thought that Sam
had a gift. But it was no gift. It was just madness. And sometime during the
course of this past day, that madness had at last burst through the fragile
casing of his will. Sam the bedbug was free at last.

There was no reality anymore. He recognized nothing, not a ship, not a building, not even the language spoken all around him. He knew no one.

"Atlantis!" he had heard the big sailor on that outlandish vessel call out. Atlantis, off the coast of Florida. *Oh, good, Sam. Very good.*

It must have happened at the grotto. That was where he had tossed away his sanity the last time.

Suddenly he stopped in his tracks. The guard poked him in the back with the spear, and pain shot through Sam's body again.

No. Concentrate. Concentrate. The grotto . . .

The Rapture. It was possible. He closed his eyes, trying not to panic. It was possible that he was still somewhere in the middle of the ocean, his body slowly filling with nitrogen while his mind escaped to this fantasy world.

That would explain a lot. He could see himself twirling wild-eyed in a bed of seaweed, playing the bongos on his air tanks.

But it wouldn't explain everything. Such as how long it was taking him to drown.

It had been hours. The shark, the ship, the long march, the fat slob who spat in his face, the woman with the gray eyes. Hours. More time than a man could live on the bottom of the sea.

He was not dying. He was just crazy.

Inside the pyramid, Sam was washed by two dour women and then led down a corridor to an immense room with walls of pale blue stone.

The first thing he saw was a huge mosaic of a gold cross circumscribed in blue. It was the same design on the pottery shard he had found on the beach. He had no time to think about this because the guards nudged him to his left, where he saw a table and twelve huge chairs, each made from different materials, each a different color, each as magnificent as the others.

The big sailor who had killed the shark and rescued him sat on one end of the table; a thin-faced ascetic type at the other. Between them were four women and five men, one of them black. One seat was empty. Next to it, in the very center of the group, sat an old man with flowing white hair. On his immaculately robed chest hung a stone the size of a man's fist and shaped like a shield, suspended from a gold chain of large oval links.

Sam's immediate thought was: *It's not glowing.* Then he blinked and squinted at it. It couldn't be the same pendant he had found at the bottom of the ocean, the diamond burning with its own green fire. This was the same shape and size, but it was as lifeless as chalk.

The big sailor spoke a few sentences, then produced a bag from which he extracted Sam's Brite-Lite, the jacket of his wet suit, and his wristwatch depth gauge and compass. Almost as soon as the objects hit the table, the black man grabbed the flashlight, examined it, then pressed the switch that turned it on.

The others whispered in amazement, and the big sailor frowned mightily at Sam. Unconcerned, the black man quickly took the Brite-Lite apart, removing the batteries and examining them while chattering excitedly. After he had replaced the components, he exclaimed over the compass and depth gauge. He was reaching for the wet suit when the thin-faced man at the far end said something in a tone of undisguised contempt that caused the big sailor to rise from his seat with a snarl. Some others got up, too, and soon everyone seemed to be shouting at everyone else.

The old man in the center of the table lifted his hands in a feeble gesture to restore order. He was trying to be heard above the din when the gray-eyed woman who had stopped the slave line to wipe Sam's face came into the room.

It quieted immediately. The woman murmured what sounded like a per-functory apology, then sat down on the empty chair.

"You," Sam whispered. His breath had caught when he saw her, and the music he had heard, the music he had followed all his life, came back to him.

She hears it, too. I know she does.

The woman made a point of not looking at him.

Sam forced himself to remember who and where he was. *Forget it, Sam. There is no music. There are no people here. There is only you, Sam, and you're lying in a hospital bed somewhere with tubes stuck up your nose.*

Finally able to be heard, the old man said something and gestured for the items on the table to be passed down to him. He studied them for a moment, then looked steadily at the new captive. Sam felt grossly uncomfort-able, as if he were being skewered by pins. It was a relief when the old man finally turned away from him to speak to the gray-eyed woman.

What he said must have shocked her. She looked up at him, startled, then blushed deeply.

The old man spoke again. This time the woman closed and opened her eyes slowly, then stood up and walked reluctantly toward Sam. She brought the music with her, faint but distinct.

Who are you?"

"What did you say?" Sam asked aloud, his voice catching in his throat.

The woman stopped for a moment, her eyes frightened, then ventured forward again. When she was close to Sam, so close that he could feel the warmth of her body, she raised her hands to his face. Her touch was like a kiss.

Don't believe this, he warned himself. *She's not real, remember? You've made her up, all of this, everything . . .*

And then the music came, bursting from her mind into his, beautiful, familiar, forceful as the ocean.

My love, I do know you. I had almost given up hope that you would come . . .

"It was you," he whispered.

A shudder ran through his body. "All these years. *You* called to me."

My love, how long I have waited . . .

Sam moved forward toward her. Their eyes held for a moment longer, and then she broke away with a cry.

The guards seized Sam by both arms.

"Please come back," he called, but the woman ran away from him like a frightened deer.

When the old man spoke again, it was to the guards. Sam was pushed roughly out of the room.

CHAPTER 5

THE KING WAITED IN ATHENA'S APARTMENTS, SWIRLING THE WINE IN HIS glass. If it had been any of his other children, he would have summoned them to him. And they would not have kept him waiting.

But this was Athena, who would not have exited the council chamber in so undignified a manner for any but the most urgent reasons. And if she was late for their meeting now, well, then, even the king of Atlantis would have to wait for her.

He glanced about at the spare orderliness of her sitting room: a divan, a table, a small oil lamp. The only adornments were an earthenware pitcher filled with water and a tapestry of himself on the occasion of his coronation. It had been woven by Athena's mother, Metis.

Metis, who had once made him believe he could change the world . . .

Athena appeared, pale and trembling.

"Are you ill?" he asked.

"No, Father. Forgive me for leaving as I did. I hope I didn't embarrass you too badly."

"Did the prisoner do something to you?" he demanded. "Did he touch you?"

"No. It was nothing like that."

Zeus closed his eyes, trying to be patient. "Then what was the problem? Were you unable to discern his thoughts? That's not unusual. The mind of a savage—"

"He is not a savage," she said. "Did you see his hands, his fingernails, his teeth? They were clean and perfect. Even his beard was shaved."

"Yes, that was most peculiar. And his hair. Short as a baby's. I can't imagine who his people are."

"He came . . . from the sea."

The king laughed. "Clever. He can even lie with his mind. He must have known you were listening."

"It was more than that." Athena hesitated. The music . . . mostly it was the music. But she had understood his words. *And he had understood hers.*

That was the terrifying thing. They were words she never would have spoken, words she had never even meant to think. But they had come rushing out, just as they had in the wild dreams she had dreamt since her youth. The same words. The same music.

She stood before the king, her hands clasped in front of her. "Father, he could hear me," she said softly.

Zeus put down his goblet. "That cannot be," he said. No foreigner had ever possessed the Power. That had come from the Stranger alone, to his descendants on Atlantis. "He's simply a well-trained spy, putting on a show for your benefit."

"Perhaps." She hung her head.

"I want you to see him again."

"No!" She looked around frantically. She did not want the strange prisoner who could read her thoughts to be in her rooms. She did not want to think about him.

"Athena, I realize it may be distasteful for you, but it is extremely important that we learn the purpose of his mission here. This fellow had some peculiar equipment with him, equipment that even Hephaestus does not understand. Whatever people he represents are very advanced, more than any we have ever encountered, perhaps more than we ourselves. They might even be connected with the earthquakes that are threatening to destroy us. Do you understand what I'm saying?"

"Yes, Father," she said. "Still, I am not inclined to use something as holy as the Power to interrogate spies."

"Nor am I. But the man apparently does not speak our language, so even torture is not likely to work. Besides, I don't want him to die before he can tell us anything." He gazed angrily into his cup. "Believe me, I am not happy about asking you to do this. If I could, I would communicate with him myself, and leave you out of the whole matter." He drank the rest of the wine hurriedly.

How it must hurt him not to have the Power any longer, Athena thought. She sat down at his feet. "I'll see him," she said quietly. "Is he in the prison?"

"Gods, no. Hades would have him on the block by sunrise. He's being kept in the palace. I'll have him brought to you." He rose and pulled her to her feet. "Thank you, Athena."

She held onto his hands. "Father, perhaps he has no people," she said, blushing.

"No people? What on earth are you talking about?" he sputtered. "He must have come from somewhere. Besides the sea, that is."

She almost spoke, then stopped herself. "Of course. He must have."

Zeus kissed the top of her head. "Sometimes you think too much," he said.

He let himself out. Athena stared after him for a long time.

Coward, she thought. *For all my displays of courage, I am yet a coward.*

She had meant to tell him, but she had been unable to speak about it. How could she? How could she tell her father that the strange man with the clean fingernails had come *because she had willed him to*?

He had always been her lover, back as far as she could remember. He had never had a face, but he had a name: *Sam*. At first, back when Athena was a child, he had been little more than a pet in her mind, a ghost-boy whose presence she could feel, if not see, because he brought the music with him.

It was strange music, unlike anything she had ever heard with her ears. It only played in her dreams, when she went to him. She could see him then. He lived in a stout, dark building made of small red blocks. There were only a few adults in the building, but many children.

She still heard the voices. *Oh, that's just Sam the bedbug. He's crazy.*

She could sense his sadness.

"Come to me, Sam," she would call to him. "They don't believe you. They'll never believe you."

Now this is the last straw, Mr. Mr. Sam Smith. A fire! Didn't you ever hear about the little boy who cried wolf?

"Hurry, Sam, run. They'll hurt you."

There was a fire, of course. Sam had seen it coming. On the night it happened, Athena tossed in a terrible fever while she watched the children run screaming out of the building.

And then Sam was beaten.

Why did you do it, Sam? What makes you want to burn things?

"Oh, Sam, please come. I'll take care of you and no one will hurt you anymore. But you have to leave now. Oh, please, please listen to me!"

And he had left. The music was very strong that night.

When Athena awoke the next morning, her fever was gone. But her Sam had not come. Nor could Athena reenter his world. She looked in her mind for the square dark house but could not find it.

Sam had disappeared from her.

He doesn't want me with him anymore, she realized with sadness. *I frighten him.*

He had the power, but he lived in a land where the power meant nothing; and so he was ashamed of it. He would hide it, try to destroy it. One day, she feared, he would forget her entirely.

Yet he had heard her once. He had heard the music. So she would wait. She would wait and listen and one day, perhaps, he would find his way to her.

The next time she saw him she was sixteen, just beginning to bud into full womanhood. She was dreaming of the ocean.

This time, he came to her as a lover.

No words were spoken. He came from the sea, wrapped in music. They had kissed, in his dreams and hers, and he had taken her in his arms and loved her until they both cried out in passion.

In the morning, finding him gone, Athena wept.

He was never here. It was just a dream. A lonely girl's dream.

She vowed never to allow it to happen again.

And yet it had happened. Again.

And again.

For years she had lain with him as the sweet music sang, loved him gloriously in the dark part of her dreams and then loathed herself by the light of day.

She had never married. The Atlantean nobles thought her disdainful. The commoners idolized her as a paragon of purity.

None knew the real reason. She could never love a mortal man, so long as the ghost-lover came to her.

Come to me, Sam. I have waited, waited for you . . .

And now, at last, he had come.

But was he the fulfillment of a dream or an evil vision come to life? Had he been born of her will, or was he one whose power was greater than her own, greater even than Zeus's, capable of destroying her and everything she knew?

T he knock at her door filled Athena with alarm, but she forced herself to appear composed when it opened and she confronted the short-haired prisoner.

"Take off his shackles and leave us alone," she commanded the guard with him.

"Your Highness, I cannot. If he harms you—"

"He is unarmed. Wait on the other side of the door. I will call if I need you."

Reluctantly, the guard removed the slave's shackles and withdrew.

Sam touched his raw, weeping wrists. Athena motioned for him to follow her toward a porcelain basin, where she poured cool water over his wounds. The pitcher she used was plain and utilitarian, decorated by a row of encircled crosses.

"The shard," he said in wonder, taking the pitcher from her. "It was from this."

She stepped away immediately. Her eyes darted toward the door.

Realizing that she was afraid he would hit her with it, Sam set the pitcher down. "I'm sorry," he said. "It was just . . . this thing made me think . . ." He slapped his arms against his sides. "Oh, what the hell. None of this is happening, anyway."

Slowly, fearfully, she moved back to him. After a moment she picked up a small clay pot beside the basin and removed its cork stopper. Then she scooped out some of its oily contents and rubbed the ointment gently over the injured skin of his wrists. It stung for a moment, but the pain was soon replaced by a sensation of cool relief, and something more. At the gray-eyed woman's touch, he heard the music again, flowing into him so strongly that he moaned.

He feels it, too, he heard her say, although her lips never moved.

"Who are you?" he asked.

I am Athena.

"Athena," he repeated.

She inhaled sharply. *So he does have the Power*, she thought. He could hear her thoughts as clearly as she could hear his.

"What power?"

Athena looked down at her hands encircling his wrists. "We are touching. That makes it possible for us to communicate through pure thought. Words like these are not necessary." Sam realized it was the first time she had spoken aloud to him.

"This gets stranger all the time," he said. But then, why shouldn't it be strange? Crazy people had crazy ideas.

"There is nothing disturbed about your mind. If there were, I would perceive it."

"Oh, right. I'm perfectly normal. I just happen to be a mindreader in Atlantis."

Sam grasped her thought: *He does not believe his own senses*. And then: *Poseidon might be wrong*.

"Poseidon?" *The big sailor who fished me out of the water. That's who she's thinking about*. "Poseidon?" he repeated, grinning crookedly. "Athena? Who's the old guy with the long white beard, Zeus?"

"Then you do know us."

He laughed out loud.

"Why have you come to Atlantis?" Athena demanded, her voice suddenly strident.

"It wasn't my idea, believe me."

Wasn't it? Nobody made you go to the Peaks.

The woman frowned. She didn't know what the Peaks were.

"I don't know why I came here, or how," Sam answered honestly. "Something happened to me in the ocean."

Athena closed her eyes as she saw his memories of the underwater place—the two divers, the shark, a cave in the depths of the sea, glowing with green light . . .

I went right through the wall, he thought with wonder.

"That is a lie!" she shouted. "You have come to my country as a spy!"

Sam smiled, astonished. "A what?"

"Even with the Power, you could not have come *through a wall!*"

There was dead silence between them. "I suppose you're right," he said at last. "Guess my mind isn't so undisturbed, after all." He smiled sadly. "You've got to admit, it's pretty bad when even the figments of your imagination complain that you don't make sense. Good old Sam the bedbug."

"Sam . . . Sam the bedbug," she whispered.

"That's me."

She touched his cheek. "Sam," she repeated. "Your name is *Sam*."

He was about to speak, but the music came to him again, more intensely, shooting from her hands into him like sparks of light.

"I called you," she whispered. "From the house filled with children, where you were blamed for the fire."

Suddenly Sam felt himself trembling. "Don't do this to me."

"You came to me for a long time . . . at night. . . ."

"Give me a break, okay?" he said harshly. "Just send me back to that dungeon, or wherever I was, and leave me alone. Before long, they'll pull the plug and this nightmare will be over. But don't tease me with that. Don't make me start believing you're real."

She threw back her head in haughty indignation. "You think *I* am not real? *I*? It is you whose reality is in question."

Sam made an effort to get his bearings. "Wait a minute. Are you saying you imagined *me*?"

"Well, haven't I?" she demanded. "Have you lived any sort of life apart from my dreams? Do you have any memories?"

"Do I . . ." For a moment, an image of Darian and the others on the island washed over him like a tidal wave. He was safe now, rendered impervious by his insanity; but they were still waiting. Waiting for the attack that would snuff out their lives. Waiting for Sam, who would not be able to help them.

"There *are* others in your thoughts," Athena said with relief.

"Of course there are. A whole world of others . . ." He stared at her. "But you were in my dreams, too. All my life."

His eyes pricked with tears. Suddenly the music swelled inside him, whole and perfect, not at all like the distant echoes that had tormented him whenever he'd passed over the Peaks. The music pulsed with the heartbeat of the gray-eyed woman whose touch was like sunlight on his face. He put his arms around her and pulled her close to him.

"Sam," she breathed the moment before their lips met. *I have loved you from the beginning of time.*

I, too, he told her with his mind. *And I will never leave you.*

The music swirled through them and around them, chords from the sea and the stars. Tears ran down Sam's face into her hair.

His existence here was real, he understood at last in the depth of his soul. It was all real.

And he had been waiting for it forever.

CHAPTER 6

HADES HAD LEFT THE COUNCIL MEETING IN A FURY, AND HIS ANGER STILL had not subsided.

"What manner of carnival has the Atlantean royal house become?" he shouted, tossing a gem-encrusted statue of an ox against the wall. One of the rubies in the ox's eyes shattered.

Ares laughed. He touched the exquisite golden sculpture with a toe. "What did you expect, Uncle? You didn't think the king would continue the meeting without his precious spoiled poppet, did you?"

"Athena's a witch," Hades spat. "You can be sure it was her wheedling that got that common soldier buried here in the royal tombs."

"The king can never refuse her," Ares said, his mouth twisting bitterly. "She'd steal the throne from me if she were allowed."

Hades laughed. "Allowed? Do you really think a minor item like the law is going to stop her from usurping the throne? You're an ass, Ares."

"A woman can't rule!"

Hades shrugged. "No woman ever has. Not yet. But Zeus will do as he likes, with Athena whispering in his ear all the while."

Ares rose, anger blazing in his eyes. "Then I'll kill her now, with my bare—"

"Oh, sit down." Hades made a weary gesture and plopped down on his chair, his black robes billowing about him.

Ares really was quite impossibly stupid. Fortunately, intelligence and good judgment had never been prerequisites for becoming king, and despite his warning words, Hades believed that Ares would become king—at least in name. The high priest himself would actually rule Atlantis then. As he did now.

Zeus had publicly named Ares crown prince and heir to the throne when Ares was four years old. Since the king was unmarried at the time and refused to name the boy's mother, the announcement had come as a shock to the council, but eventually they got used to the idea. Zeus had many bastard sons, they reasoned, and declaring one of them his heir would prevent a series of bloody civil wars at Zeus's death.

The problem was Athena. Conceived before her mother's banishment, she might claim, if she had an eye toward the throne, that she was the king's only legitimate child. But Athena would not fight for the crown. She would only succeed Zeus at his express command, and Hades would make sure such a command was never given.

He looked out glumly at the pavement below the death pyramid where he and the other priests lived. The stones were still stained with blood, even though they had been scrubbed again and again.

"That slave falling off the altar nearly caused a riot this morning," he said.

"The gods didn't want Prometheus in their tomb," Ares pouted. "He was a commoner. And a traitor, besides. His body should be removed."

"Not possible, I'm afraid." Hades sighed. "Poseidon would never permit it. Nor would the commoners. They love having that smelly old soldier in the pyramid next to our divine kings."

"Who cares what the commoners think?" Ares sneered.

Hades shook his head, a small movement. The dolt knew nothing. He would be hopeless as king. Nevertheless, the high priest tried to explain. "It is what commoners think that creates kings," he said. "And nations. And gods. Even the heretics' fabled Stranger himself would have been no more than a stone-age wanderer had he not been able to persuade the common people of his superiority."

"How could he do that?"

"By accident, probably. He found a peculiar stone, dropped it against something, and a piece of it flew off, revealing its interior. So he cut it again, this way and that, until he produced the royal diamond."

"They call it the Eye of Zeus now," Ares said sulkily. "As if it'll be buried with him."

Hades ignored him. "Or he found a tree burning after a lightning storm and brought back a branch to amaze the people with his 'invention' of fire. It doesn't matter what he did. It's how he did it. Common people are always looking for an uncommon man. It was how your father took the crown from Cronus."

"He said he had to do that."

Hades smiled. "Dear boy, no one *has* to become king. Not while there's already a king on the throne." His tight smile faded. "And not when one is the youngest of three sons. No, Ares, Zeus saw his chance and took it. And the crowd of common men cheered him on."

Hades remembered it all as if it had just happened, beginning with the terrible shattering moment in which he found himself not the heir to the throne but a prisoner condemned to death, and ending with the coronation of his youngest brother as king.

Zeus had never been meant to rule. He had been little more than a child when the unspeakable events had come to pass. Nor was Poseidon a threat. He would never have entertained the idea of leaving his precious ships to grapple with problems like irrigation or land disputes.

Of the three brothers, there was only Hades, Hades with the best mind and a devotion to duty unmatched by even his father, King Cronus himself;

Hades, who kept accounts and watched over the too-trusted nobles who gladly would have robbed every coin in the treasury; Hades who, alone among the old king's sons, paid true homage to the gods, studying the ancient texts, forcing himself to sit at the feet of Hecate, high priestess of the heretic goddess worshippers, so that he might learn the secrets of the enemies of the king-gods.

Hades had devoted his life in preparation to wear the diamond amulet of Atlantis's kings. And so he would have, were it not for Hecate.

Because though Hades had never been her disciple, he had become her lover.

He was twenty. He had dutifully married his cousin Persephone, whom he found willful and hysterical. Within the first six months of the marriage, Hades had sent her back to her mother. Now she only visited Atlantis occasionally for the sake of appearances, remaining alone with her servants in a remote part of the old palace. The arrangement suited Hades. Their obligation to one another had been completed: She would one day be queen, and she was pregnant. If she bore a son to succeed him, Hades would never have to touch her again.

Because for his pleasure, there was Hecate. Nearly twice his age, she knew everything about the arts of love. She awakened his senses in a way that the bloodless Persephone could never have imagined. There were no boundaries; nothing was forbidden. She would make ferocious love to him one moment, then caress him with the tenderness of a spring breeze the next. She teased him with her hands and mouth until he begged for release and then she gave it to him, taking her own pleasure with him.

"If you so despise the Atlantean kings, then why have you taken me to your bed?" he asked, lying shining with sweat in Hecate's arms. It was no secret that the priestesses hated the "new" religion and its cult of royal ancestor worship. "I will be the next king after my father Cronus. And after I die, I too will become a god."

She laughed softly. "After you die, I will no longer desire your body, my puppy."

She had always made him feel small. If it were not for her sexual skill, he would not bother with her. "Old cow," he muttered. "You're as corrupt as your religion. Our priests are celibate."

"Then they know nothing of what it is to be human." She smiled and traced a line down his belly with her slender finger. His passion rose again, immediately, urgently. "This is why we have incarnated into flesh," she said, rubbing her breasts against him. "To experience the senses, and all the pleasure they bring. To feel love as only the body can feel. To know life by touching it."

He turned his face from hers. "That is the sophistry of a whore." He wished his erection would go away. "And no one still worships your fat-teated old statue anymore."

Hades felt a small triumph when she winced at his words. "It is not the statues we worship, princeling, but the Earth herself. And those like you are killing her."

"The Earth is not a woman." He rose up onto one elbow. "It is an object. It can't die."

Hecate rose from the bed and walked naked to a window. "You know nothing, young adder." she said quietly. "Gaea is dying now. The earthquakes are the shudders of her body as she falls toward the void."

"Superstitions," Hades said. "If it will ease your mind, the tremors mean nothing. I have consulted a number of scientists, and they are in agreement—"

"Atlantis will perish!" Hecate spoke with a voice like a sword on stone. The light from the window bathed her naked limbs in yellow light. "The kings of your family have forced the people to worship them and their dead ancestors instead of the Earth spirit," she said. "It is a sacrilege the Stranger would never have permitted. But his sons knew nothing of the Power. They saw how their father was revered, and desired that reverence for themselves. And so first they set themselves up as kings, and then in later generations, as gods, though there has not been an Atlantean king fit to rule for a thousand years."

"I shall be fit to rule," Hades said coldly.

"You shall never be king."

Hades threw off the silken coverlet that covered him. "How dare you—"

"Zeus will take the Eye for himself." She spoke with a distant look in her dark eyes, as she did when the Power had command of her. It was very strong in Hecate, as it was in all those chosen to be high priestess. "He will seize it by force."

Hades felt as if he were frozen in a block of ice. "What are you saying?" he whispered.

"It will be Zeus. I have seen him in my visions. He will be the first king of Atlantis to possess the Power since the Stranger." A shudder ran through Hecate's body. "And he will use it to destroy us."

Hades felt his mouth go dry. "You must tell my father," he said at last. "The king must know what you've seen."

She laughed. "Do you think for a moment that Cronus, that ungodly beast, would attend my prophecies?" she asked savagely. "He has said publicly that he does not believe the Power exists, that those in possession of it are mad, and that I and my priestesses are frauds whom he tolerates only to appease the peasants." She wiped her mouth as if the taste of the words she spoke carried an unbearable bitterness. "No, he will not listen to me."

He rose from the bed. "Then I'll tell him."

She sniffed haughtily. "Tell him what? That his favorite son will depose him? He will never believe you, Hades."

"But something has to be done!" he shouted. "Surely you don't think I'll just stand by and allow my younger brother to take the throne from me."

Hecate did not answer.

"What must I do? Tell me, priestess. I command you!"

She narrowed her eyes. "It is not easy to change the course of things to come," she said. "The price will be high."

"Tell me what I must do!"

She walked behind him and whispered in his ear. "Kill your father."

Suddenly the room went so silent that Hades could hear his own heart beating. "You don't know what you're saying," he gasped.

"I told you the price would be high. You must kill the king in his bed, and then kill Zeus. It is the only way you will rule."

"But the gods—"

"Your gods cannot help you," she scoffed. "Zeus will be your last king. Unless you stop him."

Hades felt his jaw clenching. He had always feared some treachery from his father and youngest brother. Zeus was a big, strapping, genial boy with a natural talent for leadership, and the king openly favored him. While Hades labored to learn the difficult and time-consuming tasks of a chief administrator, Cronus had appointed the eighteen-year-old Zeus as deputy to the land forces commander in charge of military training. It did not take a prophetess to realize that Zeus was a threat to him. His only surprise was that he had not seen it sooner.

"I will kill them," he said.

Silently Hecate prayed to Gaea, asking the Earth's spirit's forgiveness. Zeus was to be the instrument of destiny, she knew: Her visions of what was to come told her that. Atlantis was meant to perish at the king's hand.

But she could not bear those visions. If Hades, in his hunger for the crown, could avert fate, the land she loved might not be doomed to disappear into the sea forever.

"Perhaps it is possible to halt the inevitable," she murmured.

Hades fixed her with eyes of flint. "We create our destiny," he said. "I will be king."

How he had believed that!

His belief had given Hades the courage to steal into King Cronus's bedchamber that night. It had dispelled the wave of shame and fear that washed over Hades as he watched the old man sleeping. It had enabled him to pull the dagger from his belt and hold it high above his father.

I will be king.

He had believed it until his father's eyes opened suddenly and his great hairy arm thrust upward, grasping Hades's wrist.

"What have you done?" the old man rasped. His eyes, newly wakened from sleep, seemed big as dinner plates.

Hades whimpered and trembled. It was an effort to control his bowels. "It was to be . . . a sacrifice," he answered in a small voice. "It was . . ." But he could not go on. No explanation would be enough.

He left with a guard, who was later killed for his negligence. After Hades confessed, Hecate was killed also, along with all her priestesses. Their temple was burned. A sacrifice was prepared in the name of the true gods, the dead ancestors of King Cronus. A great sacrifice, the heralds cried, a sacrifice to end the earthquakes forever.

Hades, heir and eldest son of the king, was to have his living heart taken from him in a holy ceremony the following day. His father, Cronus, would wield the knife himself.

All the preparations were made. A special scaffolding constructed for the purpose of supporting Hades's body was placed over a stone which had been prayed over by the priests of the king-gods. All the soldiers in Atlantis gathered around it. Prometheus, who had charge of the King's Guard, kept the awestruck populace at a distance.

A royal sacrifice! Nothing like it had been performed for a hundred years. The crowd of onlookers stretched for miles.

Cronus stood atop the platform, the knife in his hands raised high. Beside him stood his two sons, Zeus and Poseidon, called to witness the execution of their brother.

As Hades climbed the scaffold, he sobbed in terror. "Help me, Zeus!" he called out. "You have the Power. Use it! I am of your own blood! Use it to help me now, I beg you!"

Zeus stood trembling.

"Do not let him kill your brother!"

Poseidon laid a hand on Zeus's arm, but it was too late. The Power was already crackling from Zeus's fingers like bolts of lightning. His man-child's eyes burned with it. A bright glow surrounded his entire body.

"You will not take my brother's life!" he shouted as the Power emanated from him in visible waves. A nearby tree suddenly burst into flame. The sky darkened in the span of less than a minute, and winds blew like the breath of death itself, sending sparks from the blaze swirling around the gathered army.

The commoners who had come to witness the sacrifice screamed in terror. "He is the Stranger returned!" someone cried.

"The boy carries the wrath of all the gods within him!"

Thousands broke through the ranks of soldiers to swarm over the scaffold. Someone snatched the great diamond from Cronus and placed in around Zeus's neck, where it glowed with a pulsating, unearthly light. At the sight of the living stone, the people backed away in awe. Hades descended the scaffold gratefully, followed by Poseidon and then Cronus himself, his shoulders hunched like an old man's. Above them all, Zeus stood alone in his own blazing light.

Prometheus knelt to him. He was the first. Then the others, soldiers, commoners, nobles, even the old king, fell to the bare ground in homage. Only Hades remained standing, looking about him in horror. His life had been saved, but he had lost the throne.

And Hecate's prophecy was coming true.

"It can't . . . it can't . . ." he whispered. Then someone grabbed the robe he wore and yanked him to the ground. A pebble cut his face. He smelled the dirt in his nostrils.

There was a new king.

Uncle."

Hades looked up to see Ares's handsome, belligerent face frowning at him. "What is it?" he asked irritably.

"Have you been listening to a word I've said?"

Hades swallowed drily, brushing back his hair with a bony hand. "No, I haven't."

Ares sighed. "I said that the foreign slave who made Athena act so crazy is still in the palace."

"Why would he be kept in the palace? The man's obviously a spy."

Ares shrugged. "Maybe he's got something Athena wants." He smiled lewdly. Hades waved a hand at him in disgust. "Well, maybe they grow them big where he comes from," Ares went on, laughing. "Two women slaves bathed him. They didn't seem disappointed."

"You've talked with the servants?"

"I've heard them talking. They're all excited."

"What do they say about the slave?"

"Everything. Some think he's a spy, some say he's a lunatic. I heard a couple of them whispering that he's the Stranger himself, come back to make things right again." He snorted a chuckle through his nose. "If you ask me, they don't have enough to do around here."

"The Stranger," Hades said thoughtfully.

The earthquakes were tearing at the very core of the Atlantean people. Now they were grasping at straws, willing to believe anyone who promised an end to the ever-worsening tremors. In their fear, they might even go back to the old religion, with some foolish outlander as its centerpiece.

"Leave me," Hades snapped. "I have to find a way to rectify today's debacle."

"Why not have another sacrifice? A big one. That'll make people forget the omen."

Hades looked up. "Another sacrifice . . ."

"I'll lead the expedition to collect the slaves," Ares offered.

The high priest considered. A great sacrifice, a spectacle unlike anything ever seen before. "Perhaps you're right," he said slowly.

Sacrifice, Hades thought after Ares had left. Sacrifice was the key to containing the people's panic over the earthquakes.

They had come by the thousands to see Hades sacrificed by his own father, he remembered bitterly. Even after their king had been deposed and the throne seized by an upstart child with a freakish bent for destruction, they had turned not on Zeus, but on Hades.

Sacrifice! they had demanded of their new godlike king. They wanted to see blood spilled. Hades had sweated in the priests' temple, where he had fled to find sanctuary, as the mob surrounded it, demanding his blood.

Finally Zeus had satisfied them by ordering a foreign slave to be ritually killed in his place.

The earthquakes stopped for a time after that. Hades was exonerated. The people were exultant.

Only Zeus suffered.

"This is wrong, so wrong," he lamented after the sacrifice had been performed.

"It was a slave's life for your brother's," Hades reasoned, offended that Zeus would even consider the alternative. "Let me remind you that I am a royal prince of Atlantis."

"Who tried to kill our father in his sleep."

Hades turned away.

"I will have no more to do with this barbaric murder," Zeus said. "From now on, if you require that another die in your stead, ask the priests to help you."

With that, he had given over the first piece of his authority to Hades. The sacrifices continued. The priests of the king-gods knew what power they held over the people.

By the time Hades became high priest, the rabble had forgotten all about King Cronus's intention to offer him up on the block. His first act as the spiritual leader of Atlantis was to perform a massive sacrifice of twenty slaves.

The people celebrated for days.

Yes, *sacrifice*, Hades thought. He would give them a sacrifice they would never forget.

Until the next earthquake.

CHAPTER 7

HADES STOOD NEAR THE LARGE WINDOW IN THE KING'S PRIVATE CHAMBER. The morning sun glared all around him so that the priest's elongated frame in its black robes looked like some sort of unearthly spider.

"A monumental sacrifice," he said. "It is the only way to silence the people's fear."

Zeus sighed. "Perhaps their fear is justified."

Hades sniffed. "Of course it is. The gods detest you."

The king turned away.

"Do you expect me to continue to hold my tongue in the face of certain disaster?" Hades said hotly. "It was bad enough that you married a heretic. But when you allowed her to defile the very walls of the royal palace with the words of her false god—"

"Spare me your sactimony, brother," Zeus said. "I gave up my wife for your religion, in order to keep peace in Atlantis. I will not have every memory of Metis blotted out."

"The words inscribed on the palace are an insult to the gods," Hades muttered stolidly. "That is why our ancestors will not save us from the earthquakes."

"Nothing will save us!" the king shouted. "Your sacrifices are a worthless farce, performed as a bloodthirsty entertainment for the vile mob my people have become!"

"They would not be worthless if you would have the Stranger's words removed. . . ."

"I command you to be silent!"

Zeus paced before the long horizontal window in his private quarters. From the outside, the palace pyramid looked like four identical triangles of gleaming alabaster, its smooth surfaces marred only by a gigantic recessed door and the balcony where the royal family stood on ceremonial occasions. Part of the genius of Hephaestus's design was that these same surfaces were made, in fact, mostly of glass, opaque and undetectable from the outside. The stone and mortar which held the structures together were on the inside, radiating from their metal cores. "If it were not for Metis, this palace—which you say she 'defiled'—would not even exist," the king said quietly.

* * *

Hades tossed his head in disdain. It was true that the former queen was the first to spot Hephaestus's uncanny ability to build. Metis had convinced Zeus to have the pyramid constructed, despite the protests of Hades and others who complained that the design was bizarre. After it was built, however, and Hades saw for himself how light and airy was its interior, how elegant its curving stairways, he demanded a similar edifice be built as a temple to the gods in the Land of the Dead.

Metis had been angry about that. She had intended for the magnificent palace pyramid to be a tribute to Zeus, whom she fervently believed to be the living incarnation of the Stranger, the being at the center of her religion. To have a duplicate of the structure used in the service of the blood-swilling king-gods was repugnant to her.

She responded by ordering the dying words of the Stranger to be carved above the doorway of the great palace pyramid.

"With a stranger will it begin again," she told Hades defiantly. "And it has. My husband Zeus has come with the Stranger's power to begin a new Atlantis, free from the filth of its corrupt kings . . . and their priests."

Hades hated Metis. He knew that as a young girl before the temple of the goddess had been destroyed, she had studied with the priestesses there. She resolutely had refused to turn away from the ancient practice of goddess worship, even after her marriage to the king. Metis openly despised the idea of human sacrifice, and refused even to keep slaves. But Zeus had always stood by her odd ways, no matter how the priests grumbled; and when he found that Metis was to bear him a child, the king's adoration for her knew no bounds.

As soon as he heard about the queen's pregnancy, Hades had gone to the council, composed of the twelve family members charged with overseeing the king's rule. "With a stranger shall it begin again," Hades quoted to the council. "Heresy, inscribed in stone to mock the gods," he spat. "She is a witch, I tell you, and she will not stop until one of her own sits on the throne in place of the rightful king—a demon brought forth from her own belly!"

The council members considered.

"But the king already has an heir," Zeus's sister Demeter said. "Ares has been recognized publicly as crown prince. The queen agreed to his succession before her marriage."

"Princes have been deposed before," he argued. "And so have kings."

He had hoped to shame the council members with that. There was not a one among them who did not remember how Zeus had ascended to the throne.

Demeter cleared her throat. "No decision will be made as yet," she said, to the relief of the council. "We shall wait to see further evidence of the queen's wrongdoing."

They did not have to wait long. Within the week, an earthquake of a magnitude never before experienced in Atlantis took place. The country was still reeling from its effects when Hades approached the council again.

"Did I not tell you the gods would be displeased?" he accused. "This is a warning to us all. The sorceress known to you as Queen Metis has plotted with her evil goddess to destroy both our religion and our monarchy. Unless she is cast out, her child will kill Crown Prince Ares and seize the throne of Atlantis." He let his gaze rest on each member of the council in turn. "The gods have spoken."

There was a hollow silence in the council chamber as the members regarded one another nervously. Zeus himself had seized the crown from his father and stolen his older brother's birthright. What would stop Metis's unborn son from doing the same?

Besides, they all reasoned silently, it would be convenient to have someone to blame for the earthquake.

The council demanded that the queen be banished. In the span of ten days, Metis and the child in her belly were gone.

The commoners rejoiced. The evil in their midst had been eradicated. To appease the true gods, a sacrifice of fifty slaves took place, to the wild cheers of thousands.

Inside the palace, Zeus sat like a statue day and night for weeks. For his country, he had sent away the only woman he had ever loved.

A year after his daughter Athena was born in exile, another earthquake shook Olympus and several other cities along the coast. Six months after that, there was another. And another. All the sacrifices Hades offered had no effect on them.

The Power which had once burned inside Zeus diminshed quickly after that. The council ruled him, and Hades ruled the council; and Zeus did not particularly care.

"Those words on this pyramid were the symbol of Metis's faith in me," the King said quietly now, oblivious that Hades was still in the chamber with him. "They are all that is left of what I once was. Or may have been."

"What are you saying?" Hades snapped irritiably.

"Nothing. Just the ramblings of an old man. How many ships will you need?"

"Twelve, each with a full crew and fifty fighting men."

"Take them. Collect your slaves. Make your sacrifices," the king said. "Just go away."

Hades smiled. "As you command, Majesty."

When the guards opened the door for him, Athena was waiting on the other side. With her was the foreign spy who had been fished out of the sea.

"Good evening, Uncle," Athena said, bowing quickly to the high priest as she entered. Ignoring the king's dismissal of him, Hades followed her back into the room. Sam tried to enter as well, but the guards stationed at the door held him back at spearpoint.

"Let him pass," Athena demanded.

"Have we completely lost our senses here?" Hades shrilled. "Majesty, the princess is attempting to bring an enemy spy into your private chambers!"

"He is no spy, father, and no enemy to us."

Zeus looked at the short-haired savage appraisingly.

"I have learned a great deal about him, and his story is quite extraordinary," she said.

Hades sighed impatiently. "You mean he has told you his lies." Zeus responded with a look of irritation, but Hades went on doggedly. "This man is undoubtedly trained to dissemble. He would have no difficulty convincing an innocent girl—"

"He doesn't speak the language," the king said. "Let him enter."

Hades uttered a sound of disgust as Sam was brought forward.

"He has the Power, father," she said quietly. "There is no doubt."

The king said nothing. Hades's eyes narrowed into slits. "Prove it."

Athena thought for a moment, then took the barbarian's hand in her own. "Very well. Ask him a question. He will give me the answer telepathically, and I will tell you in turn."

Hades laughed. "That should afford a fine demonstration—of your imagination."

She colored. "I would not lie, Uncle."

The corners of Hades's mouth twitched. "If your barbarian indeed possesses the gift you claim, have him read another's thoughts besides your own. Mine, for example."

"Or mine," Zeus said.

"My brother, you are the king," Hades said, looking shocked. "This may all be a hoax to bring the spy close enough to you for assassination."

"With my daughter as his accomplice?" Zeus asked, his voice tight. "Is that what you're saying?"

Hades's face was impassive. "It is possible," he said.

The king's eyes burned with fury. "At one time you convinced everyone that Metis's child would overthrow me," he said in a harsh whisper. "Everyone except me." He rose from his seat and walked forward. "Well, here is her chance. Come, Athena. Bring your savage."

"Majesty—"

Zeus cut him off with a gesture. Roughly he grabbed Sam's hands and placed them on his own chest, over his heart. "Prove your innocence, stranger. And my daughter's."

For a moment Sam was lost. He was frightened, frozen, aware that his failure would result in his death, and possibly Athena's as well.

It began with a stranger. . . .

Sam felt his eyes roll back in his head. He saw a barren landscape, sere and brown, its scrawny trees bent low like grasses in the high wind. Great chasms crisscrossed the parched earth. There was no water, though the ocean still surrounded the lifeless island. Along the sandy shore, the bones of men, picked clean by birds, shone in the relentless sun.

This is the fate I have seen for my land. Will it come through the gods' hands? Or through yours?

The sadness pouring into Sam from the old man's mind was like a liquid of tremendous, unbearable weight; and the worst of it was that he knew the king had lived with it for most of his life. He wanted to move his hands away, run from the suddenly oppressive room into the light and air, leave this troubled being with the tragic vision which he carried around his heart like a chain.

Sweat beaded on Sam's forehead. "How can you live with this?" he whispered.

If there were someone to rule after me, I would gladly take my life to be again with my beloved Metis. But—

Suddenly his eyes locked with Sam's.

"It cannot be," Zeus said aloud. "I have not possessed the Power in a quarter century. . . ." The diamond on his chest was glowing faintly.

"It's the same stone," Sam said. He touched it with the tip of his finger. For a moment it blazed a brilliant green.

"What do you know of this stone?" Zeus demanded.

"I found it. Under the sea." He opened his mind to the king and felt him probing, unsure at first, then more strongly, coursing through his thoughts, his memories. The stone's color deepened and radiated, pulsing with the old king's heartbeat like a strobe as he explored every corner of Sam's consciousness with a brutal intelligence.

The king felt his breath catch as the foreigner's mind poured into his own. Such memories! Automobiles and airplanes and telephones, films, television, printing, cameras, computers, submarines, radio telescopes, space vehicles, men walking upon the surface of the moon.

The savage came from the western mainland, but it was called Florida. There was a sailor named Darian who lived there, and a woman physician who treated the mind as the ancient priestesses of Atlantis had. There was a young girl with Apollo's bright hair and his gift for healing as well as Artemis's affinity for animals. A man as black as Hephaestus swam at the bottom of the sea searching for his friend who had passed through a grotto and disappeared from his world. An old crone with eyes very like Zeus's own mother Rhea cooked on a battered stove outdoors on a desolate island in the middle of the vast ocean waters.

They were all there, on that island so far from the wonders of his civilization; and the foreigner was afraid for them all. They were in danger. They had little chance of escape from what awaited them on that parched and terrible island of death where, years hence, their bones would dry unnoticed in the sun. . . .

Zeus gasped. "The place of my vision," he said hoarsely. "Atlantis . . ."

"No," Sam said, still envisioning the bones of his friends on the empty beach. "That's Memory Island."

"They are the same," the king whispered.

"Memory Island and . . . *Atlantis?*" He tried to grasp the implications of this possibility. "Then the stone didn't come from a different *place* . . ."

"But a different time." Zeus closed his eyes in despair. "The Eye of Zeus lay on the bottom of the sea because I and all my descendants had been dead for countless millennia." He looked up into Sam's eyes. "We come from the same land, my friend, I in my time, and you in yours. And we are doomed to the same fate."

He lifted his hands from the foreigner's and recoiled away. He no longer wished to know what was in this stranger's mind.

* * *

Wait a minute," Sam offered, rushing toward the old man to make contact again. The guards pounced on him. They knocked him to the floor, the tips of their spears pressing against his throat.

"Kill the barbarian," Hades ordered.

"No. He means me no harm. Let him come."

Sam stepped forward. The king extended his hand once again and placed it over Sam's. "We both have seen the course of things to come," Zeus said wearily. "There is little more to be said."

"But maybe we can do something. Something to help us both."

The king arched an eyebrow. "Such as?"

"Such as evacuating this place."

The king scowled. "Leave Atlantis? Are you mad?"

"Maybe. But I ought to tell you that in my time, people who have what you call the Power are being killed. That's why those friends of mine you saw are in such trouble. There aren't many of us, and I think that's because most of you Atlanteans died here. But it doesn't have to be that way."

The king's expression softened. "Go on."

"If you managed to get your people out of here—all of them—they'd pass on these genes you have to the whole world. By the twentieth century, everyone on Earth will be able to do what you and I are doing right now, and more. Your people would live, and so would mine. And as corny as it sounds, the world would probably be a lot better off than it is."

Zeus considered. "But to leave Atlantis . . . is there no alternative?"

"Not unless you can come up with a way to stop earthquakes."

The king's grip on his hand tightened.

"I wasn't serious, Zeus. No one can stop an earthquake. Not even in my time."

"The people of your time have not been faced with annihilation."

"But I don't know anything. I'm a sailor, not an engineer—"

"We have engineers. My son Hephaestus will build you whatever you need."

Sam looked helplessly at Athena, then back at the king. "Your Highness, I'm trying to tell you—"

"Find a way," Zeus commanded. "Or you will die with the rest of us." He pushed Sam's hands away, then signaled for a guard to take him outside.

Athena and Hades both rushed to the king. "Father, what happened?" she asked. "What did you see?"

"Unbelievable things. He comes from a time so remote that Atlantis is no more than a rumor to his people. A time where ships fly in the air and events are captured in lighted boxes that can show what has occurred again and again, and people ride in carts that move by themselves. . . ."

The high priest's eyebrows raised. "Did you say his *time*?"

The king nodded slowly.

"And you believed him? By the gods, you've both been taken in by a common spy!"

"He is not a spy." Zeus stared at the door behind which the Sam stood. "He is only a stranger, like the last Stranger—unable to return home, and doomed to live out his life with savages." The king laughed softly.

"This is preposterous," the high priest said. "Athena, call your father's attendants. He must be taken to bed."

"I don't need to go to bed. This is the first beam of hope I've felt in decades."

Athena looked at him quizzically.

"Don't you see? He comes from the far distant future—a future filled with machinery. You saw for yourself the tools he carried in the sea. He has been sent to us, by what gods I cannot know, but he has been sent as our deliverance."

"The earthquakes . . ." Athena said, her voice hushed. "Could it be?"

"No, it cannot!" Hades shouted. "The gods would not send a barbarian—"

"Perhaps it was a different god," Athena spat. "Or goddess."

Hades's eyes widened in rage.

"She brought the Stranger the last time."

"Enough," Zeus said.

"Majesty, how can you take seriously the empty promise of an enemy savage who says he can stop earthquakes?" Hades demanded.

"It is not he who says it," the king said. "It is I."

"I see. Then he promises nothing."

"He suggests that we evacuate Atlantis."

"Gods above," Hades sputtered. "I will not remain to hear this."

The king laughed. "Then go, brother. Perhaps, for once, we shall not need your slaughters to appease the people."

"I hope you are right," Hades said. "Nevertheless, I shall go ahead with our plans." He bowed perfunctorily, then swept out of the room, his black robes billowing behind him.

Zeus sighed with satisfaction. "This is the first time I've felt like a king since . . ." He blinked. "Your mother believed that it was possible to change the course of things to come," he said. "The priestesses taught her that."

"Yes, I know."

"When she left, I was given one last vision before the Power vanished in me. It was an image of Atlantis as it would be in the future. A terrible image of a lifeless place sucked dry by the earthquakes and our vain efforts to stop them. It so frightened me that I never summoned the Power again afterward, though I have lived with this vision for all the years of my life since then. But now, at last . . ." He patted her hand. "Tell Hephaestus that he is released from all other duties so that he can assist this fellow—what's his name, by the way?"

"Sam."

"Sam?" He grimaced. "Sounds like a dog's name."

"His people use two names. His other is Nowar."

"Well, that's a little better, at least." He laughed. "Tell Nowar he must work quickly. Hades is mounting another slave expedition."

"Father—"

"There's nothing to be done about that."

"You mean Sam's—that is, Nowar's—idea may not work."

"The idea is mine, not his." Zeus smiled at her sadly. "And yes, for all our dreams, it may not work." He patted her hand. "Now go. I am tired, and I wish to spend some time remembering before I sleep."

"Remembering, Father?"

He fingered the diamond suspended on his chest. Its unearthly fire had vanished. "Remembering that, for a little time, I felt the Power rise within me once again."

She kissed the top of his head. "And how did you feel?"

The old king's hands trembled. "Like a god."

Sent to deliver us," Hades muttered as he strode across the plaza toward the canal. The king was an even bigger fool than he had thought.

A stranger, like the last . . .

He turned back to face the palace. On its wall, the Stranger's words sparkled in the sun, mocking him.

The barbarian possessed the Power. At least Zeus believed he did. That made the savage a dangerous enemy. If he convinced the king that he was the Stranger come back, he might well seize the throne when the time came.

Hades could not chance leaving Zeus alone with the foreigner. He would send Ares alone on the slaving foray while he himself stayed. And watched. And prayed for an earthquake.

With a stranger shall it begin again.

"We'll see," he said, turning his back on the pyramid.

CHAPTER 8

THEY STOPPED AT THE STABLES WHERE THE COWS SURROUNDING THE BARNS made a terrible din as they trampled the earth to mud. An old man with a scraggly gray beard ran after them, calling frantically.

"That is Issa, who cares for the palace livestock," Athena said. "He has worked on the palace grounds since he was a child. My mother gave him his freedom, but his citizenship was revoked after her banishment."

She stared after the old man for a moment, her eyes full of sadness, then directed Sam's attention to two younger men who stood examining some sort of metal scoop, oblivious to the chaos around them.

Sam recognized one of them. He was the black man who had taken apart his flashlight and compass. The other was young and huge, with the physique of a bodybuilder.

"This? How can I use this?" the big one was saying, shaking the metal scoop in his hand.

"There are two hundred other identical parts," the black man said. "They all fit together in any configuration we need. I made them to build a flume to carry rainwater into the third canal."

"Can you understand what they're saying?" Athena asked.

Sam nodded. "As long as you're touching me."

"Good. In time, you'll know our language on your own. Until then, I'll stay with you."

"Good morning, Athena," the black man said heartily, walking toward them. He moved, Sam saw, with a pronounced limp.

"Hephaestus, brother, this is Sam Nowar. He is a guest of mine and Father's."

The black man bowed deeply. "I am honored, Excellency," he said.

"Sam'll be fine. You were in the throne room yesterday when my things were passed around."

"I'm afraid I've rendered them quite useless," Hephaestus said, embarrassed. "I took them apart, then lacked the materials to put them back together again. But if you show me how, I'll try to make you new ones."

Sam smiled. *Sure, just whip up a flashlight and compass. Maybe a diesel engine too, while you're at it.* "Okay, thanks."

"Your easy ways are refreshing," the black man said, not without humor. "Most visitors regard us with a begrudging sort of awe. What land are you from . . . Sam?" He looked as if he were suppressing a smile at the name.

Athena broke in hurriedly. "It's quite far," she said. "Hephaestus, the king has ordered Sam to invent a device to stop the earthquakes and directs you to help him. All your other duties are to be suspended."

Hephaestus's eyebrows shot up. "Stop the earthquakes?"

"Wait a minute," the burly young man with him interjected. "What about me? Hephaestus was going to help me muck out these stinking stables."

"Be quiet, Hercules. This matter is more important than the stables." Athena said.

"That's easy for you to say. Hera's not having *you* shovel dung till you drop."

"She would if she could," Athena said.

"Hercules?" Sam looked over the man's handsome features and glistening muscles. "Did you say his name's Hercules?"

"Yes," Athena snapped. "And I'm afraid he'll have to clean the stables alone."

"Sister," Hephaestus said, "I will be only a few minutes more. Have a little pity on the lad."

Athena sighed. It was no secret that her father's wife detested Hercules even more than his other illegitimate children, perhaps because the boy's peasant-born mother had been more beautiful than Hera herself. The queen thought about things like that. It was one of the reasons Athena had no time for her.

"All right," she said. "We'll wait until you're finished. But don't take too long." She led Sam away from the stable toward a fence, beyond which was a moat and what appeared to be a large park. Inside the enclosure roamed a number of exotic animals, tigers and leopards, wolves and bears.

"This is my uncle Poseidon's collection of animals brought back from his journeys," she said. "They're tame. Issa treats them like his children." She waved to the old slave, who had spotted them and was loping toward them, a look of grim determination on his face. "Are you in safety, Princess?" he panted as he approached, eyeing Sam suspiciously. "Lord Poseidon says I must never let harm come to you."

"I'm fine, Issa. Thank you."

"I'm a foreigner myself, and a slave, but your mother was good to me."

"I know."

Sam extended his hand. "I won't hurt the Princess, I promise," he said, forgetting that the old man could not understand him.

Issa examined the stranger's clipped fingernails from a distance, then reluctantly lay his own dirt-encrusted palm on top of it and looked away, wincing.

"He thinks you're going to punish him for insulting you," Athena whispered.

Sam shook Issa's hand. "Sam Nowar," he said as the zookeeper quickly withdrew his hand.

"Nowar?"

"Right. Sam Nowar." He pointed to himself for emphasis.

"Nowar," the old man repeated.

"'Sam' is rather an unusual name, even for a foreigner," Athena said delicately.

An enormous clatter rose up behind a nearby hill, sending the cows scurrying again. Issa bowed quickly in apology and ran off after them as the source of the racket appeared over the rise. It was a cart drawn by two oxen, loaded with fat metal pipes that clanked with each bump. Accompanying it was a score of men on foot.

"Those are workers from Hephaestus's forge," Athena explained. "I can't imagine what he wants with them." They wandered back toward the stables.

At a word from Hephaestus, the men unloaded the cart and began fitting the pipes and elbows together. In surprisingly little time, all the pieces had been joined in an elaborately looped and twisted line.

Hephaestus barked some last orders at the men, then came to stand with Athena and Sam.

"Very impressive," Sam said. "What is it?"

The black man laughed. "It's a flume. It will bring the water down from the mountain's river into the stables. In the front and out the back, and the dung will be gone with it. Hercules will never have to clean the stable again."

"Pretty neat, if it works," Sam said.

"It will work," Hephaestus answered. "My gift is meager but consistent." He limped off toward one of the constructions.

"Don't believe him," Athena said. "Hephaestus is a master builder. Architects say that a talent like his hasn't existed for a thousand years."

The various groups were assembling their metal loops and slides into one enormous whole stretching from the stables uphill to the small mountain river. During the worst of it, Poseidon came galloping up, his white stallion snorting.

"What the devil's going on here?" he shouted over the din.

Sam didn't hear Hephaestus's reply, but the old sailor laughed when he heard it, then yanked the black man up onto the horse behind him and galloped off.

"Poseidon isn't overly fond of Hera, either," Athena said.

"Hera? Oh, right. She's the one who's picking on Hercules."

"My father's second wife," she explained. "Six months ago, she ordered Issa to stop cleaning out the cow barn. Hercules was stupid enough to boast that he'd been invited along on the next slaving expedition. So now that the ships are almost ready to leave, Hera is making him clean the barn first." She shrugged. "It's typical. Unfortunately, even if Hephaestus's device succeeds, she probably won't permit Hercules to go along."

A moment later, they heard hoofbeats as Poseidon and Hephaestus galloped back. "Clear the way!" her uncle shouted. Athena and Sam followed the workmen, rushing for safety.

Hephaestus leaped off the animal's back and made a last-minute adjustment in the Y configuration of pipes at the entrance to the barn door. "Well, that's all we can do now," he said. "Let's hope the barn is still standing when this is over."

Poseidon roared with laughter. "A little late for worries, isn't it?" he shouted. His horse whinnied as the workmen pointed with wonder at the quivering, quaking flume.

Water was hurtling downward, gaining momentum as it rushed in a line over the rolling hills of the terrain, slowing around curves through the ingenious shapes Hephaestus had devised. Just when it threatened to spill over the sides, the water was made to loop in a complete circle. Then it twisted from left to right, serpentine, working its way uphill again to finally crash down with deafening power as it exploded into one side of the cow barn and out the other.

The men cheered, dancing in the cold spray of the water. Hercules grabbed Hephaestus in his arms and lifted him into the air. Issa stoked his beard in wonder at the sight.

Sam looked at the half-mile-long water slide, creaking and swaying but perfectly watertight throughout its convoluted length, and shook his head. How long ago was Atlantis supposed to have existed—eleven thousand years? The time of cavemen?

And yet one of these men had created this sophisticated structure. On a whim.

In a few minutes, the flow subsided. They followed Hephaestus through the barn, which had been swabbed down to bare muddy earth. On the far side, hay and manure were scattered over a rolling meadow. The grass glistened.

Hephaestus approached, a broad smile on his face. "Well, now that that's finished, we can get to work on the earthquakes. I take it you once had earthquakes in your own country, Sam."

"Still do."

"But your people have found a way to control them."

"No."

Hephaestus cocked his head. "Then—if you don't mind—may I ask why His Majesty selected you for this task?"

"He thinks I know things that I don't," Sam said dejectedly.

"You are not an authority on earthquakes?"

Sam shook his head. "I'm a sailor."

"Ah," Hephaestus said gently. "Then our project may take longer than the king expects."

CHAPTER 9

THE SLAVE SHIPS LEFT ATLANTIS FOR THE WESTERN MAINLAND AND, AS ATHENA had predicted, Hercules had not been permitted to go along.

Meanwhile, for two weeks Hephaestus and Sam had been drawing up and discarding various plans for earthquake prevention, hoping to come up with something usable before the ships returned with Hades's sacrificial slaves. This morning, when Sam arrived at the open field near the bay, Hephaestus had been waiting with two long metal coils and a shovel for each of them.

"What the hell is this stuff, anyway?" Sam asked after two hours. He spat on his bloodied hands.

"Metal rope. I dipped the fibers in molten lead." He tossed Sam a rag.

"A lot of good this'll do me now. I'll probably die of lead poisoning before the earthquake kills me."

Hephaestus grinned. "Well, at least you'll be able to speak your last words in the proper Atlantean tongue," he said. Sam had learned the language with amazing speed, probably owing to the unique telepathic way in which Athena had tutored him. Within little more than a week, he had become fluent enough even to joke with the workmen from the forge.

"Yeah. I'm a real linguist. I just wish I knew something about earthquakes."

The black man shrugged. "I don't know if an earthquake expert could help much anyway. Nature always has the final word."

Then you think the destruction of Atlantis is inevitable?"

Hephaestus scooped up a shovelful of dirt. "I think we'd better do what we can," he said.

They worked in silence for a while. Finally Hephaestus sent the digging team back to their regular jobs at the forge. They had dug an area around the roots of two olive trees, and now Sam and Hephaestus were connecting the roots with the metal rope. Hephaestus's theory was that if all the deep-rooted trees were joined together in a powerful underground web, it might contain the vibrations from a quake and keep damage to a minimum. It was a good idea so far as Sam could tell, but the work was backbreaking.

"Have you ever thought about how to stop the tremors before?" Sam asked, breathing hard after the exertion of knotting the cables together.

Hephaestus bent over, his hands on his knees. "Many times."

"And nothing worked?"

Hephaestus shook his head. "It's the location of the island. There's some sort of earthquake belt that runs north and south, almost in a straight line. It's as if the land on either side of the quake line were rubbing together deep underground. Unfortunately, that line goes right through Mount Olympus and through all three canals."

Of course Hephaestus was right, Sam thought, recalling his high school science classes. This Atlantean had figured out something that scientists would only come to realize during the mid twentieth century of the modern world. Earthquakes were caused by plates on the Earth's surface, colliding and slipping into each other.

And there's no solution for it. It's just the way the Earth is built. Atlantis is sitting on a fault.

"Then there might not be anything we can do," he said carefully. "What are the canals for?"

"We need them for irrigation. They collect rain and river water and carry it in concentric circles around much of the island. They've helped the agriculture, but they've made the land even more unstable. Oh, no."

"What is it?"

The black man pulled Sam away from the olive tree and pushed him toward the open field. "Get into the open. One's coming now."

Sam took a deep fearful breath. He had been on the slave ship during the last tremor. The men in the hold had smashed into one another like leaves in the wind, while seawater had gushed over them in torrents. Athena had told him later that it had been minor, as far as Atlantean earthquakes went.

He could almost smell this one. The birds screamed overhead as they flew out toward the sea. In the woods, he saw deer leaping frenziedly, heading for shelter.

The tremor knocked both men down when it struck, rumbling deep in the Earth. Sam felt the ground moving beneath him, crawling like a living thing. Trying to rise, he dug his fingers into the dirt, fighting off a sudden fear that he was about to be swallowed whole by whatever beast lived in its depths.

Ahead of him, a tree splintered with a terrible crash and then slid slowly to the side where it came to rest like a spear tossed miles by a giant.

Hephaestus was lying prone, his arms covering his head. "Get down, fool," he shouted.

"Is this it?" Sam called back as he dropped flat to the ground. "The big one?"

"I don't think so," Hephaestus answered, scrambling closer to Sam. "I've been through worse."

"That's encouraging," Sam mumbled.

It was over in less than a minute. At the far end of the plain, one farmhouse had lost its chimney. A cow screamed in pain as it struggled to stand. Other squat little farm buildings seemed to have come through without much damage.

But the metal cable had not held. Hephaestus picked up both frayed ends from a spot between the two olive trees which now leaned precariously away from one another.

"Better to find out now, rather than later, I guess," Sam said.

They stared at the broken cable for a long time. "It's no use," Hephaestus said finally. "It looks like Hades is going to get his sacrifice after all."

"Does he believe that'll stop the earthquakes?"

"He pretends he does. It will make a great spectacle. The people will see him trying to save them, and they'll regard him as their savior. Then, one day, when a giant quake comes, he'll say it's because Zeus is on the throne and has angered the gods . . . and the people might be frightened enough to believe him." He threw down the ropes. "Meanwhile, two thousand slaves will have had their hearts cut out for nothing." He ran his fingers through his wiry hair. "Life is so cheap to us," he said quietly.

Sam could feel the engineer's disappointment. It was even greater than his own because, after all, Sam had never held out any hope for finding a solution to the earthquakes, but Hephaestus had been searching for years. Now time was clearly running out. With each rumble, the land of the island became more porous, less capable of fending off the encroaching sea. There was never a day now when repair crews were not working on the canals. Sinkholes had appeared in the plain, and areas which were once arable farmland were turning into saltwater marshes.

And the best mind in the world—in Sam's lights, maybe the best mind who had ever lived—could not think of one thing to do about it.

"Maybe the sacrifices will work," Sam offered lamely. "I mean, miracles happen, don't they?"

Hephaestus snorted derisively. "Let's get out of here," he said.

It was a long walk back to the palace, but before they had gone a mile, a figure came riding toward them in a large chariot drawn by two horses kicking up billows of dust that made the figure appear to be constantly emerging from a cloud.

"She looks like a warrior, doesn't she?" Hephaestus said, smiling.

"She?"

"It's Athena. You can see the silver of her headpiece."

She did, in fact, seem to be made of silver, from the diadem in her hair to the crossed bands of silver across her breasts. Moving in the bright sunlight, she shone like a jewel.

"No wonder they call her a goddess," Sam said.

"What's that?"

"Nothing. She's very pretty, that's all."

"Athena's beauty is the least of her attributes. If Zeus were wise, he'd choose her to succeed him on the throne. That is, if anything of Atlantis is left," he added as an afterthought.

The chariot stopped and Athena ran, flushed and dusty, toward them. "Hephaestus," she called. "A message from Parnassus. Your mother's illness has worsened. Come, I will take you to her."

As they rode in the chariot over the highlands, the whole of Atlantis seemed to be spread out before them.

The main island was fairly large and crescent-shaped, anchored at one end by the towering cone of Mount Olympus, with the capital city of Olympus sprawled at its base, and at the other end by the much smaller Mount

Parnassus. Surrounding the main island and stretching across both sides of the Atlantic were an archipelago of small islands, most of them uninhabited and used only as stopovers for the great Atlantean ships on their way to the eastern and western mainlands—the bodies of land Sam knew as Europe and Central America.

The three of them rode south to the city of Parnassus, a journey of several hours overland even though it was visible across the bay from Olympus. As they passed through the small villages along the way, Sam saw everywhere the ravages inflicted on the island by the earthquakes. Buildings were overturned, roads heaped like jumbles of ribbons, land ripped apart as if it had been torn by gigantic hands. Clearly, Atlantis would not survive many more tremors.

Can't they see there's no hope except to get out while there's still time? Sam wondered. The king had refused to consider Sam's suggestion to evacuate the country, even after the terrible vision he had seen.

Well, it was easy to ignore visions, Sam knew. He had ignored them for most of his life. He looked at Athena. Was she, too, despite her powerful clairvoyance, also an ostrich with her head in the sand? Didn't any of them realize that they were facing the end of the world?

"There it is ahead," Athena said, pointing out a long, low building fronted by columns and vined with climbing flowers. "The Muses' residence."

"The Muses," Sam said, remembering what little he had learned about Greek mythology. "Aren't they supposed to be spirits or something?"

Hephaestus laughed. "Hardly. They all started out as the king's concubines. He didn't want them any more after he married Queen Metis, and no one knew what to do with them."

"Hephaestus, it wasn't like that!" Athena chided, slowing the horses.

"Yes, it was. My mother's one of them, after all. She said they were all worried sick that they'd be turned into slaves. I suppose they weren't far from slaves to begin with, even though they'd lived in luxury in the palace, but none of them were ordinary." He winked at Sam. "Zeus was a connoisseur of women. Each of the concubines had some special and outstanding talent, developed either in their homelands or here. My mother's was mathematics. She would have greatly resented scrubbing pots in the royal kitchens."

"That would never have happened," Athena said.

"It certainly would have, if it weren't for your mother." He turned to Sam. "Queen Metis had this grand house built for them, with dozens of extra rooms, and called it a school. Then she got the peasants and tradesmen to send their children there, since the nobility refused. To erase the stigma of their former status, she insisted that the retired concubines be called 'Muses'—it's an old literary term meaning 'guide.' Now it's the best school on the continent. Even royal children study here—if they can pass the tests. The Muses are very particular only to take the most gifted students." He grinned and squeezed Athena's shoulders. "Yes, little sister, your mother left her mark."

Athena blushed with pride as she drove the chariot up to the building and turned the reins over to a stablehand.

Set among the foothills of Mount Parnassus, the Muses' residence was a peaceful oasis of grace and order. Below it, the colorful tiled roofs of the city glinted in the warm sun. The sound of a nearby waterfall mingled with the laughter of children.

"You will want to see your mother alone," Athena said. "We will wait for you. I would like Sam to see Apollo's cave. Give Polyhymnia my best."

The residence was cool and airy. The music from a flute drifted past Hephaestus as he walked on bare feet over its marble floors. Farther down the hall, a group of children was singing, accompanied by lyres played so well they sounded like harps.

He had spent much time in this place of learning, surrounded by women who spoke of geometry and agriculture and poetry, who danced with the lightness of forest sprites and sang with voices like bells. Women with skins of brown and yellow and palest white, their common bond a man who loved them and their accomplishments.

Presiding over it all had been his mother, Polyhymnia. Zeus had given her that name as he had all the others: Calliope, Clio, Melpomene, Euterpe, Erato, Terpsichore, Urania, and Thalia. Beautiful names, belonging to the most beautiful collection of women from around the world, although that would have been laughable to the children who knew them now as old women.

Hephaestus stopped at the entrance to a room. Before he could knock, Apollo peered out of the doorway, his eyes as compassionate as an angel's. Hephaestus was grateful that Apollo had consented to attend his mother. He was as fine a healer as he was musician; but even when his patients were beyond healing, as Polyhymnia was, Apollo brought them comfort.

"I'm glad you could come so quickly," he said with a smile.

"How sick is she?"

Apollo's eyes told Hephaestus all he needed to know. His mother was dying.

"Let my son in," a woman's voice called behind him. "I'm not a cadaver yet."

Polyhymnia appraised her son with a cool gaze. She had arranged herself—with some effort, he suspected—in a pose of elegant grace upon a divan covered with rose silk. Her own robes were of palest green, nearly transparent in their fineness. Her hair, still black with only a few gray strands betraying her age, was pulled up into a series of gold rings atop her head. If it were not for her face—once achingly beautiful, now taut with pain and weariness—one would have thought she was still the exotic concubine brought from a distant land by a king who loved her.

"You're filthy," she said, amusement in her eyes.

"Forgive me, Mother," Hephaestus answered. "I came as soon as I received Apollo's message. The roads are dusty with summer. You look well, though."

"I have apparently made it through the latest crisis, with the help of Apollo's magic."

"I have no magic," Apollo said. "If I had, lady, I would use it to make you well."

She waved him away. "Only a fool wants to live forever. Great age is a terrible curse."

"That is often true," he said, bowing graciously. "I shall go and leave you to your son."

After he left, Polyhymnia's gaze rested steadily on Hephaestus's face. "It's the earthquakes, isn't it?" she asked. "That's why you're so dirty. There was another one today."

Her son was silent. He did not know what to say.

"Well, it does not matter," she said bitterly. "Atlantis has outlived its usefulness. It is time to turn it over to the gods for punishment."

Hephaestus frowned. "Punishment? Surely you haven't taken up Hades's belief in the wrathful Atlantean gods."

"There are other gods besides Hades's."

He had no idea what his mother was talking about. "Which gods are those?"

The old woman narrowed her eyes. "You have learned much among your father's people," she said. "And forgotten more. Even your name."

Hephaestus took a deep breath. He had heard this lament before. His mother had named him Ptah, a sound of power among her people, but Zeus had deemed the name unpronounceable and renamed him. She seemed annoyed that her son had never objected.

"A name isn't so very important," he said.

"One could say the same about an idea, a fact, a truth." Her eyes flashed. "Or have you become too much of an Atlantean nobleman to care about such things?"

Hephaestus sat down wearily. He had come to see his sick mother, and now he was being badgered as if he were a defendant in court.

"Look at me," she snapped.

He looked up dutifully, resentful that she could still make him feel like a wayward child. "Atlantis is doomed, Hephaestus, but you are not. You are not an Atlantean. While half your blood comes from Zeus, the rest is from the heart of the 'other' world where people are allowed to have different colored eyes, different hair, different skin."

"We are no longer in danger in Atlantis, Mother," he said. "You are treated with honor and respect." He did not add: *because of me.*

"I hear you behind your words," Polyhymnia said. "You feel that you belong here, that your gifts would have been wasted in the primitive land of my ancestors. That my people are, after all, not quite human, suitable only for slavery."

"You were never a slave."

"Was I free to leave these long years?" Her elegant nostrils flared.

"I don't understand your point, Mother."

"You don't understand because you think like them! You even married one of them." Her mouth twisted as she spoke the name with deepest scorn. "Aphrodite. You begged for her hand, you gave her everything . . . and yet she despised you."

"Mother . . ."

"You were never anything to her but an ugly black cripple. . . ."

"Stop it," he shouted. He turned away toward the window to hide his face.

"You weep because you believe it yourself," Polyhymnia said. "At your birth, the high priest tried to kill you. Your Atlantean wife loathes you. But even though it destroy you, yet you follow the Atlantean way and thus betray yourself every day."

"How?" he asked hotly. "How do I betray myself, or you? By building dams? By forging tools? By constructing palaces?"

"By doing those things for *them*," she said. "Look at what these people have done with the singular gifts bestowed on them by the Stranger. They can not only read and write and understand numbers, but they can build and sail and soar. With such ability, they could have led the world out of darkness, eliminated hunger and disease, made a paradise of this planet. But what have they done?

"They have withheld the knowledge that would make all men better. And why? Because they cannot be merely men. They must master men, master all they see. That was why I was never permitted to return to my people. The Atlanteans feared that like Prometheus, I would care for the savages. I would try to save their lives."

She sat back on the divan and closed her eyes. "And I would. I would have told them everything I know. Mathematics, writing, music. I would have given them the knowledge of Atlantis to build upon. It would first have benefitted them, but in the end, it would have come back to this land, because the wisdom of the Stranger would be made to grow with each generation of scholars, not diminish back into ignorance."

The corners of her mouth turned down bitterly, and she suddenly looked old. "You wanted to know which gods have come to punish Atlantis. I will tell you. They are the spirits of the air and the water and the stars, of which human beings are a part. And they have watched these prideful Atlanteans separate themselves from the rest of mankind until there is no longer a place for them in the universe. That is their offense. It is for that that they will die. And you, too, if you are one with them."

"I am sorry if I displease you," Hephaestus said disspiritedly. "But an Atlantean is all I know how to be."

"Really? Then how did you build the pyramids?"

"How . . ." He hesitated. "I don't—"

"Yes, you do know what I mean."

He looked at the floor.

"I am a mathematician," she said quietly. "And so I know that these structures are perfect. Their measurements, their relationships, perfection on perfection. I know the perimeter of the base measures the number of days in the year. I have divided the perimeter by twice the height to find the constant that measures the circle. I know that one can calculate the distance to the sun using the values of your buildings. But to do this, one must first *know* the distance to the sun, which was a secret kept by the priestesses of Gaea." Her feverish eyes bored into his. "This knowledge could have come only from one source."

"No," he began to protest.

"You have found the Stranger's own writings, haven't you?" she rasped.

He looked away.

"The high priest killed Prometheus for building a fire to save a slave woman's life. What would he do to you if he knew that you have found the lost knowledge of Atlantis and failed to give it to him?"

Hephaestus was silent for a long time. Finally, he said, "The knowledge was not lost. It was ignored." He took a deep breath. "Years ago, when I was little more than a boy, I was given the task of repairing the underground burial chambers of the king-gods. They were very old, and had been badly damaged by earthquakes. Hades gave me a list of all the ancient kings interred there, and I found every coffin . . . plus one extra."

He swallowed nervously. "It had been behind a wall that had fallen in when part of the ceiling collapsed. The odd thing about it was that the casket was made of a metal I had never seen before. I tried to chip off a piece of it so that I could melt it down in my forge, but it was impossible. That was when I found the writings. They were inside a small case beside the sarcophagus."

Polyhymnia raised her fingers to her mouth. "What did they say?"

He shook his head. "They were difficult to understand. Some parts were expressed only by symbols, which I took to be forms of mathematics and chemistry. That was how I arrived at the dimensions for the pyramid. But the written sections . . ." He looked into his mother's eyes. They gazed at him steadily, patiently. "Some of it seems to assume that human beings have more than five senses," he said.

"And so you decided not to tell Hades."

"I had no choice, mother. The priests deny that the Stranger ever existed. If I were to tell him I'd found the coffin, Hades would have had me killed to protect his religion."

Polyhymnia pressed her lips together. "Then what did you do with it?"

"Nothing, at the time. But later, when I built the death pyramid, I moved it along with those of the kings. I built a special chamber for the coffin. No priest can find it."

"And the writings?"

"I copied them onto the wall of the chamber. For a later time, when the truth is no longer required to conform to the notions of those in power. When, perhaps, great knowledge will be used for something besides the subjugation of others."

She blinked slowly, her eyes brimming. "How I have underestimated you, Ptah," she whispered. "And how proud I am to call you son." She embraced him, and within the circle of her bony, frail arms, Hephaestus felt her complete and perfect love. "I wish to make a request of you," Polyhymnia said, her voice quavering. "A very difficult request."

"Yes? What is it?"

She clasped his hands. "The end of Atlantis will come soon," she said. "Before it is too late, I want you to go back across the seas to my homeland."

"Back to—"

"To the so-called savages from whom you have distanced yourself so utterly. Teach them what you know, and learn from them what you need. Place the ashes of Atlantis in this new land, Ptah, and from them build an empire based on dignity and truth."

He was silent for a long time.

"Will you do this for me?"

He nodded slowly. "Yes. I'll go."

She smiled, then lay back, her eyes closed.

"I love you," Hephaestus whispered, still holding her hand.

She squeezed his once, so weakly he could not discern whether or not the action was deliberate, then let go.

CHAPTER 10

AFTER HEPHAESTUS WENT INTO THE MUSES' RESIDENCE, ATHENA LED SAM UP a narrow path toward a cave where to women stood. At their feet were dozens of clay pots, some of them enormous, surrounded by cut flowers. The women were tending the flowers, picking out the dead blooms, arranging the rest. Sam saw one of them drop a dead mouse into one of the flower pots.

"What's she doing?" he asked.

"Feeding the snakes."

Sam stopped in his tracks. "You're taking me into a cave with *snakes*? I don't think so."

"Don't be silly," Athena chastened. "The snakes here are sacred. It is said that the Stranger came to this cave to die. After his spirit departed, the serpents protected his body from predators until the priestesses arrived to claim it. This is a place of great power."

The Stranger, Sam remembered. The king's thoughts had contained something about that. "Is that what you call God?" he asked. "The Stranger?"

Athena shook her head. "He was never a god," she said. "He came from a place far away—no one knows where—with powers and knowledge beyond the ken of the primitive people who lived here in those days. At least that is how the legend goes."

She picked a fragrant blossom from a low-hanging branch and twirled it between her fingers. "In that time we worshipped the Earth goddess. Some of us still do, even though Hades and his priests have all but outlawed the faith. They discount the Stranger now because he had been very close to the high priestess of the old religion. Her lover, in fact."

Sam laughed. "You sound as if you knew him personally."

"My mother spent her youth with the priestesses before their temple was destroyed. They kept the Stranger's memory alive."

"Even his love affairs?"

"Oh, it was more than that. He loved her so deeply that he promised to return after his death to be with her again." She ducked her head to enter the mouth of the cave. "Some believe that was what the Stranger meant when he wrote his last words—these—with a burnt stick on this stone."

She gestured toward a large slab of rock propped against the far wall. The original writing had been replaced by words carved into the rock. " 'With a stranger shall it begin again,' " she read. "Of course, one can read many meanings—"

"Oh, my God," Sam said. He brushed the stone lightly with the palm of his hand. In his mind, he could almost see the luminescent plant life covering it drift away into the ocean. "The grotto."

"Is this place familiar to you?" she asked.

"It's how I got here. Only it was underwater. I found it in the Peaks, and I came up—" he squinted along the distant shoreline "—over there, I think. Facing Olympus."

The two women who were tending the flowers outside murmured as they slipped past him, behind the Stranger's stone. "What's back there?" he asked.

"The cavern is vast," Athena said. "This is only its mouth." She led him inside.

The inner cavern was not the dark, still place Sam had expected. Fissures crazed the slippery, slightly domed floor, out of which poured billows of seething steam and an eerie phosphorescent light. It was as close an approximation of hell as Sam had ever seen. The women who had preceded them sat on a stone bench along the glistening wet wall.

"They are waiting for my brother Apollo," Athena said softly. "He is a healer."

As she spoke, an enormous python slithered across the floor near Sam's feet. Athena laughed at the expression on Sam's face. "Don't worry," she said. "The snakes here are well fed."

"Glad to hear it." Sam swallowed. "Do all your hospitals look like this?"

"No. Apollo does not treat sickness with medicine here. He heals with the Power alone."

"Oh." Sam thought of Carol Ann. "I knew someone like that once." Suddenly he felt the memories of another life crashing down upon him like pebbles in an avalanche, stinging with its old hurt, threatening to bury him.

"This place greatly concentrates the mind," Athena said, sensing his unease. "Be careful of your thoughts." She pulled him deeper into the interior of the cave.

Sweat had been pouring into his eyes since they had walked behind the Stranger's stone, but here in the dark corridor where they walked, it was much cooler. Athena moved briskly into another chamber of the cave system, then another, each darker than the last. It was as if she were racing toward some sort of sanctuary. She held her back very straight, very rigid. Sam had the feeling that if he touched her, she might break into brittle little pieces.

By the time they reached the last cave there was almost no light, and the air was so cold Sam felt himself shivering. Here Athena finally stopped, sitting on a small natural ledge against the wall. Feeling his way, Sam sat next to her, blinking in the absolute darkness.

"I used to come here as a child," Athena said, her voice sounding hollow. "Sometimes I saw you in my thoughts." She trembled.

"What's the matter?" he asked gently, taking her hand. He could make out the faint outline of her face now.

"I almost did not bring you here," she said softly. "I thought that I might keep you with me, like a pet. Forgive me."

The implications of what she was saying slowly crept over him. "You mean you know how to get me back?"

"I am not certain. But as I told you, this is a place of power. It is also apparently where you crossed over from your world to mine. If there is any place from which you might return, it is here."

"How . . . how do I do it?"

"Try to remember the world in your own time. It should not be difficult. Those thoughts have never been far from your mind."

She was right. Behind everything he had seen and done in Atlantis had been the nagging, insistent memory of the people he had left behind. Darian, aging and alone on board the *Styx*; Cory, whom he might have loved if Athena had not called to him from the bottom of the sea; Reba . . .

Reba was kneeling on the sand of Memory Island.

And she was staring right at him.

Sam!

He gasped.

Sam, honey, wherever you are, you got to come back

"Reba?"

I see you. But it's dark there, so dark

He felt his whole body growing numb. "Athena," *he whispered, reaching out for her frantically.*

"Don't be afraid," *she said, embracing him. He could hardly hear her voice.* "Good journey to you, Sam. . . ."

He heard the music again, Her music that had called to him all his life, fading now, the tie between them finally loosening. At last he would be free, a normal man for whom the siren of the distant past did not sing. He would have his world back.

Without Athena.

Sam? Reba's voice, louder now. Sam, you hear me?

"I . . ." He clutched Athena closer to him. "God forgive me, I can't leave her now," he said hoarsely. "I know you need me, Reba, but I've waited for her too long to give her up."

"No, Sam," Athena protested. "Go. You must try. . . ." She was choking with tears.

Reba's face shrank to a pinpoint and vanished.

"Get her back!" Athena demanded. "Leave this place now, before it is too late!"

"It's already too late," Sam said.

"You are betraying your own people by not returning to help them."

"I'm staying here."

She moaned. "You don't know what you're saying, Sam. There is no future here. Not for any of us. I will show you." She pressed her hands on his face and released the full flood of her thoughts.

Suddenly Sam felt as if he were on fire.

Fire. It's all fire.

The fire was all around him: First the earth opened up in giant cracks, swallowing whole buildings while a fleet of ships surrounded by hundreds of small boats bobbed wildly in the roiling sea. Bobbed, then capsized, one by one, overcome by waves the height of mountains, washing over the square sails of the galleons until they were gone, splintered like driftwood. For a few moments, heads dotted the water, their bodies invisible, their faces contorted with terror and the certainty of death.

In the rubble which had once been the great city of Olympus were strewn bodies, thousands of arms and legs, a woman's buttocks obscenely displayed in death, a disembodied foot resting atop an ornament that had once graced the roof of some magnificent building. Then came the sea, the sea roiling over the plain, covering the land forever, taking it down, down. . . .

"That is what awaits you here," Athena whispered roughly. Her hands slipped from his face. "And the barren island of my father's vision is all that will remain of us."

He took her hands. "It doesn't have to happen that way," Sam said stolidly. "We can leave. All of us, together. There are places in the world besides Atlantis."

"We cannot change the course of things to come," she said dully.

They were both silent for a long time. The only sound was the slow dripping of water from somewhere far away.

"I brought you to my doomed country," Athena said bitterly. "I brought you here because I saw you in my dreams and I wanted you to be with me," she said. "It was as if I'd known you before, in some other life, in some other time. . . ."

Suddenly she laughed. It was high-pitched and hysterical. "Another time," she shrieked.

"Athena—" He took hold of her shoulders. "Athena. Stop it."

"Another time. . . ." She bent her head forward onto his chest and sobbed. "It was *your* time I saw, a time that owes nothing to Atlantis, a time where this land is nothing but a legend, a fairy story. Everything we know, everything we are, is for nothing." She held him close to her. "Oh, Sam, don't you see? I brought you here to die with us. If you don't go now, I'll have destroyed you!"

He felt her slender body wrack with a sadness so terrible it seemed her flesh could hardly contain it.

"I wanted to come," he said softly.

"Because I called to you."

He drew in the fragrance of her hair. "It was all I had to live for."

"Then you're a fool."

He moved his face close to hers, felt her breath on his face. "I won't leave you," he said. "I'll never leave you."

In the dark cave he took her in his arms and their lips met, hungrily, their embrace one that had waited lifetimes. Her dress slid from around her easily, settling to the floor like the wings of a butterfly.

She came to him then, naked and filled with wild love. The music that welled out of them crashed around them like waves as their bodies moved in a frenzy of desire. His mouth suckled her breasts, perfect, pliant, and when they joined in flesh, as they had been joined in their minds for so many years, it was as if the sea had swallowed them both.

"I love you," he said.

The words, whispered, echoed through the cave, softer, softer, until they were inaudible but still present.

"And I love you, Sam."

She buried her face in his neck and wept.

CHAPTER 11

At dawn, the southeast seacoast of Atlantis was even more beautiful then her cities. The Atlantean fleet, now reduced to fewer than a hundred ships because of Hades' slaving expedition, stood in the harbor, their masts pointing toward the sky, bursting one by one into flashes of light as the sun rose.

From atop a boulder protruding out of the sand, Sam watched a lone man on horseback cantering along the docks, stopping occasionally to take a closer look at one vessel or another. It was Poseidon, Sam knew. The old man could not stay away from the sea. And when on land, he always rode. It was as if he could not bear for his feet to touch dry land.

Sam smiled as Poseidon galloped toward him. The gruff old sailor would never believe that he would be remembered, one day eleven millennia from now, as a god.

"Spying on my ships?" he demanded as he reined in the stallion abruptly, engulfing Sam in a cloud of dust.

"No, sir."

"Then what's your business?"

Sam shook his head. "I've got no business."

"My brother thinks you'll end the earthquakes. Can it be done?"

Sam looked out into the harbor. "No, sir. Not by me."

The horseman snorted. "Well, that sounds honest, at least." His gaze followed Sam's toward the water, where the first of Poseidon's sailors were heading toward shore, sacks of tools slung over their shoulders.

"Are you planning to build more ships?" Sam asked.

Poseidon looked down at him, his eyes narrowed. "We're repairing the ones we've got."

"What about the rest of the island? Do you have other shipyards?"

The sailor crossed his arms over his chest. "I think all you need to know is that the Atlantean fleet is the biggest and best in the world."

"Big enough to get everyone out of here?" Sam asked baldly. "Look, evacuation is the only hope you people have. And that depends on your ships."

Poseidon looked at him crookedly. "Have you told the king of your fears for us?"

Sam picked up a pebble and tossed it. "I've tried. So has Hephaestus. Zeus won't listen, and that bat-winged priest keeps telling him I'm some kind of enemy saboteur."

The sailor laughed. "My men would agree with him. The ones who don't think you're a spy are convinced you're a sorcerer. And I'm not sure you're not both."

The approaching seamen passed them. They touched their fists to their chests in salute to Poseidon while eyeing Sam suspiciously. Then they slid into the water around the first ship, their hammers and tar pots on backs as they climbed the squat masts. Poseidon turned his stallion to follow them.

"The sails," Sam said suddenly. "Your sails are wrong."

Poseidon turned back toward him, frowning. "The sails aren't even up."

"Doesn't matter," Sam said. "It's their shape that's wrong. They're square, and stuck on the masts like shields. Spinnaker sails would maneuver better."

"Spin . . . what?" he asked irritably.

"Kind of like this." Sam drew a picture in the sand with a stick. "It's sort of like a lopsided rectangle, so that one corner points upward."

"That's a ridiculous shape for a sail," the sailor scoffed. "It would overbalance at the first gust of wind."

"Not if it were allowed to rotate on the mast." Sam made some refinements on his sand drawing. "You'll need some spars here . . . and here . . . to provide support for the sail, so that when you hoist it, the upper spar is lifted by the rigging. These ropes—" he added more lines "—will adjust their position. Each sail would move in a full circle around the mast, and you could let them out according to how much wind you have to work with." He set down his stick. "They'd make your ships go a lot faster than those big rags you've got up now."

Poseidon glared at him. "By the gods, you even talk like a sorcerer."

"What I am is a sailor, Poseidon, and I can help you if you'll let me." His words hung in the silence. "Look, I'll prove this sail works," Sam offered. "Give me one ship. I'll fit it out and you can see for yourself."

"Give a ship to a spy?" the old man roared. "Do you think I'm an idiot?"

"No, you're not. That's why you ought to consider what I'm saying."

For a moment Poseidon sat motionless on his stallion, examining the crude drawing in the sand. Then, without a word, he reached down and pulled Sam up onto the horse with a powerful swing of his arm. He galloped the stallion down the beach until they were beside the remains of an old fishing boat lying on its side in a bed of dried seaweed.

The boat was only fifty feet long, Sam noted, barely larger than Darian McCabe's *Styx*, with a shallow keel. There was a hole on the bottom three feet wide. The single mast had been broken off near its base. It had no rudder.

Poseidon tossed him onto the beach beside the wreck. "You can have this one," he said with a grin.

"Very funny."

"You said you needed a ship. Here it is."

Sam felt the broken ends of the boards around the hole in the hull. The wood wasn't rotten; the boat must have been pulled out of the water fairly quickly after it was wrecked.

He put his hands on his hips. "All right, I'll take it," he said.

The old man laughed heartily. "Excellent! You have three days." He galloped away.

"Wait," Sam called after him. "Three days isn't . . . this tub's a wreck . . . I can't. . . . "

But all he heard in response were hoofbeats and Poseidon's laughter.

"Damn you," he shouted. But the laughter didn't stop.

Sam went to see Hephaestus. The engineer had been brooding in his palace apartment ever since his visit to his mother, but Sam told him this was an emergency. He drew pictures of the sails and rigging he proposed, and diagrammed the wind dynamics as well as he knew how.

Hephaestus looked at the drawings for a long while, at first with little interest, then coming to life with question after question.

"The problem is that the boat's a piece of junk," Sam complained. "And I've only got three days to repair the hull and rig the sails."

Hephaestus smiled. "We'd better get to work, then," he said.

Hephaestus had one crew of men from his forge repair the hull of the boat and coat the bottom with pitch while another team constructed a rudder which responded to a helm fashioned by yet a third group. The sail, cut from ordinary sailcloth, was being sewn by a fourth crew. Sam marveled to watch their big, permanently-blackened hands work with the skill and precision of embroiderers.

The masts were in the hands of Sam and Hephaestus. From Sam's designs, Hephaestus fashioned two lightweight masts made from a metal alloy that was sturdier than aluminum, with half its weight. With bolts, Hephaestus attached the rings that accommodated the rigging.

They were finished in two days. They had two telescoping masts, twenty and thirty feet long, which swiveled smoothly in all directions and would support a ton of canvas.

But it still had to be assembled.

They began near sundown, the men from the forge carrying the restored hull on their shoulders to a makeshift dry dock on shore. By nightfall, the rudder had been attached and the underpinnings that would support the helm fitted into the empty hull.

Issa, the ancient slave who tended the livestock and the zoo, came by with a tray filled with oil lamps. He exhausted himself scurrying about, trying to hold a light over one section of work and then another, but the night was starless and the men, already growing slow and clumsy with fatigue, were bumping into each other in the darkness.

"Fitting the masts is going to be impossible without light," Sam said. "Maybe we ought to wait until daybreak. . . . "

He squinted into the distance. A smattering of light, like a swarm of fireflies, emerged from the pyramid palace in the distance, then made its way slowly forward toward them. As they watched, the tiny lights grew in number until they took the shape of an immense serpent winding its way down the mountain.

"What is it?" Sam asked, feeling the flesh on his neck rise.

Suddenly Hephaestus laughed and pointed. "Look. The leading light."

And then Sam saw it: a band of silver just above the glow of quivering flame and the face of a goddess.

"Athena," he whispered.

"It looks like she's brought every retainer in the palace with her."

"And every lamp," Sam said.

The workers welcomed the torchbearers loudly. Sam watched Athena's serene face blush in the glow of flames. "How did you get them all to come?" he asked.

"None would stay away," she said. "All have heard of your wager."

"Wager?"

She gave him a look of mock surprise. "Why, don't you know? It's all around. If your boat can't sail faster than my uncle's best warship, you've promised to turn yourself into an ass."

Sam laughed. "It won't be the first time." He felt himself getting lost in her eyes again. "I've missed you."

"You had to be left to your work."

"I thought you didn't believe we could change the course of things to come," he said.

She smiled at him shyly. "Perhaps I was wrong." She backed away, positioning herself and her lamp at the opposite end of the boat.

By first light, the masts were locked in place, the rigging mounted, and the new sails ready to unfurl. Only a few of the volunteers, among them Athena, remained. She was standing, as still and beautiful as a statue, the lamp in her hands infusing her with radiance.

"We're finished," Sam said. He was bone-weary. It was a struggle to keep his eyes open. But even as he leaned against the keel, he heard the sound of hoofbeats.

"Let's hope she floats," he said to Hephaestus.

"If she doesn't, don't count on anyone pulling us out," the black man said.

Sam looked at him. "Us?" he said.

"Do you think I'd miss the maiden voyage of a ship I built with my own hands?"

Sam grinned and turned to face Poseidon.

The old sailor circled the small boat, his face deliberately expressionless. But Sam could see in his eyes the admiration for the workmanship and a barely contained curiosity about the lightweight metal masts and the sails furled tightly to them.

He examined the mechanism beneath the helm that controlled the flared, curved rudder, so different from the crude boards used in even the newest fleet ships, then turned back to Sam.

"Well, let's see how this strange fish swims," he commanded.

As the men from the forge lifted the boat into the water, Sam glanced at Athena. Slowly she inclined her head in silent benediction.

Sam and Hephaestus climbed into the boat and Sam untied the first sail. The wind was good; it flapped noisily as it opened. Then it filled as Hephaestus untied the second sail. Observers on shore gasped at the two delicate parallelograms which filled with air, then settled as Sam luffed the boat around into the wind and then filled again as Sam at the helm raced across the harbor mouth.

He guessed he was doing twenty knots, three times the speed of Poseidon's fastest warship, and when he looked back toward shore he saw the old sailor, standing near Athena, staring after him.

He did not know that Poseidon had been hoping, too, that Sam's idea would work. The old sailor had known for some time that evacuation of the island might become necessary.

"Let me take some people now," he had pleaded with Zeus weeks before. "A few hundred at a time, moving them out of our colonies. There's Iberia, Phoenicia, Egypt, Attica . . . all with tracts of good land."

Zeus answered by covering his head with his hands.

"Brother, you must consider—"

"I do consider. I consider every night as I cannot sleep," Zeus said.

"Then save the people while you can!"

Zeus looked up, red-eyed and angry. "And what if this calamity does not happen for a thousand years? My visions—and the foreigner's—are without time. Should I exile our best citizens to savage lands now for no reason?"

Poseidon was astonished. "But the earthquakes—"

"The earthquakes have come and gone for generations. Perhaps they will go on for generations to come." He slapped his hands into his lap. "Who knows? Perhaps the ancestor kings will save us, after all."

"Is that what Hades is saying?" Poseidon asked with disgust.

The king sighed. "Why do you insist on mocking the gods?"

Poseidon's eyes were hard. "I know no gods, brother. Certainly not Hades's moldering kings. I know only the sea, and the sea in an earthquake frightens me."

Zeus touched the diamond pendant around his neck as if hoping for a sign from it. The lifeless rock gave none. "We will wait," Zeus had said, wearing his weariness like a shroud. "We must hold on to Atlantis for as long as we can."

Poseidon had obeyed, but on that day, he began working his men mercilessly from daybreak to night, repairing every vessel in the fleet. He vowed to himself that when Ares returned from his latest expedition, there would be no more slave runs. Every ship would remain moored at harbor in perfect condition, awaiting the king's command to evacuate the island.

Now he smiled as he watched Hephaestus and Sam Nowar sail their boat back and forth across the harbor with a speed he had never seen before. The new sails gave him hope. They, not the mountain of sacrificed bodies that lay in the Land of the Dead, would save his people from destruction.

A soft arm draped gently around his waist. Athena rested her head on his shoulder, her hair smelling of smoke from the lamp she had held through the night.

"Does it make a difference, Uncle?" she asked. "We still cannot stop the final earthquake."

"No, we cannot," Poseidon whispered into the wind. Sam and Hephaestus were coming around, tacking against the wind, slicing forward through the sea without a single rower. A laugh rose from deep in Poseidon's throat as the watching crowd of sailors cheered. "But with these sails, we can outrun the bastard!"

S tanding atop the death pyramid, Hades looked out of expressionless eyes at the bay.

The foreigner was going to convince them all to abandon their homes and live like savages in some distant colony. Then, no doubt, the barbarian's own people would move in—a bloodless coup of the greatest nation in the world. And this treacherous savage would sit on the throne of Atlantis.

He had never forgotten Hecate's prophecy. Half of it had already come true—Zeus had usurped Hades's place as king. But there had been another part to which the high priest had paid scant attention at the time. Hecate had forseen that Zeus would not only rule Atlantis, but would destroy it.

Now he saw how that would come to pass—not through Zeus's own hands, but through those of a stranger whom the mindless rabble would follow into oblivion.

The people must be persuaded not to leave.

For that, he needed an earthquake.

Return soon, Ares, he commanded silently. *Bring my slaves*.

F rom a window in the palace pyramid, Zeus also watched the small boat that sailed with the speed of a bird in flight.

He knew his brother. Poseidon would be impressed and would surely rerig the ships of the fleet to use the odd new sails.

Perhaps it is time to think of escape, after all, he thought. *So it has come to this*.

He fingered the diamond amulet. The Eye of Zeus no longer saw anything.

Once his mind had boiled with visions, plans, decisions. The stone had glowed brightly. "Ah, Metis, why did I let you go?" he cried aloud.

With her, he had banished his self respect. And with that, even the Stranger's great gift had left him.

Now Hades and his sacrifices were all he had left to wish upon.

His heart felt as dead as a hollow tree.

CHAPTER 12

HEPHAESTUS WAS CALLED AWAY THE NEXT DAY TO ATTEND THE FUNERAL of his mother in Parnassus. Apollo told him that she had never regained consciousness after her son's visit to her. It was as if she had saved the last of her strength to see him.

Upon his return to Olympus, he found the naval yards in a welter of activity. After Sam's demonstration of the efficacy of his new sails, Poseidon had ordered the hundred large warships which remained in the harbor to be similarly outfitted. Now, Hephaestus's forge worked day and night to build the navy's new masts. At night, the glow of its furnaces colored the sky around Mount Olympus.

Zeus had even asked the commoners for their help in refitting, but they had not cooperated. Instead, they had gathered on the banks of the canal facing Hades's pyramid and raised their plaintive voices, praying for the gods to deliver them from destruction.

"Why don't they help?" Sam asked, seeing the crowd kneel before the black figure of the high priest. "Don't they understand? These ships can save them."

"They'll accept salvation if someone gives it to them, the way Hades has promised to," Hephaestus said dryly. "It's easier to sacrifice a slave than rerig a ship. Besides, they don't want to accept the idea that they may have to leave. There's not much out there, you know."

"Then the hell with them," Sam growled. "The best will want to go."

Will they? Hephaestus wondered. *Will I?*

His whole life and more was bound to Atlantis. This was where he grew from an unwanted bastard child into the genius of his age. When the time came, would he be willing to leave? Or would he, like the commoners, like the king himself, continue to hope for an end to the earthquakes, look for a way to repair the damage done, hang on for another day, yet another day. . . .

Hephaestus had promised his mother he would go. He had meant to keep that promise, but . . . *Africa?* Why, the whole gigantic uncharted continent was so savage that the Atlanteans had not even established slave routes there. To leave the greatest civiliation the world had ever known to live in a jungle with people who had not yet developed even the concept of the wheel was a prospect too unpleasant to contemplate.

Still, he had promised.

He owed more than his life to Polyhymnia. He owed her his knowledge. For it was his mother, one of the jungle people his Atlantean sense of superiority held in such disdain, who had taught him the magic of mathematics as she herself learned it. She had opened his eyes to the perfection of geometry, the arcane mysteries of algebra. She had shown him the stars and revealed to him their absolute connection with the Earth.

And she had never been a slave.

Zeus had found Polyhymnia by accident, in the remotest area of the deep jungle, far to the south. She had been a queen of sorts, according to Zeus, although she herself had rarely spoken of her life before she had come to live in Atlantis.

The king had seen her, carried in a great chair, her hair braided into a hundred loops, like snakes, dotted with gold nuggets and gems of brightest blue and green. Her eyes, Zeus told him, were wild like a panther's, and her limbs, longer and more graceful than any Atlantean woman's, were covered with bracelets of hammered gold.

Zeus had been on excursion with Poseidon. They had blown off course, and Polyhymnia was the unexpected treasure they found. She offered herself to Zeus in exchange for his promise to send no others to the land she called Timbuktu. If he did not comply with her bargain, she said, she would kill herself.

Zeus never doubted that she would keep her word. Years after her arrival in Atlantis, even after the king took other concubines to slake his lust in her place, neither he nor Poseidon ever had revealed the location of her native land.

Or perhaps they simply did not remember it.

Hephaestus sighed. In the end, he knew, he would go. Polyhymnia had not been an Atlantean; promises had carried weight with her.

A sharp nub of metal from one of the masts he was unloading cut his palm. He cursed and held his other hand to it to stanch the flow of blood.

"It's a sign," a voice said behind him.

Hephaestus did not turn around. He knew the velvet of that voice and the poison it carried. He tore off a piece of his tunic and wrapped it around his bleeding palm.

"You're defying the gods. Perhaps you'll lose those precious hands." She laughed in that overblown, exaggerated way he had always hated.

He whirled to face her. "Aphrodite," he began. He wanted to tell her to stop bothering people who worked while she idled but, as always, the sight of her took all his words away and left him staring like a fool.

She was wearing the belt he had made as his wedding gift to her. It was a broad expanse of beaten gold, seven inches wide in its center, ornamented with polished red star sapphires in a sunburst pattern around a massive pear-shaped pearl that gleamed like the moon. She had kept the gift when she left him. In fact, she had worn it on the day she sailed away with Ares to one of his pleasure homes on an out island.

Her infidelity had come as no surprise, really. Aphrodite was a beauty, the most beautiful woman the royal house had ever produced. She would have been a prize if she had been a peasant's daughter; as a noblewoman of Atlantis, she was unreachable.

From the time she was a girl, Aphrodite had been courted. Songs were written about her breathtaking beauty, her golden red hair, and eyes as blue as the sea, her porcelain skin which never freckled, her lissome figure.

And so everyone was shocked when Hera, wife to Zeus, announced that Aphrodite would marry Hephaestus, who walked with a limp, whose nose had been crushed during his fall in infancy, whose right eye drooped somewhat, whose dark skin still bore the pink stretched scars from that fall.

Hephaestus!

He knew why he had been chosen. Hera, in her jealousy, had played one of her cruel jokes on the one woman who was unqualifiedly more beautiful than she herself. Hera had made the choice to punish Aphrodite for her youth and perfection, but Hephaestus did not care. He loved her anyway, and hoped that with time Aphrodite would come to love him in return. He had asked nothing of her. He did not even demand his marital rights to her body, although he hungered for it.

Once she had kissed him. It was a tease, a long, slow tantalizing kiss that left his whole body hard and throbbing, his need so urgent that he feared he would explode. And then she had danced away, laughing, taunting him with her naked legs, her hair swirling in waves below her hips.

It was an old story, and he should have known the ending. Aphrodite despised him. She openly consorted with other men, particularly Ares. And after a while, Hephaestus no longer cared.

"What do you want, Aphrodite?" he asked quietly.

"Is this your best solution to the earthquakes? Rebuild the navy?"

"Yes." He went about his work, conscious that his hands were trembling. It was the scent of her, not human, nothing to do with sweat or tears, but the scent of jasmine and rose and bergamot, as if she were some exotic blossom planted among weeds.

"It's a waste of time. No one's going to leave Atlantis except for the king and his precious Athena. And good riddance to them both, the scared rabbits!"

"If they leave, we all leave."

She laughed. "Do you think they'd let *you* on board?" Her voice was high and tinkling as a bell. "It stinks here."

"Then go back to the palace. Or wherever you're lying down these days."

She pointed to Sam, fitting a mast at the other end of the ship. "It's his doing, isn't it? He's the one who's been talking Zeus into abdicating his throne."

"So far as I know, the king is not abdicating anything."

"But he will. When that spy says it's time, Zeus will leave, and our enemies will move in without sacrificing a drop of blood."

"You're talking nonsense."

"Am I? Well, Ares will be home soon. We'll see what he has to say."

"What's that supposed to mean?"

"It means that some of us still care about Atlantis. We're not willing to destroy it because some foreigner who claims to have magic powers tells us to."

He wiped his hands on his tunic. "Fine," he said wearily. "Now if there's nothing else, I have work to do."

She regarded him with disgust. For the first time, Hephaestus noticed the fine lines around the corners of her mouth, the occasional glint of silver in her abundant hair.

"You're not young anymore," he said with amazement. Her only gift had been her beauty, and already it was fading.

Aphrodite's eyes flashed with anger. "Ape," she hissed as she turned away.

As Sam ambled over to Hephaestus, he watched Aphrodite pick her way awkwardly through the laborers on the docks.

"Your wife?" Sam asked.

"She was." Hephaestus felt ashamed of the catch in his voice. "A long time ago."

Suddenly a man who was shimmying up Sam's newly set mast called out, "Ships!"

On the shore, the supplicants praying to gods inside the death pyramid bounded to their feet. "Ships! Ships!" They raced toward the docks, knocking over the masts which stood waiting to be mounted, trampling the precious handwoven sailcloth. "The crown prince has returned with the sacrifices!" they shouted. "We are saved. Saved!"

"I was hoping we would be done before he got back," Hephaestus said quietly to Sam. "Now, if an earthquake of any magnitude comes, they'll have to choose between Hades's way and ours."

The crowd, shrieking and running like mainland savages, threw themselves into the water of the harbor, waving their arms wildly at the returning ships, shouting through the tears that streamed down their faces that the catastrophe had been averted and that the gods had taken pity on them.

"Bring the sacrifices," they screamed. "Let the temple run with blood for the gods to feast on."

"I think they've already made their choice," Sam said.

And then the ground began to shake.

CHAPTER 13

IT WAS WORSE THAN THE OTHERS.

The earthquake lasted for nearly nine minutes. When it quieted, the city of Olympus lay in ruins. The walls of ancient temples on the surrounding hillsides had fallen in. Boulders had rolled loose from the volcano of Mount Olympus and smashed into government buildings below. Whole sections of the city were engulfed by fire. At first count, more than two hundred people had died. The other cities on Atlantis were damaged just as badly.

More than twenty of Poseidon's newly rerigged ships were sunk at their moorings when inundated by building-high waves. Forty others suffered some sort of damage.

For the next twenty-four hours, Poseidon's seamen worked alongside the fire patrols to dig through fallen rock and debris to retrieve the dead.

The twelve ships returning from the slaving expedition turned away at the first sign of the quake. There was talk at first that the ships had sunk, but Poseidon knew that the crewmen who manned the frigates could tell the difference between the normal turbulence of rocky shoals and the wild water that surrounded an island in the throes of earthquake.

Two days later, although most of the dead had been buried and the rubble cleared, the city had not yet recovered. In the city squares, toppled statuary lay bound in rags, awaiting the attention of workmen. The torso of Atlas, first son of the Stranger, rose up, headless, from its ruined temple. A marble likeness of the sea-god, Oceanus, lay half buried in broken stone.

Hephaestus surveyed the destruction around him. *We will die here*, he thought, *in this place which was supposed to bring the light of the universe to the Earth*. His eyes filled with tears.

Gods of my soul, how miserably we've failed.

Sam was in the fields with the zookeeper, Issa. He had seen the old man struggling to splint the quake-broken leg of what appeared to be a lion cub. The animal—only a hundred pounds but already possessed of four-inch fangs—clawed and spat at the old man while he tried to set the bone.

"None but this one got hurt, bless me," Issa said, finishing the splint while Sam held the cub still. "I suppose it's not much use fixing them up, though. If we have to leave, there'll be no place on the ships for animals." He turned his face to the sun and blinked. "I guess I've grown fond of them." There were tears in the crinkles of his eyes.

"I think there's going to be a lot of water," Sam said. "And maybe not just here."

The old man stared. "Is this a prophecy?" he asked meekly, bowing his head to the man so many regarded as a wizard.

"No. It's . . . well, okay, yes. I think we're going to have a lot of flooding, and I don't think you should leave all the animals behind. There might not be any when you get where you're going."

Issa gasped and took a step backward. "You mean . . . the whole *world* . . ."

Sam touched his shoulder. "Issa, I have that boat that Poseidon gave me. It's small, but it will carry many of your finest specimens. Build cages for them. You can get the materials from the shipyard. If the worst happens, you'll be ready."

"What animals would I take?"

"You'd know more about that than anyone else," Sam said.

Issa screwed up his face in thought. "Well, I do have this god."

"What?"

The old man looked suddenly flustered. "You won't tell the priests, will you?"

Sam chuckled. "Not likely. Hades isn't exactly beating down my door to make conversation with me."

"That's true enough," the old man considered. "Him and his priests are telling people you made the earthquakes happen so everybody will leave Atlantis and turn it over to you."

"Right. They probably believe him, too."

"Some do."

"So what about your god, Issa?"

He made a gesture for Sam to keep his voice down. "Slaves aren't supposed to have gods, but I've got one. He talks to me sometimes." He added conspiratorially, "He's invisible."

"Ah."

"Tell you the truth, I don't even know for sure its a *he*. It's just this kind of voice in my head. When I need to know something, really need it, I ask him. And sometimes he answers." He grinned broadly. "So I think maybe I'll ask the invisible god what animals I should take with me."

Sam nodded. "Sounds good."

"And I'll pray for you too, Nowar."

Sam smiled his thanks.

Even in a land of mind readers, some people were just plain nuts, Sam thought as he walked back toward the harbor. The first of the expeditionary ships was arriving, and the populace had gathered at the shore in welcome. There were no cheers, though. The people who waited for the slave ships wore expressions of despair as if their lives, along with their city, had fallen to pieces.

* * *

While Poseidon was busy with the king, the expedition's command ship sailed into harbor alone.

Ares was the first to walk down its ramp, looking about him in silent incredulity at the damage the earthquake had wrought. The people, many of them swathed in bandages, supported by sticks, their scars still crusted with dried blood, bowed at his feet.

Suddenly Aphrodite ran through the immobile crowd, shrieking,. "It was *his* doing! The foreigner made the king lose faith!" Sobbing, she threw herself at Ares's feet. "We were ordered to prepare to leave Atlantis, my lord. To leave behind the bones of our ancestors, to turn our backs on the gods themselves."

Ares stared at her, confused. What did he care for the bones of their ancestors? He had eighteen hundred slaves in tow, and needed to get rid of them. Then, behind her, he saw Hades emerge from a black palanquin.

The crowd immediately turned to the high priest, stretching out their hands to him in supplication. Hades exchanged the briefest of glances with Aphrodite before she melted quietly into the throng.

He had deliberately stayed away from the populace in the aftermath of the earthquake, whetting their hunger for the sacrifices while the slave ships remained at sea. The tremors had come in answer to his deepest prayers, and at the most opportune time possible. It was his chance to make the move he had been planning for more than forty years, and it was imperative that he make the most of it.

His priests had been busy spreading rumors among the disheartened populace about their weak-willed king and the barbarian who had turned Zeus against his people and their gods. They painted a picture of Athena as a wanton harlot who consorted with the enemy, and of Poseidon as a senile dupe no longer capable of commanding the armed forces. To ensure that none of the three would be present for this moment, Hades had sent a priest with a message to Ares to bring in the expedition's flagship ahead of schedule, at the hour when Poseidon always conferred with the king in the palace.

Ares, too, if he had followed Hades's instructions, had played his part. The contingent of fighting men sent with him on the expedition had included all of Poseidon's most loyal commanders.

"How many casualties?" Hades asked the prince.

"More than a hundred." Ares's lips twitched. "Most of them officers."

Hades closed his eyes and let out his breath. At last his day was finally coming to pass. He spoke so that all the multitude could hear his voice. "Welcome home, future King of Atlantis!"

The noise of the crowd swelled into a deafening roar of welcome. Some among them wept openly with gratitude as the first of Ares's troops swaggered down the gangplank to stand behind their leader.

Then Hades raised his hands for silence and cried, "Where is the enemy spy who has visited this curse upon you?"

In the distance, the crowd writhed like a pit of snakes around the spot where Sam had been working alongside Hephaestus. They shoved him forward, kicking and spitting at him, until he landed on his knees in front of the high priest.

"Is this true?" Hades demanded, each word ringing out in accusation. He had fixed the glare in his eye so that his face presented a perfect picture of outraged justice. Slowly he lifted his arm, and from his long black sleeve a bony finger pointed. "Have you persuaded King Zeus to abandon his people and his country, as the Lady Aphrodite claims?"

"Of course it isn't," Hephaestus said, jostling through the crowd to reach Sam, but the jeering of the closing mob drowned him out.

"Spy!" they shouted.

Hephaestus backed up, pushing Sam behind him. "What's the matter with you people?" he shouted.

"The foreigner has brought evil with him!" someone screamed.

Quickly Hephaestus reached out for Sam's arm, but a hand in the closing crowd snatched it away. The mob swarmed past Hephaestus to circle Sam and engulf him, cursing him and tearing his clothes. Urged on by his neighbors, a fat farmer raised a stick.

"Stop!" Hephaestus screamed. "Don't kill him."

Hades halted the farmer with a gesture. The people fell aside silently as the tall priest glided toward Sam.

Hades looked down at the dazed and bloodied face. "Your days as a guest of the palace are over," he said, his voice low. "Your new quarters will be among the kind of savages you represent." He turned to the cadre of Ares's soldiers. "Take him to the temple of the true gods," he commanded, then turned to the crowd as the soldiers grabbed Sam and lifted him over their heads, his arms pulled behind him, his feet trussed up behind his back.

Hades spoke to a young priest who followed behind him like a shadow, and the shadow carried the message to another black-robed shadow, who brought it back to the galleon at the dock where another priest in a black robe, his face invisible beneath his spread hood, cried out: "Bring forth the sacrifices."

With the beating of drums they were led out, their hands tied with rope, stumbling down the gangway, blinking in the fierce sunlight, marching toward the Land of the Dead behind the soldiers who were carrying Sam.

Hephaestus moaned as he watched.

Then in the distance he saw Aphrodite, standing on a rock, her gossamer robes blowing around her like the wind itself. The slaves passed before her, not daring to look up at the vision of beauty.

But she was not watching them, nor the mob that followed. Her eyes were fixed on Hephaestus, half-kneeling on the sand, his brown skin turned ashen, a rivulet of blood trickling down the side of his face. Her lips curved into a small smile.

CHAPTER 14

Sam sat alone again in the darkness. Somewhere beyond, he could hear the low murmur of voices.

He was in a small cubicle in the depths of the death pyramid. He had been dragged into this black room past hundreds of men crowded together in a vast, stinking outer chamber which he reasoned must be the holding area for slaves.

They had all looked so *different*, he remembered. Some were very tall, while others appeared to be almost miniature human beings. Some were extraordinarily hairy, their arms long, their foreheads sloped back. Most were dressed in skins, although a few wore fabric tunics or garments woven of reeds. They spoke a babel of tongues.

But Sam knew they had one thing in common with each other, and with him. They were all going to die.

The Great Sacrifice had begun. With each scream, as a slave's heart was cut out by a sacrificial bronze knife, the voices inside the pyramid stilled as these men, so different from one another, joined in mourning the fate they would all share.

Sam leaned his head back against the cold stone. A few weeks ago, he might have convinced himself that this, too, was part of the nightmare he was experiencing. But he knew now that there was no hope of waking up to find himself safe in a hospital bed. He had come to Atlantis through some undersea window in time, and he would never be permitted to go back.

Athena, he thought, remembering her somber gray eyes. Athena had warned him that his life would end here.

We cannot change the course of things to come.

Maybe he had known, somewhere deep in his mind, that he could not change that course.

But he had never thought he would die so far from her.

Did he regret it, then? Was he sorry he had allowed Reba, offering to bring him back to his own world, to slip away when he'd had the chance?

Sam turned his face to touch the damp wall. No, no regrets. For the moment of love they had shared together, he had relinquished his existence in two lifetimes.

But they had shared that moment.

"Athena," he whispered, and the name brought him comfort.

Athena stood proudly in the barge slowly making its way across the narrow canal to the Land of the Dead. The sun reflected off her silver headband in brilliant light.

"Why is she coming?" Ares asked nervously. He had stood beside the high priest during the sacrifices as a symbol of the royal house. Since Hades's dramatic welcome of the returning slave ships, the public knew that times had changed. Zeus was a pariah to his own people; Ares would soon replace him as king.

Hades smiled. "She's about to launch a protest, I imagine. The foreigner is her lover, you know."

Ares looked up sharply.

"She'll want me to release him." He laughed softly.

"I don't see what's so funny," Ares said uncomfortably. "The king probably sent her."

"The king? What power does he wield? The kingdom he stole from me is in ruins. The people hate him. The army belongs to you."

He watched the small boat reach the shore, its lone passenger standing like a goddess. "Look at her," Hades said with scorn. "So arrogant, so sure of herself." He descended the steps to await her arrival. "Come with me, Ares," he said. "I think we should prepare a special welcome for the princess."

Athena walked up the long flight of stone steps which branched halfway up the structure's side. One way led straight to the apex where the sacrifices were being made; the other wound downward into the pyramid itself, through a small door into a labrynth of corridors lit by smoky torches. Hephaestus had designed this well, she noted. Without a single visible mark on the exterior, the building was actually honeycombed with entrances and stairways leading in all directions.

Deep in the interior, in a spacious chamber that was dry despite the lack of windows and the enormous stone wall blocks, she found Hades waiting for her. His hands, she saw, were brown with dried blood. The odor of death was strong on him.

"I have come to ask that you release Sam Nowar," she said without preamble.

Hades did not answer for a moment, instead staring at her, his blue eyes pale in the torchlight.

"It is not within your province to detain him," she reminded him.

He made a small gesture conveying his indifference. "In these times, the law is of small moment."

"It is nevertheless the law."

"According to whom?" he bellowed with a sudden anger that made Athena's heart thump. "Your father, who no longer has even the respect of his people? Let me tell you, Athena, they do not object to your lover's fate."

"The people have become a mob," Athena said. "A mob which follows the loudest voice. Today that voice is yours. But what happens when the earthquakes begin again? They will turn against you, just as they are turning against Zeus—"

"It is not my voice, but your father's own incompetence that has turned the people against him," Hades said coldly. "Zeus was not meant to rule. He stole the throne which was to have been mine."

Athena clasped her hands together, exasperated. "Uncle, that was so long ago—"

"Not to me!" Hades snapped. "Not to my descendants, who would become gods of Atlantis were it not for the Stranger's blood that runs in your veins."

"Your descendants? You are a priest."

"I am the rightful king. And you will not usurp that right."

Athena frowned. "I?"

"The whole of Atlantis knows how you've plotted to take the crown from Ares—"

"That is not true," she said reasonably. "I am not the heir to the throne."

"You will be, if you have your way. The oracles predicted your coming. In time, you will take the throne from him, just as Zeus took it from his own father. And from me."

"Your oracles are never right," Athena said with contempt. "They said the earthquakes would end if you sacrificed enough human blood. Well, they haven't ended, and they're not going to end."

Hades narrowed his eyes. "Human blood," he said. "Perhaps that's it. The slaves aren't human enough." He looked over at her. "But a royal sacrifice may please the gods."

Athena stepped back slowly. "What are you saying?"

"First, the foreigner will be sacrificed," Hades said calmly. "Then you, for your designs on the crown. By then, the populace will have grown used to the idea." He smiled. "They'll accept the spectacle of the king on the altar."

"The king!" Athena gasped. "You dare not!"

"Only by your deaths will the gods be satisfied."

She raised herself up to her full height. "So that you will ascend the throne. That's what all of this is about, isn't it? Simple regicide?"

"Ares," the high priest called.

The young soldier entered and looked hesitantly toward Athena. "Yes, lord."

"My lady wishes to see the enemy spy."

"Very well," Ares said. "I'll take her to him."

"See that she remains with him."

The soldier smiled cruelly. "Yes, lord."

He reached for her, but Athena slapped his hand away. "How can you serve him, Ares?" she asked with disgust. "Hades means to take the throne. After he eliminates me and our father, do you not believe he will come after you, the king's eldest son?"

"But he is not Zeus's son, Athena," Hades said smoothly. "He is mine."

Athena's eyes met those of Ares. The young man's face was blank with astonishment.

"Take her," the high priest commanded.

Sam had almost fallen asleep when he heard the voice.

How many hours he had spent in that utter darkness, he did not know, but the screams of the dying, at regular intervals, had ceased to turn his blood cold with fear. As he began to drowse, Sam felt a terrible guilt settle over him because the death- screams were becoming no more than meaningless noise to him, the equivalent of a jackhammer drumming on a city street. He ached at his own callousness.

And then he heard it, sharp and clear, hurting him like a knife slicing through his brain.

Got to come home, Sam.

He sat bolt upright, inhaling, smelling suddenly the very dust motes in the dry still chamber.

"Reba!"

I can hear you, honey. Can you find your way back?

"I don't know."

Well, you got to try. Something's going to happen and you got to be here for it.

"What? What's going to happen?"

Come home, Sam. Come home.

Her voice was faint, dispersing. "Reba? Reba? Talk to me. I need you."

There was no answer. "No, don't go!" Sam was shouting, beating at the stone walls of the chamber.

Quietly, she spoke again.

It's a puzzle.

"What is?" he whispered.

A picture. Can you see it?

"I can't see anyth . . . "

Close your eyes, lamb. It's a picture. It'll take you out, bring you home . . . Her voice was fading. *Look, just look. . . .*

The silence hung about him like cobwebs. Sam pressed his face against the cold stone. His head was pounding.

Look? At what?

She had said there was a picture, a puzzle. He tried to think. High above, the muffled scream of a slave cut through the stillness.

Sam threw his hands over his eyes. "Stop it," he cried. "For God's sake."

The heavy metal door swung open. At once Sam was assaulted with sensation: the faint glow of light from torches in a distant corridor, the shadowy figures of the slaves in the adjoining chamber, the odor of their sweat and their fear, their voices, once a vague blur of sound rumbling in agitation, now separate and distinct.

And then Athena stood in the doorway, framed by a faint glowing light.

Ares threw her roughly to the floor. "Take your whore," he growled.

After slamming the door behind him, Ares leaned against it, still stunned by the impact of Hades's words.

He is not Zeus's son. He is mine.

Hades's son!

In a single sentence his birthright had been swept away like soiled straw. He was not the crown prince. He was the bastard son of the high priest. And he would never be king.

Suddenly out of the corner of his eye he saw a big slave lunging toward him, his fingers spread like claws.

Ares welcomed the attack. He drew his dagger and brought it down with a wild zeal, slicing the man's chest half open with the thrust. Then, with a scream of rage, he whirled around and slashed another prisoner's throat purely for the sense of release it gave him.

"Anyone else?" he shouted. His face was twisted in a grimace of fury. "Come, fight me, you stinking animals. The bastard Ares waits to slaughter you."

He threw himself toward the press of bodies again, thrusting wildly with his dagger, sinking it into any flesh he could find while the slaves screamed and then, finally, began to tear at him.

"Yes, kill me and I'll kill you," he panted, feeling his face slick with blood. "That's what we're for. That and nothing else."

In the melee, the dagger was taken from him. Then the slaves parted until Ares was faced by only one man, a big mainlander dressed in a tattered cloth that wound around his loins. In his hand was Ares's own knife.

"In the heart, beast," Ares taunted. "It will only make my death official."

There was a sudden light. The slave looked up, startled, and in the lantern's glow a spear flew straight into the man's neck and hurled him backward. A squad of soldiers rushed into the chamber.

"We heard the noise, sir," one said.

"Get me out of this hole," Ares croaked.

CHAPTER 15

AT MIDNIGHT, HADES CAME TO HIM.

"The screaming's stopped," Ares said. "Too bad. I was getting used to hearing them."

"What on Earth possessed you in the slave chamber?" Hades hissed. "You killed five of the sacrifices."

Ares burst out laughing.

"Was it because of what I told you of your lineage?"

"What? That you're my father and not Zeus? That I'm not the rightful heir to the throne? Why should that upset me?" He laughed again.

"You *are* the rightful heir," Hades shouted. "I was the rightful king. *I* was the eldest son. *I* was trained to wear the crown. And *my* birth was not in question."

Ares furrowed his brow. "Was Zeus's?" he asked.

"Oh, surely you have heard that story," Hades snapped. "There has been speculation about Zeus's birth for decades."

"They say Rhea had him in the woods," Ares recalled.

"Quite. She claimed to have seen a vision of doom for her unborn child, so she fled the palace to spawn him like an animal in the forest." He curled his lip. "Rather convenient, I'd say, considering that King Cronus had already approached the priests about sacrificing the infant."

"A royal sacrifice?" Ares was astonished. "Back then? But the earthquakes weren't even that bad sixty years ago, were they?"

"It wasn't a question of earthquakes, but of parentage," Hades explained disdainfully. "Everyone at court knew that the queen was in love with Prometheus. Why my father didn't just have her and her treasonous lover executed, I'll never know. At any rate, there was no witness to the birth, so no one saw if she exchanged the baby for some peasant brat in order to save Prometheus's bastard."

He sighed. "And of course, once she brought him to the king, Cronus had reconsidered and accepted Zeus with open arms. Even when Zeus started to exhibit that freakish ability he calls the Power, Cronus was too besotted with him to admit the boy wasn't his own son." He laughed mirthlessly. "I'll wager my father went to his grave wishing he had gone through with the sacrifice while he had the chance."

"We'll take care of that for him," Ares said stolidly. "Imagine, a peasant bastard sitting on the throne of Atlantis."

Absently, Hades scraped some dried blood from the dagger beside Ares's bed. "And so you see, your claim to the throne is thoroughly legitimate. But in order to secure it for you, I had to work for a lifetime." The memory brought bile to his mouth. "That was the bargain I struck with Zeus."

Punishment?" Hades had asked incredulously when Zeus came to visit him in the priests' temple after his coronation. "What do you mean, there must be a punishment?"

"You tried to kill the king," the young ruler explained. "It is a capital offense."

Hades exploded at him. "You wet-nosed pup! I let you steal the crown of Atlantis from me! Is that not punishment enough?"

Zeus ignored the insult. "When the people were calling for your death, I permitted a slave to be sacrificed in your place," he had said. "But that does not end your guilt."

"By the gods," Hades sighed. "Do you forget that you are my own brother?"

"No, I do not forget. But neither can I forget that I am king, and responsible for law." He took a deep breath. "For this reason, I must command that you remain here, as a priest, for the rest of your life."

"What? You must be mad!"

"It will not be a bad existence, Hades," Zeus said, half in apology. "I have thought it through carefully. The priests are exempt from our laws. So long as you are one of them, no one can accuse you of treason."

"You could pardon me," Hades said crisply.

The young king shook his head. "I will not begin my reign in corruption. Not even for you."

Hades had shuddered in despair. "But priests are not permitted to wed. What of my wife, Persephone? She is with child."

"She will be treated as your widow," Zeus said. "According to custom, a woman who loses her husband must be cared for by the dead man's family. I will take responsibility for Persephone and the child."

Hades considered the offer for some time in silence. Finally he asked, "How much responsibility?"

Zeus looked at him questioningly.

"If the child is a boy, will you make him your heir?"

This had stunned the King. "But I have not even married. It would not be seemly—"

"As you yourself have said, little brother, you must not forget that you are the king. You can name whomever you please to succeed you."

Zeus paced the small temple cell.

"You owe me this much," Hades said. "Were it not for my actions, you would not wear the crown today."

"Your actions! The council had advised me to have you executed for your actions!" the young king shouted.

"I see. Then listen to them, by all means. They will be pleased to tell you how much they have each stolen from the treasury. They will gladly allow you to administer their lands, oversee their appointments, watch their plots against you. I'm sure they will advise you well." His eyes were hard. "They know that you are young and completely inexperienced. They look forward to your reign as an era of wild abandon for their greed."

Zeus felt deflated. "How can I stop them?"

"I will stop them for you," Hades said. "And as a priest who possesses no private property, I will serve Atlantis without thought for personal gain. You will never look at me and question my dedication to you and our country. All I ask in return is that my dynasty sit on the throne, in your name. It is a small price, I think."

Zeus had paid that price. And it was a pittance for what he had received in return.

Hades had worked ceaselessly for four decades providing a solid background for Zeus's flashy popularity. It was he who had met through endless hours with Zeus's ministers, who had examined each provincial office for signs of corruption, who had quelled a thousand small rebellions before they required military action. It was Hades who had agonized over the daily problems of Atlantis, while Zeus was lauded for his perfect rule. And in the end, when they were both dead and their bones crumbled to dust, Hades would be forgotten, a faceless priest whose name had vanished, while Zeus would be proclaimed an immortal god until the end of time.

How Hades hated his brother.

You will be king," he said now, looking at Ares. "I have sealed that bargain with my life."

The young man clenched his fists. "And Zeus would take it from me," he said bitterly. "A bastard and his daughter, born in exile to a deposed queen, and a lying mainland savage." He shook his head.

"None of them will live out the week," Hades said consolingly. "And none of their blood will ever rule again."

In the small cell, Sam held Athena in his arms. "Hades won't hurt you," he said. "He wouldn't dare."

Athena said nothing, but Sam could sense her thoughts. Hades no longer cared if he offended the king. Through Ares, the army was his. Zeus had no more power.

"How did he let it slip away from him?" he wondered aloud.

"He was afraid to use the Stranger's gift," she said. "And now Zeus is like an elk felled by yapping dogs. The vermin have come to power now." Suddenly she sucked in her breath. "What was that?"

Sam's head felt as if it had been split open with an axe.

The picture, Sam.

Athena jerked backward. "Whose voice is that?"

Sam ran his hand through his hair. "Someone from ... my time. She wants me to find a picture. She says it's the way out of here."

"A picture?"

"I don't know what she's talking about. A—"

"Sam!"

She took his hand and pulled it over her shoulder, to the wall she had been leaning against.

There he felt it, there beneath his fingertips, chiseled into the stone: a circle inscribed with a cross.

"Hephaestus would have thought of a way out," Athena whispered.

Sam scrabbled with his hands over the surface of the immense stone block. "But these are too big," he said. "They couldn't move. ... " He chuckled. "You crazy black devil."

The stone on which the emblem had been chiseled was not the same size as the others. It was no more than twelve inches wide and two feet high. Sam stood and began pressing against the stone, but even with all his weight against it, it would not move. Finally he lay flat on his back on the floor and extended his arms over his head until they touched the far wall. Then, bracing his feet against the block containing the symbol, he pushed with all the strength in his legs.

The stone moved.

"Sam ... "

"Just follow me."

It only moved a short distance, perhaps eighteen inches straight back. Sam looked beyond it, but could see nothing. Still, he crawled through the opening headfirst. There was room to stand on the other side of the stone. He waited there for Athena, then pulled her through.

"Are you all right?" he whispered.

"Yes. We must replace the stone perfectly."

Together they moved the heavy block back into place, then sat in the pitch blackness of this second chamber.

After a moment Athena began searching the walls for another emblem chiseled into the stone.

"Are you so sure Hephaestus would have planned an exit?" Sam asked, feeling along the lower stones.

"Yes. He designed this as a tomb for the bodies of the ancient kings, the greatest treasure of our people. Once that treasure was in place, it would have been too easy for Hades to seal the architect in with it, to protect its secrets."

"So he made sure he could always get out," Sam said.

"My brother Hephaestus is not a fool."

"No. And here's the mark to prove it."

The second stone was higher, almost at waist level. Sam leaned his shoulder against it. Some thin retaining mortar broke loose and the stone slid silently on tiny metal balls until it fell with a thud into the next chamber.

"Let's go," Sam said.

CHAPTER 16

WHAT DO YOU MEAN, HE WON'T SEE ME?"

The courtier trembled. "I'm sorry, Lord Poseidon. "We have instructions that the king is not to be disturbed by anyone." He nodded over his shoulder toward two soldiers guarding the door to the king's chambers. Poseidon recognized neither of them.

"But . . ." Poseidon snapped his jaw closed. He was not about to whine in front of a palace underling. He turned on his heel and stomped out of the palace.

Up ahead he saw the harbor, guarded now by a ring of heavily armed soldiers. They had already been there when Poseidon and his seamen had marched to the docks to welcome the homecoming troops.

When he asked a smirking young officer who had stationed them there, the man had replied, "Ares."

"Ares?" Poseidon had roared. "Who do you think is commander of this harbor?"

"Ares, sir," the young officer had answered languidly.

"Diaclo!" he shouted. There was no response. "Where is Diaclo, whom I placed in charge of the second phalanx?"

"Dead, sir," the officer replied.

"Sodalus?"

"Dead on campaign."

Poseidon narrowed his eyes. "Celmus?"

"Dead."

He stared levelly at the man. "They're all dead, aren't they," he said finally. "Ares has had you kill every last one of my commanders."

The officer stared straight ahead, but there was a gleam in his eye that Poseidon had to struggle to keep from extinguishing with his fists. It was then that he heard the scream from the first of Hades's slaves as the heart was torn out of him. In the distance, he saw Ares's plumed helmet beside the black robes of Hades atop the death pyramid.

Filled with shame and impotent rage, Poseidon had gone immediately to Zeus, but it seemed the king, too, was now under the control of the new army.

He ran up a flight of stairs and burst into Athena's apartment. Her maidservant shuffled up to him, her face swollen with tears. "She has gone, my lord."

"Gone? Where?"

Iris wailed and covered her face with her hands.

"Speak, woman!" Poseidon shouted impatiently. "Your histrionics aren't helping anything."

"To the priests' pyramid," she sputtered. "To free the foreigner."

"What? Why the devil would she do that?"

"Sire, I don't—"

"Never mind. When did she go?"

"At sunset, my lord. Will you help her?"

Poseidon let out a sound that resembled a growl. "I'll try. But if she's gone to Hades's temple, she's just walked into the lion's mouth."

Iris started wailing anew. He closed the door on her.

Mad, he thought. *The whole kingdom has gone mad.* Ares had usurped command of the army, Hades had seized control of the populace with his bloodbath extravaganzas, the king was a captive in his own palace, and the princess Athena had sailed willingly to her death.

Poseidon spat on the ground. This was not the Atlantis where he had grown up, playing in the waves of its ocean, abundant with life and wonder, where he had raced his wild horses, where he had read since childhood of heroes and their deeds of glory in the sheltering walls of Olympus. This was an ugly, alien place where people lived in misery and fear and had forgotten all they had learned about civilization. Here, a man's dying scream provided all the excitement of which his people were capable.

"Damn you all," he whispered. "Damn you all."

He stalked to the stables. Issa was busy nailing crates together on the deck of the small boat that the foreigner had rebuilt. When the slave saw him, he rushed over to help Poseidon with the white stallion.

"I can mount my own steed," Poseidon barked as he clambered atop the stamping horse. "What are you doing with that boat?" he asked as a cranky afterthought.

The old man grinned. "It's for your creatures, sir," he answered. "Nowar gave it to me." His wrinkled face seemed to slump. "He been took by the priests," he said.

"I know. You think you'll need that boat?"

"Nowar told me I would, and I do believe him, lord. I don't want the animals to die. If we have to leave Atlantis, somebody'll have to take care of them."

Poseidon could not help but smile. "You're a good man, Issa, but you don't know anything about sailing."

"I'll trust in the god."

"Which one?" Poseidon said.

"It depends on who's asking, sir," the old man said evasively. "They all seem to work well enough for them that believe."

Poseidon sat back on his steed, his vision momentarily blurred. "I wish I had your faith."

He started away, then turned about. "How long have you been my slave, Issa?"

"Since Queen Metis left, sir." He bowed his head. "I was free before that."

The sailor felt an ache in his heart for the old man. When the decree came to again enslave the foreign-born citizens of Atlantis whom Metis had freed during her reign, Poseidon had been at sea. He had never given a thought to how Issa or any of his other slaves had come to be his property.

"As I recall, Issa isn't even your name."

The old man smiled. "It was the name of the stable master I worked under. When he died, you gave the name to me."

Poseidon winced. "That was pretty callous of me."

"No, sir. I don't recall having another name, anyway. Least not now."

Slowly Poseidon dismounted. "Do you have ink and paper?" he asked.

"Parchment, sir, inside the barn," said Issa, puzzled. "For keeping accounts of the feed."

Poseidon brushed past him into the barn. When the old man followed him inside, he was writing with Issa's brush. "That's your freedom," he said, handing the documents to Issa. "Give it to one of the palace clerks." He climbed back onto the stallion. "Choose a new name for yourself, too," he said.

The old man stared at the parchment with wonder. "Yes, lord." His toothless grin was as bright as the sun.

Poseidon held up a hand in salute. "Safe journey to you and your ship," he said before riding away.

Hephaestus peered out one of the foundry's windows. It was dark enough now to leave.

Outside, where the canal waters rolled gently by the heavy metal furnaces, he struggled to put a small boat into the water.

He would approach the death pyramid from the north, where no ships ever came. There were a thousand ways into and out of the structure—as long as there were no guards to see him.

And if there were?

Hephaestus checked the dagger in his belt. He had never been much of a fighter, but if he had to kill one of Ares's soldiers to free Sam, he would.

He stepped into the small flat-bottomed boat and prepared to untie it from the dock. Just then he saw Poseidon, arms akimbo, staring down at him. "Where are you going?" the sailor asked.

Hephaestus waffled. Poseidon could have him hanged for what he was planning to do. He took a deep breath. "To the Land of the Dead," he answered honestly.

"Can you get inside the pyramid?"

"I can."

Poseidon looked toward the island, a small dim speck from here, then back to Hephaestus. "Move over," he said. "I'm going with you."

* * *

They moored the boat at the rocky north shore and climbed hand over hand to reach the cliff edge where the pyramid stood.

"Stay low," Poseidon said as he dropped to his belly. "The moon is our enemy tonight."

They crawled for some distance before Poseidon grabbed Hephaestus's tunic to stop him. "Soldiers," he hissed. "They're on patrol. We'll wait here and see how long each of their rounds are." He moved back into a shallow ravine. Hephaestus followed him, sitting back and wiping the dead grass off his hair.

"A fine fix this is," Poseidon said. "When a crazed priest and a make-believe soldier can abduct a royal princess and neither the king nor I have anything to say about it."

"The princess? Athena?" Hephaestus asked, stunned.

"What'd you think this was about? That sail-rigging foreigner?"

"Well, yes," Hephaestus admitted.

Poseidon's eyebrows knitted. "You mean you were coming here in the dead of night to free a legitimate slave?"

"He isn't a slave. He was taken without right—"

"Oh, never mind." Poseidon waved him down.

Hephaestus studied the old sailor's face. "If Hades has taken Athena, why aren't you here with a battalion?"

"Can't reach them," Poseidon grumbled. "Ares has taken over the army. The only people I have that I know are loyal are my sailors, and the little bastard's sealed off the harbor."

"What about the king?"

"I think they've got him under house arrest in the palace." He noted the black man's horrified expression. "I couldn't very well storm the throne room by myself," he muttered. "If I had any sense, I'd be with my men instead of trying to get Athena out, but Hades is likely to kill her unless someone acts quickly."

"He'd kill you, too," Hephaestus said. "He'd never allow you near your men." He looked up at the waxing moon. "If Hades and Ares control all of Atlantis, what are we going to do once we get Sam and Athena out of here?"

Poseidon gave a rueful laugh. "I was hoping to come up with something." He sighed. "There are no laws anymore. Earthquake or not, I'm afraid this might be the end, my friend."

Hephaestus looked at the ground, but Poseidon slapped him heartily on the back. "So we might as well have one last run, don't you think?"

The black man smiled lopsidedly. "I wish you had a better fighter on your side than me," he admitted. "There are more soldiers around the pyramid than I'd anticipated."

Poseidon raised an eyebrow. "Not so many. Twelve I've counted—three four-man patrols, coming by every three minutes or so. Add in another four inside the pyramid . . . no more than sixteen men."

"Three minutes," Hephaestus considered. "That's awfully tight. I can't run fast."

"Then it's a good thing I'm here." Poseidon got up into a crouch.

"What are you doing?" Hephaestus squeaked. "The guards are coming."

"I'm giving you another minute or two. When they take me, run like your ass is on fire. And bring Athena out alive."

Then he stood up and walked toward the pyramid.

When the next patrol appeared, Poseidon was standing in a field of wild grass, his trident held aloft. In the moonlight, he looked like a bearded deity rising from the foaming waves of the sea.

The soldiers hesitated, looked at one another, then walked slowly toward the apparition. "Who goes?" one asked timidly.

"It is Poseidon," he answered. The young soldiers immediately saluted, their faces pale and frightened in the eerie silver moonlight.

"Take me to the priest, my brother Hades," he said. "And do it speedily, or you'll find yourselves on that bloody altar of his."

The four men hastened to escort him to the front—and only known— entrance to the pyramid, while other soldiers joined the growing entourage as they neared.

None of them saw the lone black man limping to the rear of the pyramid, where the boats of Charon, the ferryman, bobbed on the canal that wound around the island. No one saw Hephaestus slip onto the algae-covered rocks behind the oldest of the canal boats and lift a ring of iron which opened an underground stairway. No one, in the confusion of Poseidon's entrance, heard the soft steps of a man in a narrow passageway which roamed the entire structure, a passageway which led nowhere unless one understood the key to its design.

What is it?" Hades murmured low, his eyes red-rimmed and his breath foul.

"I've come for my niece."

Hades blinked once, lazily. "Your niece? Not your army?"

"The army will be mine again soon enough," Poseidon said.

The high priest broke into laughter. "Are you too stupid to know that your life is forfeit among the army, you corrupt old fool?"

"Corrupt? You're the one who murdered my commanders, you and your evil spawn!"

"Your commanders were as worthless as you, Poseidon. For years, you all pretended there were no slaves to be had. But we picked them like berries from a bush."

"Slaves," Poseidon spat. "That's all that concerns you, Hades. Are you so little a man that you cannot feel safe with anyone who is not in chains?"

Hades rolled his eyes and waved his brother away like an annoying fly.

"I will not leave without Athena."

"I'm afraid that won't be possible," Hades said. "The citizenry has already been informed of a royal virgin sacrifice to appease the gods. I'm afraid she'll have to stay until morning." He smiled.

Poseidon leaped at him, unable to contain himself any longer. Hades had anticipated the move. With a crook of his finger he signaled a pair of armed guards to intercept his brother.

"I imagine you'd like to see her before she dies," the priest said calmly as he led the way below to the cells.

In the main chamber, the new slaves parted fearfully as the door opened, pressing themselves against the walls. But when Poseidon entered, the silence gave way to astonished murmurs.

"The King of the Sea!" someone whispered loud enough to carry through the stone chamber.

"It is Poseidon. . . ."

"Poseidon. . . ."

"Poseidon. . . ."

Some of them fell prostrate, bowing their heads in obeisance. Poseidon recognized some of the faces of the mainlanders with whose villages Atlantis had once traded peacably, before the days of the slaving expeditions.

"Could there be a better argument for your treason than this?" Hades scoffed. "These savages consider you one of them."

He signaled for a guard to open the door to the next chamber. "Who orchestrated it all, Poseidon? You? Zeus? The foreigner? Did you plan the abandonment of our country together? Or were you just a puppet?"

When Poseidon did not deign to answer, Hades pushed open the next chamber door. "It's no matter. You're all where you belong now—" He looked about frantically. "What is this?" he breathed.

The small room was empty. One of the guards lifted his lantern in all four corners, but there was no trace of Athena or Sam Nowar.

"Sorcery!" Hades seethed.

In the next chamber, a low buzz of excitement traveled around the vast room.

"Guards!" the high priest called. "Guards, come at once!"

The slaves fell silent as a dozen soldiers clattered down the stairs, their weapons drawn. They found Hades quivering with rage.

"Take this man outside and lock him in irons," he rasped. "You're going to tell me what you know about this, Poseidon."

The soldiers hesitated. Poseidon was no ordinary criminal. Even the very youngest had heard tales of his feats at sea and his compassion for the men who served him. But when Hades snapped his head around angrily, one guard stepped forward and pushed the point of a spear against the old man's back. "Yes, sir," he shouted to the priest.

Hades swept past them in a fury and rushed toward the stairs, his robes billowing behind him.

"We're obliged to follow orders, sir," the guard told Poseidon in a small voice.

Poseidon fixed him with a glare. "Not from madmen."

The tip of the guard's spear quivered, then poked into Poseidon's back so hard it drew blood. The old sailor appeared not to notice. He walked forward, his carriage straight, his head high.

The slaves parted in silence to let him pass. One gave him the Atlantean salute, a mark of respect which Poseidon himself had always accorded the residents of the mainland villages he visited. One by one, each slave took up the salute, right arm extended, ending in a closed fist.

When Poseidon and his armed escort left and the slaves were again left in darkness, they remained standing, their arms still upraised.

CHAPTER 17

Sam and Athena passed through eight other chambers as empty and dark as the one in which they had been held prisoner before Sam felt the shape of a lamp in the middle of the otherwise unbroken stone wall. "There's flint, too," he said excitedly.

Athena hurried over to him, her hands feeling along the smooth stone. "Give it to me," she said. "I don't imagine you're very experienced at using flint."

He handed it over to her, their hands cradling the precious stone. A spark flashed, and then the wick burst into a tiny flame that seemed so bright they both had to turn their eyes away from it.

Then they saw the rest of the chamber, glowing softly in its opulence. There was a chaise of pure gold with cushions of lapis blue; an alabaster table inlaid with sparkling cut gems of all hues; a chest made of a red metal, banded with silver and gold; a large painted wood mask; urns and vases of translucent stone, giving off the faint scent of rare oils; and, in the center of the room, an enormous sarcophagus bearing the astonishingly lifelike image of a man in old age, with flowing white hair and large, wise eyes.

A gold plaque beneath the face read OCEANUS.

Athena gave a little gasp. "Why, King Oceanus has been dead so long, he is all but a legend. It's hard to believe this is where he's really buried." She touched the gold-bordered coffin gently. "Hephaestus knew of this, yet said nothing."

"He knows a lot of things," Sam said. He raised the lamp to the plaque. Beneath the ancient king's name were details of his deeds in the long-ago time when Atlantis was still young.

"He built the first great ships to cross the ocean," Athena said, smiling as she read. Then her eyes met Sam's, and slowly she melted into his arms. "Is it all gone now?" she whispered. "All to be destroyed by Hades and his hatred. . . ."

Sam swallowed. "We've got to find the next door," he said.

* * *

Each burial chamber was more fabulous than the last, and for the first time Sam understood the stories the Atlanteans told about the proliferation of genius during the early years after the Stranger's arrival.

In the tomb of Atlas, they found chairs with complex mechanisms which permitted them to change shape, as well as a global map of the Earth, a wall painting that showed the planets in orbit around the sun, and in a corner of the room, a compass not much different from the one Sam had worn on his wrist when he first came ashore in this strange land.

"Who would have thought the old tombs held such wonders," Athena said. "Hephaestus and his forge workers dug all this out of an underground rubbish heap."

Sam examined the compass. "But hasn't anyone ever *seen* these treasures?"

"Oh, the priests must have. Each room has a door." She pointed to the gilt-encrusted portal in Atlas's chamber.

"But the moving stones . . ."

"I don't think Hephaestus told anyone about those."

Sam felt a frisson of uncertainty. "Maybe they weren't his idea," he said. "They might be a trap."

Athena examined the wall carefully, going over it with her fingertips. "In any case, I prefer it to that dank cell." She found the symbol again and pushed the stone.

The passageway was long, longer than any of the others, and was made of metal. Athena and Sam crawled at an agonizingly slow pace through the suffocating heat until they finally reached a block of stone. Sam pushed against it, hoping fervently that they had finally reached an exit to the outside.

Nothing happened.

"Oh, no," he moaned.

"What is it?"

Sam pushed again, harder this time, bracing his feet against the sides of the shaft. There was no movement, not the slight shift of rock he felt with the stone in the first chamber, nothing. He lowered his hands in despair.

"Then it *was* a trap," Athena said tonelessly.

"Damnit!" His anger made him lurch upward, striking his head against the low ceiling of the tunnel. Stars sprang to his eyes.

And the ceiling moved.

"What in hell . . ." He felt tentatively above his head. The metal was dented. As he pressed against the dent, he felt it bang loosely under his fingers. He pushed gently to the left. The panel swung away.

Above the panel was a space of about six inches and then a flat stone surface. Sam positioned himself into a low squat and pressed upward with his back against the overhead stone. It moved easily. He hoisted himself up, helped pull Athena after him, then replaced both the metal panel and the stone.

"I've known tricky minds before, but your brother Hephaestus has got to be—"

The words caught in his throat. As they turned toward what they thought was the center of the darkened room, they saw a strange glowing, green light forming the shape of a lozenge.

"It's a coffin," Athena said.

They both scrambled to find the lamp. Athena located it first, in the far corner of this room which was vastly larger than the others. When the flame caught, they both looked around in wonder.

Every inch of the walls was covered with writing.

There was nothing in the chamber besides the sarcophagus. It was made of some black iridescent metal and banded with gold on either side of the infinitesimal crack through which the green glow came.

"There are no doors here," Athena said with quiet excitement. "Hades has never been in this room."

Sam frowned, his eyes fixed on the glowing casket. "Hephaestus sealed it from everyone except . . . *himself.*"

Athena held the lamp aloft, studying the writing. "'The effect must be envisioned,'" she read, squinting. "'And must be desired by all.'" She moved on. "Somewhere there must be a beginning to all this writing."

Sam was paying only half-hearted attention. His eyes were riveted on the sarcophagus. It glowed with the same light as the Eye of Zeus, the diamond he himself had found millenia in the future.

"Here it is!" Athena called. She looked back at him with delight. "Listen to this, Sam. 'I who write this am nameless among those with whom I have made my home. My journey was long. This place, which I have named Atlantis after a children's story in my own land, was not my destination, although I now know that it was my destiny. . . . '" She turned to him. "Sam," she said in a hushed voice, "this is the tomb of the Stranger."

Her eyes were sparkling with wonder, but the gleam left them when she saw what he was doing. "Sam, don't. You mustn't. . . ."

She might as well have told him to stop his heart from beating. The casket drew him to it like a magnet. When he placed his hands upon it, a sensation like electric shock coursed through his body, making his eyes close and his lips open, gasping for air.

"Sam . . ."

Tears streamed down his face; his hands trembled.

Quickly Athena replaced the lamp on its holder and rushed toward him, but by then he had already slid open the lid of the sarcophagus. The green light flooded the room and washed over Sam as his heart thudded wildly in his chest. He stared and moaned, low and long.

The body inside the coffin was not human.

Athena clasped her hands over her mouth to keep from screaming. Sam stood transfixed, his hands hovering over the corpse as if he were warming them in its radiance.

The Stranger had been taller than any man either of them had ever seen, easily over eight feet. His skin was pale to the point of blueness, and he had no bodily hair whatever. The orbs around his eyes were high and arched. The nose was very thin, almost like a beak. There were no lips, no teeth—merely an opening in the mask of the face, a slit, like the slits of his ears, surrounded by a network of veins close to the skin. His neck was slender, yet supported a head shaped rather like a lightbulb, swelling above his ears.

And yet, though the individual features may have seemed grotesque, the overall effect of the mummy—if that was what it was, since it was so perfectly preserved it looked as if it might sit up at any moment—was one of gentleness and calm.

Athena lowered her hands to look again. "A woman made love with him," she said wonderingly.

His hands were folded over his belly and covered with a cloth woven with exquisite refinement. Tentatively, Athena reached out a hand to the cloth. It fell apart at her touch, and she drew away.

Beneath the disintegrated cloth rested the Stranger's hands. They were long and slender, spatulate at the tips, their fine bones standing out in relief.

Sam touched them gently.

You must lead them now, a voice inside him said.

Sam trembled wildly.

"Sam? Are you all right?"

There is so much yet to teach them.

"But they're going to die," Sam answered aloud. "And I'm going to go with them."

"Sam!" Athena said frantically. She touched Sam's face, his forehead. They were cold. She leaned her head against his shoulder. There was no link between them, none of the communication that had till then flowed so freely between their minds. "Sam, who are you talking to?"

These people have their own destiny, and it is entwined with yours. But you must take the next step. You must begin it again.

Listen: I who write this am nameless . . .

For two hours he remained motionless, clasping the hands of the alien corpse. Sweat poured off Sam's face; he shivered as if suffering from cold. Only his lips moved, repeating in a whisper ever word he was hearing.

"'We can change the course of things to come,'" Sam said, repeating each word of the message pouring into his mind from the being in the coffin. "'The Power is to be used by all, together. Envision and desire one thing above all else, each of you in the deepest recesses of your spirit. . . .'"

"What are you saying?" Athena sobbed, then sat back on her heels in despair, watching the man she loved rant while he clutched the dead body of a monster.

He had lost his mind. She was alone now, in the core of the pyramid, with no way out except the tortured route which had led her here, and that would only take her back to a cell where an executioner waited. She turned away.

What did it matter now, she thought finally, straightening her back like the princess she was. Here was as good a place to die as any other. Here, where they had found the strange heart of Atlantis and she had lost her love to it.

"'In the other realm, we appear as we are truly, because we do not possess the trappings of flesh, or the fears that come of that flesh. . . .'"

Sam's voice was hoarse and raw. Saliva trickled from a corner of his mouth.

Oh, my love, she thought wearily. *How could I have done this to you?*
She had nearly closed her eyes to sleep when she saw the ceiling open.

Her first instinct was to use the oil lamp as a weapon. Whoever had come for them would not leave without an injury of his own. A pair of legs dangled for a moment, and Athena took aim.

The man dropped in front of her. It was Hephaestus.

She lowered the lamp and threw her arms around him, but he was staring at Sam and the creature in the coffin.

"Can you get us out of here?" Athena asked.

Hephaestus swallowed hard and turned to face her. "Yes, but we have to move fast. Poseidon's used himself as bait to distract the guards."

"What will they do to him?"

He exhaled heavily. "I don't know. But it was what he wanted. You're to get out alive, Athena. That was his order to me." He grabbed her around the waist and thrust her upward into the hole in the ceiling.

"But Sam—"

"I'll get him. Wait in the passageway."

Sam had taken no notice of him. Standing still as stone, he appeared to be speaking to the corpse.

"Come along, Sam," Hephaestus said gently, taking him by the arm. He shook him, then tried to pry his fingers loose from the Stranger's. It was no use. Sam remained transfixed, the words rushing out of him too fast to be understood.

With a sigh, Hephaestus stepped back a pace and clenched his fist. "I'm sorry, my friend," he said as he threw his best punch at Sam's jaw.

It never struck.

At the moment before impact, Sam turned his face to Hephaestus. Perhaps that was it, the engineer would think later. Perhaps Sam's eyes had stopped him.

They were unearthly, clear as pools of green water, with depths of intelligence and compassion Hephaestus had never, in all his life, seen before on any human face. He had looked into an elephant's eyes once and had seen something of like kind, as if the beast had understood all the suffering in the universe, but Sam's gaze held even more than that.

It held power.

His fist stopped a hair's breadth from Sam's face. For the briefest moment, he felt as if it had been stopped for him in mid-air, halted by some unseen force.

But of course that couldn't have been so.

Then Sam smiled with an expression difficult to fathom: hopeful, patient, peaceful beyond telling. "I've finished," he said softly. He let go of the Stranger's hands at last. "You knew about him, didn't you?"

"Yes," Hephaestus said. "I knew who he was. But I couldn't open the coffin." He glanced down at the weird countenance of the sarcophagus's occupant. "Where could he be from?"

"I don't think that matters," Sam said. He met Sam's eyes questioningly. "You never saw him before? You never touched him?"

"Gods, no."

"But the walls . . ."

"I found a scroll in a case beside the sarcophagus," Hephaestus said. It fell to pieces when I read it, so I copied it all down on the spot and then painted it on the walls. I couldn't understand much of what he said, but I thought it was important to preserve." He made an impatient gesture. "Come on. We have to go."

Sam saw Athena's face appear at the ceiling opening.

Hephaestus jumped to latch onto the stone ledge of the shaft with his fingers and pulled himself up. "Now, Sam," he urged.

Sam had turned back to the Stranger's sarcophagus. The creature had never been wrapped in bandages like the subsequent kings; he had not needed it. Slowly, with reverence, Sam closed the coffin's lid. Then he blew out the lamp and pulled himself through the ceiling opening.

When he replaced the slate, the chamber was again sealed, hidden, ageless, unknown.

And in the darkened room, the green glow around the sarcophagus dimmed and faded into blackness.

CHAPTER 18

THERE HAD BEEN NO SACRIFICES FOR NEARLY THREE HOURS, AS HADES HAD been occupied with his prisoner.

The high priest sat now on an uncomfortable low stool, facing his brother. Poseidon was bent over a barrel, his wrists and ankles tied to metal rings that jutted out of the stone floor. The seaman was nearly unconscious.

Hades touched his finger to one of the open slashes in Poseidon's back. There was an involuntary shiver, nothing more. The priest's eyes slid disdainfully toward Ares.

"You're supposed to keep him alive," Hades said with soft contempt.

"He'll stay alive as long as I want him to," Ares countered. The young commander was naked from the waist up, his muscled torso slick and shiny with sweat. His eyes glistened.

He was a killer; Hades had always known it. It was a virtue in a warrior, and Ares was the greatest of all Atlantean fighters. But he lost control too easily. There had been stories of Ares's inventive brutality since his childhood. Since the last slaving expedition, Hades knew that they had all been true. Ares found an almost sexual release in conferring death.

But he must not kill Poseidon. Not until they had learned the secret of the foreign spy.

"Brother," he said softly, leaning toward Poseidon, "I do not wish you harmed this way. It is the stranger I seek, the foreign devil. He has addled you with his sorcery and done the same to Zeus. At this moment, he holds our beloved Athena as his captive. I beg you, Poseidon, help me. Help me to save our country. Tell me where he has gone."

With effort, Poseidon lifted his head and met Hades's sincere gaze with frozen calm. He had known torture before. He had seen many of his own men die under the lash of pirates or savage tribal kings.

The end of torture was always death. If a man broke early, he died with contemptuous but merciful speed; if he refused to talk, death came slowly and with great pain. But there was no alternative to death.

Poseidon decided to die in silence.

"Where has he gone?" Hades repeated, this time without the posture of concern.

He waited for a moment, then nodded wearily to Ares.

The whip sang before it cracked against Poseidon, opening a fresh gash. The sailor flinched, his arms and legs pulling the ropes taut.

In a corner of the torture chamber, a young soldier turned his face away. The skin had been almost entirely flayed from Poseidon's back, exposing the raw muscle beneath.

The soldier's name was Orion. He had sailed with Poseidon, as his father had a generation before him. On Orion's first voyage he had traveled west to Ixlatan, the most civilized of the mainland cities, where the kings dressed in feathers like plumed jungle birds and ate magic black berries which they said gave them superhuman strength. The Atlantean traders were welcomed with day-long parties and celebrations and honors appropriate for kings. Thus it had always been, sailing with Poseidon.

Even with the advent of the slaving expeditions, some semblance of courtesy had remained. Instead of trading goods for goods, Poseidon had bartered Atlantean looms and machinery in exchange for slaves captured by the warriors of Ixlatan in their battles with neighboring tribesmen.

But this last voyage under Ares had been different from the beginning. After Poseidon's commanders were run through with spears and dumped overboard, the troops were constantly indoctrinated in the way they should think: The old regime was corrupt, they were told. Poseidon, along with the puppet king Zeus, worked for the foreign barbarian nations to destroy the great civilization of Atlantis. It was incorrect to call the barbarians "human." They were not human. To pretend otherwise was to undermine the sanctity of the Atlantean ideal.

After a while, only a few among them had disagreed. These were executed. By the time the fleet reached Ixlatan, there were no dissenters left. And there was no talk of trade.

Their first command was to storm the palace. The great feathered king of Ixlatan was killed in his throne room, and his nobles taken off as slaves. The golden ornaments which hung everywhere were hacked off, taken away as booty by the young Atlantean soldiers.

Ares himself had been the first to rape one of the palace women—an act which would have merited execution under Poseidon—and his troops had followed Ares's example. Orion had been caught up in it all, the violence, the heady freedom of absolute power over a subject people. He had felt like a god there, capricious and responsible to no one. Drunk on the strong wine which Ares had brought for his victorious troops, Orion had axed the wooden gods of the mainlanders into splinters. He had stood back, lost in a pleasant fog, while his fellow soldiers aimed their spears at a line of fleeing women and picked them off like birds at the hunt. He had helped to light the fires that burned the stately houses of the nobility, one after the other, to the ground.

In the span of three days, Orion saw the empire of the west, established for more than two hundred years, crushed like a primitive village. When the Atlanteans were finished in Ixlatan and the long line of slaves marched into the holds of the ships, the fabled city of the young soldier's first boyhood adventure stood in ruins.

Now Orion looked at Poseidon, hung over the barrel like a bloody slab of meat. The old man had already vomited; he probably hadn't much water left in him. Flies settled in his wounds.

The soldier no longer knew what to believe.

A priest walked slowly down the stairs and approached. "It is almost dawn, Eminence," he whispered to Hades.

Hades cast a final look at his brother, then rose slowly. "Place him with the slaves until I return," he told Ares. "I must speak with Zeus."

Ares was slapping the coiled whip impatiently against his thigh. For safety's sake, Hades plucked the whip away and gave it to the soldier. Then he picked up a pitcher of water, drank from it, and threw the rest onto Poseidon's head. "Wake up, brother," he said. "We would not want you to miss the first sacrifice of the day. Particularly since it is to be you."

Wordlessly the soldiers moved aside when Hades approached the door to the king's chamber. He found Zeus sitting in his golden curved chair, staring forlornly through the window at the death pyramid across the canal.

"Most glorious Majesty," Hades said mockingly.

As Zeus turned slowly to face him, even Hades was shocked at the king's appearance. His face was drawn, his eyes sad and tired. There was an expression of ineffable sadness in his eyes, as if he had looked into the future and seen there only death and decay. The pendant hung lifelessly from the chain around his throat, the giant diamond as dull as a piece of chalk.

"What more do you want, Hades, now that you've imprisoned me in my own palace?" he asked. The words, meant to be curt, instead sounded only weary.

"Soon the day's sacrifices will begin," Hades said. "As you see, the citizenry is already gathering below. It would be appropriate for the king to give his blessing to the first offering."

"I'd rather not."

"Oh, but I'm afraid your presence will be required. It's to be a special sacrifice." Hades leaned close to whisper in his ear. "Poseidon."

"What?" The king's eyes glimmered with shock. "Is this some sort of foul jest?"

Hades clucked sympathetically. "Alas, no, Highness. Like his friend, Prometheus, he has betrayed his country. Perhaps the gods will forgive him after his sacrifice."

"Even you cannot commit such an atrocity," Zeus said. "Poseidon is our own brother!"

Hades feigned surprise. "My, what an odd thing for you to say. I, too, was your brother, if you will recall."

"I did not take your life!"

"You took my throne! It was more than my life!" The high priest closed his eyes; in a moment, he had brought himself under control again. "As I was saying, you will watch the ceremony from the palace balcony, either willingly or at the point of a soldier's spear. And you will watch again when Athena and the foreign spy are brought to the block."

The king half rose from his chair. "You cannot do this," he rasped.

"Oh, I can," Hades reassured him.

"Athena is an innocent. Even if you took the throne, she would not stand in your way."

"She has the Stranger's power," Hades explained quietly. "That is what must be eradicated. Every drop of the foul blood that has poisoned Atlantis must be spilled on its earth."

He did not have to add that the king himself possessed that blood. Zeus knew that his own turn at the altar would come, but only after he had watched his brother and daughter die before him.

"You are mad," the king said, his voice quivering.

Hades had an answer, but Zeus could listen to him no longer. He turned away to stare out the window again.

In the slave chamber, the men were quiet. The shadow of Poseidon had seemed to linger long after he had been taken away for torture.

Some slept; the respite before the sacrifices resumed had been welcome. For a while, at least, death had not come for them.

Then the heavy door at the top of the stairway opened and Poseidon was tossed inside to fall down the stone steps.

For a moment no one moved except to clear a little space around the old man whose body was slick with his own blood. Then one of the slaves ventured forward. Bending down, he slung Poseidon's arm around his neck.

Immediately they were surrounded by others, supporting the seaman's head and legs and body, carrying him to a clean corner of the chamber.

"Is he dead?" a middle-aged man asked in the Atlantean tongue.

The slave who had picked up Poseidon looked at him. The speaker was small and dark and beardless, like many of the slaves from the western mainland, except that this man had the delicate uncalloused hands of a patrician. The man who had lifted Poseidon was himself from Attica, far to the east.

"No," he answered. "He's . . ." He searched for the Atlantean word. "He's alive."

The dark-skinned patrician knelt and tore his filthy tunic to wipe Poseidon's wounds. It was made of fine soft cloth. There was a thick band of white on one of the man's fingers where he had worn a ring. Of gold, probably, the Attican thought. The westerners were all very rich, especially those like this one who had clearly been a nobleman.

And now the man was a slave, the same as himself, waiting for death.

There were those in his country who had believed that Atlantis was the home of the gods. Well, they were evil gods, the Attican decided. They destroyed not only those who were helpless to fight them, but their own as well. He had heard how Prometheus was brought down for giving fire to a mainlander. Now they had tortured the famed Lord Poseidon, the king of the sea himself.

Evil gods.

For an hour he sat in silence next to the dark-skinned patrician who cradled the unconscious Poseidon's head in his arms. Finally he clasped his hand on the westerner's shoulder. The other man looked up in surprise, the bloody rag still dangling from his fingers, then understood the gesture. He nodded; the Attican saw his eyes well with tears.

"Bring up the traitor Poseidon!" a priest's voice commanded from the top of the stairs.

The Attican held him more tightly. As six soldiers marched down the stone steps, he knew that they were coming to take the king of the sea to the altar of sacrifice.

Poseidon's eyes fluttered open, unfocused.

The soldiers approached two abreast as the throng of slaves parted deferentially, their eyes downcast, each hoping not to be the next selected to go to the blood altar. One of the guards reached past the Attican to grasp Poseidon's arm. The slave shoved the soldier away.

The chamber fell instantly into dead silence.

At first, the soldiers were so amazed at the slave's impudence that they did nothing. Then the guard he had pushed gave him a swat on the side of his head that sent him reeling. But the Attican got up again and rushed at him, forcing him away from Poseidon once more.

"You'll not take this man!" he shouted in his own language.

This time the guard raised his spear.

And it was snatched out of his hands.

By the patrician from the west, the Attican noticed. By those smooth brown hands which had probably never borne a weight heavier than the gold of his jewelry.

"The king of the sea is not a slave," the patrician said in the clicking sounds of his native speech. "And neither am I." With that, he thrust the spear into the neck of the nearest guard.

The riot had begun.

Within ten seconds the other five soldiers lay dead. A flood of men poured up the stairs. The great restraining door shook, then bent, then broke with a deafening crash.

The soldiers on the other side were prepared with long daggers and pikes, but they were outnumbered by a hundred to one. Overcoming the guards' scanty resistance, the prisoners poured through the passageways, heading to the outside, to freedom.

In their frenzy, Poseidon was left behind.

In the pyramid palace across the canal, Hades was still hectoring the king, savoring and dragging out the moment of triumph he had envisioned for so many years.

Through the large window, Zeus saw the first slaves pour out of the pyramid entrance and head down the steps toward the plaza below. He stood up, about to command his guards to quell the riot, before realizing that the military was no longer his to command.

He thought quickly. Poseidon and Athena were both imprisoned in that pyramid. The revolt taking place across the canal might well be their last hope of escape.

He would somehow have to prevent Hades from becoming aware of it.

Keeping his back to the high priest, he swiftly pulled closed the thick, sound-muffling draperies.

"You're absolutely right, brother," he said, forcing the excitement out of his voice. "I have wronged you. But I am prepared now to make amends. Here is a proposal. Have your sacrifices. You may have Poseidon and Athena. But don't take me to the block, I beg you. Let me abdicate. I will announce you as king, repudiate any family claim to the throne, and go into exile. Would that be agreeable to you?"

Hades blinked for a moment in surprise, then chuckled. "At least you're straightforward about your cowardice."

"This is no time for noble posturing," Zeus said with false heartiness. "Not if I hope to keep my organs intact." He dashed to the door of his chamber and ordered the guards outside not to disturb them for any reason. "We'll work out the details immediately. That would set my mind at rest."

Hades stroked his chin, teasing the king. "Let us not be precipitous in our enthusiasm, Majesty. It may be that you would be more useful as a sacrifice to the gods."

"No," the king said quietly. "I am prepared to publicly acknowledge that I took the throne from you, thereby legitimizing your claim and averting civil war. It is a good offer, but you must either accept it now, and work out with me the exact manner of my abdication, or reject it forever."

Hades stared at him icily. "How dare you think you can continue to give me orders?"

"It will be my last. Decide, Hades. I have said that you were right and I was wrong. Let us now, as brothers, resolve this matter."

And let us not, under any circumstances, look out the window as your precious sacrifices escape your bloody prison, he thought.

His jaw clenching, Hades picked up a blank scroll and tossed it at the king. "Write your confession," he said.

CHAPTER 19

ARES AWOKE TO THE SOUND OF CLANGING METAL. THE YOUNG SOLDIER named Orion had just burst into his sleeping chamber in the death pyramid.

"What is it?"

"The slaves have rioted, sir. They are escaping. There aren't enough of us left to fight them."

Ares jumped to his feet and grabbed his sword. "How many have escaped?"

"All of them, sir," Orion said, terrified. "They're leaving the island in the canal boats."

"What about the military transport? Have they taken that, too?"

"Not yet, but I saw them boarding." Orion felt a great need to relieve his bowels. "I don't think any of us are going to get out of here alive, anyway," he added.

Ares shoved him out the door. "Get to the boat," he growled.

"The boat?" Orion nearly tripped over his own feet. "But the fighting is in this building—"

"Get to the boat!" Ares repeated in a shout. "I'll be damned if I'm going to get myself killed at the hands of a filthy slave."

Hephaestus was the first to emerge from the hidden passageway at the back of the pyramid where he had hidden his boat. Behind him, Athena and Sam held one another as they took in the horrific scene in the courtyard just outside the boathouse. Blood ran in rivulets along the pavement, pooling around the bodies of dead Atlantean soldiers while half-naked slaves, screaming in terror and jubilation, ran wildly among the corpses.

A flotilla of small vessels zigzagged in the canal. Ordinarily used only to ferry the dead across the canal, the unseaworthy craft were now so filled with men that they could barely float. In the empty boathouse, Hephaestus saw Charon's bloodied body. One of the ancient ferryman's thin arms hung limply over the wall of the canal.

"Charon!" he whispered, trying to determine if the old man was still alive.

The ferryman's eyes opened. "Took the boats," he said. "They killed the guards and took the boats."

Athena made her way toward him and looked at his wounds. There was little she could do for the dying man. "Do you know where Poseidon is?" she asked gently.

Charon pointed feebly to the pyramid. "Inside . . . slaves' quarters . . ."

Hephaestus made for the entrance at once. Sam followed after him.

The massive underground slave chamber was eerie in its silence.

There was a thin-faced slave with Poseidon, crouched among the bodies of the dead. When Sam and Hephaestus entered, the bloodied slave made no move to fight or run. His only gesture was a movement of his arm across Poseidon's battered head, as if protecting it to the last from the Atlantean killers.

"We've come to take Lord Poseidon to safety," Hephaestus said cautiously.

The slave's expression changed in sudden recognition of the black man. "Hephaestus," he whispered. "The architect." He scrambled to his feet. "I'll help you carry him out of here. But be careful. Everyone here has gone mad, prisoners and captors alike."

"There are no more captors," Sam said as they lifted Poseidon into their arms. "They're all dead." He cast a glance at the slave. "Why did you stay behind?"

The ragged man with the oddly noble bearing panted with the effort of carrying Poseidon up the long flight of steps, obstructed by the heaps of blood-spattered corpses lying across their path. "This began because of me," he said softly. "And him." He looked down at Poseidon. "I was a captive, and was to die. That was fate. But when the king of the sea, who had commanded respect even from the ruler of my own land, was brought in here like a common slave, I could no longer accept fate. That was the beginning of the insurrection."

At the top of the steps, after kicking aside several corpses, the three men set down their burden. There was an even longer flight down to reach ground level, but at least they were outdoors, away from the horror of the blood-slick stairway. In the distance, Hephaestus saw his ship in the open water, heavy with the weight of too many men on board. He groaned.

"What's that?" Sam asked, wiping his forehead.

"Our ship's gone," Hephaestus said. He felt like weeping, but Sam's voice cut through his despair.

"Let's get Poseidon to Athena," he said. "We'll worry about everything else later."

Hephaestus exhaled a small puff of resignation, then lifted Poseidon's legs and helped carry him away from the death pyramid.

In the wide stone courtyard in front, hundreds of slaves were moving frantically, some of them picking the valuables off the bodies of slain guards, others simply milling about, uncertain of what to do with their newfound freedom in the Land of the Dead, where there was not even one living tree.

Beyond the pyramid was a long plain where the dead were buried. Their graves were unmarked, forgotten to the living, the older ones covered with weeds, the newer ones mounded with brown earth. After the plain was the sea. There was no more.

Some of the prisoners howled in despair. The boats were all gone. They had fled the slave chamber in triumph, only to realize that there was no way home. A few of them leapt into the water and were swimming toward the harbor.

Hephaestus saw that the ships in Poseidon's fleet that had survived the last earthquake had already moved offshore. But the twelve frigates which had returned from the slaving expedition under Ares were still docked, surrounded now by swarming slaves who tried to climb the sides of the vessels.

Let them have them, he thought. It was better to lose a few ships than to have the slaves rioting in the streets of Olympus. There would be enough problems coping with Hades and Ares and their traitorous army.

But that, too, was something they would have to worry about later.

R ow,'' Ares commanded the young soldier as he settled into the large military boat.

His bare arms were covered with blood. When Ares and Orion had arrived at the canal, they had had to fight nearly fifty slaves for the vessel. All of them now lay dead on the shore as Orion punted with one oar to free it from the shallow waters into the channel separating the Land of the Dead from Olympus. Behind him he heard the death cries of the Atlantean guards as they tried to defend the pyramid from the blood-crazed slaves.

"They'll die to the last man," Orion said, unaware that he had spoken aloud.

Ares splashed water from the canal onto his arms to clean them. "Won't be much of a loss," he said. "Sixteen troops, most of them too young to be of any consequence." The boat stilled. "I said row, damn you!"

Orion turned back to his task and rowed, steeling his jaw to keep back his tears. The new commander had deserted his men during a bloody massacre.

Not much of a loss. Ares dealt with numbers, not human lives. And Hades, the high priest who was privy to the thoughts of the gods themselves, was already calling him the future king.

They know more than you do, Orion told himself. It was not a soldier's place to criticize his superiors. And yet he could not push back the feeling that this army was a different one from the army in which his father had served. Under Prometheus and Poseidon, a soldier fought with honor. In this new army, all that was required was a willingness to kill.

The men in Orion's squadron had killed tribesmen, patricians, women, children . . . even their own officers. Now they, too, had been left to die.

Orion rowed, and tried not to think.

A thena was waiting at the boathouse. Charon lay beside her, his wounds bleeding through the bandages Athena had made from strips of her own garment. She wiped his face with a water-soaked cloth, trying to bring the old ferryman some comfort, when Poseidon was carried in to her. Gently she moved away from Charon to examine her uncle's flayed back.

"We have to get him to the palace," she said.

"I'm afraid that won't be easy," Hephaestus sighed. "We don't have a boat."

Charon stirred and mumbled something. Athena knelt beside him and leaned over to hear what he was struggling to say. The ferryman gestured with a trembling hand toward the rocky far wall of the boathouse. He mumbled again.

"I think he said, *boat*," Athena said.

Sam climbed the rock pile which concealed Hephaestus's secret entrance to the pyramid. "That's what it is," he called out exultantly. He lifted the end of a small canal boat, then cursed. There was a melon-sized hole in its side.

"He must have been repairing it," Sam said disspiritedly.

Hephaestus clambered on the rocks after him. "Then he'll have tools about. Use your head, Sam." In a moment the engineer produced some planking, already cut to size, and a hammer and nails from a barrel well out of sight of the canal. With his expert hands he set to work quickly, each blow of the hammer ringing out in the cavernous rock. In a matter of minutes the boat was afloat in the canal, with Poseidon laid carefully inside. They had all gathered around Charon to lift him next, but the old ferryman shook his head with more energy than Athena would have thought him capable.

"I will stay here," Charon said with a tremendous effort, the words bringing up bubbles of blood. "Here, among the dead whom I have served." His head lolled back against Athena.

"But Charon, you must . . ." she began, but her words trailed away. The old ferryman's eyes were already beginning to glaze.

"We'll have to leave him," Hephaestus said. Athena closed the old man's eyes, then arranged his limbs into a position of dignity before stepping into the boat.

Hephaestus gestured to the patrician slave. "You next," he said.

"I?" he asked. "But I am nothing to you."

"Get in!" Hephaestus took his arm and forced him into the boat. "If you should be so lucky as to reach your home again, tell them that not all the people of Atlantis are like the ones who enslaved you."

"Yes, yes, I will do that," he said, his eyes gleaming.

Hephaestus gestured Sam to go next, but Sam unceremoniously shoved him in first. "You may be an engineering genius, but I'm not trusting you with the only boat left."

When everyone was safely seated, Sam got in. "Don't suppose we have any oars," he said. No one answered. "All right, then, we're going to have to paddle. Get your hands in the water, all of you."

The boat started out uncertainly into the canal, with Sam lying across the bow, his arms elbow-deep in the water, trying to steer the boat to the other side where the pyramid palace was.

"You row well, westerner," Hephaestus said to the slave with a grin. "What is your name?"

"I am Quetzalcoatl of Ixlatan," the man answered. "And for you and the Lord Poseidon I will paddle with my hands to the ends of the Earth."

*   *   *

While on foot they had gone unnoticed by the rioting slaves, but now the people from the palace had a boat. Five persons in a boat large enough for ten. First dozens, then hundreds of former prisoners suddenly gathered along the sides of the canal to watch them.

One picked up a stone.

"Oh, no," Hephaestus said. "They're going to kill us for the boat."

"Be quiet," Sam commanded with quiet authority. He turned from the bow to Athena. "Put your arm on my back," he said. "The rest of you, too. Get close so that we're all touching."

Hephaestus frowned with irritation as the others pulled their hands out of the water. "Sam, this is no . . ."

"Do it!" Sam snapped.

Reluctantly, Hephaestus joined the others. Athena held one of Poseidon's hands. Quetzalcoatl held the other. They huddled together, the tiny boat bobbing in the water of the canal. There were masses of men now on both sides of the small waterway. One by one, they stooped to pick up stones. They moved together, closing in on the boat like shadows.

"The Power is used by all, together . . ." Sam whispered. And speaking the words, the feeling of perfect understanding that he had experienced while touching the Stranger's hands filled him once again.

Envision and desire one thing above all else, each of you in the deepest recesses of your spirit . . .

"They won't harm us," Sam said softly.

A strength grew inside him and suffused every part of his body. It spread through him like honey, then flowed out of him into Athena's fingertips, which he could no longer distinguish from his own flesh. And from there it traveled, quick, snapping like lightning into Hephaestus, who was another part of Sam's being, and to Quetzalcoatl, who knew nothing of the Stranger, but was part, nevertheless, of the new entity which the five of them had become. Somewhere, in a part of Sam beyond the realm of physical touch, he felt Poseidon stir. The sailor's life force, weak but growing stronger with each beat of his heart, added to the new being.

Sam felt the entity that was himself and the others glow with colors, each hue contributed by one of its parts—Athena's a pure blue, Hephaestus's an ever-changing purple. Poseidon emanated a yellow which was changing rapidly to gold, and Quetzalcoatl added a fiery red to the mix. They were all part of each other, yet also part of this new, unique life form that throbbed with invincible power.

When the first rock was hurled, it came straight at Sam's eyes, then caromed away as if it had struck a shield. He never blinked. Another rock hurtled toward them and also was repelled.

Some of the slaves made the sign of the evil eye; others set their jaws and threw their missiles with greater determination. They fell like bubbles on the five in the boat, sliding over them and into the water.

"That is Poseidon," one of the slaves murmured. "You have cast your stones at the king of the sea."

At that, many of the attackers dropped their rocks and backed away, but their places on the bank were quickly filled with others. A red-haired slave from the eastern mainland whose face bore the scar from an Atlantean whip stroked the blade of a dead soldier's knife. The tip of his tongue showed between tight lips. "I don't care who he is," he said. "I want that boat." He stepped forward, his chin thrust out.

Athena turned and looked up at the savage with the knife on the shore beside them. The men around him shrank back, awestruck at the sight of her face.

"Her eyes are made of moonlight," someone said.

The slave swallowed but stood his ground. Grunting, he jabbed his weapon into the air.

"You will not harm us." It was Athena's lips that moved, but the men who heard her would have sworn that five different voices had spoken.

With a cry, the slave with the knife flung himself toward the boat. All five inside raised their arms at the same moment to catch him. The weapon fell from his hands as he passed among them like a current of water, then slid out the back of the boat. There he clung to the side of the canal, wearing an expression of utter disbelief.

One of his countrymen pushed his way through the crowd to pull him out of the water but when he extended his hand, the man only stared up at him.

"I have touched the gods," he whispered.

The slaves on shore dropped their stones, one by one, all of them, so that they made a sound like rain on the barren plain. Then one man waded into the water of the canal and pushed the boat gently forward. Others followed in silence as if performing a sacred ritual, moving the vessel out into the channel.

When it reached open water, they stood on the banks of the Land of the Dead, watching as the tender current carried the immortals to the palace on the far shore.

CHAPTER 20

THE FIRST TREMOR HIT AS THE CANAL BOAT WAS NEARING SHORE, CAPSIZING the ferry and bringing the five out of their entranced state with terrifying abruptness.

"Get my uncle!" Athena shouted, wading frantically back toward the boat.

"I'm here." Poseidon rose out of the water, shaking droplets off his hair and beard. Quezlcoatl, who had been trying to upright the boat, suddenly dropped the bow. Then he reached out and touched Poseidon. The skin of his back was nearly healed, with only faint pink marks to show where Ares's lash had cut into his flesh only hours before.

"The whip . . . my wounds from the whip are healed," Poseidon said. He turned to face Sam. "What did you do?"

"I don't know," Sam said. "It was something we did together. Something we must have always known how to do. . . ." He could still feel the Stranger's spirit infusing him as the long-hidden words had poured into his mind from an unknowable source beyond death.

Hephaestus stepped onto the bank and put his arm around Sam's shoulders. "Let's go," he said. "There might be another tremor, and we don't want to be in the water when it comes."

They began the slow walk to shore but fell back as, in silent agreement, everyone stood aside to let Poseidon pass. When the old sailor stood on the rocky ground, he raised his arms to the sun, as if infusing himself with the light and warmth of life. "Go to the palace and wait for me," he told the others.

"What about you?" Hephaestus asked.

Poseidon's eyebrows knitted in anger. "I'm going to get my army back!"

At the barracks, Orion called the surprised troops to attention. They had been either asleep or preparing for furlough, eager to shake off the dust of the long slaving expedition, when the small tremor hit. A portion of the ceiling had collapsed, and at the time of Orion's announcement that Ares himself stood outside, the men had been scrambling for their garments and weapons. When the battalion finally stood ready for inspection, Orion fell into his usual place among the men.

"The slaves have escaped," Ares said, preparing them for the riot which he knew would take place shortly in the streets of Olympus. "They have murdered your fellow soldiers, who now lay slaughtered in the Land of the Dead. Now these savages are on their way to murder your families in their homes as they murdered your comrades."

The soldiers tensed, ready to do battle.

"The corrupt devil Poseidon let loose the foreign wizard to work his evil sorcery on the brave Atlantean troops—"

"That's a lie!" Orion called out.

It was not something he had planned to say. Years later, after he had taken up a quite different life, Orion would still be puzzled by this rash action of his youth. He had been trained to obedience, taught to question nothing spoken by his superiors. Yet he had called the high commander of the Atlantean military a liar in front of an entire barracks!

Ares swiveled slowly toward the young soldier, his expression one of rage. Orion's fellow soldiers looked at him aghast, their feet moving imperceptibly away from him so that he appeared to stand alone in a small, empty space.

His cheeks blushed wildly, but he had started and, since he knew that he would pay for the remark with his life, he saw no need to stop. "Lord Poseidon came to the death pyramid to find the princess Athena, who was locked in a cell. She was going to be sacrificed."

Orion spoke at the top of his lungs. "Then the high priest Hades and Commander Ares tortured Poseidon with a whip across his back. But he wouldn't talk. Even when they threw him in with the slaves—"

Ares drew his dagger and lunged forward. One of the soldiers pushed Orion aside, out of the way. Incensed, Ares waved the dagger from side to side, examining the faces of the troops to see who had come to Orion's aid.

Even the officers were struggling to retain their composure. For weeks they had been drunk with power and adventure in foreign lands, drunk enough to obey whomever had appointed himself in charge; but back on land, they remembered Poseidon.

"That's what made the slaves go crazy," Orion went on, righting himself to stand at attention once again. "They recognized Lord Poseidon. They called him the king of the sea."

"Because he was in league with them!" Ares shouted.

"Because he was a good man, sir!" Orion shouted back.

Ares came at him again. This time, a dozen or more men stepped between him and Orion. One of them pried the dagger out of his hand.

The soldier's voice was hoarse. He wiped away tears that had sprung involuntarily to his eyes as he recalled the senseless agony in the Land of the Dead. "And so they rioted. And when they did, the commander left the troops to die, every last one of them except for me, so I could row the boat. And I swear by everything that's holy that's the truth, and I don't care if you kill me now, sir, because I've said it."

The knife lay in the dust at Ares's feet. He bent to pick it up, but an officer casually placed his foot over the blade as he cleared his throat. "Sir, I suggest we take the soldier into custody so we can question—"

Ares came up swinging a fist that connected with the officer's chin with a bone-crushing thud, then staggered backward as the man slumped to the ground.

"You swine!" he shrieked at the troops. "I'll see you're all flogged before you die, traitors! I'll kill every one of you myself, do you hear me, then hang your worthless skulls from the palace, where your wives and children can look at you while they're beaten in the public square!"

His mouth was foaming with rage, but little by little the troops had ceased to pay attention to him. For over the horizon walked a man with a set to his shoulders and a stance they all recognized before ever seeing his face. Emerging calmly into the sunlight, his long white hair streaming like the whitecaps of the sea, strode Poseidon.

Ares gasped. "Kill him!" he commanded.

No one moved.

Poseidon never deigned to look at him. "Captain, take four men and escort Commander Ares to King Zeus in the palace and wait for me there," he said. With his toe, he kicked Ares's knife away.

The order was carried out at once.

"You'll die for this, old man," Ares seethed as he was unceremoniously trundled away.

At that moment, another tremor rumbled beneath the Earth, sending some of the soldiers tumbling to the ground like toys.

"Stand at attention!" Poseidon snapped, riding the quake like a wave at sea. "What's happened to him?" He indicated the unconscious officer.

A young lieutenant stepped forward. "Commander Ares attacked him, sir. For preventing the Commander from killing young Orion there."

Poseidon raised an eyebrow when he recognized the guard who had forced him into Hades's chamber of horrors at spearpoint.

"He said you were tortured, sir," the lieutenant said, frowning.

"So I was."

"But . . . but . . . ." Orion stammered. "Your wounds . . . I saw them myself."

"You inflicted one of them, if I'm not mistaken."

Moaning, Orion fell to his knees. "Kill me, lord. I beg you—"

"Get up, fool, and act like a soldier," Poseidon said irritably. "Alert the other barracks. The runaway slaves are beginning to swarm the city. All troops not presently defending their ships offshore are to assemble at the south gate of the palace. I will meet with them presently."

"Yes, sir." Orion took off at a run.

The quake had settled quickly, but the waves at sea were rising. Poseidon raised his voice. "The rest of you, crew members of the galleon *Oceanus*, secure your ship immediately, before the runaway slaves have a chance to steal it. And don't kill them unless you have to. You'll be sailing with them back to the mainlands."

The young lieutenant glanced sidewise at the bay, where the waves were crashing white against the shore.

"Think you can remember how to sail in weather?" Poseidon bellowed, staring hotly into the officer's eyes.

"Yes, sir," the lieutenant answered with pride. "I sailed with you to Ixlatan once, sir."

"Good! Then you'll know the way." He addressed the troops again. "You'll be stopping off at the priests' pyramid to pick up the rest of the slaves, then sailing west. When you reach the mainland, every soldier on board is to remain in Ixlatan until whatever damage you've wrought on your last expedition has been repaired. Once you have completed your task to the satisfaction of the present ruler there, you will set sail for Attica to return the eastern mainlanders to their home. Is that clear?"

"But . . . but that will take years, sir," the officer stammered.

"Then I suggest you get moving," Poseidon answered. "Dismissed."

It's settled then," Hades said. He looked up from the parchment scroll on which he and the king had been writing. "You will speak to the people today. You will abdicate and name me as the rightful king. In return, you will be exiled to the eastern mainland. Is that agreed?"

"In essence," Zeus replied. "But exactly how will I get to the mainland? Will I have escort vessels in the event of attack? Will I—"

"You're being exasperating, brother," Hades snapped. "I have no more time to waste with you on such nonsense. This is your proclamation." He tapped the parchment. "Read it, sign it, and later you may—"

The door to the king's private chamber flew open. Two soldiers tossed the struggling figure of Ares on the floor. Behind them stood Poseidon.

"You!" Hades exclaimed, unable to take his eyes off his brother who seemed, miraculously, to be in perfect health.

"He escaped with the slaves," Ares reported bitterly.

"What?"

"They're rioting, Hades, overrunning the city. I came back to get reinforcements, but Poseidon showed up and took the fourth battalion from me. They were always weak. . . ."

Hades ran to the large window and pulled back the draperies, revealing a nightmare scene of absolute chaos. In the plaza below, fear-maddened slaves fought with Atlantean soldiers. Citizens lay dead in the street. Already a half dozen fires had been set, and smoke poured from the small wooden buildings of the marketplace.

His face twisted in fury, Hades turned to the king. "You knew this," he accused.

Zeus's face was inscrutable. "How do you like your kingdom now, brother?" he asked quietly. He reached down to the table, picked up the piece of parchment on which Hades had been writing, and tore it in two pieces.

"Father?"

He looked up to see Athena entering the room, along with Hephaestus and the foreigner. With a cry of relief, he rose to embrace his daughter.

Then came the third quake.

CHAPTER 21

SECURE IN THE STRUCTURAL PERFECTION OF THE PYRAMID PALACE, ZEUS and Hades had not even felt the previous tremors, but this latest earthquake was enough to buckle the pavement of the plaza below. Athena fell into her father's arms as outside, a wagon drawn by oxen tumbled onto its side.

Poseidon clenched his jaw as he looked through the window at his ships, so carefully preserved against attack, now bobbing crazily in the mouth of the harbor.

"I have spoken with the troops," Poseidon said, forcing calm into his voice. "The navy is at your command, Majesty."

Zeus felt a rush of love for his brother whose loyalty had never wavered, even when the king had proven too cowardly to accept his sage advice. Now he knew Poseidon was silently offering it again. "How many ships is that?"

"Eighty," Poseidon answered with a gleam of hope in his eyes. "Enough."

"Enough for what?" Hades asked suspiciously, not privy to the current that was flowing between his two younger brothers. Then, like a hammerblow, the realization of what they were planning struck him. "No!" he shouted. "You will not evacuate Atlantis. This earthquake is minor. With time—"

"There is no time," Zeus snapped.

Everyone present turned to stare at him, and at the diamond hanging on his chest. It had begun to glow with a faint green light.

"We must leave now," he said quietly, "before the ships we have left to us are destroyed. The Iberian coast is relatively unpopulated. Our people will be safe there, and we can build shelters before winter comes."

"You must be mad," Hades said. "No one will leave Atlantis for the wilderness of the mainlands. If you wish to abdicate your rule, then do so. But don't expect anyone with any intelligence to go with you."

"Those with the Power will go," Zeus said, touching the pendant. "The Eye will draw them together. The others . . ." He turned back to the window. "The others must follow, or they will die here."

His heart sank as he watched the continuing carnage in the streets. Greedy youths crawled over the overturned oxcart, helping themselves to its contents. A contingent of soldiers had collected twenty or thirty runaway slaves who were walking across the plaza, their waists tied together with rope. Passersby threw stones at them as they shouted their scorn at the foreigners. At the eastern end of the docks, distinguishable by their square sail riggings, were moored the two remaining ships which had sailed with Hades on the slaving expedition. On their decks, washed by wild waves, pitched battles were taking place as the slaves attacked and fought for control of the vessels.

We have had our chance at paradise, he thought. *And we have thrown it away*.

There was so little left of Atlantis to save.

He cleared his throat. "Hephaestus, bring all the royal family to the harbor and help them to board safely."

Hephaestus stood frozen, trying to absorb the impact of what the king was saying. He would be leaving Atlantis, not at some time in the vague future, but now. His pyramids, his dams—all his accomplishments would be left behind for the sea to swallow and the winds to erase.

"Go now, my son," the king said gently. "The palace must be evacuated."

Their eyes met. Hephaestus's were brimming. "Yes, Highness," he said, and left. His long journey to Timbuktu was about to begin.

Zeus turned his attention to Poseidon. "Make room for any troops who remain loyal to you, and their families as well." He glanced back at the window. "And get the slaves."

"The *slaves?*" Hades howled.

"They were brought here in violence and against their will," Zeus answered curtly. "We owe them at least that much."

"I have ordered the crew of the *Oceanus* to sail for the west with the slaves, once they are subdued," Poseidon said. "It shouldn't take long. They are unarmed, and most of them aren't trained fighters. One of them, a former nobleman from Ixlatan, is talking with them now, urging them to surrender."

"Oh, by all means, take your slaves with you," Hades hissed. "Go live together with them in their thatched huts and bow down to their feathered demons. You will find out how much your freakish Power is valued among the savages." He laughed. "In their land, they will make slaves of *you*. And while you toil in their fields and carry the stone for their buildings, while you watch the foul-smelling savages fondle your women, my son and I will rule Atlantis."

Poseidon snatched a sword from one of the guards. "Give me permission, Zeus, to kill these dogs now!"

The king shook his head. "No," he said softly. "It is too late for our squabbles and our dreams. Our day is done. Even yours, Hades." He gestured to the soldiers to release Ares. "The two of you are free to go. The punishment for your crimes is that you are not to leave Atlantis with the ships that sail."

"Brother, I implore you!" Poseidon said, aghast at the king's leniency. "These two vermin tried to take control of the entire military. They imprisoned your daughter, tortured me, and openly plotted to take your throne. Surely they must not be allowed to remain and rule the country!"

Zeus's eyes were cloudy and distant. The stone on his chest pulsed with a life it had not shown for a quarter of a century. "There will be nothing left here to rule," he said.

Out to sea, past the fleet of ships that stood ready to take his people away, he saw once again the island of his vision—a bare, unpopulated place all but covered with water, its once great cities sunk deep in the abyss of the ocean.

The first time the vision had come to him, it had filled him with terror, but now he saw it for what it had always been—the truth, nothing more nor less. Atlantis was not theirs to keep. It belonged to whatever gods had first brought the Stranger, with his knowledge, to a primitive island archipelago in the middle of the ocean. That knowledge was given, for better or worse, to Zeus's ancestors; now their descendants, in their turn, were commanded by those same gods to pass it on to other lands, other minds.

He turned back to the people in the room—Hades, smirking at the lightness of his sentence; the others, puzzled and disappointed at what they considered the king's weakness. Even Athena and the barbarian, with the Power strong in their blood, were too young to see beyond the calamity of their own lives. But Zeus understood. For the coming generations of man to live, Atlantis must die.

So it was to be a sacrifice, after all, he realized, the greatest sacrifice possible: the body of Atlantis for the spirit of the Earth.

"We cannot change the course of things to come," he said quietly.

Hades sneered. "We'll see about that." From the king's desk he picked up the torn parchment on which Zeus had written the announcement of his abdication. "When you leave, I will consider you banished from this kingdom, as you agreed. *My* kingdom. Those who follow you will be regarded as traitors."

Shoving the soldier's swords aside, he walked regally to the door. "You'll wish you had killed me, brother," he said. "Because I swear I will kill you. You and everyone who carries your blood."

The guards accompanied him and Ares outside. Through the window, Zeus watched Hades walk out onto the plaza. Around him, despite his armed guard, people by the dozens threw themselves at his feet, begging him to avert the earthquakes with more sacrifices.

"Look at them," Poseidon said with disdain. "He'll give them what they want, even though it means a death sentence for them all."

Zeus knew the truth of that. Nothing would stop the earthquakes. They would come again and again until there were no crops at all, no animals, no clean water. Those who stayed behind with Hades to satisfy his hunger to sit on the throne would die of starvation and thirst in a barren land. By the time the last of them decided to leave, there would be no ships for their journey, and no resources from which to build them.

And that time was coming soon, soon.

"We will save who we can," he said. He stepped forward and embraced Poseidon. "Fill your vessels, King of the Sea. You yourself captain the ship carrying the royal family."

"Aye, brother. The *Dolphin*'s the best in the fleet." He hesitated. "And you?"

"You will see me." Zeus nodded to all of them. "Collect your belongings, all of you, and be quick."

Athena clung to him. "Father . . ." A terrible feeling of unease was settling around her like ashes. "You will come, too, won't you?" she asked anxiously.

"I said you will see me." He kissed her forehead. "Safe journey to you, my precious one." Gently he disengaged himself from her. "The gods— your gods—be with you."

As they were leaving, he touched Sam's shoulder. "Please stay for a moment," he said, closing the door behind the others.

He walked to the window. "You come from the future," he said. "I believe that truly. And so I must ask you: Will any of my people survive?"

Sam hesitated before he answered. "I don't know," he said finally. "I don't know what will happen to any of you. But you'll be remembered. Even in my time, people will know your name."

"The last king of Atlantis," Zeus said, smiling bitterly. "How cruel." He picked up the amulet on his chest and let it fall again. "I wonder if the Stranger, too, was no more than an ordinary man."

Sam looked at his hands. "I don't think he was ordinary," he said.

"No. Probably not. But he wasn't an Atlantean, and I doubt he was a mainlander. Since I met you, it's occurred to me that possibly he, too, came from another time. Another Atlantis, perhaps, which had made the same mistakes we have." He turned to face the window. "Do we ever learn from the past?"

"Someday we might," Sam said.

The king nodded slowly. "Yes," he whispered. "Someday." He bent his head forward and removed the pendant from his neck, then placed it on Sam's. The stone sprung into fiery life, its glow throbbing with Sam's pulse.

Zeus touched the diamond. "This will keep our people together," he said. "There are others with the Power. Athena, Apollo . . . others. They will be drawn to you. You will not lose one another so long as you have the Eye to see clearly. Do you understand?"

Sam felt himself trembling. "I think so."

"It is you, Stranger, who will begin it again. You, not I, will bring back Atlantis, with your people who are not doomed as we are, but waiting to be born."

He clasped Sam's hands in his own. "You must go now," he said. "There is a ship waiting for you. And a new life. Use it well."

The king would not be leaving the island, Sam knew. He would never be part of the new world into which he was sending his people. After they sailed, he would cease to be a man with a man's cares and sorrows. From this day, he would be known as Zeus, king of the gods.

Sam bent his knee and bowed before him.

Alone, Zeus walked from the palace toward the peak of Mount Olympus.

In the city below, soldiers, rioting slaves, and the angry citizenry clashed together over the neglected bodies of the dead into one screaming, dangerous mob. The crowd around Hades was swelling. Others, following Ares, were striking down the few families who were trying to make their way toward the ships.

This is not the end of the world, the king thought. *It ended some time ago, when no one noticed.*

He turned his back on it and resumed the wearying climb among the rocks of the mountain. Perhaps the Atlanteans deserved the inexorable future that awaited them. Once noble and magnanimous, they had become indifferent to everything except their own vicious pleasures. Their king, by forgetting his kinship with the Stranger, had led them into this.

Now he must lead them out.

At last he stood on the rim of the great volcano, his feet bare and his head bowed. He would never know if he was right or not, if what he was about to do would be known as an act of faith or of mass murder.

Perhaps the Stranger had felt something of the same trepidation, Zeus thought. He must have known that men could use his knowledge for evil as well as good.

In Atlantis, evil had won.

But the knowledge was still alive. And someday people would learn from the past.

Someday, the Stranger would be welcome again.

He raised his arms in the ancient attitude of prayer. "Gods, the gods of the Stranger, do not destroy Atlantis!" he shouted. "Take me in its place!"

Inside the dark hole of the volcano appeared a spot of red. Heat steamed up, searing Zeus's face. "Scatter us to the winds if you must, bury our treasures beneath the sea, punish us for forgetting you and debasing the gifts which our ancestor brought us. But this I beg you: Do not take away the Stranger's land forever. One day when we are clean again, when we have given our gift to the world as we were meant to give it, bring us back to our home."

His body shook with uncontrollable force as the Power surged through him, up his spine and down his limbs. Light crackled from his fingertips. His eyes, glowing with rapture and gratitude, looked into the heart of Mount Olympus.

In that void, the spirit of the Earth beckoned to him.

CHAPTER 22

BY THE TIME SAM CAME OUT INTO THE PLAZA, POSIEDON'S FLEET WAS RETURN-
ing from its offshore mooring back to port. A long procession of royal family
and servants, carrying their masters' personal treasures, all surrounded by soldiers
loyal to Poseidon, marched from the palace toward the docks.

Beyond them, on the grazing grounds for the royal cattle, Issa led Poseidon's
white stallion on a rope. When he spotted Sam, his spine straightened and he
quickly wiped his tear-streaked face.

"This is the last of them," he said stoically. "I killed all the others this morning.
My wife dressed the meat to take with us."

"But the king just now gave the order to leave," Sam said.

The old man smiled in a toothless grin. "A king higher than Zeus told me
what to do. I said I'd ask the invisible god, and I did. He sorted everything out
about the animals. The boat, too." He pointed to the bay with pride.

Ahead, moored on a sandy stretch of beach some distance away from the
harbor, was a huge ungainly rectangle, the strangest looking craft Sam had ever
seen. He had to look twice to realize that it was the same boat he had given to
the old gamekeeper. A superstructure had been built on the deck, so high it
looked like a wall, unbroken by even a slit in the boards. Only one small perch
appeared above it. The sails had been removed.

"No wonder the slaves didn't take it," Sam blurted out.

"My sons were guarding it," Issa said, oblivious to his friend's dismay. "My
sons and two bears."

Sam smiled wanly. "I think there might be a problem with the design," Sam
said, rubbing his forehead. "You're not going to be able to see out of that."

"Don't need to," the old man answered. "Don't know nothing about sailing,
anyway."

"You mean you're just going to . . . to float along?"

"That's my plan." He took a deep breath of salty spray. "Well, I guess I'll be
setting out."

"Where to?"

Issa spread his hands. "Wherever the sea takes me. I'm a free man now."

Sam looked at the wide ocean. "That you are, Issa."

"Oh, I changed my name, too. As part of my freedom. I don't want to go by a slave's name no more. Nor a master's. I'm going to be a stranger where I'm going, and I want to have a stranger's name."

Sam smiled. "So what should I call you if we ever meet again?"

"You won't forget it," the old man said, bursting into wheezy laughter. "I plan to call myself Nowar."

"Nowar?" Suddenly Sam's face blanked. "Nowar . . ." He looked again at the odd craft in the water. "The ark."

"I took your name. It's the closest to the Stranger's I could think of."

Sam looked into the old man's eyes, as hopeful as a boy's. "Good luck to you, Nowar," he said.

Issa shrugged. "It's out of my hands."

"You're going to make it."

The old man beamed. "Is that a prophecy?"

"Guaranteed accurate," Sam said. "Watch for a bird."

They bade each other good-bye, and Sam went to look for Athena.

The first frigate to sail out of the harbor was filled, not with members of the royal family, but with slaves.

It had not been easy. Many of the captives who had been brought to the docks by Poseidon's soldiers had died by their own hands before Quetzalcoatl could persuade them to board. Even Poseidon's presence on the docks had not convinced the slaves that they were not going to be sent back to certain sacrifice on the high priest's pyramid.

Quetzalcoatl had pleaded with them to believe that they would be taken home, not to the Land of the Dead. He had sworn by his god Tlaloc that he spoke the truth.

"The gods have abandoned us," one of the slaves had shouted as he held a knife to his own breast.

"They have not," Quetzalcoatl explained patiently. "They are speaking now through the king of the sea and through me. You must believe that there is good in the world, as well as bad." His voice broke. "You must believe this, or your lives are no longer worth living."

With his patient efforts, they came. Those from the nearby western shores who had dreamed of Ixlatan and its wonders; and the wild tribesmen from the far lands across the ocean, from Attica and Iberia and Egypt, from Sicily and Italy and the vast wilderness of the uncharted European plain, all willing to die for the chance to see their homelands again.

When they boarded the Atlantean ship, Poseidon pointed to Quetzalcoatl and instructed the ship's crew. "This man is to be in charge of all passengers. He will see to it that these *free men* do you no harm. In turn, you will defer to Quetzalcoatl in all matters not related to the running of the ship."

"Yes, sir," answered the young lieutenant from the fourth batallion. The sailors saluted Poseidon. Clenching his jaw, he returned the salute, knowing he would never see any of them again. He clapped his hand on Quetzalcoatl's shoulder.

"Thank you," he said quietly. "I know what you did for me in the pyramid."

"I believe you would have done the same," the patrician answered. He stood up straight. "We will rebuild Ixlatan, and your men will be safe there. I hope, Lord Poseidon, that one day you will consider making your home with us as well."

Poseidon looked out to the sea, which he knew would be his only home from now on. There would be no scrabbling in the dirt of a farmer's field for him, no bending to the laws of a feather-caped king. He was a sailor.

A woman passed by on the docks, carrying a basket of grass for weaving. She sang as she walked, her voice breathy and low:

> The wind blows
> And we are scattered like seeds
> To clutch the Earth
> To bloom for a moment
> To die like dust in the wind
> And the wind blows. . . .

"Farewell, my friend," Poseidon said.

And so the freed slaves came to the ship *Oceanus*, their muscles taut, their hearts pounding as it pulled from its mooring. As it neared the Land of the Dead, the stranded men on shore gathered silently, prepared grimly, prepared to fight what they thought was the approaching Atlantean army with just the stones in their hands.

Quetzalcoatl disembarked and spoke to them as he had spoken to the others, and in time they, too, boarded. And when the ship finally rode the wind out into the open sea, they cheered, the former slaves and the Atlantean crew alike, the cheer of free men sailing into the unknown.

Athena was not at the docks with the other royals who waited patiently for Poseidon to see off the ship of slaves. Smoke from the fires all over the city was thick as Sam walked from the harbor to the back lawns of the palace, where Athena's rooms faced. In the distance, he could hear the lowing and braying of Issa's menagerie.

Not Issa, he corrected himself: Nowar. The old man who bore his name would become the most famous survivor in history, and on a boat that looked as if it had been designed by a committee.

He smiled. So one of the Atlanteans will make it to land, he reflected.

And the rest? The slaves escaping from the Land of the Dead in their tiny canal boats? Would any of them reach the far shores of the desolate wilderness that would come to be called Europe, or the weird civilizations of Central America? And what about the others, the inhabitants of the great Atlantis? Could they bring themselves to cast off everything they owned, everything that was accepted as their due, to live as pioneers in harder conditions than they could ever imagine? Could exquisites like Apollo make a life in a place where there was no music except for the wind whistling through a clump of water reeds? Could Athena . . .

No, Athena would survive. Sam would make sure of that, one way or another.

He would never see his own home again, but he would stay by her. And the rest.

He pulled the diamond on its chain from beneath his garment. This was the Stranger's legacy, and Zeus the Thunderer's.

Sam was not its rightful owner, he knew. This object, this repository of the Power, would someday belong to someone greater than himself. But until he found that person, he would be its guardian. With it, the Stranger's descendants would stay together. He owed that to the king. Sam would keep them together and try to persuade them to use the Power together, as the Stranger had intended. Together, they would all possess it, and its scope would be magnificent.

These strangers, for they would all be strangers now, would fulfill the promise of the world by sailing to all its distant shores.

It would be a new beginning for all of them. Perhaps, even, for himself.

Suddenly he felt horribly cold.

The diamond dropped out of Sam's hand and thudded heavily onto his chest. Sweat poured off his face. His hands shook violently; his knees nearly buckled. It was difficult to breathe.

The shivers. Even here, he recognized them.

Earthquake, he thought. Back at the docks, Poseidon's command voice echoed through the mist. *Hurry*, Sam wanted to shout. *The big one. The big one's coming*. But he could not speak. The shivers had its icy hands gripped around his throat.

Then he arched his back and a dry gasp hissed out of his throat as something struck between his shoulderblades. Something that felt like a hot iron burning into his flesh.

The blade twisted, and Sam knew it was not the shivers. It was a knife.

Ares's face peered over Sam's shoulder. "Don't pretend you didn't expect this," he said.

Another voice spoke through the agony of Sam's pain. "How did you get the Eye of Zeus?" As Sam's vision dimmed, a shadowy figure robed in black came out of the smoke into his line of sight. "Did you kill Zeus for it?" Hades demanded.

"What difference does that make," Ares grumbled as he withdrew the dagger from Sam's flesh. "He's saved us the trouble."

The pain was horrifying. Sam screamed as the blood rushed out through the pulsing wound. He felt only vaguely the tug of the chain around his neck as the pendant was removed.

"Perhaps you're right, Ares," Hades said, hefting the diamond. "The Eye will draw those with the Stranger's blood to it."

Oh no, no, Sam thought through a swirl of light and darkness. To show his domination over Zeus, Hades was going to kill Zeus's children and everyone else with the Power. Wipe them out until nothing remained of the Stranger, and all the magic of Atlantis was gone.

The magic . . .

Because that was what the Power was, ultimately—a speck of magic inside the human race which made them hope and dream and imagine. People in his time had seen angels. Reba Dobbs spoke with the spirit of her dead grandmother. Carol Ann Frye could heal with some unknown force within her own body. Harry Woodson, Jamie McCabe . . . names from another life, now never to exist. Because without the Atlanteans, the Stranger's blood would never flow through the veins of any human being who would ever walk the Earth.

Hades would kill them all. The human race would go on without any trace of the Power, beings with intelligence, but without any inkling of something greater than themselves, something binding them together as part of the infinite universe.

Mankind would lose its soul, now and forever.

Sam caught hold of the priest's robe and pulled Hades to him. "Don't do this," he rasped, tasting his own blood. "You don't know. . . ."

He never finished. The Earth began to rumble again, deep in its heart. The sound grew stronger, and the ground began to quiver like the fletching of an arrow when it strikes a tree. It rolled by in waves, each one closer to the surface than the last.

Ares cried out.

"It's nothing," Hades snapped, flinging Sam away from him. "This will pass in a moment."

"But . . ." Ares pointed upward. "Look. The mountain."

Hades craned his head to see, above the pall of smoke, the peak of Mount Olympus. At its summit stood the figure of Zeus, his body glowing with eerie green light. The light radiated out from him, growing, finally encompassing the entire island. He turned to look down on the ravaged city. His eyes were visible, even from such a distance; they burned like coals. Lightning shot out of his upraised hands into the sky, burning it black. The clouds raced down, and the balmy summer day turned in an instant to terrifying night.

Sam pulled himself up to his knees as he witnessed the fulfillment of the vision he had seen in the grotto under the sea: Zeus the Thunderer, commanding his people into exile.

The mountain roared. Zeus bowed to it once, humbly. Then, as the low clouds flashed and boomed, he stretched his arms out to his sides in a gesture of supplication and stepped out over the rim.

In the city, a collective gasp rose from the populace. Soldiers dropped their weapons. The citizens of Olympus fell prostrate. The sea itself seemed to still as a plume of fire spewed out of the volcano's cauldron, and the darkened sky lit up like a fireball.

Sam closed his eyes. The Atlanteans would leave now, he knew. Hades would not be able to kill everyone with the Stranger's gift. They would go to the far corners of the world to suffer and die, but they would take the magic of their ancestor with them.

"Good-bye, great king." Sam moved his cracked lips, but no sound came.

He felt cold. Death was coming quickly for him. He wished he could have saved the diamond, but it was out of his hands now. He smiled with the thought. It was what Issa—Nowar—had said. Out of his hands.

He fell against the ground and pictured Athena's face. *No regrets*, he thought.

Not a one.

CHAPTER 23

POSEIDON, HURRIEDLY RUSHING HERA'S SERVANTS WITH THE QUEEN'S END-less baggage onto the fleet's flagship, looked up suddenly at the blaze in the sky and knew instantly, with a moan in his throat, what Zeus had done.

"What is it?" Hera screamed, running out on deck. "Another earthquake? Now?" Her attention was seized by two servants stumbling along the gang-plank with a particularly heavy chest of inlaid wood. In the first tremors of the explosion, they lost their footing and were scrambling to keep the chest from falling overboard.

"Be careful with that!" she shrieked. "Those are my best lamps!"

Without a word, Poseidon yanked the chest out of the hands of the slaves and heaved it into the water. "Hercules," he called. "Take the queen below. If she gives you any trouble, throw her overboard." Then he shoved the slaves up the gangplank. There was no time now for an orderly progression into reserved berths. Whomever the gods chose would survive.

Poseidon wiped the sweat from his face with the back of his hand. In his mind, he could still see the figure of Zeus, glowing with an unearthly light as he was immolated in the heat of the volcano's eruption.

"Peace be with you at last, my brother," he whispered. It was the only prayer he had ever spoken.

"No baggage except food," he shouted, taking a silk-wrapped bundle of gowns from another servant and tossing it on the ground like a heap of rags. The volcano rumbled again.

Hephaestus found Aphrodite in her apartment, seated before a silver mir-ror. "What do you want?" she asked his reflection.

"We are leaving the island. There is room on the ship for you."

She laughed. "Thank you, but I don't think I'd enjoy the life of a mainland farmer."

"Then you'll die here," Hephaestus said evenly. "The ships are leaving. There won't be any more after the fleet goes."

"What a pity. I've always liked sailors."

He stomped away, slamming the wall with his fist. "By the gods, if anyone deserves to be left behind, it's you," he muttered.

A moment later, the palace shook again. The windows filled with red light from the erupting volcano, and all the lamps burning in the corridors were extinguished by a massive swat of air.

From somewhere in the palace someone screamed, "The king!" but Hephaestus was thinking only of Aphrodite. He ran back into her rooms, picked her up bodily, and slung her over his shoulder.

"Put me down, you disgusting beast!" she shrieked.

"Nothing would give me more pleasure," he said, racing down the broad stairwells. "Nevertheless, you are my legal wife, and as such I am responsible for your safety."

He had barely reached the docks when Mount Olympus roared to life again, this time sending a wall of lava a hundred feet into the air. The crack in the pavement of the plaza broadened into a crevasse wider than the height of a man. Two buildings sank toward one another and collided, their roofs shearing off like pieces of tin and falling to the street below. For a moment, the thousands of windows in the two pyramids shimmered with light in rainbow colors, then exploded outward in a violent burst, carrying with them the bodies of those who had not left in time.

Aphrodite hung motionless on Hephaestus's shoulder, her face blank with shock. As the children from the palace and their nurses crowded, whimpering, up the ship's gangway, Hephaestus set her down.

"Are you all right?" he asked.

Her face was ashen. "Hephaestus, you . . . you saved my . . ."

Her interest in her husband vanished when she caught sight of Ares leading a contingent of rogue soldiers. She waved to get his attention, but Ares and his men were marching determinedly toward the last remaining vessel from the slaving expedition.

"Excuse me," she said hurriedly, "but since we're all leaving, I think I'll join Ares on *his* ship." She danced away.

"Ares isn't going," Hephaestus said flatly. "It's his punishment for torturing Poseidon and plotting to kill the king."

She turned around. "He's not leaving?"

"I'm afraid not," Hephaestus said.

"Oh." She sauntered back, displaying her brilliant smile. "In that case, I'll sail with you. I'll have my own stateroom, of course."

"I doubt that."

"But you can arrange it, can't you?" She held out her arms invitingly. "After we're underway, I'll show you how grateful I am."

Hephaestus sighed. "I'd rather you didn't," he said, moving out of her reach. "But if it becomes necessary, I believe the stable servants will be on this ship. You might ask one of them to accept your gratitude."

He left her, crimson and speechless, and loped back over the plain to help the injured.

On board the *Oceanus*, already sailing far out to sea, the jubilant freed slaves were stunned into silence by the eruption of Mount Olympus. As the waves beneath them rose to unimagined heights, they saw the windows in the distant pyramids in the land of the gods shatter like a spray of water.

"Get below!" Quezalcoatl ordered his passengers. Slipping along the rolling, wave-lashed deck, he heard the navigator shouting to communicate with the captain, who stood at the helm less than a foot away.

"Should we come about, sir?" he called, squinting against the wind which had begun to blow them wildly out to sea.

The captain took a final look at the towering buildings of Atlantis, now crumbling like sand castles before his eyes, and shook his head. "Just try to keep us on course," he answered gruffly.

He glanced over at Quezalcoatl, clinging to a mast like an insect on a twig, his clothing soaked, his face blackened with the ash that was engulfing the ship in a thick cloud. The captain gestured angrily for the fool mainlander to get below decks, but a fifty-foot swell soon diverted his concentration from the thin-faced man from Ixlatan.

Quezalcoatl watched the land of his conquerors disappear into the black mist, and hung his head. He tried to pray, but the only thing his mind could hold was the song of the woman at the docks.

The wind blows, and we are scattered like seeds . . .

He heard it again and again, and even the screaming of the wild sea could not drown it out.

Nowar, too, was in the open water, headed east. He saw only a plume of smoke in the far distance, which he took to be Hephaestus's forge.

"Funny how lively the sea is out here," he said. His wife smiled and put her arm around his waist. Neither of them had been on a ship since being brought to Atlantis as children. The motion of the craft was exhilarating to them both.

Then the ark lunged forward, bobbing like a cork on the suddenly billowing waves. Nowar's wife shrieked with laughter and hung onto the sturdy rail.

He chuckled, too. "Why, you aren't afraid at all, are you?" he said, trying to make it sound like an accusation.

She straightened up and shook her head. Her kerchief blew free and her gray-streaked hair flowed out behind her in the wind like a girl's.

In the palace library, Athena witnessed her father's suicide.

She had been carefully packing some fragile scrolls into a box when she looked outside to see the king on the rim of the volcano.

"Father!" she whispered, too stunned to believe her eyes.

Then he jumped.

You will see me, he had said in his chamber. And so she had, at the moment of his death.

She slumped to the floor. As the fireball erupted, consummating Zeus's union with his land, Athena stared emptily into the hot, red light. Outside the library people stampeded down the stairways, forgetting their baggage, anxious to arrive at the docks before it was too late, but Athena did not move. Only the shouting of her maid, who was shaking her by her shoulders, finally roused her from her numbing grief.

"Princess, you must help!" Iris shouted hysterically. "The Queen Mother Rhea has dismissed her servants and locked herself in her room. She refuses to leave the palace!"

Athena got to her feet. "I'll see her," she said. "Take your things to the ship and wait for me there."

The maid wrung her hands. "Oh, lady, you'd better hurry—"

"I will," she said, shooing Iris away.

Rhea was lying on her bed, calmly embroidering a baby's gown.

Athena noted that the draperies were drawn and that the old woman stitched by the light of a single candle. That was some relief: Perhaps Rhea had not seen her son's death.

She sat down on the bed beside her grandmother. "We have to go now," she said, placing an arm around the old woman.

Rhea smiled and shook her head. "No, I won't be making this journey." Slowly she completed a perfect flower on the hem of the tiny garment. "When you have all gone, I will walk to the sea and wait."

"Wait?" Athena could hear the impatient edge in her voice and forced herself to be calm. "Wait for what?"

"For Prometheus." She held the cloth near the candle to examine her work. "He often talks with me there." She laughed lightly. "Sometimes I think we've spent more time together since his death than before it."

"Come with me," Athena urged gently. "Wherever you are, Prometheus will find you."

Ignoring her request, Rhea held up the gown. "I dressed Zeus in this on his naming day. He'd been swathed in nothing but rags. I gave birth to him outdoors, you know, in the woods."

"I know," Athena said.

"Prometheus was with me. He helped with the birth."

"Did he?" Quietly Athena rose and went through her grandmother's things, gathering a few items Rhea might need on the journey.

"He was always there when I needed him," the dowager queen said, so quietly she might have been talking to herself. "The council wouldn't permit me to leave the palace, even when I told them my baby would be in danger. They didn't believe that I'd seen a vision. A terrible vision."

Her hands grew agitated. "I walked through the woods halfway to Parnassus. When the labor began, I was all alone. I was afraid the wolves would come after me, but I needn't have worried." She smiled shyly. "A few hours before dawn, when Zeus was ready to be born, Prometheus found me. He built me a fire."

Her eyes sparkled with unshed tears. "I've often thought that he might have been thinking of me when he built the fire for that woman and her babies on the mainland. The fire that got him killed."

"Perhaps you should ask his spirit," Athena said.

"I have. He tells me only that it is the destiny of Atlantis to bring fire to the world. What an odd thing to say, even for a ghost."

Athena bent over her grandmother. "Please, we must go now. There is no more time." She tried to pull Rhea from the bed, but the old woman firmly pushed her away.

"Hush, Athena!" she whispered excitedly. "He is here now. Prometheus!" she cried with delight. "And Zeus . . ." Rhea frowned. "But why are *you* here, my son? The vision was overcome. I bore you in the woods, away from the palace."

"Grandmother, we really—" Something brushed against Athena's cheek like a caress. She dropped Rhea's carefully folded robes. "Father," she whispered. The image of the king's final act came back to her, and her heart broke all over again. "Father, why did you do such a thing?"

A dry, fragile hand fell softly into her own. "Don't you see, child? It was the vision," the dowager said softly. "I could not cheat fate, after all."

"What was it?" She knelt on the floor beside Rhea's bed. "Tell me, Grandmother. What was the vision? Tell me!"

It took a moment for the old woman to acknowledge her, as if the pull of the spirits she saw were almost too strong to release her. "The vision, yes," she said at last. "I saw Zeus atop Mount Olympus. He was to be sacrificed to the volcano for the expiation of Atlantis's sins."

Athena's breath caught. "A sacrifice . . ."

"But he's here now." Rhea leaned back against her pillow. "Well, I suppose it's all right," she said contentedly. "There are so many people here I never thought I would see again . . ."

And then came the boom from the mountain above them. The draperies in the room glowed red with the fiery blast, and the walls shook. In the corridor outside, the few who remained in the palace screamed in terror.

"Grandmother!" Athena gasped. Rhea did not respond. She rested against her pillow, her eyes closed, a slight smile on her face.

"Grandmother . . ." She released the old woman's hand. It fell limply to the bed. There was no heartbeat, no life force left in the queen dowager. She had simply gone away.

Carefully Athena arranged the coverlet over her and kissed the wrinkled, lovely face. "Thank you, Prometheus," she murmured, "for taking her when you did." She blinked back her tears. "Farewell, Father. Good journey to you."

As she approached the door leading from Rhea's room, a tremendous crack resonated through the palace. Two gigantic pillars tumbled like twigs onto the marble floor which seemed to writhe in a bizarre dance. She tried to pull herself back, but it was too late. One entire stairwell had collapsed, and she felt herself sliding toward the hole it had left.

"Sam!" she called, unaware that she had even uttered the name.

The pressure inside the pyramid became suddenly suffocating. The force which had been dragging her out and down inexplicably reversed and propelled her up off the floor. Then, in one ear-shattering instant, all the windows of the palace blew out at once. Athena was slammed against the stone casing above her grandmother's bed, then hurled into space in a shower of glass, but she saw none of this.

All she saw was Sam Nowar's face.

*   *   *

Sam, peering over cards on which were printed symbols of stars and triangles and circles.

"How'd I do, Doc?"

"I think you know."

"How would I know? Think I'm a mind reader?"

She threw down her . . . what was it? A thin piece of wood with a black point. It made a mark where it touched the snowy white paper cut into perfect rectangles.

"I hope you're happy, Sam."

She? It was her own voice; she could feel the sounds coming from her throat, but in a language Athena had never heard before. And the face wasn't hers. Not exactly. The same green flecks in the gray eyes, perhaps, but the features were different. The woman was older than Athena and she wore an odd garment that covered her arms and fastened in the front with white bonelike disks.

Don't let go. . . .

Her hands were touching Sam's across a table littered with evenly shaped rectangular papers, and through them both a music was flowing, raging like a river; the same music she had heard the first time she touched Sam's battered face on the plain where the slaves marched.

Music.

She had heard it, too, in a place called Rome, where Sam held her clasped against the metal armor covering his chest. She was dark then, as was he, and she never would have recognized his face if it weren't for the music that called him to her in that life, as in this.

He was her son, splashing naked along the yellow mud shores of the Huang River as she tried to hold him still, feeling her heart leap as high as the trees to hear their secret music.

He was her commander in a legion of Huns. Wounded, she had carried him across her saddle as she rode, listening to the hoofbeats of her horse keep time with the music of the wind.

He had been a woman, dressed in blue finery, come to be married in the church where she served as priest. At the moment the priest touched the hands of the couple, the music flowed between the thin, celibate hand and the ring-bedecked fingers of the bride. The woman looked up, gasping, and the priest choked down a feeling of irredeemable loss.

And, too, he had once come to her in a grotto protected by snakes, where she prayed to the Goddess for a sign that life was everlasting. He came, following the music of her soul, a stranger to fill her heart with love and her belly with a new beginning for mankind.

Again and again: a grandfather, a daughter, a friend, an illicit love . . . always Sam had been there, in lives before this and lives yet to come; yet always the music was the same.

She could hear it now, rising around her in waves. And then his voice:

My love, I have waited so long for you. . . .

Her own words, in the fevered dreams from which she had called him from the depths of the sea.

Come to me now, one last time. . . .

Sam," she murmured, dragging herself along the grassy plain before she was quite conscious. She tasted the blood in her mouth. Her eyes, too, were sticky with it, but she did not need to see in order to find him. Hand over hand, she pulled herself over the ground, now thick with ash, feeling the hot embers burn her palms and the legs that dragged behind her.

"Athena!" A pair of voices called to her.

Dimly she saw two figures running toward her from different directions, but she did not stop for them. One figure was bathed in a yellow glow. Apollo, who could feel others' pain; he would understand. The other was limping and lame, but nevertheless running with the power of an athlete over the roiling earth.

They both would live long lives. This would end and they would go on, just as Zeus had wanted them to. It was something Athena knew, surely, without thought, just as she knew her own time to die had come. And Sam's.

That was the terrible regret of her dying moments: Knowing that, after such a short time together, they would have to wait for yet another lifetime to be together again.

Make it soon, she prayed, inching closer to the bloodied man she saw before her on the burned grass.

"Sam." She was with him at last, her fingers entwined in his hair, her lips nearing his, touching his.

I love you, Athena.

I love you, my darling. Forever.

Don't leave this life. Not now.

I will stay with you, Sam.

Then silence.

"Are they dead?" Hephaestus's voice.

"No. Not yet." She felt Apollo's deft healer's fingers probing her. She wanted him to stop; she wanted both of them to go away.

"Can you do anything?" Hephaestus asked plaintively.

Apollo shook his head.

"Not for either of them?" He bent down to disengage the two mangled bodies.

"Don't move them," Apollo said. "She doesn't want that."

It will be soon, Sam.

No. You have to go . . . out into the world. It was what the Stranger intended.

He struggled to lift his head, and she felt a desperate surge of energy flow through them both.

Don't Sam. The music is so strong now. Don't take it away.

Another surge. *I can't do this alone. The power wasn't meant to be used alone. Remember the boat?*

"Hephaestus," Apollo said quizzically, sitting back on his haunches. "What happened on the boat from the Land of the Dead?"

"The . . ." He looked at Apollo, then at the nearly lifeless bodies of Sam and Athena. "Poseidon was injured."

"Yes, I know."

"Sam told us to—"

Just then, the big figure of Poseidon flung himself on the ground at their side and wrapped his sinewy arms around the two. "Hold them," he commanded. As the men obeyed, Poseidon shouted over his shoulder at the sailor and laborers who had followed him in his mad dash from his duties on the ships.

"You, mate! Come here! You, too."

Dutifully the seamen wrapped their arms around the others.

Hephaestus understood at once. "Come, Apollo," he whispered as he joined the circle.

Apollo knelt beside him. A small cry escaped his lips. His was the gift of healing, yet never had he experienced the Power in such abundance.

He felt his own golden essence growing as it left his fingertips, growing and mingling with the others like strands of hemp entwining to create a rope. The rope was made of light and color; it was life itself, pouring out and flowing into each of them, diminishing no one, adding to each, until it throbbed through them all like a single heartbeat.

One of the sailors burst into tears, trembling in that web of life. Hephaestus sighed. Slowly Athena's eyes opened. She saw the violet aura around his wooly head, and Apollo's dazzling smile, but they were not separate from one another, nor from other others gathered around, nor from Athena and Sam. All of them had become one being, as they had been on the canal boat sailing from the Land of the Dead. And once again they had journeyed back to life, this time as a different collection of souls, a new consciousness, but their species had been the same: man, yet more than man.

They had become the Stranger.

Athena sat up, bringing Sam with her. The two seemed to float on the bed of energy created for a moment, then settled softly to the ground as the crowd around them separated once again into individuals.

Around them the ground cleaved, shooting up a spray of rock as the massive plates of the Earth ground together. Mount Olympus exploded again and lava poured red, crawling slowly down the mountainside toward the city, covering with a burning hiss everything in its path.

The screams of terrified people running wildly, some carrying the lifeless bodies of children, the whistling wind from the sea, the shouts of the crowd at the docks—suddenly they all boomed to life again for the handful who, for a moment, had transcended to a place of mute and timeless power.

Hephaestus knelt beside Sam. "Are you . . ." He plucked at Sam's blood-stained clothing, searching for the wound.

"We can change the course of things to come," Sam whispered, holding tight to Athena.

The sailors who had joined in the miraculous healing were looking at their hands, watching in wonder as the vibrance of color drained from their fingertips, when the volcano erupted yet again. "Hurry, all of you, back to the ship,'' Poseidon growled above the din of the endless earthquake. He was pulling Athena to her feet when he spotted something over at the docks. "Damn him," he said through clenched teeth. Without another word he raced over the buckling ground toward the ships, with his men struggling to catch up.

At the far end of the harbor, on the bow of the last slave ship, stood Hades.

Ringing him was a line of soldiers led by Ares. At his command, they were casting their spears into the hysterical throng of people storming the gangway, pleading for a chance to escape the destruction of the volcano.

A woman carrying an infant pushed through the frantic crowd. "No passengers not necessary to the running of the ship!" Ares shouted at her. In a frenzy of fear, she tried to slip past him. One of the soldiers knocked her backward with the shaft of his spear. When she tried to get up, Ares drew his sword and, with one motion, sliced off the woman's head. Still clutching the baby, her decapitated body fell into the harbor.

"Get those traitors off that ship!" Poseidon shouted to his second in command, who had already lost several men trying to halt the piracy while attempting to launch the rest of the fleet. "I'll not have it sailing half empty because of that priest and—"

With a sound like the dying groan of some huge, immortal beast, the ground around him cracked and pulled apart. Poseidon threw himself down as a gush of salt water exploded out of the earth like a solid wall. Gasping, he finally stumbled to the splintered pier just as Hades's ship set sail, rocking wildly on the waves in the enclosed harbor.

"Ready to cast off, sir," his second reported. "The ships are boarded with all the passengers they can carry. I don't know how long they can hold up here."

"Send them on their way," Poseidon said with disgust, watching Hades's spacious, nearly vacant ship sail off. "Get everyone who's left onto the *Dolphin*. We'll manage somehow."

He shoved Athena and the others up the gangplank, screaming orders at the top of his voice, while on the plain beyond the Earth turned to quicksand, swallowing up the people who were running vainly to reach the docks.

Except for the pyramids, the buildings had all gone. The Hall of Justice, the Academy, the marble shrine dedicated to Atlas, first king of Atlantis— buildings believed to have stood for a thousand years had fallen in the span of an hour, crumbled to dust. The statues and fountains, the mansions of the nobles, the wide-paved streets, the elegant plazas with their gold-tipped obelisks, all gone. The houses and farms had caught fire; now the blaze had spread to the plain where the gushing water doused some of the blaze in clouds of steam.

So this is how it ends, Poseidon thought as he made his way through the delirious mob to the helm. This is what had come of the greatest civilization ever to grace the earth.

"Damn all the gods," he muttered.

As if in response, another roar rose up and, with a blast of heat from the raging heart of the earth, the top of Mount Olympus blew apart.

The palace exploded. Its huge blocks of stone, glowing red as coals, scattered through the air like feathers, leaving nothing behind but its perfectly wrought metal core. On the Land of the Dead, the priests' temple trembled as if in sympathy, then shattered.

The pyramids were gone.

On board, the crowded passengers covered their heads as chunks of flaming mortar rained down on them, but no one spoke. There were no more words to encompass the horror which their eyes and ears conveyed.

Poseidon called for his crew to pull anchor. The *Dolphin* leaped in the water like one of his impatient horses. As the vessel was freed at last, he saw the two lonely towers which had once been the great pyramids of Atlantis sink slowly into the rising sea.

All that was left now was the sagging, blackened cone of Mount Olympus, standing sentinel over the dead dreams of a thousand years.

CHAPTER 24

WITH THE FINAL MOMENTS OF DESTRUCTION, THE SKY WAS SO DENSE WITH vapor and smoke and ash that seeing was impossible. The captains of Poseidon's remaining ships, all setting sail at once through the boiling surf, did the best they could to avoid colliding with one another, but they had little to aid them except the calls of the sailors and the screams of the passengers.

Perhaps it's for the best we can't see, Poseidon thought grimly. There was nothing to be done now for those floundering in the water, calling out with their last breaths for rescue. There was nothing to be done for the ships that were sinking, their passengers wailing belowdecks as the sea invaded their broken wooden hulls to devour them. Nothing for those left on Atlantis, clinging to a tree limb or a fallen pillar, waiting wild-eyed for death.

No, he thought. *It is better not to see*.

Athena stood on deck next to Sam. There was no room below; she had given her berth to a young servant who was in the late stages of pregnancy. The deck was filled with passengers in similar straits, doing what they could to help the crew, or simply trying to stay out of the way. Many of them were soldiers who had stayed in Olympus, trying to save the city when others had simply fled. They still wore their armor and carried their spears wearily, grateful to be given some task by the crew.

Two of the soldiers stopped at the rail beside Sam and Athena to hurl a corpse overboard. The ship had not been ten minutes out of the harbor and already there were six dead.

"Perhaps they're the lucky ones," Athena said, thinking of her grandmother. Her last sight of Atlantis sinking into the ocean had been a devastating experience for her, as it had been for everyone on board. Hephaestus had gone belowdecks in despair, carrying a misshapen piece of glass which had once been the mortar in his perfect pyramids. It was all that remained of his immortal creation.

"Even if we reach the mainland, what can we hope to find there?" she asked, not expecting an answer.

"You'll find how to use the Power," Sam said. "And you'll pass that knowledge on to your children."

She smiled and leaned against his chest. "Yes, our children. Yours and mine. We'll start over with them."

He put his arm around her. "We'll do that," he said.

Yet he knew somehow that would never be. He remembered calling to her from some faraway place where there had been a tunnel of light filled with the promise of peace. He knew now that that light had been the tranquility of death.

It had been difficult to turn away from the light, to come back to the pain of his living body drowning in its own blood, but he had forced himself, made himself come back and wait, wait for her, so that he might touch her one last time.

And she had come to him. Her lips on his were their final moments together. Even when the circle of life collected around them and infused him with their own vitality and brought them back, he knew that his time with Athena was over.

His eyes welled with tears.

"I will never leave you," Athena said on the deck of the ship bearing them to the southwest, over the place where Parnassus and the cave of the Stranger had once stood. Sam held her closer, filling up with the music that bound them together.

With the screeching sound of a ship scraping an iceberg, their vessel bumped roughly against another ship's hull. Athena went sprawling on the deck. Sam rushed after her, but as he was picking her up, a wind from the east gusted to blow the smoke momentarily away.

The clear air was a blessing for the sailors. On both ships, they ran toward the point of impact to push away from each other with oars. The passengers were squeezed aside by the crewmen, jammed so tightly together they could hardly breathe. Sam felt his ribcage compressing painfully against the rail. Athena was lost somewhere behind him.

He began to shout her name, but the words caught in his throat. Standing exactly opposite him at the rail of the other ship was Hades, his eyes widening in outrage when he spotted Sam. Around Hades's neck hung the diamond pendant.

"I found Athena," Hercules said, pulling her through the throng back to Sam. "She was . . ." His gaze followed Sam's to the priest on the square-sailed ship. "By the gods, he has the Eye of Zeus," he remarked in astonishment. "I wouldn't have thought the king would make *him* his successor."

A murmur circulated around the deck. Finally a man called out, "Hades is the new king!"

"Like hell he is," Sam said in a language no one understood as he clambered to the top of the rail.

Poseidon's own crewmen tried to push him back, cursing at him as they swung their oars around to stop him, but Sam was already in the air, leaping toward Hades's ship.

"Sam, don't!" Athena screamed as the pressing crowd separated her from

Hercules. Crushed against the rail, she watched, not quite believing what she was seeing, as Sam landed squarely atop Hades on the opposite deck. The two of them skidded, struggling, toward the main mast.

"I think you've got something that doesn't belong to you," Sam said, snapping the chain.

The priest grabbed for the pendant. "Sorcerer! Do you think they will ever accept you as king?"

"I don't want to be king," Sam said. He had held the priest by his collar; now he let him go with a push. "That's not what this stone is about. Leave it alone, Hades. Go be king of whatever hellhole you land in." He climbed the rail again, but but by now the ships were too far apart to make the jump.

"Kill him," Hades ordered. His gaze swung malevolently around toward the oarsmen on his ship but they only stared at one another, then at Poseidon on the other deck.

Poseidon watched Hades's silent frustration with some amusement. The crew members had never had a vote as to which vessel each was to serve. Ares may have persuaded the soldiers accompanying him on his slaving expedition to abandon Poseidon, but he had never thought to gain the loyalty of the men who worked the ships. If he had, he would have known that to a man, they stood solidly behind the great sailor who had trained them.

"Give him an oar," Poseidon said.

"Aye, aye, sir," one of the crewmen on Hades's ship said with a slight smile as he extended his long oar across the void to bridge the distance between the two vessels.

It was more than twenty feet long, enough for a hand-over-hand bridge, if Sam could traverse it quickly. Sailors from both ships held it steady as Sam climbed over the rail and suspended himself from the slender but sturdy shaft of wood, the pendant's chain wound tightly around his wrist.

None of the passengers spoke while they watched Sam inch along the oar as the two ships bobbed together. Even the gods seemed to be holding their breath in this pocket of calm, clear air. Only Hades's eyes shifted momentarily from Sam toward a line of figures moving in a silent crouch along the deck.

Then suddenly the oarsman on Hades's ship arched forward, a dagger buried in his back.

Ares rose from the deck.

"My troops are behind me, in case the rest of you have any ideas." His soldiers stood up, their spears poised at Poseidon and his deck crowded with civilians.

Sam was still hanging, not moving, while the oar shifted back and forth on the railing, dancing closer to the edge with each movement of the ships. He looked up through the cascade of perspiration flooding his face. Ares met his gaze, and a smile spread over his handsome features. "Hold the oar steady," he ordered. The onlookers sighed with relief.

A crewman obeyed, replacing the dead man who had held one end of the oar. Ares reached across him to snatch the diamond from Sam. The chain snaked around Sam's wrist, burning his skin as it unwound. He tried to hold onto the amulet, but at that moment the ship lurched and he instinctively brought both hands back to the oar. The pendant snapped loose, and Ares held it.

"All right. Let him come across," Poseidon called. "You've got what you want. We'll part in peace."

Ares made an exaggerated bow. "How gracious of you, Uncle."

Hades moved to Ares's side. "Give me the diamond," he said cautiously. He knew Ares would not stop now. The smell of blood was in the air.

Ares held the diamond to the light. "I think not, Hades. You seem to have become overly fond of it."

That was when Sam moved. With a swing of his legs, he hurled himself toward Hades's ship, catching the rail with his fingertips, then pulled himself over. Without a second's pause he whirled, smashing Ares's cheek with both fists clenched together.

Ares staggered back. His soldiers surrounded Sam, but Ares halted them with a gesture. "No," he said, wiping blood from the corner of his mouth. "He's mine."

He placed the diamond on the deck between them. "Come and get it," he taunted.

Sam lunged at him. Ares feinted, laughing. As they circled the stone, it moved, first toward one, then the other as the ship rode the growing swells beneath them. The wind was changing. Wisps of mist and smoke snaked onto the deck. As the ships began to drift apart, the oar fell into the water. Poseidon groaned. Even if Sam managed to get the Eye of Zeus away from Ares, he would not be able to get back to the *Dolphin*. "Bring a rope," he ordered a crewman.

In the mate's wake, Hercules muscled into the spot next to Athena. He was carrying a fisherman's trident.

"I wish that was me over there," he said. "Your friend doesn't have much of a chance against Ares." Someone shoved against him and he cursed. "Found this on the deck, though. If those curs try anything . . ."

"Don't be a fool," Athena snapped, taking the trident from him. "If you do anything, they'll kill him."

Aboard Hades' ship, the two men wrestled, parted, and came together again. Sam was tiring. Ares was bigger than he was, and he knew from Sam's first blow that this foreigner needed space to fight. He would keep his arms pinned and straining until his muscles weakened.

It shouldn't take long, Ares thought. The savage's excitement had given him a temporary strength, but he had been wounded. *After all, I put the knife in him myself.*

Sam fought to free himself from Ares's grip, but the soldier was used to combat. He pinned Sam's arms behind his back until his shoulders screamed with pain. When they were too numb to move, Ares released them and punched Sam in the stomach.

Sam flew across the deck, both from the blow and the sway of the ship, crashing with a thud against the keel. He saw Ares coming at him again. Blindly, he groped for a weapon. Anything . . .

His hand closed on the diamond which slid toward him. He felt its cold fire, heard again Zeus's words.

It is you who will begin it again . . . with your people who are not doomed as we are, but waiting to be born . . .

My people, Sam thought. The king must have been talking about the frightened refugees on Poseidon's ship. Sam's own life was nothing, a small, twisted anomaly that belonged neither in his old world or this new one. But the others in his charge were the survivors of Atlantis, the only beings on Earth who carried the knowledge of the Stranger deep in their blood. The stone belonged to them, them and their descendants. It would be a magnet, keeping them together so that the would not be scattered around the world, their great gifts diminished through generations until, in his own time, those blessed with the Power would be regarded as lunatics and charlatans. Instead, they would be strong and certain, and one day would create a civilization capable of understanding the depths of the universe.

They had to have the stone.

Ares jumped, crushing Sam with both feet. Before Sam could recover from the nausea and the blistering pain, Ares dragged him up by the scruff of his neck and pummeled him with his fists.

Sam went down again, rolling with the dizzying waves. He blinked, searching for Poseidon's ship. It was drifting away. With each roll of the sea, the two frigates drew farther apart. He got up, staggering, trying to move toward the rail, but Ares caught him just below the eye with a fist like iron.

Seeing the blood running down Sam's face, Ares took a moment to pick flecks of his opponent's skin from the gold of his heavy insignia ring. Then he looked up and shrugged in mock apology for the benefit of his soldiers, who laughed heartily at the charade. They leaned lazily on their spears as if to underscore their contempt for the interloper.

But Sam still held the diamond, and with each new blow, he moved closer to the rail.

"Where's the damned rope?" Poseidon muttered from the deck of the *Dolphin*. Already the two ships were so far apart that it would be next to impossible to get the crazy foreigner back. To make matters worse, the wind had shifted direction, bringing with it the soot and ash which had temporarily cleared from the air. In another few minutes, Hades's ship would not even be visible.

Finally the crewman with the rope appeared. Poseidon tied one end to a cleat on the deck and knotted the other around a grappling hook, then circled it over his head, letting out some of its length with each revolution. Finally he let it fly. It sailed out over the water, just missing the railing of the slave ship. With a curse he tried again, but the rope fell even more short of its target. The ship was simply too far away.

Poseidon gritted his teeth and was preparing for a third attempt when Hercules took the coil from him. "Let me try," he said quietly.

The sailor grunted. He'd heard the boy was strong, if empty-headed. "Try to get a good swing," he said, handing over the rope.

Hercules swung. The rope grew longer as it rose into the air, picking up momentum, then fell clamorously against the rail of the slave ship and held. The passengers on board the *Dolphin* cheered as the rope yanked taut and the two ships jerked to a standstill.

As the fight between Ares and Sam went on, one of Hades's soldiers strolled over to the rail and casually began to saw at the rope with his knife. Poseidon's heart sank. "Take the rope, Sam!" he shouted. "Throw the blasted stone away and get to the rope!"

The soldier only sneered.

But Hercules was not yet finished. Hand over hand, he pulled on the fraying rope, his huge muscles straining, his body lathered in sweat. Poseidon watched him for a moment, then realized with amazement that the slave ship was moving nearer. With nothing except the strength of his arms, Hercules was towing the frigates together.

Quietly Poseidon told his first mate to gather the soldiers on board the *Dolphin* around Hercules. If Ares's men got the idea to kill him, they would be answered by a hail of spears.

Glad to be of use, the troops showed up with miraculous speed, their weapons poised for attack.

"I'd get away from that rope if I were you," Poseidon called to the soldier with the knife.

Looking up to see an array of armed men well within throwing distance of his body, Ares's man sheathed his knife.

The ships moved closer together.

"Come over!" Poseidon called to Sam. "Drop the damned stone if you have to. Just get over here!"

Sam scrambled toward the rail, but he was too battered and exhausted to escape Ares. With a kick to Sam's kidneys, Ares heaved himself onto the body of the oarsman he had killed and pulled the knife from the man's flesh. "I think I'm tired of you," he said with a smile. "I'll take the king's stone now, if you don't mind." He moved forward for the kill, the blade in his expert hands.

Sam got to his knees, gauged his distance to the rail, and knew he could not make it across before the knife struck.

"Move, man!" Poseidon roared.

Sam stood up. His life was over. Only the stone mattered now.

Keeping his eyes fixed on Poseidon's, he threw the amulet to the old sailor on the other ship and prayed that it would reach Poseidon's waiting hands.

For a moment the diamond seemed to hang suspended in air, sparkling with all the colors of the rainbow. Then the wind gusted up, so strong that both ships listed dangerously. The frayed rope snapped.

Flying on the current, the stone veered, blowing westward toward the *Dolphin*'s bow. Every arm at the rail extended to reach for it, but it fell just out of their reach, tumbling end over end, winking in the light. Finally, as the passengers groaned in disappointment, the Eye of Zeus dropped into the sea.

"Oh, God, no," Sam whispered.

No. It couldn't be. The stone was the reason he had been brought to Atlantis in the first place. It had been his destiny to keep the Power intact, to change the dreary course of things to come. After anguishing for a lifetime, he had finally understood that things happen for a purpose, that each life mattered, that there was, in fact, a force which could only be called God.

But the stone was gone. By hazard, luck, chance . . . gone. Like Atlantis. Like the future he had thought to change. As he watched the dark bubbling waves swell beneath him, he never heard Athena's scream.

"Sam!" she shrieked as she watched Ares rushing up behind him with the dagger. Sam did not move. By losing the stone, he had seemed also to lose any will to live.

She lifted the trident in her hand, pulled it back, and threw it with the true aim at which the soldiers on the practice fields had marveled when she had been little more than a child. It caught Ares square in the chest, three spikes that pierced his armor to his beating heart. His lips parted slightly; his eyes stared forward, unblinking; then he tumbled forward as Hades ran to him, emitting a keening moan like the cry of a sacrificed slave.

Hades's soldiers bolted to attention.

"Ready your spears," Poseidon commanded his troops as the ships began to bob away from one another in the mist.

Slowly Sam moved to the rail and climbed up. The soldiers on the slave ship, greatly outnumbered by Poseidon's force, glanced over at Hades for direction.

"Come to me, Sam," Athena pleaded. "Jump now. You can still make it."

Sam blinked at her fuzzily.

Hades looked up from his son's body. "Kill him," he growled to his troops. "Then kill them all."

Athena covered her face. "Oh, my love," she whispered.

Poseidon tensed. "Ready your shields."

Sam listened to them all with complete indifference. He balanced on the top of the rail, defeated, suspended between the sky and the sea. He felt the shivers creeping up his body, engulfing him, but they meant nothing to him now.

Hades's soldiers loosed their spears. Sam closed his eyes, waiting for the blades to pierce his back.

And then the wave came, a gigantic wave bursting out of the calm water between the ships, an eruption so sudden that it swept away the spears in their flight as if they were straws. It washed over both ships in a torrent, pushing them wide apart.

The wave lifted Sam off the rail as if cradling him in its monstrous dark hand. It held him aloft on its crest, almost gently. Sam did not struggle. His last sight was of Athena, her face buried in her hands.

I will never leave you, he told her with the voice of his undying soul.

Then the wave bore him down, down into the sea, and the mist followed it, thick and white, to cover its secret work.

"Throw the rope into the water!" Poseidon ordered, although he already knew it was too late.

The deck was curiously silent now. It might have been the mist, Poseidon thought, so thick. He had sailed in heavy fog before, and he knew it could play tricks with sound. Sometimes it would envelop a ship in a silence so impenetrable that a man's voice sounded feeble from even a few feet away; at other times, the most faint sounds from distant places could be heard with absolute clarity. Now he could not hear even the roar of the ocean, but a baby's cry cut cleanly through the white air. Then it, too, faded to nothing and there was only silence.

"I'll kill you."

Poseidon's back tensed with a jolt. It was Hades's voice, shrill and filled with menace.

The sailor remembered his last glimpse of the priest holding the body of the son he had never been permitted to recognize. Hades had expected to be king. He had expected the same for his son. Neither dream, the only ones Hades ever cherished, had come to pass.

The priest screamed with rage. "Zeus has done this! Zeus and his murdering daughter and the demonic Power they used to destroy everything we knew, everything we owned . . ." The scream diminished to a sob. "To the world we were gods. We could have ruled like gods."

"That is past," Poseidon said into the mist, his voice not without gentleness. "Let it be, brother."

"I will *not* let it be!" Hades rasped. "I'll kill you. I'll kill you all. You and your children and theirs, through all time, through all eternity. Every bearer of that foul blood will die. . . ."

And then the voice died away, vanishing into the mist like a memory. Hades was gone.

P oseidon stared into the fog. There was nothing. His ship was adrift and directionless.

Oh, he would find a port somewhere. He would leave his passengers on dry land, and stay himself, perhaps, for a day or two, and then move on. That much he could do. But no more.

To the world we were gods. . . .

The world was mistaken. They were not gods. They were only men, like the slaves in the Land of the Dead, like the savages in the new lands. Seeds in the wind, to light and bloom and die, and then blow away.

He breathed deeply, smelling the air, acrid with smoke and bitter with remembrance, yet carrying still the scent of the eternal ocean.

Only men, for whom life was short and painful and precious.

He shouted into the fog. "All hands, back to your posts."

"Aye, aye, sir." Feet scrambled around him.

This, too, would be a new day.

GENESIS

Deep.

The devil lived here.

Sam floated under the waves, carried back by the power-ful current drawn to Atlantis. The sea was reclaiming its own, and he was part of the sea.

All spirit now, his body visible, naked in the dark water but no longer quite a part of him, he saw beneath the sea the vanished city of Olympus: its broad paved streets, its temples reduced to jagged lumps of stone, its citizens hor-rific cadavers, already bloated with death.

That would pass. The bodies would feed the fish. There was a purpose for even the most useless of creations.

The souls, though, that was different. They went on, intact, scrambling for a place to dwell, complaining when they found it, then bitter to leave. The cycle of birth and rebirth was endless, or could be.

He thought perhaps he would not come back another time. There had been so many lives, after all, and each one a pitiable struggle, usually for foolish ends—a soldier's death at the heartfelt but idiotic command of some general or other; a priest's suicide because of some imagined sin.

And this one! Twenty-nine years spent in the wrong time. It made no sense, even now with his head finally clear and able to think.

He had gotten back—or forward, or sideways, depending on how one looked at time—but it hadn't seemed to make much difference. He hadn't changed a thing. Hadn't done any good whatever. A waste of a life.

He wished that the tenuous strings holding him to his body would let go. Sam Nowar had been a particularly resilient receptacle, at least physically. He wanted to shake it loose, this flesh, get on with things, be free.

Free . . .

His thoughts vanished at the sight of a curious structure, an odd assortment of stones inside a cave. It came to him then. The Stranger's shrine. That small misshapen pile of rocks where a man with no name had come to write his testament. It was still intact, still as it had been.

Some things always survive.

Sam and his body moved closer to it. Even here, under the ocean, it was a place of peace. No wonder Athena had loved it so. . . .

The eyes in Sam's body began to weep.

Athena.

I will never leave you. . . .

He had told her that, but in the end he had left. He had left without even a struggle because he had lost the stone.

Oh, Athena.

The music played for him now, tinny and frozen. He was so far from her. His body swam down, closer to the grotto.

Come back, my love, my love forever

Closer yet, the body scraping against the ancient walls of the cave.

We can change the course of things to come.

Athena . . .

And then the music swelled and carried him through the grotto, trembling, terrified, suddenly burdened again with the body he had longed to shed, shaking in spasm, bug-eyed, screaming finally when he saw the man in the wetsuit swimming toward him.

The mouthpiece went in. Sam breathed and let himself be pulled back to the submersible and put inside.

It was warm there, and light. As he lay on the floor of the metal ship, a familiar black face leaned over him and said: "You're alive."

CHAPTER 1

WHERE'D YOU GO?" WOODSON ASKED.

"Where . . ." Sam laughed weakly.

"When I first went into that cave, you were gone. And then a second later you were there, right in front of me. Buck naked."

Sam looked down at himself. Naked. He had lost the robe he had been wearing, lost it in the water . . . with his body. . . .

"Where's your gear?" Woodson persisted. "What happened to the shark?"

"Shark?"

Had there been a shark? Yes, there had. Weeks ago, or months, or somewhere in a dream. He could not quite remember.

"The shark, man. It followed you into the cave. I expected you to look like Tuna Helper by now."

"The shark . . . okay, yeah." Sam ran his fingers through his wet hair. "We were diving. There were two guys. You killed one."

"I killed both of them. Sam, is this the Rapture?"

"I . . . I don't know. No, I don't think so." He squinted his eyes at Woodson. "Did you say I was only gone for a *second?*"

Woodson shrugged. "Well, it took me a couple of minutes to reach the cave but . . . what am I talking about, of course you weren't actually gone. . . ."

"But I was, I left for a long time. I was living in . . . Atlantis," Sam said with wonder.

Woodson reached for the control panel. "I'm taking you to a hospital."

"No." Sam grabbed his arm. "It isn't the Rapture. I don't know how to explain how it happened, but it did happen. Right here. Those metal cylinders we saw are the cores of two cantilevered pyramids. The cave where you found me was a shrine."

He studied the underwater scene on the other side of the submersible's glass bow. "Over there was the harbor where the fleet docked, and beyond it were the canals, three of them, ringing the city of Olympus."

"Olympus," Woodson said flatly.

"And in the center was the volcano."

"The what?"

"The volcano. You saw it. So did I. And Carol Ann. All the Rememberers did. That's what we were all remembering, Harry. The volcano that destroyed Atlantis."

He stared out into the sea. "It stood right where Memory Island is. The island. That's all that's left of Mount Olympus."

Woodson looked at him quizzically. "You're serious, aren't you?" he said.

Sam met his eyes. In them, Woodson saw the pain of a thousand lifetimes. This was not nitrogen narcosis, he realized. This was a man who had experienced the impossible.

"I'd better surface," Woodson said. "Keep talking."

As he brought the sub up, Sam began to relate his experiences on the other side of the cave.

"That's why our blood is different," he interrupted himself. "It's the Stranger's blood. The same blood Zeus had. And Athena . . ."

He felt his heart break.

Why did I have to go back, just to leave her again?

"Look," Woodson said as they reached the surface. "The speedboat. I'd forgotten about it."

The powerboat belonging to the divers bobbed only a few feet away from the sub. Far away, in the place where Woodson had submerged, their own rowboat drifted idly.

"We can take their boat back," Woodson said. "They sure won't be needing it anymore."

He maneuvered the submersible close to the powerboat, then rigged up a towline between the two vessels as Sam crawled out of the hatch.

"They left their clothes on board," Sam said, picking up a sweatshirt and a pair of jeans that were folded neatly over a pair of deck shoes.

"Good. I was getting tired of looking at your bare white butt."

Woodson hoisted the small anchor, revved up the engine, and set off with the submersible bobbing along behind.

"Beats rowing," Sam said with satisfaction.

Woodson cocked his head at him. "You were talking about our blood," he said. "Who did it come from?"

"No one knew his name. He was a stranger, like me. That's what they called him. The Stranger."

"And he was a psychic?"

Sam thought for a moment, then nodded. It was better, he decided to keep the more exotic aspects of the Stranger to himself. "The first psychic. And then the trait was pretty scarce down the years, until it appeared full-blown with Zeus. But a lot of them, not just Zeus, must have carried the gene, or whatever it was that produced the blood we have."

Sam's face lit up. "That means they made it," he said excitedly. "The survivors from Atlantis found their way to other places. That's how civilization really happened. They brought farming and metalworking and writing and mathematics and music to every piece of the Earth they could reach." He thought of Prometheus. "In their way, they all gave the gift of fire."

"Zeus?" Woodson shook his head. "Now don't get too far ahead of me."

"Zeus was a real man, Harry. A king, just like it said in your book. And the diamond was his thunderbolt. They called it the Eye of Zeus." He looked away. "And I lost it."

"The diamond that was lost in the sea," Woodson said thoughtfully. "You're the one who lost it!"

"Right," Sam said expectantly. "So?"

"And you're the one who found it again." He smiled. "Don't you see? It's come full circle. That's probably why so many weird things are happening now."

"With a stranger it began . . ." Sam whispered.

"What's that?"

"A saying. It was carved in stone in their language. 'With a stranger it began; with a stranger shall it begin again.'"

"What does that mean?"

Sam hung his head. "I still don't know."

Unable to sleep after Sam and Woodson had left in the predawn blackness, Darian had climbed to the small plateau atop the island and begun to construct a rock and mud barricade.

As daylight began to insinuate itself over the sea, first Cory came up to help him, then Carol Ann. Working together, they built their crude fort, but Darian knew it would be a paltry defense against whatever St. James was sending against them.

"I'm sorry, ladies," he said. "I wish I could do better for you."

"It's all right," Carol Ann said. "We all knew this time was coming. Reba's right. No matter what happens, we need to be here now. Together."

They all looked at one another with the same unspoken thought: *But we're not together. Two of us are missing. We're not whole anymore.*

Just then Reba puffed her way up the hill, her eyes frightened as she approached them.

"What's is it?" Darian asked.

"It's Sam," Reba answered, almost in a whisper. "Something's happened to Sam."

"I feel it, too," Carol Ann said. Her hand flew to her forehead and she looked at Cory, who nodded.

"*What's* happened?" Darian growled. "He get hurt out there?"

"Not hurt, exactly," Reba said. "More like . . . *vanished*. He's gone, Darian."

McCabe scowled. "I don't know what you're talking about. Is he dead? Is that what you're saying?"

Cory shook her head. "No, he's not dead. Just . . . gone. I didn't know how much I'd felt his presence before, but it's not there any longer." She looked at Reba, her countenance imploring.

"Kind of like he stepped in some kind of bubble," Reba said.

"There's music, though." Carol Ann looked at Darian with her far-seeing eyes. "Beautiful music that just keeps getting louder, until . . ." She turned to the old woman. "You have to find him, Reba."

"Me? How?"

"The way you found him before. That's your gift."

The old woman thought. "Then it's going to take all of us." She linked hands with the girl. "Me to find him, you to protect him, Cory to love him."

Cory blushed as she took Carol Anne's hand.

"And you too, Darian McCabe."

"Hogwash," Darian said. "I've got no gift."

"You understand him," Cory said. She held out her hand to him. Reluctantly, he placed his big bony palm over hers.

"This better not take long," he muttered. He glanced at his wristwatch. Seven fifteen. "In case you haven't noticed, it's a hell of a time for a seance."

"Sam," Reba said softly, ranging her mind over the sea. "Sam, honey . . ."

They all felt the water at once. They gasped, choking, as they came up facing two pyramids, then turned to see the shark swimming up fast behind them.

A man on board a strange-looking sailing ship came into view. Darian jerked upright.

"McCabe, it's *you*," Reba said.

Darian could not answer that he looked nothing like the sailor in the vision they were seeing. He was gulping salt water with Sam, his pulse racing as he tried to flee the attacking shark.

The man on the ship threw a weapon and the tiger shark thrashed wildly, streaming blood. A few minutes later, the body that encased the four of them along with Sam was hauled out of the water and dropped onto the deck of the ship.

"We're *inside* him," Cory said in a small voice that sounded very far away. "Sam's eyes are seeing this."

The tall gray-haired sailor who had saved Sam's life was examining him suspiciously from a distance. When he finally turned away, he spoke one word that they all understood: *Atlantis.*

It came on them then, all at once. Huddled together, hands joined on their little piece of rock, Cory, Darian, Reba, and Carol Ann lived inside Sam's mind, viewing his new world as he himself saw it: the sacrifices, the king, the rebellion, the fires, the inside of the dungeon with Athena. Twice Reba called out to him and tried to bring him home, but both times she sank back into silence, defeated.

The images continued. The fires, the battle, the eruption that blew the kingdom apart, and then Sam, washed off the railing of a ship, hurtling finally into the sea.

And there it ended. The vision faded. The four of them on Memory Island sat mutely in a circle, their eyes closed tightly in pain and sadness.

Then Reba shouted, "Hold on, folks. Something's out there."

"Woodson!" Darian exclaimed.

Carol Ann swallowed. "Sam's back."

"He's safe," Cory said, falling back against the rock behind her. Carol Ann embraced her, trembling with joy.

Darian shook his head and breathed deeply for the first time in what seemed like weeks.

Well, it's been weeks, hasn't it? he thought groggily.

He looked up at the sky. The sun was in the same position it had been before the group had begun its strange odyssey with Sam. He checked the time.

It was still seven-fifteen.

Darian shook his watch. It was ticking. "Don't make sense," he muttered. "What don't?" Reba asked.

The minute hand on his watch clicked over one notch. "Seven sixteen," he said numbly. "How long were we with him, Reba?" he asked.

"I don't rightly . . . why, it must have been a couple months," she said, surprised. "But we didn't none of us eat nothing in all that time." She squinted into the sun. "And here it is still daylight."

Darian stood and leaned against the waist high-barricade.

It was the island, he knew.

Jamie had seen visions here. Darian himself had heard the voice calling through the fog those long years ago. There was something on Memory Island that increased the Sight in those who had it.

Including himself.

There was no point in denying that anymore, particularly since they were probably all going to die here.

On the island.

He picked up his rifle. Sam was alive. There might still be hope.

Stiffly, he walked away from the circle. "I'm going to take another look around," he said.

He walked for a few feet along the beach, then snapped rigidly to attention. Less than a mile away, a ship was racing toward Memory Island. From thirty degrees east came another.

Darian loped along the shoreline. Another ship was visible just over the horizon.

They're going to surround us, he thought, feeling sick.

He kept walking. To the west, close enough for Darian to read its name, was Aidon St. James's yacht, the *Pinnacle*.

About a mile south of Memory Island, Woodson cut the boat's motor. "Trouble," he said.

The island was ringed by ships, ocean-going yachts of two hundred feet or more. There were five of them, and space for a sixth.

Sam picked up a pair of binoculars left on the speedboat. "That's St. James's tub. Looks like he's brought reinforcements, too."

"He's going to a lot of bother for six people."

"Can we call the Coast Guard?" Sam asked.

Woodson sighed. "I've been trying, but I can't get anything out of this radio. Those ships must have all the frequencies jammed." He walked back to the tow rope. "Still, if they're out here, it means our guys are probably still alive. Give me a hand here."

"We've got to go in," Sam said.

"We will. In the sub. We can shoot back through to that vacant spot to the west. That's where I got the rowboat. There's a channel there. They'll never see us."

He was right. Stacked on either side of the channel were the rotting hulls of four rowboats, covered with tarps and secured by wires. They surfaced the sub inside the channel, then covered it over with loose brush and crawled on their bellies between boulders toward the interior of the island.

"Hold it," a voice barked above them. "Don't move one muscle."

Poseidon?

"Now get out here where I can see you."

Sam rolled over and looked up. It was Darian McCabe.

"Sam," the old man said softly. He extended his hand, then pulled Sam up and caught him in a hug. It was the first time in Sam's life that Darian had ever held him.

"I'm okay, too," Woodson said, brushing off the front of his jeans.

Darian laughed and swung an arm around him as well.

"Who do they belong to?" Sam asked, indicating the ships.

"Hell if I know. But St. James is one of them, so you can bet they're not here to throw us a party. They sent a diver to take the propeller off my boat. And they've jammed the radio."

"Sounds like you've done a great job looking after things while we were gone," Sam said drily.

Darian grunted. "Shouldn't have been gone."

"We could take the propeller from the submersible," Woodson offered. "I could put it back on underwater."

"No point, least not while those ships are here. Brand new, the *Styx* couldn't outrun a one of them. But I was thinking about rigging up some tripwires out of fishing line, in case some of these fancy-ass sailors decide to pay us a visit. Want to give me a hand with that?"

"Sure," Woodson said.

"There are some blasting caps, too," Sam said. "We used them on that canal job. Might even have a few sticks of dynamite left."

"Interesting," the black man said. "Let's see what else you've got."

Aidon St. James held a pair of binoculars to his eyes. "Here comes the last of them," he said to Penrose, who squinted to see past the island onto the sun-dappled ocean. To the east, a huge pleasure craft sped toward the hole in the ring of ships surrounding Memory Island.

"Every one of those vessels is equipped with enough explosives to level a square city block," he said.

Penrose lowered his own binoculars, frowning. "Do you think that will be necessary, sir? There are only six people on the island."

St. James looked amused. "Then we'll be sure to get them, won't we?" He waved the man away. "Get in communication with the ships. Have them stand by for my orders."

"Yes, sir," Penrose said.

Six people, St. James mused. The idiot thought it was about six people.

But then, it had taken some time for St. James himself to understand. He had gone through the testament dozens of times in the past days, piecing together odd bits of information, inferring others from pages which had been copied incorrectly or nearly disintegrated with age.

But he knew now.

He knew how to keep Hades's promise.

There will be no human gods on this Earth again, St. James had vowed at his initiation, as his ancestors had, as just yesterday his son Liam had also vowed.

No human gods. It was the only way to ensure that no one with the Stranger's Power would ever again come to claim the Earth as Zeus had claimed Atlantis.

Hades had written his testament during his last years in a primitive place now known as Egypt, where he had suffered from an ailment which would have been easily cured in a civilized country. But there were no civilized countries any longer. Zeus had seen to that. He had destroyed Atlantis in order to send the Power out into the world.

That Power had remained scattered and dilute for millennia, seeping into the population generation by generation, until those who possessed the Stranger's blood hardly recognized it in themselves. The Consortium could only find them one at a time, with painstaking effort. Without the Eye of Zeus, the people of the blood would always remain separate from one another.

But the stone had come back.

And so, strangely, had the land.

According to everything Hades had written about the location of Atlantis, its midpoint—Mount Olympus—stood exactly at the spot where St. James's ship was now facing.

Memory Island. It was the last remnant of the brilliant nation which had once dominated the world.

And Zeus's people found sanctuary there.

They had found it before, during the time of Edward Bonner's famous experiment. St. James's father had eliminated the Rememberers then, but even he had not guessed the island's secret. How many times through the ages had that insignificant-looking rock sheltered Zeus's kin, strengthening their power, forcing them to "remember" a time before most of mankind possessed even the knowledge to plant wheat?

It was the land that kept their power alive. St. James knew that now. *The land itself.*

It was their home, their place of belonging.

Without it, they would die.

The others were already coming, he knew; the stone called to them from the far places of the earth. The stone would lead them to the land. That was the prayer Zeus had invoked during his final moment.

But there would be no land. Within an hour, this pustule on the Atlantic would be gone beneath the water. The voyagers would come, not knowing why they were making the journey. They would come to the stone.

And Aidon St. James had the stone.

No human gods.

The promise would be kept.

Liam sat in his stateroom where he had been all day. His senses were still numb after his initiation into the Consortium last night.

The blood, there was so much blood. . . .

His nose was running; he did not notice. He rocked back and forth on the bed, trying to block out the memory of the man whose body had jerked in spasm as the curved blade in Liam's hand cut into his beating heart.

The image had never left him, not for a moment. It was there behind the words—a mountain of words—which had been spoken to him, words that had addressed all the questions of his life: who he was, what he did, why he lived.

He wished now he had never heard the answers.

His lessons had been in the history and language of Atlantis.

Atlantis!

The very sound of it had always sent a thrill up his spine. The lost continent, the place where the legends began.

Now he knew that the legends were true. Zeus, Athena, Apollo, Hephaestus, Poseidon . . . they had actually lived, long before the Greeks worshiped them. And there had been another, too, one he had never read about in books of mythology. He had no name. He was called only the Stranger.

The Consortium hated the Stranger. In the testament, he was called the seed of evil. In the testament written by Liam's ancestor, Hades.

That was whom the Consortium worshipped. Hades, God of death.

Liam rocked on his bed, hearing the sacrificed man's muffled screams, seeing his pulsing blood.

The Stranger had the Power. It was what made him inhuman. Or maybe he *was* inhuman, a revolting, atavistic monster, or some gross-looking mutant from a swamp somewhere.

But he could heal. He could understand a person without hearing words. He could communicate with the stars.

He was like the girl in the hospital with the golden hair. The Consortium was going to kill her. Today, on the island the *Pinnacle* was facing.

He was like Sam Smith, who had saved Liam's life by listening to words never spoken. Sam was on the island, too.

And he was also like Liam, in ways no one knew.

Last night Liam found the answer.

It would be his life's work to kill people like them. Like the Stranger.

Like himself.

Because of his fear of his father, he had mouthed the words of a vow to eliminate their kind forever.

Now it is possible, his father had said, holding before Liam the diamond that Zeus the Thunderer had left his people as his legacy. *You have the answer now*.

The answer was to destroy their island, the last vestige of the living earth of Atlantis.

There will be no human gods on this Earth again.

Liam would be the last leader of the Consortium. After him, there would be no one with the Stranger's blood left to kill.

No more gods.

Slowly he rose from the bed. He wiped his nose. He stood erect.

"That is not the answer," he whispered.

His father was on deck, talking on his portable phone. Liam walked past him into the dining room, then up the stairs and down a corridor to St.

James's office. There he smashed the lock on the gold chest. Inside was a soft leather pouch containing the diamond.

Liam took it, then walked aft, on the starboard side where his father could not see him. He removed his shirt, tied the cords of the leather pouch to a belt loop on his trousers, and dove into the sea.

When Darian entered the bridge of the *Styx*, Woodson was sitting in the captain's chair, surrounded by a litter of electronic debris.

"What the hell have you done to my radio?" he demanded.

"It wasn't working anyway," Woodson mumbled. "Just a sec." He bent over something in his lap, his knotted fingers laboring painfully over a series of fine wires. He wiped the sweat from his forehead. "Tricky bugger. There."

He held up his creations. "Ta-da. One remote detonator with a transmitter, one receiver. Sam, you about ready?"

"Coming." Sam trudged up from the hold carrying two buckets of yellow goo. "Nothing like a little homemade napalm to clear the sinuses," he said, setting down the buckets. "I've got four more of these." He went back below.

"I sure hope you two Einsteins know what you're doing," Darian said.

"Elementary science, Captain McCabe. We stripped the styrofoam off the storage lockers, then mixed it with some diesel fuel we siphoned off the tanks and added a little ether-based dry gas you had down there. The styrofoam melts, and presto—we've got a nice little surprise for St. James's goons. Are the firepits ready?"

"We've just about finished digging." Darian noticed a clump of dirt on his nose and brushed it away. "Want me to take this stuff?" He motioned toward the buckets.

"Please. And stick the dynamite in your pockets before you go."

"Just these?" Darian asked, picking up six sticks.

"That's all you had. Otherwise, we'd be able to blow up their fleet."

"Damn," Darian said as he left with the buckets.

Sam emerged with two more buckets. "These are for you. I'll be right behind you."

"Don't forget the blasting caps and fishing line," Woodson said, lumbering to his feet. Over his shoulder, he slung a fat coil of wire cannibalized from the boat's electrical system and added to some wire fishing leader from the storage lockers. Then he picked up his two buckets of napalm and headed for the island.

Darian and the women were leaning, exhausted, over their shovels and picks near the last of six pits they had dug around the crown of the island, some two hundred feet in diameter.

"Good work," Woodson said, pouring the contents of one bucket into the pit. "Now listen up." He took one of the dynamite sticks from Darian's shirt pocket and began to uncoil the wire. "I'm going to rig this dynamite to the wire, one stick to a pit."

He wrapped the wire around the stick and dropped it into the napalm, then proceeded to the next trench, playing out the wire as he walked.

"All the pits will be connected by this wire. At the last pit, I'm going to make this bomb live by inserting a receiver into the dynamite. It won't go off unless I transmit a signal from this detonator, but I don't want any of us tripping over the wires and pulling out the dynamite."

He looked to each of them in turn. "We'll be safe inside this circle as long as we're dead center. That's the barricade you built. Everyone got that?"

They all nodded. Sam came up with the last two buckets.

"Now I'll need one of you to help me. The rest of you split up into two teams and lay tripwires around the perimeter of the island. Sam will show you how to set them up. Okay?"

"I'll stay," Carol Ann said, dumping another of the buckets into the second pit. She stared at the gelatinous mixture with distaste. "Are we going to kill them?" she asked softly.

"If we can," Woodson said.

He did not add that whatever damage their little group inflicted would probably not change the ultimate outcome.

They would all die.

But they would all die clean, in the one place on Earth where they all belonged.

Liam struggled in the water.

Fifty laps.

To avoid being seen, he had made a broad loop away from the *Pinnacle* so that he would come in from the far side of the next yacht flanking his father's. It may have been good strategy, but he had increased his distance to shore by a half mile or more. There was a strong undertow too, so that every stroke Liam took was a tremendous effort.

I said fifty. He could hear his father's voice taunting him. *You disgust me, Liam.*

That's fine with me, he thought as he sliced through the water. *Because you disgust me, too. And I've already come a lot farther than fifty laps. Sir.*

His breath was loud, gasping. The muscles in his calves were beginning to cramp. In his heart he knew there was no way he would make it all the way to the island. It was just physically impossible.

"Then I'll go down to the bottom, damnit," he muttered, clamping his teeth together. "But I'm not going to stop now."

One arm after the other. Push. *Push.*

For once, Aidon St. James was not going to get what he wanted.

Cory and Sam were on the far side of the island from the *Styx*, setting up tripwires fashioned from nylon fishing line.

Each was no more than three feet long, but there was enough line to virtually circle the island.

Working at a frantic pace, they carefully tied the ends of the line to heavy stones, pulled the lines taut, then set blasting caps slightly forward of the stones. Anyone tripping the line would dislodge at least one stone, making it fall onto one of the blasting caps.

The tripwires would not deter anyone, but at least the loud bang from the blasting caps would alert the six that someone was coming and give them time to head for the shelter of the barricade.

As Sam put the last stone in place, Cory covered the wire with sand. Then she sat back on her haunches and smiled. "Guess we're ready," she said softly.

Sam studied her face. Its serenity, its pure beauty, filled him with pain.

Death meant little to Sam. He had lost the purpose of his life in the depths of the sea off the sinking shores of Atlantis. Athena was gone; the voice that had sustained him since his childhood would never sing to him again. He would die gladly, relieved that his useless life was finally over.

But Cory deserved to live. She and the others, the Rememberers, possessed something wonderful, something that could change the future of the entire planet for the better if they were allowed to develop their talents fully.

They would pass on their knowledge even to those without the blood. Together, the Remembers of the world could build a civilization greater than Atlantis itself, because the power of Zeus would be shared by everyone.

But that was not going to happen. Hades had promised them death. And death, not a new world, was what awaited them.

"I wish it didn't have to be this way," Sam said.

Cory bowed her head. "Me, too." She stood up abruptly. "Come on," she said, forcing a smile. "Let's get cleaned up. The lagoon's nearby."

Easily she made her way down the boulders protecting the shallow pool where Carol Ann had gone fishing. She waded into the deepest part of the lagoon and sat down, ducking her head under the sun-warmed water.

"God, that feels good," she said to Sam, who was splashing his face. She pulled herself out of the declevity and took his wrist by both hands. "Here, your turn."

"No, that's okay. . . ."

With a tug, she yanked him off his feet. He fell into the little pocket of sand, legs up in the air.

"See? Just like a hot tub." She crawled out onto the sand beneath the big rocks and slicked back her hair.

He was laughing.

She had never heard him laugh before.

She had never done anything with him, really. One guilty kiss in a hospital office.

That was all there would ever be.

Even that had meant nothing to him, Cory thought sadly. How could it, when someone like Athena had been with him all his life?

Sam was not a man who loved easily, she knew. He had not been reared to tenderness or affection. But he had loved the princess from Atlantis, loved her with every cell of his body and brain. Cory understood; she had lived inside him then. She had seen the woman through his own eyes.

Sam loved Athena beyond death, beyond time itself, and he would never love anyone else.

His smile faded. He was staring at her.

"What is it?" she asked.

"It's . . ." He shrugged. "It's just the light, I guess. You looked like . . . someone. . . ."

She stood up. "We ought to find Darian and Reba. They might need help."

Sam got to his feet. "Cory, while Woodson and I were diving this morning, something happened to me. I went somewhere. Somewhere very strange." His face struggled with emotion. "This isn't easy to explain. . . ."

"You don't have to," she said, taking his hand. "We were there with you."

Sam could not speak.

"It was as if we were all connected," Cory went on, "and when you came up out of the water into Atlantis, you brought us along, in some corner of your mind. All of us."

"Darian?" he asked finally.

She smiled. "He's the one who saw the marks on the stones inside the pyramid dungeon. The hard part was getting Reba to understand enough to communicate it to you."

He heard her words, but they passed through his mind like ribbons of mist. The light was falling on Cory again and there was something shining behind those smoky gray eyes, something deep and far.

My love, I have waited so long for you. . . .

"What did you say?"

Cory trembled. "Nothing."

I love you. I have always loved you, and even after death, I will love you still, for all time.

"For all . . . time . . ." Sam repeated.

Cory clutched the sides of her head. "Don't listen!" she cried. "Those are my *thoughts*! You don't have a right to them."

"It was you," he said in wonder. He was looking at her as if he were seeing her for the first time. "All along, it was you."

"Don't try to pretend I'm someone else," she rasped, the tears bitter in her eyes. "I saw Athena. I know you lost her, and I'm sorry. But I won't be a substitute for her."

She started to scramble up the boulder, but he caught her and held her by both arms. The music rushed into them both, loud, dizzying. He put his mouth on hers and she felt a circle of light emanating out of her to embrace them both.

"Sam," she whispered.

They took off their clothing and knelt, facing each other, the light pouring out of them both. They were immortal, glowing, the music visible around them. They loved each other then, each possessing the other's body with a pure fire.

His spirit spoke: *You've come back.*

I was always with you, she answered silently. *I was your mother, your soldier, your priest. You were my friend, my student, my wild lover, my wife. You are Sam Nowar and Jamie McCabe. I am Cory Althorpe the physician and Athena of the royal house of Atlantis, and I have always been with you.*

Tears streamed from Sam's eyes. "I've waited so long," he said.

"We both have."

Afterwards, they lay together in the sand. He stroked her arm, still golden with the light that was slowly passing back into her skin.

"We had a child, Sam," she said, not knowing where that knowledge came from. "A daughter, born in Attica. I named her Pallas, for purity. . . ." She blinked.

"Cory?"

She stared at him for a long moment. "A child . . . I don't remember. . . ." She touched his face. "You were filled with light, like a star. Made of light."

"Maybe that's what we really are," Sam said. He picked up a handful of sand. "Star stuff, from some place in the universe where time doesn't exist."

" 'Each of us is composed of all the sums he has not counted,' " she said. " 'Subtract us into nakedness and night again and you shall see begin in Crete the love that ended yesterday in Texas.' "

She smiled. "Thomas Wolfe wrote that. 'Each moment is the fruit of forty thousand years. . . . The minute-winning days, like flies, buzz home to death and each moment is a window on all time.' "

He held her closer to him. "Do you think Thomas Wolfe had the blood?"

"I wouldn't be surprised," she said. "There's a lot of genius in the world. Bach, Mozart, Galileo, Leonardo, Einstein . . . I think they might have been connected with something bigger than human thought. There might be all kinds of Rememberers out there, not just pure psychics, but everyone with something special about them."

Sam toyed with the sand he held in his palm. Each grain separate, he thought, each sparkling with the life of a thousand galaxies. "That's everyone," he said.

She smiled. "Then I suppose it would be possible for everyone to develop extra senses if they wanted to."

"And knew how."

"Oh, Sam," Cory said, her face radiant. "Can you imagine what the world would be like if we could all become what we *might* be?"

Then, feeling the thread of hope inside her break, her eyes dulled. "But there won't be time for that, will there? Not for us." She touched his eyes. "This moment is all we're going to have."

"It's all anyone ever has, Cory."

He kissed her. A bubble of light surrounded them. It had always been there, he realized. It would always be.

He opened his hand and the sand in it blew away.

Like seeds in the wind.

Keep . . . moving . . . keep . . . moving. . . .

Liam's arms moved mechanically through the water. His legs had turned into knotted logs some time ago. They trailed limply behind him as he willed himself to windmill his arms, ignoring the sharp pains that shot through his lungs with each breath.

The shore of Memory Island was close. Already the water was warming, though Liam thought he would never feel warm again.

His foot touched sand and seaweed. Then his knees scraped against a bank of pebbles. Still he pushed forward, straining with his arms until his hands brought up sand, and then he lay on his belly, tasting the salt water that lapped up rhythmically over his face.

Gotta get up, he told himself. *Someone on one of the ships is going to see you.*

Wouldn't that be just great, he thought, pulling himself to his knees. To swim all this way, only to be returned to his father by a vigilant crewman on another yacht.

He made himself crawl another ten feet to a pile of charred planking and plaster before he collapsed. The huge diamond inside the leather pouch dug into his hip.

Get up!

He forced one eye open. There was a length of nylon wire stretched taut between two rocks in front of him.

He opened the other eye and raised his head. Behind each rock was something that looked like a piece of black pumice. It was rectangular, with wires curving out of it like a spider's legs.

"Blasting cap," he said, panting. One of the boys at school had booby-trapped the toilets in the faculty men's room with some.

He examined the device more closely. Except for the fact that it had been placed too near the shore so that the wind had blown off its camouflaging layer of sand, it was pretty ingenious.

Liam grinned. These people weren't going to go down without a fight. Now, maybe, with himself as a hostage, they would not have to go down at all.

And they would have the stone. He had done at least that much for them.

Quickly he looked behind him. No dinghies from the ships. Maybe had had not been seen. He covered over the tripwire with sand, placed a small piece of planking in front of it, then picked his way cautiously up the bank to an enclave of rock, where his legs gave out.

The muscles in his calves went first, cramping violently from the instep of his feet to the backs of his knees. He went down keening in pain, pounding the knotted lumps with his fists.

"Damnit," he choked. "I can't stop here, I *can't*. . . ."

Then Liam noticed a pair of trousers. His trousers. On the legs of the girl from the hospital.

She stared at him in astonishment.

God, I wish I'd kept my shirt on, he thought. He had pimples on his shoulders. He tried to cover the worst of them with his hand.

She was so beautiful, the most beautiful thing he had ever seen.

I've tried to be brave, he wanted to say. *I did it for you. And me. And all of us.*

But all that came out was, "Charlie horse."

"I'll help you," she said.

Mr. St. James!"

Penrose skittered along the deck, the portable phone still in his hand. "We've just had a call from the *Odeon*. Someone on board spotted a figure swimming to Memory Island. They seem to think it was Liam."

"Liam?" St. James rushed inside. "They must be mistaken."

Penrose followed him. "The mate who saw him called the *Odeon*'s owner. Monsieur Messaline himself identified the boy."

They raced through the walkway, nearly knocking over one of the stewards, and burst into Liam's empty stateroom.

"Oh, no," St. James moaned. "Whatever could have possessed him to . . ."

With a gasp, he shoved Penrose aside and dashed back the way he had come.

Penrose caught up with him at the office, where St. James was standing over the gold casket on his desk. It lay open. Pieces of the broken lock lay beside it.

The diamond was gone.

St. James put one hand to his forehead.

"We can send a team in to get him," Penrose said. "There are two former navy SEALs in your employ. . . ."

"Shut *up*!" St. James shouted between clenched teeth. "Don't you see? He has the stone! They'll kill him for that."

He closed his eyes and breathed deeply. "We will send a message to the six people on the island," he said calmly. "And then I'll go to see them. Alone."

"Alone, sir?"

"I'll make them a deal." He examined the corners of the room as he thought out loud. "Yes, that's it. They'll deal."

He scribbled a message on a piece of stationery and handed it to his assistant. "Take that to the bridge," he said. "Then get on the phone to the other ships. Tell them to hold their fire until I'm back on board. I'll give the order for that personally. Understand?"

"Yes, sir. Of course."

"Meanwhile, I want them to get their men ready for an assault, in case I need them while I'm on the island. If I do need them, I'll ring you on my direct line. That's all you'll get, one ring. When that happens, signal the ships to send in their mercenaries. They should be prepared to kill everyone except me."

"And Liam," Penrose added.

St. James stared at him blankly. "Didn't you hear what I said?"

"Yes, but—"

"We must recover the stone," St. James explained. "I can have another son if I have to."

* * *

Inside the barricade, Reba passed around paper plates of clams and fish.

"Hope Carol Ann don't mind if we start without her," she said. "I told her we didn't need no more."

"It won't take her long," Woodson said, chuckling. "Have you seen how she fishes?"

"Damnedest thing." Darian raised a clam to his mouth.

"I think maybe we ought to say a grace," Reba said sternly.

Darian lowered the clam with regret. "All right. Make it a short one."

She lowered her head. "Lord, thank you for this bounty in the midst of our trouble. Help us be strong now that we need to be. And when our time comes to meet you, show us the path to your golden door."

"Amen," the others murmured. Darian grunted and picked up his clam.

"One more thing," Reba went on. Darian looked over at her irritably. "Gram, if you're listening, I been wondering for a while now why this is happening to us."

"For God's sake," Darian mumbled.

"I mean, we ain't denying that we got these gifts. I'm talking about the Sight. We got it in different ways, but we all got it. And to tell you the truth, we're in one heck of a pickle now because of it.

"Now, I know there's a reason and you must know what it is, 'cause you always do. There was a reason for Sam going back to that place with the volcano. There was a reason for the Rememberers all seeing that volcano blow. There must have been a reason why so many of them died, though I don't expect to know what it was till I can talk to you face to face in the land of glory."

Darian leaned back on his elbows, his eyes slitted, his fingers clenching the clam.

"What I'm getting at, Gram, is that I think something happened back then, in that place where Sam went, and whatever it was, it's still going on. And us six are part of it.

"Is that right, Gram? 'Cause if it is, I truly don't see no reason why we got to die. Now, it's not that we're feared of dying. We're all ready to do that. But it don't make no sense that we got to go just like the last Rememberers. If we all get killed, us and everybody like us, then nobody on this Earth is left with the Sight. What kind of a place will that be, with no seers, no dreamers, where the dead just disappear like smoke and the living just use up time? We're the connection between this world and yours, Gram. There's got to be a place for us here."

"Wind it up, Reba," Darian snapped.

She glanced at him angrily.

"So I'd surely appreciate it, Gram, if you'd send us a sign that somebody up there is still with us. It's getting scary around here, and we need some light in this dark tunnel where we're at. Amen."

Darian sucked up his clam. "Damn thing's cold," he said. He was reaching for another when a whistle sounded and a brilliant flash of light exploded overhead.

Darian dropped the clam and grabbed his rifle.

"A sign," Reba squeaked.

"More like a flare," Sam said. "Stay put."

In a matter of seconds there was another whistle and then a thud as something hit into the soft earth not far from the barricade.

It was a small metal canister, still steaming with heat. They ducked down, prepared for a blast. Nothing happened.

Cautiously Sam got up, carrying the cup of water he had been drinking. He walked to the cylinder and dumped the water on top of it until it was cool enough to pick up in his hands.

Its two sections came apart. Inside was a sheet of paper.

"It's a note," Sam said. "From St. James." The others clustered around him. "He wants to come on the island. To talk terms, he says."

"Terms?" Darian scoffed. "Six people and two rifles. What kind of terms have we got?"

Sam shrugged. "He says he'll come alone. If we agree, flash a light three times."

"I have a mirror we can use," Cory offered.

"To hell with him," Darian said. "He's been trying to kill us for days. Why would he change his mind now?"

"I think we ought to let him come," Woodson said. He pointed to the canister. "Because he sent us two messages."

Sam looked at the empty container, then at Woodson.

"You're holding one of them. The other message is that he has firepower on that yacht, and equipment sophisticated enough to aim it wherever he likes. If he wants to, he can blow the hell out of us."

Sam touched the canister with his toe. "Wouldn't it be kind of extreme to *bomb* us?"

Woodson shrugged. "There'd be no bodies."

"But the Coast Guard . . . the police . . ."

"He'll be long gone by the time anyone gets here. And there are five other ships to corroborate whatever he tells them."

"That's crazy," Sam said.

"Maybe. What's new?"

"It wouldn't be the first crazy thing that bastard has tried," Darian said. "The whole idea about killing us in the first place is . . ."

"It's the land," Reba said, sinking to her knes. She scooped up two handfuls of earth. "He wants to sink Memory Island."

She looked up at the incredulous faces around her. "Don't you see? It's this *place*."

Cory took a step backward. "Oh, my God, yes," she said. "All of us have become psychically stronger since we've been here. There's something about the land itself that's increasing the powers we have."

"That's why we all felt we belonged here," Woodson said.

Sam looked at Darian. "This is what's left of Atlantis."

No one spoke for a long time. Finally Darian slung his rifle over his shoulder. "Get that mirror," he said.

* * *

St. James stepped out of the dinghy and walked onto the island alone, as he had promised.

The tripwires near the dock had been removed for his visit but the other precautions had not been dismantled. Unseen, the barrels of two rifles followed every step St. James took. When he reached the high ground near the barricade, Sam was waiting for him.

"Where are the others?"

"You can talk to me," Sam said.

"All right. First show him to me so I know he's still alive."

Sam cocked his head. "Come again?"

"My son," St. James spat. "I want to see my son."

Sam sighed. "You're even crazier than I thought. Which of us do you think is your son?"

"Liam!" he shouted. "Liam, get out here. Now!"

"You think we have *Liam*?" Sam asked.

"This joke is becoming tiresome. I don't think I have to remind you that you're surrounded here. Every ship you see is armed with enough explosives to send you all to hell and back. Now if you want to deal your way out of that, you'd better show me what I came for."

"Which is Liam," Sam said, feeling his way.

"And the diamond."

"Ah. The diamond, too."

"That's part of the deal. You give me the boy and the stone and I'll see that you're all taken care of."

"I'll bet," Sam said.

"No harm will come to you. We'll give you safe passage out of here, to wherever you'd like to go. And your incomes will be assured."

Sam laughed out loud.

"I have no reason to lie to you," St. James insisted. "The lives of six people mean nothing."

"Unless you happen to be one of the six."

"Now you're beginning to understand." He smiled. "You see, you don't have to die. In fact, you can live very well, all of you. Better than you ever imagined." He touched Sam's shoulder. "Better than your wildest dreams."

"I can't wait to hear this," Sam said.

"Don't trivialize what I'm offering," St. James warned. "I head an organization that can give you virtually everything you've ever wanted. A mansion on the beach, fancy cars, anything. I can arrange for you to talk with some of our members, if you like. They'll tell you what the Consortium can do for you. It's a lot. An association with us would have definite rewards."

"What kind of 'association' are you talking about?"

St. James's eyes flashed. "We would ask you to do some psychic work for us from time to time."

"Such as?"

St. James gestured with his arm over the broad vista of ocean before them. "People will be coming. Thousands of them, all with ICDL blood."

Sam blinked. "Because of the stone," he said, remembering what Zeus had told him. The diamond would keep the Power intact.

"Yes. I'm glad you understand."

"And our job would be . . ."

"To identify them," St. James finished. "That's all. Just let the Consortium know who they are."

"So that you can kill them? Is that what you're saying?"

"What difference would it make to you what happened to them?" St. James reasoned. "You wouldn't know them."

"Yes, we would," Sam said. He took the man's measure with his eyes. He remembered the night when he was on St. James's yacht and, in a vision, had seen the man wearing a feathered mask and cape. They were Hades's robes. St. James was one of his. "We would know them," Sam said. "We know our own kind. And we know yours."

"Maybe the rest of your people should have something to say about this."

"We do," a voice called out as a figure walked from behind the barricade. It was Liam. In his hand, he held the leather pouch containing the stone. St. James sucked in his breath at the sight of it.

"It's still about slavery with you, isn't it, Father?" the boy asked. "That's what it's always come down to—whose life is worth something and whose isn't. Well, if you want it, you can have mine. I'll go with you and you can cut out my heart the way you did that poor geek who threw in his lot with you. But you can't have these people."

St. James stared, speechless, at this boy . . . no, this man whom his son had become.

"That's the offer, Dad. Me for them. Are you going to take it or not?"

"You . . . and the stone," St. James said.

"No deal."

"Don't be a fool, Liam. They'll kill you for that diamond."

"I don't care. They keep the stone."

St. James's face hardened. "Then they can keep you, too." He pressed a button on the phone in his pocket. Aboard the *Pinnacle*, his direct line rang once. Penrose heard it and sent the signal to the other ships.

"You were never worth a damn," St. James said.

The boy turned toward Sam, opened the leather pouch, and offered the stone to him.

Sam shook his head. "It's not mine," he said. "I was only supposed to hold it until the right one came along."

He looked hard at the boy, staring in his eyes. As if reconsidering, he reached forward and took the pendant from the pouch. Then he hung it around Liam's neck.

The stone instantly began to glow.

But before anyone could speak, around the island, the tripwires set off their blasting caps as St. James's mercenaries leaped off their dinghies and rafts and thundered up the slopes of Memory Island.

"Take cover!" Darian called and stood beside the barricade.

Liam did not move. He stood in the open, his head high, the diamond on his chest glowing stronger, shining more gloriously than it ever had, so brightly that St. James had to squint when he looked at his son. The light seemed to pulse from the stone in waves, encompassing more and more of Liam until his body was entirely ringed with raging light. And still it grew, spreading like a flame into the air around him.

Sam gasped. The stone had never shone so powerfully, not even when it had been around the throat of Zeus as he stood over the volcano.

Carol Ann stepped out from behind a cluster of rocks and stood beside Liam. She joined hands with him and the light spread from Liam over to the girl, illuminating her as it grew brighter, stronger, filled with power.

Their hair stood on end. In the brilliance around them, their outstretched fingertips made long shadows. Their faces glowed with an inner fire.

Reba left the barricade to join them. Then Cory and Sam came, together, feeling their power intensify into combustion.

Only Darian and Woodson were left. Before them, the Rememberers stood like huge, light-filled angels. Beyond them, Aidon St. James was motionless, transfixed, blinded by the light.

He's one of them, he thought. *My own son.*

Darian walked out from behind a tall bush, his rifle cocked, the sight square on St. James's forehead. Woodson came into the clearing from the other side, the detonator in his hand.

The mercenaries were coming. Their shouts were growing louder with every second.

"Well?" Woodson asked. "You going to shoot him?"

Darian hesitated, then lowered the weapon. "No. I ain't about to kill an unarmed man in front of his boy." He threw down the rifle. "It don't matter much in the end, anyway."

Harry smiled sadly. "Good-bye, Darian."

"Good-bye, Harry." Darian stepped forward and joined the others.

Time to die, Woodson thought. He had hidden from death for twenty-nine years, but his moment had finally come.

Reba's prayer had not been answered. They would indeed die just as the other Rememberers had, slaughtered on this island without a hope.

Over the hill, he watched the first wave of mercenaries climbing toward the clearing. St. James tore his gaze away from the five people pulsating with their eerie light and waved on the soldiers.

Only one thing's going to be different, Woodson thought. *This time, it's not going to be easy for them.*

Not this time.

He activated the transmitter. Within a split second, the dynamite in the firepits exploded, showering the attackers with napalm. Their screams rent the air like sirens. Horrified, St. James turned back, his face a mask of outrage.

"Enjoy your victory, you son of a bitch," Woodson said as he took Darian's hand and stepped into the light.

He felt himself vanish, felt all indecision, all bitterness, all guilt, all fear leave him as the white fire, powerful now as the sun, engulfed the seven of them. They were complete now; they were one being. And one thought passed through them all, pure as starlight.

This is the beginning.

As the second wave of mercenaries approached, the sky seemed to turn to stone. What had been a limitless expanse of blue transformed within seconds into a single roiling black cloud, hanging low and sparking with lightning.

Some of the soldiers looked up; others turned toward the sea, which suddenly roared with gigantic gray waves that overturned the dinghies. They tried to climb to the hillside as the waves reached up, swatting them away like flies. They bobbed on the water, shrieking, bodiless heads.

Tears streamed down Darian's face as he listened to their screams. Around him, beyond the great elemental light, bells were ringing, and the fog was thick in the harbor.

Aidon St. James also saw the fog. It swept in fast as the wind, coating both island and ocean in a vapor so dense he could almost touch its surface. Somewhere out there was his yacht. Its bell tolled wildly as it rocked on the waves, but he could not see it. All his eyes took in was the white fog and, through it, the blinding light of the seven people he had planned to kill.

"Where are you?" he screamed to the mercenaries. "Get up here, damn you! This is Aidon St. James and I order you . . . I *order* . . ."

The Earth swelled beneath him. It writhed and churned like the belly of some huge beast giving birth. Its skin cracked and whole trees fell into the new crevasses. They sucked the fog in with them as they tumbled down, down so far he could not hear them hit bottom.

The beast bucked. St. James was thrown high into the air and then the ground came up to meet him. In the shallow water surrounding the island, enormous shafts of rock thrust upward through the fog. A vast plateau emerged to the east, out of his line of sight, breaking up the yachts which had anchored there.

Then, somewhere far out in the ocean, the red glow from an underground volcano shimmered on the surface, boiling the water above it as it spread like a wound beneath the blanket of mist. It grew to nearly a mile in diameter, then shook the earth again as it shot upward, spewing lava that fell back into the water in billows of steam.

Beside it, another volcano erupted. And a third, and a fourth, all in a row to where the *Pinnacle* floated at anchor. The ship burst into flame at once. Aboard, the man named Penrose ran shrieking down the deck, his clothing afire.

St. James clung onto the bare ground with his fingers. But the earth did not want him; not this earth. It recoiled beneath him. It shuddered, revolted by his presence on it.

The lava from the four volcanoes formed a glowing red spit sprouting wings on either side, leading directly to the island. St. James looked down to see it, crimson, pulsating, like a long obscene tongue. It pointed at him. It wagged its tip of flame.

He screamed once more as he felt the earth under his hands turn to sand and shrug him off, down the hillside, down onto the beach, now white-hot, down into the place where the water used to be, replaced now by a shelf of burning rock. He thudded there, his blond hair frizzing to cinders. His skin crisped. His eyeballs exploded in their sockets. Blood burst from his ears and mouth, boiling as it arced in the air. The fat from his body sizzled on the new rock. When he was little more than a mummy, his bones caught fire.

He remained on the rock for some time, gray ash forming the outline of a man on the cooling lava. Then a wind gusted up and blew his remains into the sea as the sky opened and rain sank the cinders to the bottom.

Through it all the seven Rememberers stood, a wall of living light.

Like gods they stood, impassive, solid, protected against the rain by their massive aura of light. It grew around them until the entire island glowed with their essence.

Gram put her arms around Reba and laughed, her big breasts jiggling, her hair redolent with the scents of cinnamon and fresh bread.

Dr. Edward Bonner, dressed in a white suit and a straw hat, kissed Cory's cheek.

A host of angels, winged and magnificent, gathered around Carol Ann, singing. Their music surrounded her like pieces of colored glass.

Two divers, gray-faced and suffering, knelt at Harry Woodson's feet. He watched his heart open in his chest and out of it flowed forgiveness. The divers caught it in their hands. It glowed there for a moment, shining in their outstretched palms like liquid silver, then traveled up their arms and down their legs and into their faces, which Woodson had never before seen. They rose, whole and clean, then drifted skyward until they were only specks in space, particles of stardust.

Lars and Marie Nowar came to Sam. They touched him, and with that touch poured into his soul all the love they had been unable to give him in life. He trembled with the weight of it. Marie brushed her lips against his face and placed a small object into his pocket.

"This is for you," she whispered.

Then out of Sam's body stepped a twelve-year-old boy. He was a wraith at first, barely visible, but his flesh colored as he walked, unerringly, toward Darian McCabe and put his arms around him.

"Jamie," the old man whispered.

"You knew I was here. All these years."

"Yes. Yes, I suppose I did."

The boy held out one hand and a woman joined them. A pretty woman wearing a yellow enameled daisy on her collar.

For Liam, in the center, a swirl of air like a tornado descended from the sky. It crackled with electricity, shooting off sparks. When it slowed, a man stood inside.

He had reddish hair shot with white, a muscular lion of a man with a square jaw and the eyes of a god. He looked over Liam critically, seeing to his core, then smiled.

He nodded once, as if deigning this vehicle suitable, then merged into the boy's body.

At once the light around them increased a thousand times over, filling the sky and turning the sea to gold.

And Liam shouted, in an ancient language that all recognized, with a voice that could command the very heavens.

"Come, people of the new Atlantis! Come to your land with your visions and your dreams and make it live forever!"

And the Earth rose beneath the seven, thrusting them higher as the light spread to encompass the whole horizon, higher, touching the clouds and passing through them, higher still, until they stood alone in the pure and rarefied air of Olympus.

Then the clouds below them parted, became soft trails of white, vanished. The fog was gone. All that remained was land, new land, raw, steaming, still quivering with life. It stretched for miles in all directions. To the east, toward Europe, a series of smaller islands peeked out of the sea like stepping stones. To the west, a single metal column rose up like a sentinel.

"The Peaks," Sam said, stepping away from the others to get a better look. "This is just how it was."

Slowly, the glow around them faded. Reba clapped her hands over her cheeks. "Lordie me!" she whispered.

"I'll be damned." Darian pointed down, laughing, to where the small harbor of Memory Island had once been. The *Styx* was perched atop a ledge of silt-covered rock, its sides charred but intact.

Woodson surveyed the scene with a grin, his engineer's mind already designing bridges and roads.

Carol Ann and Liam scampered hand in hand down the mountain to a large level expanse, thick with mud.

"This is going to be land," Liam said, wiggling his toes in the ankle-deep soup. "Our land."

"Everyone's land," Carol Ann said. She reached into her pocket. "I almost forgot about this." She showed him a seed. "A seagull dropped it into my hand on the way to this place." Gently she placed it into the mud. "Maybe it'll become a flower."

Cory came to stand beside Sam. "What's that?"

He was turning over a piece of lead, bordered with a thin strip of ancient gold. He had recognized it at once as a fragment from the Stranger's coffin. In its cold smoothness, he could still feel his connection with its occupant.

We can change the course of things to come.

"Just a relic," he said. "And a reminder."

Cory pulled away from him suddenly, her hand shielding her eyes. "Sam, look!"

He moved beside her. For a moment, the sun on the water obscured everything with its dazzle, but then he saw them: boats and ships, hundreds of them, thousands, curving over the horizon. Liners, fishing boats, tugs, sailing vessels, catamarans . . . all filled with Rememberers headed for a dream each had always thought he dreamed alone.

They were all coming, coming to the place of their beginning.

Coming home.

"But why are they coming here?" Cory asked.

Sam put his arm around her. "Maybe for a second chance," he said.

Together they climbed down the mountain to meet the ships.

AFTERWORD

Poseidon was a good sailor. Many Atlanteans of the royal house survived both the final earthquake and the long sea journey.

Hera settled in Attica, where she was almost immediately worshiped as a goddess. With her former rivals, the Muses, attending her, she assisted in childbirths, settled domestic disputes, and was greatly admired by the native women, who believed her to possess the secret of eternal youth and beauty. In her old age, she talked incessantly of the wonders of Atlantis and the great deeds of her countrymen to the crowd of acolytes who sat daily at her feet, listening to her tales from the land of the gods.

The Muses filled their ranks with local girls, whom they trained carefully in the knowledge of their disciplines. The school they founded continued for more than two thousand years.

To his dismay, Hercules also remained under Hera's yoke for many years, although her harsh punishments did little to curb his rowdy ways. They led him into numerous troublesome adventures which endeared him to young men throughout Attica, and in a final irony Hera, by then quite elderly, finally embraced him as the son she wished she had borne.

Hephaestus did return, through a roundabout route, to Timbuktu, where he developed a unique civilization combining the magnificent technology of Atlantis with native African customs. Because of a dire threat from the developing Egypt, Ptah rendered the city invisible by means outlined in the Stranger's writings. This society—which worships both Ptah and his mother, known as Malana, as a single deity—still flourishes in the mists where the engineer from Atlantis placed it.

After a tragic romance with the ardent Orion, Artemis journeyed away from Attica to the Carpathian mountains. There she lived, first as a hermit, and later as the leader of a band of women warriors known as Amazons.

Her twin brother, Apollo, made his way to distant Persia. He became renowned as a physician, and his skills were developed even further by his son Aescalapius, who became known throughout the world as the greatest healer of his time.

Aphrodite, who was not granted a private stateroom on board the *Dolphin*, was even more bitterly dissatisfied with the primitive conditions on land. She demanded that Poseidon take her from Attica to the more sophisticated Phoenicia, which had not been destroyed by the great flood. There she was known alternately as Astarte and Ba'al and became the darling of the Phoenician court, introducing new delights into their worldly entertainments. Inadvertently, though, she did contribute a great deal of knowledge about ships, having sailed often with Ares. Through her tutelage, Phoenicia replaced Atlantis as the supreme power on the seas, even though the sails of the Phoenician navy remained resolutely square.

Athena remained near Hera for several years, raising her daughter Pallas as a free person. She taught Pallas weaving, at which the girl excelled, as well as fighting. In later years, Pallas would become known as Pallas Athena. Her protection of a tribe of Atticans resulted in the founding of the first of Attica's great cities, Athens.

Meanwhile, Athena herself traveled far, helping thousands along the way with her skills and knowledge. She never married. Eventually she lit upon the soil of Egypt, whose civilization was blossoming at astonishing speed and in a bizarre direction. There she met both Hephaestus and Hades and made her greatest contribution to the history of that country by passing on the Power to a group of earnest seekers. Not long afterward, she inexplicably disappeared and was not heard from again.

Hades's ship sank off the coast of Egypt. He alone, of all the soldiers and sailors on board, survived. There he quickly aligned himself with Osiris, the most powerful of the primitive kings, and helped Osiris defeat his enemy and brother, Set. As a result, Hades—who changed his name to Thoth—acquired great power and eventually ascended to the throne. As Pharaoh, Thoth brought Egypt to world eminence and built an entire society devoted to death. He dotted his kingdom with pyramids, though, without knowledge of how to build them, they required thousands of slaves and vast amounts of time to construct.

He had a son who ruled after him in his name, and his son also produced a son who called himself Thoth. The line continued; eventually it would be written that the king-god Thoth ruled Egypt for thirty-seven hundred years.

Poseidon never found another home. Or, rather, it was the same home he had always known: the sea. He sailed the world many times and wherever he went, sailors acknowledged him with reverence.

Of all the survivors of the great catastrophe, only Poseidon ever returned to the waters where Atlantis had once existed. The sea there was a horror of churning mud which even the great Phoenician sailors had deemed impassable. Only Poseidon could find his way back to the tiny island on which a boat-shaped rock commemorated the passing of a great civilization.

There, on the rock, he placed a single seed that had blown into his hair during the harrowing departure from its shores more than a year before. He had kept it for this moment.

For the future, he said as he laid it upon the granite surface.

Overhead, a gull circled.